AUNT SARAH

Woman of the Dawnland

by

Trudy Ann Parker

Dawnland Publications
P.O. Box 223
Lancaster, NH 03584

ISBN 0-9662523-8-1

Printed in the United States of America

2 3 4 5 6 7 8 9 10 98 99 00 01 02 03 04 05

Photos of the author and Aunt Sarah's basket by Jill Brooks

AUNT SARAH

Woman of the Dawnland

This book is dedicated to the People of the Dawnland, or the Abenaki Indians, wherever scattered, in their ongoing struggle to keep alive their traditions, culture and proud heritage, in a land they considered their own, long before the coming of the White man.

"Who but one who loved the reeds that grew

beside still waters and the damp roots of the

shrub and tree could save it from seasonal death

and weave it into timless art."

Chief Luther Standing Bear

Special Sources

The trail that led to the publishing of this book was long and the money was short. It is only because those listed here believed in me and in my subject matter, that this has come to be. To God, my Great Spirit, who sustained me. To my husband, Don, who endured with me. To my dad, Jack Call, for his pride in his Native American blood and my mother Celina Call, for her Native American heart. To Kenneth and Arlene Lewis who read this before anyone else and gave me hope and courage. To Velmore Forrest who gave me the ending of my story. To John D. Harrigan who copy edited *Aunt Sarah.* To Kenneth Powers, my computer man and Susan Powers, my sounding board. To John Moody who made me believe even more in myself.

To Everett Rowley who advised me and took a disk and created a book. To Alice Fogg, and Dana and Melody Fogg and to Sandow & Terry Call, John & Sandra Call, and to Jacques & Theresa Racine who believed in me even if the banks did not.

To all of you my heartfelt thanks...mine and Aunt Sarah's too, because your sweat and faith and contributions have given a heart, a soul and a voice to a people long silent — the *"People of the Dawnland."*

Trudy Ann Parker

AUNT SARAH

"This we know. The earth does not belong to man;
man belongs to the earth. This we know.
All things are connected like the blood that unites one family.
All things are connected. Whatever befalls the earth,
befalls the sons of the earth. Man did not weave the web of life;
he is merely a strand in it. Whatever he does to the web,
he does to himself.

Every part of the earth is sacred to my people ...
every shining pine needle, every sandy shore,
every light mist in the dark forest, every clearing ...
and every winged creature is sacred to my people.
We are part of the earth and it is part of us.
The fragrant flowers are our sisters,
the deer and mighty eagle are our brothers;
the rocky peak, the fertile meadows,
all things are connected like the blood that unites a family."

Chief Seattle

The Warning of 1665

"I am an old oak that has lasted the storms of many winters. My eyes are dim and my limbs tremble. The scalplocks that dried before my wigwam told the stories of my victories over the Mohawks who invaded our hunting grounds. Then, in their place, came the Palefaces. The lands of our forefather's were taken from us....I tried the magic of my sorcery in vain. I, who can take in my palm as I would a worm, the rattlesnake. I, who have seen the Great Spirit in dreams, and talked with him awake; I as brave as the bravest, as strong as the strongest, as wise as the wisest. I am like a reed before their tempest. Now, my children, heed my dying words. The oak will soon break before the whirlwind...I commune with the Great Spirit. He whispers to me, 'Tell your people, peace. Peace is your only hope...Your forests shall fall before their mighty hatchets. At your fishing places, they shall build their houses!'.....We must bend before the storm....Peace, peace with the White man is the command of the Great Spirit, and the last wish of Passaconaway."

This warning was delivered by the Great Chief and Medicine-Man of the Penacooks (one of the Abenaki Groups), at a great gathering of New England tribes, on the plains above Concord, New Hampshire, in the year 1665, when Passaconaway was nearing the 100th winter of his life.

Preface

Once upon a time, long before the coming of the White Man, this place we know today as the Sate of Vermont, parts of New Hampshire, Maine, and New York, was known only as "Indian Country." Even if your old green history book did not say so, this is a fact and not a fairy tale.

The Declaration of Independence was just that for the New Americans but for those Native peoples who had inhabited this land for generations, it proved to be not the beginning at all, but in fact, the beginning of the end of a way of life that had been their own since beyond memory.

For most of us, American History began with the incursion of the European settlers upon these shores and yet, through family legends, many of us knew that the American Indian was here first and that the elusive Western Abenaki (St. Francis Indians) had a history of their own, long before that. It didn't have to be documented for an Indian never forgets.

In the *Lunenburg Town History*, published in 1976 there was brief mention made of an ancestor of mine. Her name was Sarah (Jackson) Somers and she was a well known part of local lore and history.

Most who knew her called her "Aunt Sarah," and she was a renowned medicine woman and basket maker. She was a full blooded St. Francis Abenaki Indian, born in the village of St. Francis, Canada, in the year 1823, according to family legend, but her death certificate, filed at the Lunenburg, Vt. Town Clerk's Office, states that she was born in the village of St. Francis, P. Q., Canada, in the year 1828.

This document declares that at the time of her death in February of 1931, she was 102 years and three months of age, but from the time I can remember hearing about her, the way I heard it was that Our Aunt Sarah had lived to see 108 winters.

Her grandfather, (whose name I do not know), was one of the retaliating warriors that pursued Major Robert Rogers and his Rangers, after their surprise and devastating attack on the sleeping Village of St. Francis, in the year 1759. History called this massacre an attack.

Aunt Sarah's father's name was "Polani-Taxos-Kohla-Kost," (wolf) and he was the chief of a family band of St. Francis Abenakis, all of the Bear Clan.

Legend has it that in the spring of her first summer, Sarah went down the Connecticut River in a canoe, strapped in a cradleboard on her mother's back, to a place called "Tarritine Ledge," perched on a high bluff overlooking the snake-like back of the Connecticut River and directly across from the early town of Lancaster, New Hampshire.

This is a history, a family history of her's and of mine, and I have endeavored to bring it alive to you, just as I was told they lived it.

Actual written documentation on this tribe of Indians is scarce, except that which was written in the memory, burned therein by the glowing embers of their nightly campfires. And yet, history was being kept alive here from one generation to another.

From the picturesque shores of Lake Champlain, and all its tributaries, on through the Champlain Valley and across the Green Mountains to the Connecticut River Valley and eastward to the coast of Maine, a tribe of Algonquian-speaking Indians, inhabited this soil. They were the Native Americans of northern New England and their homelands were what we now know as the state of Vermont.

These people were called the "Abenakis," and the translation means "Woban or Aben" meaning East or Dawn and "Aki" meaning Earth or Land. These Indians called themselves "The People of the Dawnland."

These Dawnland People's ancestral ceremonies of giving thanks before a hunt or giving thanks and feasting after one, was sacred to the Indian, but more and more he was forced to live in a new way. In his life- style he had order and continuity, but that had all been changed when the White Man entered his world with his beads, tools, rum, guns, and pestilence. Everything was new from God to epidemics.

This was a more terrible time for the Abenaki than all the wars. Sarah's father could understand war, but he could not understand this constant internal fighting and drunkenness that plagued St. Francis now.

Peace, everyone talked of peace and in all of his life Sarah's father had known less of that than of anything else. And he ultimately decided to take that small family band in his charge and they would go and find their own damned peace.

Peace to this Chief was fishing on the banks of the upper Connecticut River and at night seated by the campfire and telling stories of better days.

Because of the scarce documentation available to me, I have found it necessary to work fiction with facts, to bring my characters alive. This story comes from legends told about my family band and my main characters all lived and died, but legends live forever. And, in keeping with the legend, in the spring of 1824, that troubled chief who was my great-great-grandfather and little Sarah's father, saw the changes that had taken place, just in the span of his own thirty-five years.

Since the French and Indian Wars against them, the English had despised the St. Francis Indians. These were indeed the most feared and dreaded of all the Algonquian tribes. For three quarters of a century they had terrorized the English settlements, burning, killing, scalping, and carrying off White captives to be sold in Montreal later for ransom.

Twice in their tribal history the "War Cry" of the St Francis Indian had forced the evacuation of the entire Maine coast and for more than eight decades their "Hit and Run Warfare Tactics," had been so successful that they had completely stopped the advancement of the English settlements in the Connecticut River Valley.

But that was the past, and this was the present and Chief Polani-Taxos-Kohla-Kost was contemplating on going back to the ancestral land of his forefathers, and there to live in peace if possible with the White settlers along the banks of the "Long River."

He did not know what the future would bring, living so near and most likely being met with suspicion, prejudice, and downright hatred, from the new landowners of the valley. What he did know was that soon the fish would be biting, and his people were hungry and it was time to go.

Farewells were said. Indian farewells like:

"Until we meet again may the Great Spirit make the sunrise in your heart. And may your moccasins make tracks in many snows yet to come."

And so, in search of food and a better life but most especially in search of peace, these followers of my great-great grandfather, took one last look at the village of St. Francis. The season of this final migration was upon them. They would stop and leave gifts of tobacco at the Great Rock on the edge of Lake Champlain. "Odzihozo" (the Owner), had turned himself into that rock after he made everything else, and so they needed to feel the blessing of "Odzihozo," before they began this life-changing trek into history.

And before they left that site, the People sang and danced there in the full view of the rock. They feasted and they prayed and their prayer went this way:

"Oh Great Spirit, Creator of all things; Men, animals, fish, trees, grass and berries, Help us, be kind to us. Be our guide in peace. Let us be happy and walk a good trail. Let us lead our children to a good life and old age. These our people; give them good minds. Give them good hearts to love the earth and each other. Oh Great Spirit, grant us the favor to see green trees, flowers, berries, green leaves and sweetgrass this spring and to meet each other once again, we ask you."

Feeling at peace for the first time in many moons, this chief led his little "Bear Clan" family band down the trail of peace, to the place of his childhood, overlooking New Hampshire's Crystal Hills.

His task was truly arduous and filled with awe and he was too intelligent not to know that he would be leading his people into more changes than they had ever experienced before. But, on that bright spring morning in 1824, he was leading these "People of the Dawnland" to a ledge-covered bank on the Connecticut River, a peaceful home called "Tarritine Ledge," the place where the sweetgrass grows.

Part I

Child of the Dawnland

Part One

Child of the Dawnland

TARRITINE LEDGE, 1831 — For seven summers Chief Polani-Taxos-Kohla-Kost's (Wolf) band had been there, high on that steep and rocky bluff overlooking the winding Connecticut (Long) River in South Guildhall, Vermont. For the most part, life had been peaceful, except for the terrible nightmares, that is. This was a time in the history of man when the whole world was changing, and for these Abenakis assembled here there were far more changes than in most lives.

The man of which I speak, my great-great grandfather, was still the leader of his "Bear Clan" people but now he had taken an English first name. More and more the exchange of commerce and greater dependence on the White settlements of young Lancaster, New Hampshire to the east and early Lunenburg, Vermont to the west had necessitated that he should have an English first name. He chose the name of Peter and this is why. He remembered that Roman Catholic converts and friends of his from (Odanak) or the Village of St. Francis, Canada, had said "The Black Robes claim that the Great Spirit trusted his friend Peter and declared 'Upon this Rock I shall build my church.'"

This grandfather was much impressed with the "Rock" theory. In the religion of his Western Abenakis forefathers, it was believed that "Odzihozo" (The Owner) had turned himself into a great rock on the edge of Lake Champlain. It seemed that both Great Spirits, each in his own way, respected the strength and endurance of the rock. And so Polani was no more, and in his place stood a man called Peter.

Peter was descended from the "Taxos" family, often spelled Taksos or more properly Tacshouche, depending on whether the recorder was French, English or had any knowledge of the Algonquian language. Peter was Takso's son and he would keep his own last name— "Takson," he thought.

Speaking of nightmares, it had been one to try to get his White neighbors to call him Peter Takson. They could not say "Takson," and constantly called him Jackson, and at first this made him angry. He was not Jack's son, he was the son of Taksos. The more he insisted on his name being pronounced "Takson," the more they persisted in calling and writing his last name as Jackson. This was done because his White friends thought that they were right of course, and he was just some dumb Indian—with a lisp. And now, not one but two family names were gone.

Peter consoled himself with the fact that Indian men often had name changes, one as a child, one after the vision-quest and one as a warrior, but they were usually called by nicknames anyhow. Tacshouche his father, was called "Tach," by the Abenakis, but this got turned into "Jack" by White friends, so in a way Peter was Jack's son.

Perched on this high slope, as the night sounds engulfed him, he cast a large shadow, because Peter was a big man, tall and barrel-chested like so many other Taxos men before him. A few grayish strands now wove their silent way along the temples of his once coal-black hair and he knew that he was not the lean and muscular man that he once had been. He realized himself that he drank too much, but he had to have an escape from those terrible nightmares that dogged him. He missed his old hunting partner Miles Hunter. Miles, if he were alive, would help him find out why Peter woke up in the night in stark terror, his body glistening with sweat and his stomach churning. He was always fighting for his life, and always in the same place with the same monster that drew him close like a magnet, pulling him nearer and nearer to the whirlwind core of it. Peter was flailing his arms at it, this terrible roaring cyclone that shook the ground upon which he stood. He always called out to the Great Spirit and also for his animal helper the eagle, and even to the clan's trusted totem, the "Great Bear," but the eagle never appeared and that mighty bear was utterly powerless against the shrill scream of the wind demon. Its one bright eye blinded Peter and it was hot, very hot, like the White Men say "Hell" is. Was this his own private Indian devil out of hell? He needed help—the help of a mighty Shaman.

This troubled man was neither handsome nor homely with his high and prominent cheekbones, deep, dark eyes and a wide, generous mouth. His face was one that trusted too much.

It was to this ledge he brought the baby Sarah, and it was here that two more children had been born. They were both men children: one was called Peter and the other Dennis.

This father's heart had been almost broken when he realized that the baby, Peter, would always be a baby because there was a vacant look in the child's eyes, as Peter was retarded. Little Peter's mother had taken a bad fall on ice in the early stages of her pregnancy; and not only that, but she herself had willed him not to be born in the winter, saying "I want a healthy child. I do not want a snow child," and as a result, she had carried the baby not for nine, but for eleven months within her body. She had willed it so, and it had been.

It might be a punishment. It might just be fate, but the grieving parents did not dwell on it. He was their own, a gift to them, and they would take care of him always.

When Dennis had arrived two years later, robust, alert and handsome in every way, Peter was elated. Dennis was good of nature, slow to anger and the spitting image of old Jack. The parents could relax as the "less fortunate" brother had a "whole-man" brother now to defend and protect him when they had crossed to the other side.

Sitting cross-legged on that ridge, Peter reflected on his life, knowing that two more families had recently left the encampment and gone to make a permanent home in Canada.

There were now nine families here trying to survive, clinging to the "Old Ways" as long as they could, hating to let go and yet, knowing that each day they became a little less Indian and a little more White. And still, this chief knew that the forty-one men, women and children living here on the fringes of these English settlements did have a free lifestyle.

No society is perfect and it is never easy living off the land as they did, and the hard times came and then they passed. It was a transient and gypsy-like way to exist, but that had been the way the Native American had lived for centuries; life some times good, others bad, but always free.

At will, these Dawnland people left the Tarritine encampment and went fishing on the Androscoggin River (Fish Curing Place). Here they camped and often smoked their catch right along the shores of that river. These were still good family times in spite of the fact that they were always changing and always resisting those changes too. For the most part, most White people were so suspicious of them that they left them alone. Some even called them gypsies but this did not matter, these Abenakis know who they were and where they came from.

The Tarritine income was subsidized a great deal, as the men hired out as day laborers on nearby farms and also as guides for private hunting, fishing and surveying expeditions. Their women had built a wonderful market for their sweetgrass baskets, and the smell of that sweetgrass was so strong here this evening that Peter thought you could cut it with a knife, but it was a good smell, a sacred smell, in fact.

They were a funny sight to behold, these cliff-dwellers, who were dressed in cotton, muslin and the wool garments of the White Man and not in their own traditional fur, fringes and buckskin. The men and the women both loved hats especially, hats with feathers and their proud copper-colored faces probably looked funny and quite strange indeed, peeking out from underneath these "paleface" head pieces.

These Dawnland survivors used utensils almost all made of iron now, and this was fine. If a tool was good; better than what they had, then they would adopt its use and quickly.

Every Eden has its snake however, and one had come to Tarritine. This serpent was more deadly than any timber rattler. This is not to say that the Abenakis did not respect the snake, because they did. In times of war they dipped their arrow points in snake venom and for hundreds of years they had used snake blood in their medicines, but this "No Good Snake," poisoned you from the inside out, and its name was "Firewater." It was easy to purchase and Peter, like so many of the other men had a fondness for it and took advantage of every celebration to sneak away from the disapproving tongues of their women and drink this rot gut.

Peter took another pull from the small flask that he now always carried on his person. The crimson sun was setting and the brilliance of this September day was gone, replaced suddenly by a chilly breeze that swayed the saplings.

He drank again from the flask, then wiped his mouth and put the cork back into the flask and stuffed it into his inside coat pocket.

Peter was returning from guiding a surveying party through the Paul Stream area in Maidstone, Vermont and he was tired and glad to be back in this make-shift village that he called home. He could hear the night sounds from the encampment all around him as he sat there in the shadows. The children were playing their last games of the day and the women were scurrying around, stoking the kindling to build up a bed of coals in their nightfires. As they did this, they called for their children to come to the evening meal.

Peter grimaced as the high and raspy voice of Old Bessie, filled his ears. Everyone in the encampment knew her as "Crow Woman," because she was the most malicious gossip and "pot stirrer" in the whole village. He remembered how happy he had been when a family of Cowasucks enroute to Canada, almost took her with them. That family had an old uncle with them who lived alone by choice, and he thought at first that he liked Crow Woman. What a relief to get rid of that old crone thought Peter, but at the very last minute that Cowasuck had changed his mind, stating flatly "She no go. Her mouth too big for my ears!"

Rising to his feet, Peter heard his sister Nelemano, calling his three children (by his first wife) and for just a minute, he was bitterly sad. She had died, that good and gentle creature, after being stricken with a sore throat which Nelemano and no other Shaman could cure and she had gone to the other side, with a part of Peter's own heart, leaving him with Peter, Dennis, and Sarah.

He never spoke her name again, but in his heart he remembered her as a gentle and obedient woman, not really beautiful but very easy to love.

The second wife that Peter took was also Abenaki, but she was so mean that many times he thought that she was a Mohawk! She was the mother of John and Winona and as pretty as she was headstrong. She was a loner and she went alone berry picking and there she had died after being brutally mauled by a black bear. She had always been a brave and willful woman, that Alwildia, but she did not know that fateful day that the bear she was arguing with was carrying lead in him and was almost as contrary and ugly as she was. Alwildia and that wounded bear began picking blackberries from the same bush and he refused to share them with her and she refused to share them with him. He growled, but she would not listen and she would not run; instead she sassed and threatened him and a fight ensued. She was armed only with a small kindling ax and of course, she was no match for that wounded bear.

This had happened over in Androscoggin country and her bones were lying there in Androscoggin ground nearly three weeks before Peter even knew about it. At the time, he was away guiding a party of surveyors through an area north of Stratford Bog.

When Peter returned his shock quickly turned to guilt and in his grief he drank more and more.

Peter took out the whiskey and took another swallow, and savoring that hot liquid in his mouth, he regretted that he never saw his wife again—alive or dead.

Peter knew that Alwildia was always threatening to "split the blanket," or divorce him, and walk away from him and all the children, but still he missed her. He did not speak her name ever again, but if his thoughts could have been put into words, they would have said "Woman, hateful and hard-hearted as you were, you were brave and you died well."

Once more Peter hid the flask under his coat and reaching into his tobacco pouch, he put a dab in his mouth. Soon he would meet Nelemano, that rigid and bossy sister of his who cared for his children now. And, if Nel smelled liquor on his breath, he would think that Alwildia was back from the grave, or as the White Men say, "there'd be Hell to pay!"

He could see the long, lean shadow of Nelemano, as she poked at the coals in her evening fire. He squared his shoulders and looked straight ahead. His sister had the coldest stare in the world.

Peter walked toward that little cluster of wigwams and the sounds of children romping and laughing, filled his ears. Children playing, mothers calling, dogs barking, yes, he was home.

He heard a bird take off across the forest and just as it landed in another tree, he heard a child's voice taunting "Jackson, I'll get you back for this," and Peter grinned, because he knew that Dennis had probably just won another round of boys wrestling.

John was too little to get into too much trouble yet, and tiny Winona was hitching along the ground and although she could not yet take a step, the child could climb like a damned raccoon and was just as full of mischief as "Azeban," that trouble-making raccoon that had gone down through history in Algonquian legends.

The "peepers" were gone with late summer, but now and then a cricket could be detected. Peter smelled all the different foods cooking and the scent of birch and beechnut fires. He inhaled slowly. These were the smells and sounds of life—life at Tarritine, that is.

And then he heard the sweetest sound of all, the voice of little Sarah, who now had seen seven snows. She was the epitome of her mother who waited on the other side. Sarah was a gentle child and yet, she had a quiet forcefulness about her. If she had a fault, it would be her stubbornness, thought Peter and one day who knew, she might possess those rare gifts of healing and mysticism as did one of her Sokokis grandmothers, who was a highly reputed Shaman.

His thoughts, as he approached the wigwam where he lived, were "Daughter Sarah, I hope your little moccasins make happy tracks in many, many snows."

Perhaps, that warbling night-bird in the distance, knew something that Peter did not know and that was that indeed her moccasins would make tracks in many, many snows—in 101 more snows.

He stepped out of the night shadows as soundlessly as the flutter of a butterfly's wing, his gaunt frame casting eerie shadows on her cooking fire. Nelemano sucked in her breath, and in a startled gasp said "Peter!" It had taken a few minutes before she realized who he was. His dark clothing and his hair, the color of her wood smoke, made him a part of the immediate scene, a part of what saw and yet of what she did not see. "Good thing he is my friend," she thought and she was just a trifle chagrined that she had let herself be "snuck up on," as the children would say.

She smoothed her greying temples and her only greeting to her brother was "Brother, you kept your word." When Peter left on the 20th day of August, he had promised his children that he would return to them when the hills all around them were painted, and they were, and Peter was here, true to his word.

From all corners of that cooking fire they came rushing at him, his children, his legacy. Children were wonderful, he thought. On a day when a man knew he was not the one he used to be, he sees that glow of vitality still alive and burning in the faces of his young ones.

Peter picked up baby Winona and swung her high in the air with her short and stubby legs flying like her thin little pigtails. She squealed with delight, and no sooner had he sat her down than his person was attacked by sons Dennis and John, who were hugging his legs like two ducks on a June bug.

Standing apart and looking so hopeful and shy was young Peter, his handicapped son. The older Peter went to him, picked him up and swung him higher and longer than any of them, asking the beaming boy "Peter, did Dennis and John take care of you?" With the broadest of Indian smiles young Peter nodded his head "Yes." And the only sad thing about this greeting was that this child didn't realize that he could never take care of himself.

Like a flash of sunlight, Sarah came flying out of that part of her home that she shared with Aunt Nel, away from all male family members.

Sarah was slender like the Kohla women had been, and Peter was glad of that. Nelemano had inherited the bone structure of the Taxos side and she had shoulders bigger than most men. Nel had always been tall and not fat, but "raw-boned," while Sarah, even now at the spindly-legged colt stage had the finer bones of her mother's line. She had her mother's doe-like eyes, but she had Nel's pout if she was starting to get angry. Peter smiled softly to himself, because he could see so many of Nel's traits in his daughter. He also knew that if he had ever said this to Nelemano, that she would have said it was not so.

Sarah's hair hung free, flying around her face, and that hair was as black and shiny as a crow's wing. Without the bear grease that the Kitsia "old ones" used, her hair might get that reddish tint to it, thought Peter.

He hated that reddish-black look and he hoped that his daughter would protect her hair from the elements, so that she would never have it.

As Sarah embraced her father, the child exclaimed "Father it is so good you are here. We missed you!" Her face lit up with a smile of joy.

Peter slung the sack he was carrying to the ground. "We will eat and then I have presents for all of you."

Nelemano stirred the cook-fire and said nothing. Peter was too happy. Peter was bearing gifts. Peter was half-drunk and would probably spoil the taste of his food by the tobacco that he had stuffed in his mouth to fool her, but not for one minute was this Dawnland woman fooled.

Peter seated himself by the cook-fire. He averted Nel's eyes as the children joined on both sides of him and they watched the stew bubbling. It was the same old stew that they had eaten last night, with one more partridge breast thrown in, but it smelled so much better tonight, the children thought. Peter could have told them that food was always better, when shared with those we love.

He drank a full cup of hot herb tea and it was good. It helped to take the tobacco taste from his palate. He grimaced.

Aunt Nel took her place at the circle around the fire after handing bowls and spoons to all the others seated there, and then from the cooking pot that simmered she served each one their supper.

Peter smelled the sweet corn cakes that Nel had prepared with maple syrup and apples, and he had to say that she was a very good cook. And in his heart, Peter realized that she was not only a good cook but a good person, for she had dedicated her whole life to the upbringing of his children.

They ate and spoke as they did. Indian children, though usually well behaved never had to be "seen and not heard." They were seen, and when it was time for them to speak they were heard, not scolded and not expected to be as smart as adults. These Dawnland children, were made to feel that their input also counted in the life of a family.

When Peter asked "All is well, Sister?" and Nel looked squarely at him and said "most ways, so." Peter knew that all was not quite well here.

The father asked each child then what had happened in its life since they last spoke, and he listened as they told him about this world of Tarritine, at least as they saw it through their children's eyes, and sometimes they had the sharpest eyes of all.

By the time the sweet corn cakes were gone, Peter knew that there had been some family trouble during his absence, concerning his niece Nancee and her half-French husband, Giroud. Nel's lack of interest as the children talked, told Peter that she would explain this business to him later.

"John, you have a cut over your eye, and Dennis, your forehead is bruised," the children's father said and then asked "What happened?" John and Dennis exchanged glances and then, John never being one to talk, Dennis said "Crow Woman told Josh that our grandfather was a Mohawk!" Dennis paused and then went on "I hit him, he hit me."

Peter knew the rest and he was glad that his sons would stand up for themselves against that old liar. Gossip was an evil thing.

"I hate that Crow Woman and I put a lizard in her water jug." This was young John's only comment on the story, and Aunt Nel gave one of those disapproving snorts, high up her nose like those Indians do, while Peter had to fake blowing his nose in a large bandanna to keep them all for realizing that he was laughing. He should have put her in her water jug.

When he recovered he said, "Next time they tell you that, you tell them "Better a Mohawk than a fool or a Magpie!" This brought all those seated around the fire into uncontrolled laughter, even the stoic Aunt Nel.

The children had finished eating, and they filed out and seated themselves beside the outside fire which crackled within a circle of blackened dirt and hissing rocks.

This was the way most "good weather" days ended, with the whole family assembled for the story hour —the bewitching hour that kept the heritage and culture of a Native American people alive. These stories were unwritten history, legends, and lessons of life, educational and often humorous and at other times quite spiritual in nature. These Abenakis believed that old Indian proverb or adage: "Have time for your children in their youth, and they will have time for you in your old age."

These were a people who practiced what they preached much better than the White Man, and a very big part of "making time for their children in their youth" were the lessons and legends and history passed down from one generation to the other at the story hour.

Before the stories could begin tonight there was a matter of gifts to be given out, and Aunt Nel was presented with a tortoise shell comb. Small Winona, perched upon her father's lap was waving the ugliest new rag doll that Nelemano had ever seen, but the baby girl liked it just fine.

Peter, the child, was given his own real leather belt and Dennis, and John both beamed when they were handed beautifully beaded knife sheaths.

Sarah was delighted when she realized that her father had given her a small medicine or wampum pouch, as handsome as it was practical. It was made of soft doeskin and had long slender strings of rawhide attached to it, and she would carry it either around her neck or tied securely around her waist, like Aunt Nel wore her own. This pouch was trimmed with porcupine quills and baby otter tails. Sarah clutched the bag silently to her heart, for she had been asking to have one of these for almost a year now, but Aunt Nel had said that she was still too little. It was nice to realize that in his astute wisdom, her father could see what Aunt Nel could not, that Sarah was growing up. Little Sarah felt very old and very proud right at this particular moment in her life.

The youngest Peter, that slow child, played a few minutes on the reed flute that his brother Dennis had whittled for him, and then taught him how to play. This reed flute had been hand carved with two chambers.

Native American music, true Native American music, is always more haunting than melodious; and this "handicapped boy" got a higher and even more of a haunting sound than most, from the home-made flute. As he played he actually captured the treble of the nightbird; and the father was happy, for he knew that young Peter, who had been cheated of so much, had been given a fine gift by the Great Spirit. After all, he had been given the gift of music. It was a beautiful night, this clear September evening, indeed a bit too warm for the season known for frosts.

The night stars looked down upon them huddled here before the glowing embers, and as partially-painted Autumn leaves around them rustled, the smell of burning beechnut wood crackled and filled the nostrils with the familiar aroma of home.

There was no other sound now but the wind, and it was time at last for the same stories and legends to be repeated again and again, but at each new fire and with each telling, the old stories were new and fresh and magic all over again.

No night fire ever burns or smells exactly the same way, and each bed of coals leaves something different burned into the memory of the mind. Things written here are never forgotten, because it is a time of magic for the young and for the old. Was it perhaps that the fire actually did mesmerize one, or was it that those eternal stars above put the glow of a child's heart into the heart of any adult that sat before a fire with children.

Somewhere, someone knew the answer, but if this was a form of hypnotism then let the coals blaze ever brighter as the nightfire sings its song and the spell of the story hour weaves its fire magic into all hearts.

As night pulled her black curtain over all below, the story hour began. The first legend was always about "Azeban," that mythical-trickster raccoon, because this was the one that young Peter, John and Winona too enjoyed the most. These three always fell asleep quicker than Dennis and Sarah, and that was perhaps the most important reason that the adventurous raccoon got top billing.

This poor Azeban was always scheming and getting himself into the worst of all possible situations. Because of his mischievous nature, he was always plotting and playing tricks (that usually backfired) on all the other forest animals. The stories always had it that every time Azeban set a trap for someone else, he ultimately got caught in it himself. The moral of this story was to warn children against being a sneak or a trickster, either one, but instead to strive to be straight-forward in all that they did. It was for their benefit to realize early in life that if one always sets out to do bad things to others, that misfortune will always fall back upon the evil perpetrator.

The younger children howled with laughter as Peter told them about the time Azeban sneaked over to fox's nightfire. While brother fox lay sleeping, Azeban tried to stamp out the fire as a great joke on fox, who was supposed to wake up to a cold fire, but who instead was awakened abruptly by the bellowing and roaring of Azeban, who was running off screaming loudly with his tail on fire.

Why only the last snow, Azeban had his nose frostbitten because he stuck it into a beaver's lodge in the middle of the winter. In other words, if he had kept his nose in his own business and out of brother beaver's, he would have been fine. On the other hand, if he had done that he would never have been as famous or infamous as he was. He would not have been "Azeban"...

Aunt Nel settled her large frame back against the shadows and worked the sweetgrass strips in her capable hands. " It was good to see Peter here with his family, telling the stories that should be told by the father to his children," she thought.

She gazed up momentarily at those night stars, and wondered briefly if they themselves had any idea of the magic that they brought to every story hour. Those night lights could be old story tellers!

The children giggled with pleasure and delight as their father went on to tell them more and more antics of that trickster raccoon. Then, as the coals burned lower, Winona began her little chant, the one she always sang herself to sleep with. For this little Woman of the Dawnland, tonight old Azeban had done his last mischievous deed and when her little head drooped in sleep she was carried by Aunt Nel, and placed in a small basket-bed made of white ash which Nel's big hands had made. The bed sat directly beside Aunt Nel's and when Winona was tucked in snugly the child's Aunt returned to the gathering by the fire.

Peter added some kindling to the coals and poked the fire until flames once more burst from the glowing embers. As the fire built up to his satisfaction, he banked it and then sat down cross-legged before that fire and told the children about the swamp beast.

And as the smoke rose from the ring of blackened rocks, so did the story of that phantom who lived in the swamp, the "swamp menace." Children, if they listened on a clear night, could hear him calling to them. He was always in the bogs and wetlands, hidden by the swale grass and the dead-tree forest. And he would sing, a soft song he would sing, and his voice could be heard calling for miles and miles. If he would sing from Cat Bow Swamp in Lunenburg, children on Tarritine Ledge in South Guildhall, could hear that eerie call.

He called to the children in this way:

"Come, come to me, away from your mother and your father. Do not listen to them, listen to my song and then to your own heart. Come to the mists of the swamp. I am here and I am your friend."

Peter puffed his pipe and then looked at his children. "Is he really your friend, Dennis?" asked the father.

"No, Father, he is not my friend," was the boy's answer and Peter asked "Then why does he try to pretend that he is?"

"Because, we trust our friends. He wants us to believe his lies, but if we listen to our parents and stay away from the swamp at night he can never hurt us." said Dennis.

"This is true, my son. He cannot come and get you, and you must never be the fool and go to him. If you do not listen to him, he will get tired of it all and go off and call to children not as smart as you, my children."

No sooner had Peter said this, than the youngest, Peter, departed for his bed, leaving Sarah, Dennis and John to listen to the legend of the crow.

The two boys looked at each other. They knew the story of crow. They knew that was why Old Bessie was called "Crow Woman," but perhaps if they listened to it one more time they could better understand why that old woman was so hateful and such a troublemaker.

Nel shut her eyes in a contented half-sleep herself, and pulled her bright red wool shawl a little tighter around her shoulders, for suddenly the air of this clear September night had gotten cold and damp, it seemed.

Peter continued to puff on his pipe and while he told the crow story the smoke from the pipe rose in circles that forecast rain. It mattered not if the smoke went straight up or formed a ring, this was Peter's way of sending his stories to the Spirit World on the wings of the pleasant and sacred scent of tobacco smoke.

In his deep and rumbling voice Peter began "In the days when the world was young The Owner, Odzihozo (the Great Spirit of our Grandfather's) made all things. He made the crow a beautiful bird, sleek and magnificent to behold. The crow of long ago had a beautiful melodious voice and powerful wings, and just like its brother the eagle, it could soar. Crow was as big and even as powerful as the eagle, with a massive wingspan. He was not brown like some hawks, or brown and white like the mighty eagle, but instead he was black, the color of the Great Bear himself." At this point, Peter made a long pause so that the imagination of the children could focus upon the crow of long ago.

The story began again: "The crow now, for all of his gifts, had some very bad things about his person. He was by nature a sneak and a gossip, and worse yet a liar. He listened to all the little birds when they talked in hushed whispers about matters close to their hearts and then he flew swiftly away and all over the forest he went taking great pleasure in repeating these secrets. He screamed them across the sky and even in the tree tops to the chipmunks and the porcupines, who stopped their work and listened in despair. It was sad. Nothing or no one was safe from his vicious tongue."

The only sound was that of the night wind, picking up sparks from the coal bed as Peter went on, "Soon, the birds of the forest were learning that they could not trust that crow at all. Too bad, he was such a beautiful feathered creature, but he had a reputation now of being a malicious gossip and a troublemaker, who added his own two-cents worth of lies to every story he heard. He was very proud of himself and he felt important indeed, since he knew everything about everybody! Well before long, the birds would not talk at all when he was around; and worse yet, they even stopped their singing as they worked, lest he make something bad out of the songs they sang." Again the father paused so his audience could reflect the enormity of what that crow hand done.

As young John's head bobbed and he fought off the dream weaver, Peter finished his story.

"The Great Spirit, Odzihozo, was very angry at the crow. It appears that the crow had a brain smaller than his ego and a mouth bigger than both these things. The Owner missed the singing of the little birds and the chatter of the small woodland creatures, now also reluctant to speak. The once noisy forest was as quiet as could be and he, that crow, was the cause! So, Odzihozo summoned that offending bird and said to him 'Crow, my heart is sad. I am sorry for you. You are now and always will be your own worst enemy. I made you as majestic as the eagle, but you have a small heart. You delight in others misery and you thrive on refuse and create your own in addition, so I will make you a small bird like your heart. And you will live the rest of your life feeding on carrion. Because of your love for gossip and rotten things, I have made you a scavenger bird and your descendants shall not have a mellow voice. They will not even be able to talk plain, because I have slivered your hateful tongue. From the crow's mouth, will come the most monotonous rasp in all the forest, and you will never again fly across the woodlands below, telling either confidences or untruths, because no one will listen to you or be able to understand you. And you are the cause! You are the cause and from this day on, the only cry from your mouth will be 'Caw, Caw, Caw,' and now crow, it is finished.'"

And for that evening, at least for these children, it was.

There was a lull in all but the crackle of the fire and the wind that stirred the dry leaves around the camp. Nelemano worked in silence and Peter pressed the flask in his pocket, and to her cool muteness, he asked "What is going on with Nancee?"

Aunt Nel never looked up from her intricate basketry, but answered flat and to the point, "Her husband Giroud, he wants to leave and go and live over Androscoggin way—Berlin town."

As her brother listened, Nelemano continued "Nancee wants to stay with the family and head for Springfield, Massachusetts, with us in two weeks and Giroud accuses her of being a 'bad woman' and he is insane with jealousy and makes threats against her."

Peter's face turned into a black cloud. Nelemano stopped work on the basket in her hands and remembered "Peter, I said the day she married him against our counsel that the time would come when he would beat her."

"And, I said, 'only once!'" was his reply and then with a quick glance, he asked "Nel, has he dared to do this?"

She shook her head no, and explained "Only just threaten, but that Nancee, daughter of your sister Skyry, she says she is not 'bad woman,' she is good woman and she is tired of his accusations and lies. She says she will never go away from her family with Giroud."

Nelemano paused and then went on "They have been waiting for you to return. Giroud wants a council meeting and he is going to split the blanket and leave Nancee. But, cocky smart one that he is, he wants her family to hear his side at council," she finished.

"That Giroud, he just got his request." Peter said.

The entire camp would listen to all of Giroud's grievances and Nancee would be there listening with the rest and would have a chance to refute his complaints with a rebuttal of her own, or to sit in silence with her head down and let the entire family council decide who and who not talked straight.

Splitting the blanket or divorcing, was now starting to be a more common practice than it used to be, but if one was unhappy in the partnership of marriage and worse yet two, then it was the right thing to do.

Nel put her partially constructed basket down and said to Peter "Brother, take your hidden rum out of your shirt pocket and drink yourself to sleep if that is your pleasure, but my bones are already aching here in this Tarritine country and I look forward to leaving. The ducks have gone over, the first ones, and I am eager to follow. And now, Peter Jackson, this winter when we get to Massachusetts or New Jersey, I want to live in a wooden house with a stove. I am cold and my bones creak in this climate and I am ready to live in a house. I was not ready last year, but this year I am ready."

Peter almost smiled at the flatness with which his sister had told him that she knew about his "secret flask," and of her decision to live like a White Woman. That was Nel, and the White Man's clock meant nothing to her, for Nelemano Jackson lived her life on "Nel's time," and as stubborn as she was, by God— that was a good thing.

He would not drink in her presence, but he did say "Nel, I know that I drink too much, but it helps me to sleep. The dream of the bright whirlwind becomes more frequent in my old age."

Rising from her sitting position, she said "Peter Jackson, it is the poison in your hidden bottle that rots your brain and makes the dream." She was a soft-spoken woman, straight and to the point.

Peter controlled his temper and simply shook his head no, adding, "No, Nel, it is not so. Only when I am drunk do I have any rest from it. I know this dream means something; it has to mean something very important in my life."

"Well, when you find out what that is brother, I hope you are sober enough to remember it," snapped Nelemano, and then she abruptly disappeared into the wigwam where she and her brother's children slept.

Peter did not hear her leave, because she had not intended that he would. After several minutes of staring into the white coals, Peter tapped his pipe and began to drink from the much discussed flask in his pocket. She did not understand. Why should she? Even he didn't.

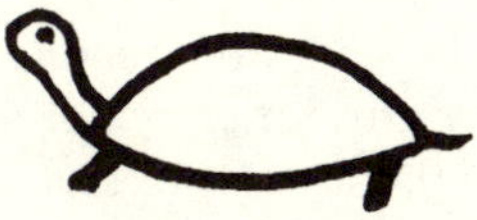

Long before the first rays of the morning sun fell softly on the "Dawnland People" of Tarritine Ledge, the camp was alive with daylight sounds.

In the old days, the men were up before dawn and off on their fishing or hunting trips at this hour, but now these summer campers were off to the nearby farms to work as day laborers. Some just loaded themselves up with baskets, and in the course of a day they would walk miles to the neighboring towns and outlying farm houses and sell their baskets as door-to-door salesmen, or even perhaps swap for apples, maple syrup and other food supplies that they were fond of. Trails where warriors once roamed were now trod by peaceful vendors, still trying to stay free and survive as best they could.

Peter awoke with a dull headache. He had them often, but after some strong coffee or "Nel's tea," this pain in his head would usually go away. He dressed in the semi-darkness and decided by the feel of his own aging bones that the weather of this early Autumn day was going to be fine. Good, he would take the boys hunting.

Then Sarah burst through the divided part of the wigwam and bounded up to her father, who had his homespun trousers on and was in the middle of buttoning up her shirt. She was as frisky as a newborn colt and for just one moment, Peter wondered if ever in his life he had felt as good as she seemed to feel this morning?

Sarah stepped back from her father, for the first time noticing the stench of stale whiskey and clothing badly in need of washing.

"Father, good thing you came home on wash day or a crow would eat you!" the child exclaimed and Peter, now fully awake, was embarrassed that it took a child of only seven snows to inform him that he was a dirty stinker!

Peter had to grin to himself at her observance of his somewhat dishevelled appearance.

"Your father needs a bath and a change of clothes, Sarah, and I may even get a haircut, but first I need some tea. This old carrion has a headache."

He made his way toward the inside bed of coals in the first part of the wigwam. There sat Nel's teapot bubbling, and the smell of blueberry cakes was strong and comforting, even to a vile-smelling old critter like himself.

Sarah was all compassion for her father's headache. She knew he had those morning headaches quite a lot, and she also knew that Aunt Nel had no sympathy for them. That made no sense, for Aunt Nel was the kindest and very best doctor that Sarah knew of.

"Father, you drink your tea! I will get you something from Aunt Nel's tote bag and it will make that headache go away fast," she said and snapped her fingers as she did. This was a new habit, acquired just since Peter had been away this last time.

As she bounded off she said "You need spirea, Father!" And even at that tender age, Sarah was right, for spirea or meadowsweet contains salicin. Salicin is also found in the bark, leaves and roots of poplar and willow trees and we know it today as aspirin.

Peter didn't know it, but his headache didn't have a chance, for little Sarah returned with a cup containing a powder substance and then poured Aunt Nel's "boneset tea," over it and half an hour later, Sarah's first patient was heading for a bath and a haircut, minus one headache.

"Father, you don't take care of yourself." the child told him, and he nodded "I'll try harder, Sarah," he said as he beheld the serious face of his oldest child of seven— going on thirty-five and already giving a man orders like a bossy White Woman— or was it bossy Aunt Nel?

Shortly after breakfast Nelemano took Sarah aside and helped her to tie the new medicine pouch around her waist and said to her "This morning child we go to collect herbs and roots and many good green gifts from Mother Earth. You are now responsible for your own private medicine bag, but you can only put one thing at a time into it, because you are young Sarah, and you have much to learn. Many times the berries or leaves of a plant are a miracle cure for something, but the roots of that same plant could be deadly. You my child, must know the difference—and the dosage."

Taking Sarah's hand, Aunt Nel led the child toward the swampy soil surrounding Tarritine Ledge. And though many people feel even today that a swamp is a useless tract of land, Sarah Jackson would be told repeatedly by her Aunt Nel the herbalist how incorrect this theory was, because swamps have always provided a tremendous supply of medicinal plants and herbs that needed the moistness of wet earth in which to grow.

"If it were not for the swamps growing the medicine, the people who tend the maize might grow sick and die," Aunt Nel continued.

Nelemano then smiled at her small pupil and asked "Now Sarah, do you have any questions before we begin our first lesson?"

For a few minutes the child was silent and then her serene little face broke into a proud smile and she said "Aunt Nel, how do you know so many things? Did you just wake up one morning and know everything?" Nelemano Jackson smoothed her hair and smiled softly. It was a darn good thought, but it was not true.

" No Sarah. It has taken many, many mornings to learn this little bit of healing that I know. My grandmother taught me one day at a time, one green plant at a time, just as I will show you."

They walked on and Nelemano continued "Indians learned from watching our brother animals, for they knew how to use the fruits of the earth to heal their sore hides and cure their sick bodies. The oldest grandmother's oldest grandmother observed this, and it is from the animals that we have learned to heal ourselves."

As silent as shadows they moved among the grasses glistening with dew. Someday, when this child was older, Nelemano would tell her how the old ones had noticed animals suffering with ticks and heat rash and how they had seen the animals roll in the yarrow leaves which healed their hides, and so the Indians made a powder and a poultice from the leaves of the Yarrow plant and rubbed their own affected hides and likewise they were cured. Moving along, Nel thought ahead to a day when she would point to the white acorn and ask "Sarah, what is made from this—and why? And someday Sarah would reply "sweet oil," for minor skin irritations." speaking of cures, Nel thought to herself that she would have to chew some water lilies soon to help her indigestion.

Today's lesson would begin with a favorite plant of the marshlands, the cattail. The Abenakis ate the raw shoots and boiled the roots as a vegetable. The cattail's fluffy head was swallowed to stop a diarrhea and during Nel's own infancy, these were used as a soft padding for her diapers.

Someday Sarah would know that the yellow plant or goldthread which prevailed all over Cat Bow Swamp, was a soothing gargle for sore throats, and also dried up canker sores and healed irritated gums. But, this root in the wrong hands was extremely poisonous. "Trial and Error," was Indian medicine.

As they gathered their precious cargo of cattails, Nelemano said "Close to the sickness lies the cause and also lies the cure." This line is not engraved in many books of medicine but it was a saying burned forever into Sarah's mind, and one that she remembered all her life, because again and again, it proved itself to be true.

The day progressed warm and pleasant. Peter Jackson took his three sons with him into the forest to perhaps shoot a partridge or, even better, a duck. The wild turkey was long gone and about as plentiful in the woods as was the elusive white fox. It didn't matter, the boys would still enjoy this day. Peter, the slow child, would stay with his father, but Dennis and John would fan out. Peter would tell them where to go and just what to do if they saw game. They did not carry a weapons; only Peter carried a shotgun. Today the boys were scouting and in doing so, were learning to seek out some food, stay with it, and lead their father to it. Above all they must be quiet, as quiet as a woodsmunk, and as stealthy as any of their oldest grandfathers had been. The thundering drum of a partridge told young Dennis that he had overlooked one, as he took a higher trail than his younger brother John.

John passed where a huge male bear had marked his territory, and by the way the claw marks had dug into the flesh of the tree bark the boy knew that it was a large one and that standing up this bear would be taller than he was. He kept walking but he was more alert now, for he knew the legend of his mother, Alwildia, and that she had been mauled to death by a black bear. He was afraid, but he was more mad at the bear now than he was possessed by fear. John, with his child's ax, whittled as quietly as he could the end of a sturdy limb that lay on the ground.

He did not want to fight this bear. He was of the Bear Clan himself, and had the bear that killed his mother not been wounded, that probably would never have happened, but if this bear too was crazy, then John would hold the stake before his chest with both hands and hope as the bear closed in to grab him that the sharp end of the stake and the bear's own strength would pierce the mighty animal's heart, and so avenge his mother. If the bear got him, then Alwildia would know that he too was brave and that he had not backed down.

A grunt behind the boy spun him around and he was relieved to behold only a big old porcupine, and that stubborn quilly pig would have walked right up to John, if he hadn't flailed his arms at it and threatened it silently with the stake. After a few minutes it waddled off in another direction.

John, while whittling the end of the stake very sharp so as to use as a lance, had in his haste cut his own index finger on the left hand. It did not bleed much; it just smarted and burned.

He knew what to do, and upon passing the first balsam fir he cut a small piece of the gum or pitch that ran down the sides of the tree and applied it to the puncture to draw out infection and to heal.

Just then John heard the mewing of the slate-colored catbird, but he knew it was not that; it was a signal from Dennis, high on the ridge above him. Dennis had found a bird and John would hold his position until he heard the crack of his father's shotgun. It was a good sound as it split the air and there was only one shot. That was very good because two blasts is maybe and three is goodbye. Suddenly, John could taste that bird roasting for supper.

He joined his father and Dennis shortly and Peter told his sons that after they had skinned and woods dressed the partridge, young Peter would carry it home.

This father was just a little vexed as he silently remembered when the time spent dressing a catch was much better spent getting another meal. However, the last time he threw a feathered-carcass at Nelemano she had thrown it right back into his face and said cooley "Brother, I don't do that no more. You do it!" Peter scowled mightily and thought to himself that Nelemano acted just like a White Woman most of the time. The world was getting to be a crazier place all the time, Peter Jackson had decided and he at this moment felt very old.

"Why do you carry a sharp spear, John?" the father questioned his youngest son. John explained about the bear markings on the tree, so high up on the tree.

"Were the marks fresh?" was Peter's next question and John answered, "Yes father."

As Peter's eyes surveyed the stake, the sharpened end told him that his son John was preparing to go to war with the bear if it showed up.

"John, next time you find a tree that will hold you and not the awasos (bear) and you go for it!" Peter took the stick from the boy and threw it on the ground.

Young John Jackson stopped in his tracks, looked straight at his father and replied "My mother did not climb a tree; she did not run."

"My son," said Peter and then went on "Your mother has been a long time dead, a long time dead!" Peter's voice was sharp, almost scolding and then in a softer tone he continued "The bear that killed your mother was wounded John, and your mother, for once in her life—should have backed down! Courage is a fine thing, but there are times when good judgment should be exercised instead of bravery." He spoke gently but firmly and John listened.

Peter tousled the boy's unruly dark hair in a playful gesture to let him know that although he admired his son's determination and valor, the next time he could trust him to do the smart thing.

As they walked along together Peter felt a sense of pride that they were still together, and living off the land just as their ancestors before them had, since beyond memory. Mixed thoughts weaved their way into Peter's memory as they walked toward home. The look of beaming pride on young Peter's face as he carried home the woods-dressed bird to Nelemano's fire was fine to see.

Peter, the elder, was remembering the very first deer that he had ever killed. It was so long ago. He was eleven years old and hunting in the woods near the Village of Odanak or St. Francis, P.Q. Canada. As was the custom of the Dawnland People, he as the hunter, was not allowed to partake of any of the meat himself. That was a no-no for a hunter's first kill. If he partook of it he would not inherit the deer's spirit or woods wariness. It was the way it was done back then. He would divide the meat with all the families gathered there, and the next deer he killed, he too could enjoy the taste of venison. He remembered how he had said the "Deer Prayer" to the Great Spirit, to thank him for allowing Peter so much success in bringing down that fat young buck.

That very night, the whole village gathered at his parent's cooking fire to share the feast that Peter had provided them. He thought back to how the most tender parts of the meat was given to the Kitsia (old ones) with poor teeth and the little ones, because they needed the special cuts. This was a good way, for it showed that these people cared about each other, and a man who lived in a caring way would never have "withered hands or baby fingers pointing at him." It was what the old ones said, because their grandfathers had told them so.

There had been much singing and dancing after the meal on that night of Peter's first deer kill, and he had been made to feel like a mighty hunter.

Like it had happened only yesterday, Peter remembered how he had risen and told his story to all gathered there and somehow he managed to keep his voice steady, although he was sure that they could see his knees trembling.

It was funny now to think that his father had insisted that he say the "Deer Prayer," in his own words to thank "Odzihozo" for granting him the favor of brother deer.

Odd, he reflected how his heart had leaped within his chest when he saw that beautiful animal fall, and yet he was sad at the same time. Like the drumming of a distant tom-tom, these words of thanks and praise washed over Peter's brain like a tide. He recalled kneeling before the carcass of that fleet-footed one and saying, "Oh, Swift One, make Me like Yourself, Proud, and Sure and Strong. Put into My heart the Wisdom of your

Ways, Until our Spirits meet again, Old Friend, I thank you for this Chase and Kill."

Peter's eyes stung with tears, for it had been years and years since he had said those words. These were the words his grandfather had told his father and someday he too would tell them to his sons, he hoped. Who knew? He did not even know that he could remember those words until now. So many things were left unremembered by the People of the Dawnland. No more celebrations the night before the hunt and no more "Thank You" feasts after, for the White Man thought such things were foolish and no one must offend the White Man.

Dennis spoke and brought his father back into reality. "Father, tonight please tell us about you and Miles Hunter and the first moose you killed." Peter nodded that he would.

He would never forget the fear and the thrill that had swept over him and Miles. They had tagged along on the February hunt when the men could out-maneuver the huge moose, usually floundering in the deep snows of winter. That had been an exciting time, but not their time. The moose of which Dennis had spoken was one that he and Miles had killed from a canoe in the early morning mists of Lake Memphremagog. How cleverly his father Tack (Jack) had tricked that bull to come close to where his paddle now lay silent in the water and swalegrass. They had rubbed the scent of apples on their elbows and Peter had questioned the big bull's wisdom of smelling an apple in a lake. He grinned to himself as he recalled the way old Jack just looked at him with his sharp, bird-like eyes and said "Male in love don't think, him only smell."

And that is just what the moose that Miles and he brought down was doing, he was not thinking, he was smelling.

Ever so lightly, Jack had touched his paddle to the water and when he stopped his canoe, he took from his storage bag a tube of birch bark, rolled up funnel-like and resembling a big powder horn. He placed the small end of the cone in his mouth and blew through it, making soft and haunting sounds which anyone would have taken for a cow moose calling. He would then dip his birch bark tube into the water noiselessly and hold it up in the air and let the water run along through it. When a nearby feeding bull heard that call, the young boys knew that old Jack was right.

About the fourth time that Jack made that call and dipped the cone in the water, the bull could stand it no longer. He was sure that the sound of the water drizzling along through the tube and splashing into the lake was the sound of a cow moose urinating. This was his lucky day, and he went charging straight toward the call, the "dripping water" sound and the wonderful smell of apples!

He was there, and Peter and Miles were ready for him and a carefully placed shot from each youth brought the big bull down.

That night, after the celebration old Jack had given Peter the rifle he made the kill with, and Miles and Peter decided that they would be best friends and hunting partners from then on. That was nearly forty years ago and Miles had gone to the other side only three snows passed, but that bond of friendship had never changed. In fact, there were times when it was the only thing in Peter Jackson's world that indeed did not change.

Sarah awoke early on the morning of the council meeting. In fact, she was the very first one awake. Her father had gotten that bath and haircut that he promised, and when he appeared later in his freshly laundered clothing Sarah thought that he looked indeed like a chief, clean and wise and strong.

The preceding evening, Peter had visited each of the families and gotten a household-by-household account of life and recent happenings here at this ledge. He even went and sat a few minutes at the outside campfire of Giroud and Nancee, and there he could feel tension so strong that it seemed to spark and crackle louder than the burning embers that flew from the cooking fire that Nancee was poking at.

She seemed very nervous at Peter's arrival, but she was happy to see him; that was apparent for all her apprehensiveness when her uncle appeared before her fire. Nancee invited him to eat and Peter politely declined. He was some saddened when he thought of this particular niece trying to defend herself against Giroud.

Speaking of Giroud, he sat quietly in the dark shadows, his small and beady eyes watching and baleful, and he seemed to be enjoying the discomfort that his wife was experiencing. After the meal, he picked his teeth, very unconcerned about the upcoming council meeting that he had requested. He talked of stupid things, like the cold snap that was coming, and of course, how very smart he was as usual.

Peter had not stayed long at their fire for he was ever so conscious of the smirk on Giroud's face, a face that had always reminded Peter of a muskrat with stringy mustache. He was such a sure and cocky one that bird, thought Peter, and he had a long thin neck, just right for twisting. Yes, Peter would leave this fire now that he had satisfied himself that his niece bore no marks, at least none that could be easily seen.

Shortly after the noon meal a cold wind and a rain came up and the council meeting was moved inside a temporary wigwam that Nel and four other women had erected that afternoon. This large communal tent would give comfort and protection from the elements to the family and Bear Clan members gathered there for the purpose of hearing all the complaints from Giroud against Nancee.

Rocks were placed in a circle in the center of the tent, and a little before meeting time, a fire was placed within. At dusk they assembled there. The men sat around the circle of fire, and the women and children sat in back of them. Nancee the accused, was allowed to sit in the circle with the men. The mood was very serious and the setting was almost deadly quiet.

The Sacred Pipe, that pipe of peace, with its slender reed stem and its clay bowl, was lit from the fire by the chief, for this was the way it was done. Then, all the men seated around the fire drew from it after Peter, and the smell of tobacco and sweetgrass burning intermingled with the aroma of rock maple and birch blazing in the leaping fire around which the council sat.

Aunt Nelemano sat back in the shadows with Peter's children, and she was proud of her brother. Not since yesterday had he touched his flask, and she knew that if Peter was sober that he could match wits with Giroud any day. Giroud could read a little and he could write his name in English as well as in French. He was the smartest man in that Bear Clan camp and he told them all so, at least once a day, just in case they forgot. "Too bad he wasn't smart enough to shut his mouth, because then perhaps, someone might like him," thought Nelemano.

Nel sat very straight and looking across at her niece Nancee as she was, Nel could vaguely see a resemblance of Skyry, Nancee's mother, in the side profile.

For the most part, Nancee sat with her head down and her eyes downcast. She had always been the shyest one of all the family and to have her accused of being an immoral woman was hard to imagine, and sad too, thought Nelemano, because as bashful as the young woman was, she probably wouldn't even have the spirit to stand up for herself, at this her time to do so.

The smoke rose from the long pipe in circles, meaning this rain would stay awhile. After a long moment Peter spoke. "Family, friends, we are gathered to hear why Giroud here would divorce his wife— our daughter and niece."

With no further ado Giroud got to his feet. He sneered at his subdued-looking wife and then he bowed to his audience. This was his moment and he was going to milk it for all it was worth. The very thought of publicly humiliating his spouse gave him the courage to not only go on, but to attempt to be eloquent about it, so he thought. Giroud paused a moment before he began his long list of grievances, to let the enormity of why these people were gathered here sink into the thick skull of his bride of one year, Nancee.

Then he began, "Family, you know what an honorable man I am, me, no?" Already he was blowing his own horn, thought Aunt Nel.

Giroud paused and then he went on, "It is my unpleasant duty to inform ze family of dis infidel why I will divorce dis damned ting." Here he pointed a bony and accusing finger directly at Nancee. "See, family, your Nancee is a trollop-prostitute—dat one, she!" His voice was rising now as temper forced its way into his broken French accented speech.

While faces looked at him with little or no emotion showing, Giroud continued his tirade and now that the eloquence had departed from his voice; it took on a mocking tone. If it hadn't been such serious business, if he hadn't been so vicious, to see him there huffing and puffing and expounding as he was, would have been laughable.

With a great sweeping motion of his hand Giroud continued, "She is yours family! Giroud, he give her back to you. She should go with her husband but No, she go south with you. Good to be rid of dat one, me! She find more men with you. She always look at ze other men, dat shameless bitch!" Then he turned to Nancee, his face contorted with rage and jealousy. He could barely contain himself now and the hate was spilling forth from his mouth like a mad dog frothing.

"Nancee, deny my words! Say someting so your family can hear from your own lips what a poor excuse for ze woman zat you are!"

Nancee sat with her eyes cast down but when she raised her head, she stood suddenly erect before them all. She faced her husband and there was nothing shy about her now. She was angry. She looked at Giroud a long minute and then at all of them seated there and with plain contempt and disgust upon her face she said, "Giroud, you are a small man, with a small heart. You lie! You are a 'crow man' and you make things up in your own sick mind. Here me, Giroud— I am a good woman! Now you go away, you not my man no more. You Giroud— you dirty my path!"

She sat down then, her defense over, and there was a soft rumble of approval from around the fire, or was it surprise? When Nancee again seated herself, she did not lower her head or her eyes. She held her head proud and erect and she knew that from the close of this meeting, she would never be called a dumb, stupid, damned squaw by that ignorant person Giroud, who was so proud of his French blood and so ashamed of his Indian blood and was such a disgrace to each bloodline.

As Giroud came out of shock and realized that he had been called a liar, and in fact told off pretty damned good, by this timid sub-human creature, his rage intensified. His face was getting beet red and his eyes that were usually narrow slits, were now almost bulging with temper as the blood in his temples pounded. He then started calling names first in French and then in English, "Liar, slut, pig!" He fumed and then said a few words in the French dialect that no one understood. His mustache twitched and he was roaring like a bull now, and the children, never having seen or heard such a display, leaned closer to their mothers. He was crazy!

A menacing grin curled the corners of his mouth as Giroud finished his lament. "Nancee, you lil' bitch, I was jest going let you go, me, but now since you call me a liar, I will punish you! Girard, half Frenchman, quarter Abenakis and quarter Mohawk, he split ze blanket and walk away dis night, but before he go, Giroud, he leave ze mark of ze whore on your damn face!" With glittering eyes, he pulled the knife from the sheath in his belt and continued, "It is my right, and I will slit your nose three times! See how pretty you look to ze other men then, eh slut? I Giroud, I cast you away, but first I will cut your nose!" A hush fell over the shocked assembly and the children were sitting like bronzed statues. Nancee met his gaze without a flinch.

Suddenly, soundlessly as a big cat, Peter Jackson rose to his feet. He was not smiling and towering over Giroud, in a voice that was deadly calm he said, "You Giroud, You cut my niece's nose....I'll cut your throat!"

Sarah sucked in her breath and let it out slowly. She had never seen her father angry before and it was a terrible sight to see!

Nelemano watched from her position and she knew already that the smart one, that Giroud, he would be backing off shortly. He would be backing off or he would be dead. She did not know Giroud's honorable ancestors but she knew hers, and Peter Jackson was an angry Indian.

Giroud regained some sanity and realized that he was looking into the ugliest face of any man that he had ever seen. He wasn't looking at Chief Jackson now; he was looking at death, and suddenly Giroud was not ready for it. He put the knife he was waving back into its sheath, and trying to summon up a final semblance of something he lacked all along —dignity— he began to smile and to make light of the situation by saying "I don't really mean dat, me. Giroud fool you. I have changed my mind. I jes try scare you Nancee! You are all my friends—I go now!" And with that, Giroud went hurriedly out into the night. Peter glared after the half-breed and there was a dark and foreboding look on his usually placid face.

Glancing at his niece, Peter was suddenly proud of her. She was truly the daughter of his sister Skyry. She had stood her ground! Peter rose to his feet once more and said "This marriage—it is finished!"

Outside it was raining hard and getting cold. Inside it was warm and Nancee, her ordeal over, knew that although she must go alone now, that she never ever would, not as long as this family band existed. "it is finished," she said silently, as tears slid freely down the hollows of her cheeks. And then Nancee, that good women smiled because she knew now why her uncle was the Chief.

With the sudden departure of Girourd, once more the council's ceremonial pipe would be smoked and then this council would be over.

Nelemano got up and began passing baskets of popped corn and nuts and the gathering began to relax. The women and children, after the council meeting closed, moved in closer to the fire and when the long pipe was smoked again that evening it would be the beginning of the story hour.

Nancee, that free woman, wiped her eyes and sat up erect to hear the legends and as she did, Aunt Nel smiled softly to herself and her big hands reached for her basketry. Sometimes that Peter Jackson, he was all right! Not all the time—but sometimes.

Two weeks to the day following that most memorable meeting, the birds and the chipmunks in residence on Tarritine Ledge, talked only to and about each other, because the Dawnland People had packed up their summer camping equipment and followed the Connecticut River in a southerly direction. No one saw them getting ready or heard them leave; they were there on the ledge one evening and gone come sunrise. Local farmers woke up one morning and noticed that the makeshift dwellings that had been scattered about the ledge since early June, had vanished as soundlessly as the wood smoke that curled softly from the wigwams that once stood there.

The second wave of Canadian geese had gone over honking and was now ahead of the Bear Clan band, who followed this "Long" River that had always been their lifeline and which once more was their highway. All along those winding shores, they could sell their baskets and their beadwork and crafts at the farms and villages they passed.

The length of their journey there were fish to catch, but they would not stop and smoke the fish on the shores this time; no, they would eat what they needed and trade the rest for vegetables and other useful things along the route. The Connecticut River was their market place.

With the ducks ahead of them, the painted hills of Vermont and New Hampshire surrounding them and the threat of snow chasing their backsides, these last remnants of another culture headed south toward Springfield, Massachusetts, where they would rest before going on to winter in New Jersey.

Save the blackened rocks where their fires once burned, they left no mark upon that ledge they loved. The wind whipped and howled around Tarritine now and it was indeed a lonesome place. The setting was one of dried earth in shades of antique gray and this bitter frost and cold would soon be accompanied by snow.

Was this the place where children romped and women sang as they went about their chores each day? Was this the place where the smell of sweetgrass was so thick you could cut it with a knife?

Yes, this was the place; only the season had changed. This golden summer too had passed away, but another would return to the "Place Where the Sweetgrass Grows," and the Dawnland People would also return, until the oldest members of that family band, come spring, could not make the long journey home.

For five consecutive years these "People of the Dawnland" arrived silently each spring at Tarritine and then disappeared just as quietly in the Autumn. Their individual lifestyles were always changing, but all over the world especially, in these United States of America, transitions and variations in customs and lifestyles were taking place.

A young British engineer and inventor by the name of James Watt had been more or less the catalyst for those explosive changes with his ingenious invention of the steam powered engine. Man had the wheel, and now he had a force to turn it and not by hand.

From this invention came the steam boat and the locomotive as the Great American Railroads came to be and so cris-crossed this land. These new creations had as noiselessly as a shadow replaced the rivers as the mode of transportation, especially for the Indian. These new highways called railroads could take a man, willing to ride their steel ribbons in any direction that he wanted to go. This brought the world a lot closer and now the changes came faster and faster.

Eli Whitney, an American inventor, gave us the cotton gin, a sleek machine that separated the fibers of the cotton from the seeds, and as a result opened up a new world of employment in the form of textile mills that were rapidly dotting the landscape. Any material suitable for weaving was used and most able bodied men, women and children were hired. There was little worth placed on human life or dignity in many of these work places which were commonly referred to as "sweatshops." Child labor was especially promoted, offering low wages, long working hours and often unsanitary and very unfavorable working conditions. These would eventually destroy a person's health, but long before that they would demolish the spirit and so the body died twice, within and without. Had the White Man really won?

Historians referred to this time in the history of an ever-changing world as the Industrial Revolution, and it came right on the heels of the American Revolution with the Native American again caught in the middle, unschooled and unprepared for either one.

The words of Chief Passaconaway, that wise old Penacook, had already come true. Indeed, the "White Man's houses now stood at the best fishing places." In addition to that, the waste products and disease-carrying raw sewerage from his homes and factories was being channelled directly into the once pure streams and rivers. Where a fish could not swim and a horse refused to drink was water unfit for human use, and by the hundreds the fish were dying and their swollen bodies could often be seen floating dead on top of these polluted waterways; and the Indian (that man who respected all fish and animal life) realized that any who ate of these contaminated fish would also die, be it a scavenger bird, a hungry bear or a hungry man. It seemed, only noticed by the Red Man was Mother Nature's—revolution.

This was a sad and a traumatic time for Chief Peter Jackson. The dispersal of the New England Indian tribes had begun long, long ago, but this was the dispersal of his own family band and the force of this blow was terrible to withstand. This group had dwindled in size and now only the Jackson family and two others stood together on the fringes of White society, clinging against hope to their heritage and culture.

All the rest, had been forced to go to work in the sweatshops and mills of Springfield, Holyoke and Boston. They did this because they had to. They could no longer live off the depleted forests or the poisoned rivers. A few decided to become farmers in the fertile and flat lands of New Jersey, where they decided they could survive the longest. Many of these had in turn married into White communities and were swallowed up whole by that culture. Every day there were a few more White Men and a few less Indians.

One short decade following that summer encampment, in the spring of 1831, found the remnants of this family band making yet another migration north to their old hunting grounds in South Guildhall, Vermont.

It was not quite the same this time, however, because on this journey home they had been forced to ignore the winding back of the Connecticut River, because of dams and other constrictive structures along the waterway. This trip was started by train and would be finished up by horses and wagons.

These survivors of another culture and heritage were still free at this time and this season in their lives. They were an inherently proud and determined people, these fragments of the "Dawnland" even though they were becoming more like the White Man every day that they lived. They spoke his tongue now much more than their own and they wore his clothing and used his tools and, in their furor to survive, they were adopting his customs without question—and forgetting their own.

Sitting in those wagons in their mis-matched and most often second hand garments, they probably looked more comical than they ever did proud. But they were proud, proud of what they were and where they came from, even if it wasn't popular. Hidden just underneath this White Man's apparel were usually good hearts and always copper skin and a simple philosophy about life which was; love of family, appreciating this beautiful earth and respecting it and all living things that had been placed upon it.

You can be sure that they were pointed at and made fun of, and there was certainly suspicion about these Native Americans, because against all odds they tried to hang onto their own heritage for as long as they could and they changed only to survive.

We must keep in mind, that the men and women and children perched on those hard wagon seats were just White look-alikes, because if you cut them they would bleed —Abenakis.

And so they journeyed on, these determined People of the Dawnland, who would probably never inherit the earth, but who lived their lives in harmony with it—an extension of it.

That little wagon train stopped in front a small general store at a dot on the map that we know as Wells River, Vermont. The dusty and bedraggled occupants of the wagons crawled down to stretch their cramped legs. They were well looked over by the locals on the street.

Some onlookers actually chuckled at the bear claw necklace that hung on a rawhide cord around Chief Jackson's neck. That string of claws did not belong on a white dress shirt, thought the townsfolk assembled there, but the chief's grandfather, in a fight for his life, had killed the bear the claws belonged to. He had done this with an ax and it did belong there, close to his grandson's heart. And, they laughed of course, at this proud Indian and his strangely dressed family and even at his daughter Sarah, who tended to her elderly Aunt and ignored them all. "Such a foolish lot," she thought.

Sarah did not know that a century and a half later the snickering and the ignorance would still go on. Immigrants were welcomed with a "Statue of Liberty," while Native Americans were exiled in their own land and met with ignorance and intolerance. Perhaps we were a foolish lot.

And yet, all these things this little family had seen before. They were used to ridicule and so they accepted and overcame, and even good-naturedly shared the cheese and fruit that they purchased at the store, as the wagons rolled on toward the north—toward home.

They thought about sweetgrass and laughed about the old times and joked about the good times yet to come, they hoped. But if instead bad times lay waiting for their arrival in Tarritine Ledge country this spring, then they would meet those bad times head-on, like they met the good ones, as a family— a family then, a family now and a family forever.

At seventeen Sarah was not what one would call beautiful, but there was a quiet dignity exposed in her face that was, I suppose, inherent in her. She was tall and slender and always carried her head high and her back very straight. The shape of her face was not round but oval, and this face was framed by high and very prominent cheekbones, a well proportioned nose, and deep, dark eyes. When she smiled her eyes turned up at the corners and dimples appeared at the corners of her mouth, giving Sarah a most mischievous grin.

More than the glow of beauty, the glow of health radiated itself from Sarah. In fact, her mouth was her finest feature, the lips neither too thick nor too thin, a feature very common in many Native Americans. Sarah's strong white teeth which so enhanced her smile, also protruded just a little bit, but few men ever noticed this.

With her hair as black as a crow's wing and the natural tawny-flush of her flawless copper-colored cheeks, indeed it was said of Sarah that "She was one who looked altogether fine."

Her hair this morning was combed straight back and gathered up into a French twist. She wore a tortoise-shell comb to secure it, and in a plain cotton dress and apron she planned this day to go and do some herb and root gathering up on the Tarritine itself.

She had carried water from the well and helped Aunt Nel to bathe and dress and then Sarah prepared breakfast for the whole family. Aunt Nel as the day wore on would feel better, but in the mornings, her swollen arthritic joints were slow in getting going.

Sarah had paused a minute while standing on the crooked old porch and she breathed the scent of apple blossoms, her favorite of all the flowers that grew.

It was good to be home, she thought. There truly was a strength about the black dirt of Vermont near Tarritine Ledge on the Connecticut River. Just by looking, one could tell that only the Great Spirit, with much love for (Aki) Mother Earth, could ever have created such a winding and magnificent waterway as this river that she loved. She breathed long and deeply, her steady gaze looking across the valley to where New Hampshire's Crystal Hills, rose towards the sky. The Agiachook (Mt. Washington) was the place where the old ones said the Great Spirit lived. Here Sarah reflected, if he didn't he should have, because the strength of the people who lived here was undoubtedly drawn from these mighty mountains.

The morning sun hit her eyes, and even as she squinted against its brilliance, her lips formed a prayer that she had known since childhood;

"Father, for this day so bright and so alive with new and growing things, I thank you. Thank you that my eyes can see the beauty of your handwork."

Sarah only mouthed these words, she did not speak them aloud. There was no need too. The Great Spirit who could hear the cricket and the frog above the roaring wind had heard every word.

Here in this landmark year of 1841 Sarah's thoughts were sometimes conflicting. In this decade from the child of seven snows, she had changed into a young woman having seen now sixteen winters. And in all that time there was nothing in her world that had not changed. She was no longer the spindly-legged girl child, and the metamorphosis of her transformation from adolescence to a wholesome young woman was a natural and a good thing.

This would be the first summer that the Jackson family would not actually live in a make-shift tent or a wigwam, on the very pinnacle of Tarritine Ledge. This year they would live in a wooden house. Peter Jackson, like the rest of his family, accepted the changes in their lifestyles, and enjoyed the comforts of indoor living and having water from a nearby well, and especially the wood-burning stove.

Through old cohorts of his, Peter had been able to rent an old house on a farm located on a dirt road in South Guildhall, Vt. The homestead was about one mile up a narrow road (with grass in the middle). As a matter of fact, the road the farm was located on began only about 1500 feet or so from the cut off they had used as their walking-trail to the ledge.

This road is known as the "The French District," but more commonly it is called the "Morin Road" and most of the buildings there are now just seasonal hunting camps. Peter realized that it sat just a matter of feet over the Lunenburg-Guildhall, town line, and if they didn't camp on the ledge itself, then this was truly the next best place because from the ramshackled house it was only a twenty-five minute walk, straight as the crow flies, to the pinnacle of the ledge of his childhood.

The buildings were old and crooked and part of the barn had fallen in, but Peter's younger sons, now twelve and fourteen, could brace it up enough to keep Old Bess, their horse in out of the rain.

The setting was that of old grey barn boards and leaning buildings, but still there were enough shingles left on the roof so that it didn't leak too much.

The day before, the entire family except Aunt Nel (who rested and gave orders from the wagon) had brushed away cobwebs and swept dust out in such amounts that they all got laughing at each other and were sneezing up a storm. "We are human tata' balls," quipped Sarah.

"It needs work but it can be fixed." was Peter's one statement about his new home. The water from the old well was very good. The woodstove inside was fine, and there was a long and rough cut pine table and two benches, broken chairs and beds. Everything here was old and used but still homey.

Sarah would get some cloth over in Lancaster and she and Aunt Nel would make some curtains. Perhaps she would get bright red material, because it would brighten the drab gray of the interior.

A great supply of baskets that slid around in the back of their wagon had made the trip with no problem. They were made to be used and to be tough and they had proved that already.

Sarah would take all the baskets that she could carry on her head and then Peter, (the younger Peter) would carry some on his head too, and he actually had a basket-rack on his back and he would accompany his sister on the selling trips to Lancaster. They would sell their baskets and bring back food and cloth for new curtains and some heavy flannel to make new shirts for the boys.

As Sarah stood there surveying this place that her father had decided they would spend their summer, she suddenly realized that she must approach her father, (when he was not drinking or having a headache), and try to talk him into buying this homestead before it fell to decadence.

None of them spoke of it, but Aunt Nel lost ground every winter and Sarah doubted that she could make another trip. This was their real home and if they could make it comfortable enough to spend the brutal winter, then why couldn't they spend all their time here?

Sarah knew that each spring and summer the boys and Peter would catch fish at Cat Bow Swamp and from the Connecticut River and she and Aunt Nel would make their sweetgrass baskets to sell. And of course, they could grow some vegetables — there was still time — and there was a good root cellar right under the kitchen part of the house.

Yes, this was the time to stop the migrating, and this indeed was the place to settle down, but what would Peter say?

Peter, that aging chief was known to be a very stubborn man when he was young and he was worse now that he was older. Never in her life before had Sarah ever thought of arguing with her father, but as she headed across those bright green fields toward the ledge, she knew in her heart that if Peter resisted then too bad, her mind was made up, and Chief or no Chief, that man had a fight on his hands! Her name was Jackson too.

As she stepped over a rotten log, an old black snake was disturbed. He slithered out in front of her and he was angry, for he had been sunning himself. He was not too big, but he was startled and he lifted his head and hissed at her, and for just a minute she thought that he would indeed attempt to bite her.

Sarah chuckled to herself and stepped lightly out around him. "Sorry, Old Grandfather, my mind was on fighting, but not with you!" and she continued her journey toward the ledge of her childhood days, and on toward the first real battle of young womanhood waiting up ahead.

"Surely Father can't be in a worse mood than Old Grandfather," she thought—or could he?

Sarah stooped and examined many tiny ferns along the way. It had grown up so much, just since last spring, when she and Aunt Nel had collected herbs together.

She bent to notice the pipsissewa weed. It was still too small to pick but in early September she would come and get some of them. These were excellent to induce sweating, and their worth had been testified to by the old Grandfathers and Grandmothers both, who claimed that when boiled, the roots of this weed did induce perspiring and could rid the body of evil spirits.

Sarah had tried this already, when her father woke the whole family sometimes with his terrible nightmares. He had sweated mightily and she had hoped that he had gotten rid of the "whirlwind demon" but no, it was still there hidden in his mind in the daylight and coming out in his dreams night after night to rob him of his sleep.

She saw the beginning shoots of what would later be cattails. These also she would pick at the right time, because when the shoots were ready they could be boiled as a healthy vegetable and their fluffy heads could chase a diarrhea out of one's body almost as well as strained blackberry juice, or the famous blackberry root itself.

The small medicine bag (that long ago gift from her father) for herb collecting had long since worn out. She had another now and it was made of doe-skin, no frills, but it was always tied around her small waist with "good medicine," from Mother Earth's garden inside its soft folds. This was concealed under her outer garments, but like most Shamans, it was with Sarah, waking or sleeping.

The morning sun rose higher in the sky, and Sarah picked and chose the herbs that she selected to put in the gathering sack that she carried. It was getting quite warm now, and she rolled up her sleeves and let the sun hit her already bronze colored arms.

She carried with her a small basket which contained her mid-day meal. And just as the sun was exactly overhead she was seating herself on a high point of Tarritine Ledge— her real home, she thought.

For a few minutes Sarah just sat there in silence, gazing down on the fertile farmlands and the narrow road below. She took from her lunch basket some cold biscuits, spread with butter, molasses and honey, because she could never decide which one of these spreads she liked the most, so she ate all three.

She brushed the crumbs from her lap and drank some almost warm tea for there was no way to keep it either hot or cold up there. A piece of sharp cheese and an apple completed her dinner and Sarah decided to take half an hour and let her food digest as she settled herself against the early grass protruding from the rich black dirt of Vermont.

She removed her high, black and uncomfortable White ladies shoes, and since they were wet, Sarah decided that she would make the trip back in comfortable shoes—her bare feet.

Sarah gazed over at Lancaster, that little town that she always remembered with fondness. As she looked across the river and upon early Lancaster, she was always impressed by the fact that it seemed to be a natural fortress, surrounded by mountains on all sides. The most impressive sight from that high vantage point, of course, were the Crystal Hills (Mt. Washington Range), and on those towering peaks, Sarah could see the white of snow, just before the mountain seemed to drift off into the clouds.

The Connecticut River swept along below her, and she could see the banks where the spring thaw had unleashed water and the marks of that swollen water, could be seen half way up the trunks of the many elms that dotted the "Long" River's banks. Sarah had seen the anger of that raging river during flood season, and it could be as deadly as it was picturesque. It was a precious and a beautiful thing, this Connecticut River, and she hoped that it would be kept clean and pure, because this is what the Great Spirit intended, when he placed it there.

She reflected that Aunt Nel especially, would miss the two families that came with them as far as Passumpsic, Vt. These were cousins and second cousins but all good friends, and they had made up their minds that after this last summer, here in the northern country, that they were going to go back to Springfield, Mass., and join the circus, if they could. Sarah wondered silently, how it would be to go with them?

Sarah, hated to think about Winona's words "I am going with the circus after father and Aunt Nel are gone." And, as she sat there breathing the crisp air Sarah knew that with each winter that passed, those words came closer to being true. Winona wanted to fly like a bird, to just up and fly away. Well, perhaps they would, perhaps they would some day.

A frown crossed Sarah's smooth brow when she thought about her father. He still drank too much and too often, and he still had constant headaches. His hair was nearly all white now, and he never bothered to put bear grease on it. He was growing heavy around the middle and he was often very ill-humored and sometimes distant and remote. Sarah realized that this new and surly Peter was not the arrogantly-funny head of their household any more. She guessed that a decade of those persistent nightmares of the "Screaming Whirlwind," that belched fire and ate him alive had taken much of his self-esteem and his wonderful sense of humor away. Sarah sighed when she thought about this sad and bitter man.

She could help him with his headaches, and she could help him with his hangover's too, but if there was only some medicine that could rid his mind of his tormenting dreams, then perhaps Peter would be his old self again, that gentle smiling giant of her childhood, the man that she called "Father."

She was well aware that this strange dream could be some close friend or relative of Peter's, trying to warn him about some impending disaster, but if Peter could not grasp the meaning, then what good were these repeated warnings?

Sarah faced the fact that liquor did not help her father escape from his dreams anymore than it had ever helped him escape from the realities of life. He was awakened by his arch enemy, that evil whirlwind, drunk or sober.

Sarah was watching, like all the rest of his family, as Peter withdrew more and more into himself as this hateful thing in his dreams kept grinding away at his sanity. She also had to admit that each time one of her traditional Indian cures failed, that her father lost a little more faith in them and probably in her. This coupled with the fact that Peter Jackson had lived like a White Man for so long, perhaps meant that the horrible demon called "the Devil," really was after him. She would make a plea and ask the White Man's God to help her father since his own would not listen.

Frustrated and helpless and extremely powerless was exactly how Sarah felt, knowing that she could not ease her father's dream-sickness and realizing sadly that at least once a week now, when her father slept—he dreamed of Hell.

For one precious hour of time Sarah rested. The tranquility of this ledge in early spring was a wonderful place to relax and reflect on the past and to see all the little green gifts, growing, sprouting forth from that sun-kissed earth and giving hope for the future and the promise of life ahead.

By this time in her life, Sarah had lived in the states of Vermont, Massachusetts and New Jersey and she had also lived in three wooden houses, but they didn't feel like home. Now, this old ramshackle house she left this morning, that felt like home.

A frown crossed her smooth brow as she looked across the lush, green valley below and saw all the white houses over in Lancaster. She counted three church steeples and wondered if she could find the school or not. School, why had she mentioned that word, thought Sarah. How that word did coil itself, almost cobra-like, around the White Man and his way of life. They sent their young off to school to learn to read and write and spell and to be taught the history of mankind. Many also expected the very values that should be taught at home to be taught by teachers. They wanted their children to know all about history, but never took the time to tell them their own. A teacher could not do this, after all, these "teachers," had also been taught history by a group of outsiders.

Sarah chewed on a straw and did not know if she was glad that at seventeen years she had only three years of schooling, or if she had in some way been short-changed. And then suddenly she knew that every day spent in the confines of a hot classroom was one day robbed from Aunt Nel to show her the medicines that often learned men of medicine longed to know about. The reason for only three years of schooling was the migration of the family from one community to another. By the time the school authorities in Springfield, noted that the Jackson family had children who should be in school, Sarah was already turning twelve and she took her place very reluctantly in the second grade. Her father could write his name and read moderately, and he had taught Sarah, so she was spared the total indignity of starting in the first grade.

She grimaced as she thought about that awful first year of school, with an impatient teacher and children five years her junior, who loved having an idiot around to poke fun at.

On introduction day, she was told to address the class, telling them who she was and where she came from. The Abenaki pronunciation (Ch) was still very strong in her speech, and when Sarah told the children that her name was Sarah Ann Chackson, a loud giggle went up from the class, because these children knew that she was not only a tall, gangly Indian kid, but she couldn't even talk plain. Oh, what a great day! They needed something or someone like this around here.

Under her cotton dress, Sarah always wore her little medicine pouch, hidden away from sight and taunts beneath her undergarments where no one could detect it. That part of it was all right; she loved her medicine bag, and it was exactly where it should be, close to her heart just as her father wore his beloved bear claw necklace, only Peter wore his on the outside of his clothing for all the world to see.

Sarah's teacher was a spinster called Miss Day. She had over fifty students in her class and she did try to take extra time to help Sarah with her reading, but Sarah in many aspects was behind her class and so that whole year it was a case of hurry up and catch up, Sarah.

Miss Day put a stop to the giggling outbursts when she was aware of it; and because of the age difference, she made the other children call Sarah Miss Jackson. This helped a little but poor little Miss Jackson, that confident child, began to withdraw into herself. Her grammar was poor and her self-esteem was even worse. Her only friend that awful year was the big clock on the wall, because each and every move of the hands brought her closer to the bell, the bell that set her free from this purgatory called "school."

A slight smile crossed Sarah's face as she remembered the turning point in her school career. That was some two years later when she was in the sixth grade at the ripe old age of fourteen. She was, however, slowly progressing. She read pretty well now and her spelling was called average, and although math was her poorest subject, she could pass it and she made change very well, which was a necessity to a vendor in the basket trade.

The teacher at this point in Sarah's life, was a young and nervous woman in her early thirties. Her name was Miss Greene and she was a soft-spoken person with a very kind heart. This teacher would never knowingly have hurt any living creature, and she had almost a fascination about Native Americans and their free and nomadic lifestyle.

Miss Greene was a Christian, and believed in the Great Spirit, and she lived what she believed; and because of that, there was always a great respect and admiration in Sarah's heart for this special woman.

One day Miss Greene asked the children to create something with their own hands. She was the best kind of a teacher, helpful and always encouraging her students to do better, and create on their own. She called these tests where she asked her students to be creative, "Yankee Crafts," and except for three of the children who could draw quite well, the teacher found that most of the children in her classroom could create absolutely nothing.

In the case of Sarah Jackson, things were very different. She had brought with her to school a moderate supply of already prepared sweetgrass, and while most of the class sighed and struggled, Sarah created a beautiful and delicate little basket that would hold jewelry or trinkets, complete with a cover that fit perfectly. She did this in less than one hour by the teacher's own gold timepiece. The class was awestruck, and Miss Greene could not get over the speed and the dexterity with which Sarah's slender fingers moved. Her artistry poured forth as she placed narrow strips of sweetgrass which were shaped into tiny curlicues on the bottom and top of the dainty basket that had been created before everyone's eyes.

Miss Green picked the little vessel up and said "Sarah, this is beautiful, a true work of art— but where did you learn this?" Sarah explained that she was taught by her Aunt who was a basket maker.

With pure, unadulterated admiration in her pale blue eyes, the thin, frail teacher began passing the handiwork of the one the other children called the "Dummy" around the room for all of them to see that indeed, she was not! "Your Aunt is a very clever lady, Sarah, and she must be very proud—because she taught you so well, and now you are clever." Sarah smiled and blushed, and this was the most wonderful day in her whole "school life." Miss Greene and Miss Tukesbury, the prune-faced Principal, both tried to buy that rare little basket from Sarah, who graciously refused and who took the new basket home to the one who really deserved it, Aunt Nel. On the last day of school however, Sarah gave another one just like it to Miss Greene, and this good woman had hugged the child and thanked her, while big tears ran down her cheeks.

The next fall the family migrated back to New Jersey, but Sarah did not return to school. Aunt Nel was often confined to bed a week at a time now with her arthritic condition, and Sarah took over the chores of sending her younger siblings off to school.

School was no hell for any of these. Dennis was as smart as a whip, and excelled in music. John was a good student who had occasional run-ins and fights, but that was John—sometimes his fault, sometimes not, who knew? Winona got excellent marks in everything, but she still yearned to climb high and soar like an eagle. "I'm going to ride a flying trapeze. I'm going with the Circus, Sarah— I am!" And Sarah would chuckle as she braided Winona's hair for school each morning and heard these words over and over, and though she would try not to dwell on the this, some part of her own innermost heart seemed to say "I know you will you "bird child", I've always known."

Young Peter did not go to school. School would have done him more harm than good. He loved to be of help to his family in all the ways that he could. Peter was not lazy and he did his chores slow and steady as he split firewood, toted water or hauled baskets to market. He was proud of the things that he could do, and he always did them well.

This young man felt good about himself and he lived a life of simple dignity, doing the things that he could, not doing the things in which he failed, but never feeling like a failure— because he knew that he had tried.

Sarah stared across the terrain at the Crystal Hills, and thought to herself, "Agiachook" someday that Winona will probably walk to your top and sit there like the bird she wants to be."

"When they are gone Sarah, I will fly away!" Winona would threaten and Sarah would caution her not to speak of the future or death, by hushing the child and saying "Winona, never speak of that, never!" But she knew that Winona would speak of it again, and someday it would happen. Peter and Nel would go to the other side, but not today—today there was life to be lived and roots to be gathered. Again in the fall Sarah would have to fight with Winona to go to school, and she would win by saying as she always did "Winona, if they didn't make you go to school, then they would make you do something else. It is their way."

From somewhere in the background she heard the familiar grunt of a porcupine as he descended a tree, and Sarah knew that it was time that she got back to her herb gathering.

She got up, stretching to bring herself awake and took up her gathering sack. She made a quick check of her digging tools and with a small whet-stone she began to sharpen her dull weed and herb digging knife. The black dirt on this ledge produced the gifts of healing, so well, but it raised pure hell with the gathering tools, for hidden in that rich, black dirt were tiny little stones that enriched plant life and shortened the life of a digging knife.

Sarah inhaled all the sounds and smells of her childhood home and decided that it was a fine place to be on a day like this. As she gathered she heard the birds above and once she laughed out loud at a chipmunk she had startled, and he had told her off in grand style.

As she bent to touch and examine more closely the tender stems of the new cattails Sarah smiled, for it would be a good year for these. In this tranquil atmosphere she reflected too on another time in her life, a thing that had happened to her only two summers past. It was right after a season of torrential rains, and arthritic Aunt Nel was confined to her bed with swollen, aching joints and Sarah was medicine or root gathering alone on the flat plains just north of Springfield. She was looking for "queen of the meadow" and "spirea" which is more commonly known as "meadowsweet." These were widely used among the Abenakis for relief of colds and other flu-like systems. Sarah scanned the area for the precious "cohosh" or "black snakeroot" which could be a deadly plant, but when properly administered was a most effective weapon against bronchitis, whooping cough and other respiratory illnesses She tried to find some "coclebur root" for Aunt Nel's stomach trouble, and when she saw that the "meadowsweet" was everywhere, Sara smiled, because this was an early form of aspirin.

Sarah was remembering the day she brought home "squaw root" for her friend who had a bad time each month. Aunt Nel checked Sarah's concoction and nodded her approval, but many times she had warned Sarah "Be careful of this, child, too much squaw root, no more squaw!" Sarah hoped that Doris her friend would at least try this medicine. She had seen Doris leave the store and go upstairs in tears while clutching her abdomen as one in great pain, and it happened every month so Sarah simply reasoned that it was something to do with the menstruation process, and Aunt Nel confirmed her suspicion.

Sarah appeared at the market one morning and gave the frail young woman a tea that Aunt Nel had supervised the making of. "Doris, this will stop the cramps and vomiting and you will not sweat with fever or chills either. It is medicine especially for women. Take this a few days before your time. It will keep you comfortable until next time." Doris, a thin and gentle seventeen year old, thanked Sarah but after she left, Doris promptly poured the tea down the sink at the back of the store. After all, she thought, what could an Indian know about menstrual problems. And, Doris suffered unnecessarily with "the curse" for over twenty-five years, taking pills from many doctors that never did help her condition half as much as the "Women's Medicine" that got thrown down the sink.

To her sharp right twigs cracked and Sarah, from her digging position, looked in that direction without moving a muscle. There was no danger here, for her own body told her that. This was probably just some careless deer or other forest resident, not used to her presence. She went back to her work of filling the sack with the roots and leaves and stems from Mother Earth's medicine cabinet. As she continued, the disturbance reminded Sarah of another time when she had been alone digging in the damp clay soils above Springfield, Massachusetts. That time was different because it was not a sound she heard, it was a feeling that she was being watched. Instinctively, she felt the eyes, and would have bet her life that they were human ones. And Sarah also sensed that these eyes were timid and held no malice.

Rising to her full height, Sarah had brushed at the wet sods that clung to her digging knife. "Who is there?" she asked and at the sound of silence Sarah started to get angry and she said "If you have a voice.... you had better answer me!"

Then a voice, a quavering voice did answer her "Yes'um, I done sorry you be upset ma'am. We jes hongry—me an mine, heah," The sound of that trembling voice came from a thick growth of bushes to the side of her, and Sarah turned and looked quickly into the face of a frightened young colored man about her age or even a little younger.

"I am not upset, I am Sarah—Sarah Jackson," she responded. By that time Sarah was aware of other sounds as an elderly black woman and a young child appeared out of the corner of her eye.

"I'll do da talkin' son," said the old negress, who walked steadily toward Sarah in a pair of men's boots. She was as black as a piece of coal and her face was as wrinkled as a bulldog, but as she approached, it was obvious that she was not really an old lady, she was a young woman who had seen a very hard life. Somehow Sarah knew that this young woman was very frightened and bewildered and probably very hungry.

The smaller child hung back, hiding behind his mother's patched calico skirt. He was as cute as a new born kitten, but he was afraid of people, and Sarah thought "You bright-eyed boy, who broke your spirit?"

The woman wore a bandanna around her head, and made a small curtsey to Sarah and said "We mean ya'll no harm Ma'am, we's jest hidin' out and passin' thru to Canada and freedom. We's honest folks Ma'am, jest hongry and lost, dats all, Ma'am." and their was a sob in her voice.

So, that was it, poor devils. This was just a little family of runaway slaves, probably half-starved too," thought Sarah and from that day on, after seeing these pitiful, wretched creatures, the word "slavery" took on a whole new meaning in her life.

Sarah smiled and then she asked "Where did you come from and how many are you?" She learned that they had been on the run for twelve days now, from a plantation in Georgia, and had been chased by hounds for three days and nights and that they had eaten nothing since they crossed the Connecticut state line, two days prior. Three days with no food was not funny!

Noticing that the older boy limped and hobbled Sarah asked, "What ails your son?"

"Dis my boy Lester, him shot bad in da leg two nights ago Ma'am, tryin' ta steal us a chicken. I'm so shamed, ma'am, but we'as jes so hongry!"

I understand," smiled Sarah, and she did, and the woman introduced herself as the mother of these two boy's and said her name was Unice-Mae. Sarah smiled at the woman. She didn't uphold stealing, but she upheld starvation far less than that.

On closer inspection, Sarah found that the one called Unice-Mae was in her early thirties and had two front teeth missing, but when Sarah had looked the women straight in the eye, she had seen a strength of character along with pride and courage. Sarah saw her soul, and it was a good one. The poor ragged negress, when she saw that she was not going to be condemned for "chicken thievery" began to cry and when she had control of herself once more Sarah spoke "I was born in Canada, and I will help you to get there." The broken little women said, "I knew da Good Law'd be takin' care of us Sarah, cause he done sent us a Angel."

"My Aunt Nelemano is a Shaman or a medicine woman of sorts, and we will fix the wounded boy's leg," said Sarah, who had gone to examine it and saw the angry streaks of infection starting up the leg. She knew that beneath that swollen flesh was birdshot which was festering and that would have to be "dug out" for the leg to heal.

"Your husband?" Sarah asked, as she helped Lester to walk along and the mother and the child followed, close at her heals. After a long moment, the negress said "He jest died, Angel Sarah, he jest plain died! It nearly kilt my man when Massa Greeley dun sold our oldest chile Molita and den he got all dem whippins wid da cat-o-nine-tails." Eunice-Mae stopped and sniffed and then she finished, "When dat Ole Massa Greeley done hitted my lil' Walter, heah, on da side his head wit a chunk a stove wood, poe lil' Walter, he knocked cole for two days, but I prayed and an I prayed an finally my lil' boy him wake up but he ain' never heard no living sound since, an dats when my husband, he jes die Ma'am, fever done took him quick, cause he jes plain gived up. But my man he was so tired, he jes couldn't take no moe—no moe atal!"

Sarah felt pity and sorrow and anger, all in this order, and she felt hate for a man that she did not know, only his name Greeley. In fact, the thought of slitting that bastard's throat right now with her digging knife brought a perverse smile to her lips. She was indeed growing up. Sarah was having emotions that she did not understand. Playing heavily on her mind right now was the question, "Husband of Eunice-Mae, whose name I do not know, how could you just give up and die and leave her here to fight alone, that small and brave little woman?"

On the trek home Sarah learned that they were farmers, tillers of the soil, but that they were really not used to living off the land. They told her once on this journey to freedom they had eaten some poisonous berries, and so she gave them a warning to heed: "If the leaves grow in clusters of three, it is most always a poisonous plant, and if not the plant then the root is. Never eat of things in three."

They paused several times, and the wounded boy lester had beads of perspiration dripping from he face; but he would make it, he was not uttering a sound, and Sarah knew that he had much of his mother in him.

Poor little Walter, however, was a far more pathetic picture, for his injuries were of the spirit as well as the body. He would steal shy glances at Sarah, as though he could not believe that one human being was doing a kindness for another, or at least for a black-skinned one.

Sarah felt tears stinging her own eyes as she thought about that little boy lying unconscious for two days because of an adult's own apparent hatred. Had it been one of her brothers, she knew that Peter Jackson would have killed the man who did this with his bare hands.

What an example of a "superior" race. It was incredible that the child would never be able to hear the rustle of the Autumn leaves, or the sound of geese as they flew over honking, or the robin's first song in early spring all because of a word called — slavery.

Sarah knew Massa Greeley was a madman. Things like this a monster could identify with because he had no dignity, no heart, no soul.

Thus, when sarah returned home that evening just before supper, she had the runaway slave family walking along behind.

She went into the little house they rented first, and told Aunt Nel and Peter Sr., and immediately Peter came out and bid them to come inside "Come in, you are welcome here. We haven't much, but we will share it with you, my friends."

"They haven't had a meal in three days, and one is wounded with bird shot. The little four-year-old is stone deaf because their owner hit him in the head with a block of stove wood." As she finished, Sarah saw her father's dark eyes slit, and his big hands became fists. "I told them that I would help them to go to Canada, and freedom. I told them that you would help them too, because I know you will." Peter nodded his head and Aunt Nel set about preparing some supper for them all.

After supper, Peter told Winona and John to go and play a game with little Walter, and to be very kind to him in ever way, and to teach him all that they could about listening with his eyes.

In the dim glow of a kerosine lamp, Sarah commenced the task of lancing and removing the birdshot from Lester's inflamed leg. Peter had given the boy two cups of whiskey with hot water and sugar, and Lester promptly passed out. This was good, thought Sarah because her patient would be still.

Aunt Nel no longer had the mobility or dexterity in her hands to work with the sharp lancing knife, but Sarah did, and she was swift and steady with it. And, it did not seem like a long time at all to Aunt Nel until Sarah had the wound cleaned and lanced and all the hateful lead removed. Aunt Nel, with nods of her head, had coached Sarah and she was very pleased with the good job that her niece had done. After, as Nel took the pan of bloody water to be disposed of she said "Sarah, you are truly a "Medawanno"—Medicine Woman.

Lester woke up with a smashing headache, but his fever had gone down and his leg was much, much better. The threat of blood poisoning was gone.

This pathetic little group of freedom-searchers left the Jackson household some four days later. Unice-Mae had in her hand a map that Peter had drawn of the Connecticut River Valley to the Canadian border. He had told them where and where not to make the crossing. The Jacksons had given these slaves food, and a pouch of medicinal herbs and some of their own clothing, but the finest thing that they had given them, in fact, was none of these. They had given them hope, hope in themselves and faith in their fellow man.

Peter told them, "When you get to Vermont, you don't have to be afraid. You can trust those farmers all the length of the Connecticut Valley. I have heard that there are " underground railroads" and if that is true, they will take you there." And here Peter stopped and shook hands with Walter and then he added "Those Valley people, they are slaves themselves, to that black dirt they till, but they are slaves by choice and they believe in no other kind of slavery." And Peter was right.

Her sack nearly overflowing now, Sarah headed her bare feet in the direction of that old abandoned homestead that was the Jackson family fortress right now. The eyes on her today were only that of a fat doe, and the deer bolted away in fright. Sarah saw her and was pleased that the deer's red coat looked healthy and she knew that the doe was living well, and wild and free.

She often wondered if Eunice-Mae and her two sons ever did make it to Canada and freedom? Sarah hoped so. Even the "Good Book" called the Bible said "Seek and ye shall find." Eunice-Mae knew the Bible. Eunice-Mae would make it. And of Sarah Jackson, Eunice-Mae, had said as she departed on her long trek to freedom and the far north, "Sarah, if'n I die and da Good Law'd don' know who you is chile, I's gown tell him, you is a Angel!"

Chuckling to herself, Sarah quickened her steps toward home. "Angel," she was thinking, "the Good Lord, I'm sure knows Unice-Mae and He probably knows about you too, because if you don't get washed and changed, he'll be able to smell you from here!"

Dennis romped up the grade to meet her, his long legs flying as he called, "Sarah, you there?" And she answered "I am here Dennis, I'm over here," and then Sarah went to meet her younger brother, never knowing that twenty years to the very day that she greeted him here, Dennis, that man of peace, would enlist in a Volunteer Regiment, leaving the peaceful Green Mountains, to go and fight against slavery in a great Civil War.

Sarah knew her brother's heart. Their forefathers had also gone to war in a vain attempt to keep their culture and Hunting Grounds and regardless of the sad ending, this had been the right thing to do.

It was right to go to war again to stop the enslavement of another race.

In the south, slavery flourished and as it did, so did the abolitionist movement in the northern states as rumors of war finally turned into civil war itself.

When that terrible time did come, the word slavery did not seem all that remote to Sarah. She could close her eyes and see again the brave and wrinkled face of Eunice-Mae.

She thought about a young man who was shot for stealing a chicken to save his homeless family from starvation on their trek to freedom in another country.

Slavery— that word always flooded Sarah's mind with vivid memories. And more imprinted than anything else was the unforgettable memory of a little kinky-haired boy with black-button eyes, shiny black skin and two small black ears that because of a word called "slavery" would never hear the bark of a dog, the song of a bird or the chirp of a cricket.

The next morning, bright and early, Aunt Nel was up and about her task of commanding this new fort. Her crippling condition was much better than yesterday, so there was no reason why she could not cook the breakfast and give orders around here, so she did. It smelled so good to Sarah, those pancakes and that coffee, rich and black and strong enough to wake the dead.

Sarah and young Peter and Dennis were going to walk into Lancaster today. Peter would be piled high with baskets, and all three of them would carry the extra ones on their heads.

In the early dawn light, Sarah had bathed and combed her thick coil of dark hair back into its French twist, held securely with a tortoise shell comb. She could not tell in that streaked old mirror that the summer sun was indeed, already streaking her once coal-black maine. Sarah's hair, so exposed to the elements as she gathered her basket materials and her herbal medicines, was now aglow with red highlights, and no longer the color of a crow's wing. It would darken up again in the winter months but right now it was the color of all dark hair that is exposed to the sun without a hat.

Sarah chose a pale yellow blouse with a jewel neckline and rolled the long and slender sleeves up, for she had a job to do. Her skirt was just a standard muslin that hung about her ankles and this was a dark brown color, the same color as those butternuts she loved.

She would tie on her straw hat just to keep Aunt Nel and Father happy, but once out of their sight, she would loosen the strings on the big sun protector and it would lay across her back most of the day while the sun quietly streaked her shiny hair.

Breakfast passed without incident and Aunt Nel, realizing that her little family would soon be dispersed in all directions, set a five o'clock deadline for them all to home. Sarah smiled. It seemed good to see Aunt Nel, sitting at the table and telling all the other Indians, where to go — including the Chief.

Sarah had reluctantly put on her White ladies shoes that had high button-up tops and certainly were not designed for feet with five toes, or walking either. They were not only ugly, they were also painfully uncomfortable. She had always noticed this about the dress of the White race. For the men it was not quite so bad, but the White women wore constricting garments called brassieres that were designed to protect and support the breasts, and then they put on another coiling snake that wrapped itself around the middle of their torso and they called this a corset. The corset was worn to again support the middle of their trunks, and White ladies then put on a girdle to cram their hips up into their corsets, so the upper part of their abdomen, their abused breasts, could be pushed and squeezed out through their brassieres; and to cover that fact, they wore a camisole, which was an ornamental undergarment, worn beneath a thin outer bodice, so that their bodies wouldn't apparently fall into a pile of mushy flesh. White women were always referred to as "the weaker sex," and Sarah guessed that (if they couldn't stand alone without being supported from their thighs to their armpits) they quite possibly were.

She had often thought to herself that so many White ladies, she had met, especially on a hot day, looked just plain miserable, and by God now she knew why!

Sarah marvelled, it was such a funny and yet such an unfunny culture. She once had ridden on a train beside a Roman Catholic nun. The temperature was over ninety degrees and the nun had confided to Sarah that she had on fifteen pounds of clothing. The nun prayed on her Rosary beads and later explained to Sarah that she was doing this as a "penance for her sins." Sarah said nothing but had thought quickly, "In those clothes, you are already doing that!"

She was in a good mood today, light-hearted and looking forward soon to be stopping in at all the farms along the Vermont side of the Connecticut River, leading to the town of Lancaster. She wondered, if many of them would notice how much she had grown up this summer.

Sarah knew most every farm family from Guildhall to Lunenburg. Her family had sold them baskets, and her Aunt Nel had been a midwife and a substitute doctor to many of them over the years. And now the kindly farmer's wives that used to offer her cookies and buttermilk outside, saw Sarah the young woman, and they invited her inside for cake and tea and of course conversation. She felt welcome and accepted here in the home of her childhood—the upper Connecticut River Valley.

As she and her two brothers walked along, Sarah noticed an impatience in Dennis today. He was hoping that she wouldn't waste all day talking to the farmer's wives, because there was a musical instrument that he wanted to show her in a shop over in Lancaster. He would bet that they could swap some baskets for the that fiddle, but how many baskets was a fiddle worth?

Sarah good-naturedly cautioned her younger brother "Dennis, you don't even know how to play a fiddle, and besides you are left-handed, Brother."

Dennis was ready with his reply. "Sister, I play a guitar left-handed and I could learn to play the fiddle." The sincerity in his dark eyes was very plain to see. Sarah thought "Oh, us Jackson children and our almighty dreams! Winona's is to join the circus and be an acrobat, and Dennis wants to play the fiddle, and John's is to build tall buildings. And you Sarah, your dream is to find a cure for your father's constant nightmares."

Peter Sr., still dreamed, and dreamed again, of the great belching "whirlwind menace" and the more he dreamed the more he drank and he was often a surly and slovenly stranger, caught up in his own world of "bad dreams and good whiskey." Ironically, these were her father's own words.

Walking along that narrow dirt road, they could hear the murmur of the Connecticut River as it moved along beside them, looking sapphire-blue and silver in the mid-morning sunshine.

Sarah had taken the time this morning to literally fill her medicine pouch with herbs and young and tender leaves, and the roots that she had ever so carefully wrapped. She had not seen any of her Vermont friends and neighbors along that winding river road for over a year, and she knew that just as many changes had come into her own life, many changes would have also come into theirs. They would tell her of them all, it was their way.

There would be new babies with aching gums, fevers and teething rashes and always, a few of the older ones would be gone and she would not see them again until they met on the other side. She would be greeted and asked many medicinal questions as she sipped their tea. She would be told about some doctor's remedy and if it was or wasn't working, and she would be asked to speculate on what Aunt Nel would have thought about this White Man's medicine.

It was commonly known, that Aunt Nel had the healing touch, and all these locals that lined the river knew it. She had been the most capable and respected herbalist in the valley, and now, her niece Sarah, who had learned from Nel, was a much sought after healer herself, because she also had "the gift of healing." These farm people who tilled the soil just plain trusted the judgment of a people who lived close to the earth, a race that knew the medicines of the earth, and because of this, Sarah's opinion on herbal cures was as much a valued product, as were the baskets that she so skillfully created from the very grasses of the topsoil itself.

At the first farm they stopped at, three baskets were sold. The first basket was a very large one and it was to be used to carry in fireplace wood. It was sturdy and strong, while the second was a smaller basket but yet, large enough for a seamstress to hold all the tools she needed for her sewing. The third basket sold was one so tightly laced that it could be used as a decorative vase to hold flowers, and these were traded for a gallon of raw milk, one dozen fresh eggs, and a pound of butter that had been churned that morning. These commodities would be picked up by the Jacksons on their way home.

Summer had officially arrived in the small hamlets of South Guildhall and Lunenburg, when the basketmakers were back. And at each friendly stop, when Sarah explained that her family would stay this winter, most were glad. For there was not one of them that did not know that in the case of a hard birthing or a sudden sickness, a call upon this Jackson family at any hour would be answered.

And so on up that winding road that followed their old highway, the Connecticut River, went Sarah and Dennis and young Peter. They stopped at each farm and then continued along past the old familiar homesteads, each one complete with its outlying backhouse. But here Sarah just smiled and looked away, for they reminded her of sickness and death and the stench of the dead fish lying on the top of the waterways of Holyoke and Springfield. She would tighten her lips and say "Bad as they are, those fly-catching, disease carrying little stink houses, they must be a better idea than to pipe human waste directly into the water system of any handy stream, lake, river or ocean. The "pipes of death," Aunt Nel had said. Sarah would glance across at the swift-flowing river, now not a stone's throw from her. "At least the fish are safe up here for now," Dennis was heard to say in a voice not much more than a whisper.

A look of stubborn pride crossed Sarah's young face and her gaze fell upon the mountains rising on all sides. The place that she called home, was still clean and still healthy but she knew that it was just a matter of time before the land, the sky and the water would all be threatened because of a thing called — progress. And yet it was not that so much as ignorance of the land and carelessness toward all that lived upon it.

A faint breeze stirred the early leaves of the mighty elms as the three dusty figures, still burdened with a heavy cargo, made their way across the old wooden bridge between the towns of South Guildhall, Vermont on one side and Lancaster, New Hampshire on the opposite bank.

In 1948 a new bridge was constructed here, made of steel, and it was named in honor of Major Robert Rogers and his Rangers. Ever since I can remember, this bridge has been called "Roger's Rangers Bridge," but in actuality in 1841, no one was thinking about building a steel bridge here or of dedicating it to anyone.

The history books told the story of Roger's Rangers sneak attack on the hostile and sleeping Village of Odanak, or St. Francis, Canada, in 1759, and how they killed over two hundred St. Francis Indians. Later, it came out; that Rogers and his Rangers burned the church there (for many of these Indians were Christians). In addition to that, a statue of the Madonna, weighing close to fourteen pounds of solid silver, and some gold coins and candlesticks were also stolen from the church and carried away by the soldiers.

As Sarah's heavy high-topped shoes clicked over the wooden boards, she could not have told you the future, about the dedication of this narrow bridge to none other than "the White Devil himself," but she could have told you another side of this story, a verbal account, as she heart it.

It was said that her Grandfather on the Polan side, had lost his only sister in that raid. Yes, it happened in the night, and most of the men were away hunting. A handful of old ones were left behind. Yes, St. Francis Indians were killed, but less than a hundred, all told. The victims were massacred as they slept in their blankets, and most of these were women and children.

Sarah's grandfather was among the absent hunting party, and when the warriors returned and found the church in ashes and the mission village in flames, these warriors set out hard on the heals of the fleeing Rangers. A few of the Rangers got away, however many were caught and all that were caught ——were killed.

The Rangers were supposed to have buried their ill-gotten loot on the long journey home, and to my knowledge the coins and the Madonna Statue have never been found.

The Great Spirit is said to have looked down upon the soldiers with loathing and disgust, and placed a curse on the conquering heroes. The St. Francis treasure is still being searched for, but the Kitsia (old ones) say that it will never be found, for it is guarded by the Spirit of a St. Francis Indian.

One thing has been proved and that is that the successful attack, although devastating, did not rid the earth of the St. Francis Indians.

On this bright spring morning in 1841, three St. Francis Indians walked peacefully across a little wooden bridge and into history. If in their hearts they held a grudge, in their hands they carried baskets, coming in peace to trade for the necessities of life, but their heritage would never— be for sale.

Sarah brushed off a fly that had been buzzing around her head for a few minutes. "I'd forgotten what a long walk it is!" she exclaimed. Peter said nothing for a few minutes, but as they started down the stretch of road now called Bridge Street in Lancaster, he said, "Sister, Peter, him need water, him." Poor Peter, thought Sarah, he was loaded heavier than any of them, and all his life he would have to do the hard work of the hands and the back, because poor soul, he would never have the mental capabilities of making an easy life for himself.

"Over in the Pines," said Sarah, for there were many of these that grew in clumps along the narrow entrance to the town. She pointed towards a section where three tall aromatic trees stood and she said, "We will stop and have dinner here, Peter. We are all thirsty and hungry too."

They ate in silence. The two boys had helped each other get the basket packs untied and it seemed good to just sit and eat and drink in the shade of these mighty pines.

They all ate with care so as not to get their clothes dirty and Sarah sat almost rigid on her blanket, so afraid that she would pick up some pine pitch on her light-colored blouse.

No one expected a person to be dressed up fancy on a business trip, but one was expected to look clean and presentable, and on this first trading trip of the year into the village of Lancaster, Sarah indeed wanted to look her best.

After dinner, these vendors continued their journey until they turned the sharp right corner taking them onto Lancaster's North Main Street.

This town had been indeed laid out with vision, for the streets were wide enough for two wagons to meet and no one had to get off the road, to let a third wagon pass. This was a good thing — in so many towns the streets were so narrow that even on foot a person felt cramped.

"Lancaster is beautiful!" Sarah remarked, and Dennis agreed. The nearer they got to that little shop where the "fiddle" was, the better indeed this town did look to Dennis.

This New Hampshire town prided itself with being the county seat, and it therefore had its share of professional people in residence, lawyers and doctors and the like. Now farmers also came to Lancaster so that the lawyers and doctors and everyone else had plenty of fresh meat and vegetables to purchase in the shops and this meant that there was plenty to do for everybody and the town prospered as goods and services were bought, sold or swapped in the free enterprize of commerce.

They started down the long street which was lined with stately elms. The very air itself seemed to spark with excitement and that brisk feeling of a small town when it is buzzing with life.

A very snappy team driven by a man with a high black hat passed the three basketmakers and the horses snorted, and as the clop of hooves drifted further away, Sarah brushed the freshly kicked-up dirt from her dress.

"Dennis, you don't know how to play that fiddle, if we do get it!" Sarah exclaimed but once more her brother reiterated "Sister, I can play a guitar, and a flute and you know well that I can learn to play a fiddle." Sarah could see that her brother was very determined.

Dennis knew that the stores and shops in Lancaster would always swap commodities with the Jacksons for baskets if they preferred this to actual money, but what Dennis could not figure out was how many baskets was one fiddle worth?

Sarah did not have her mind on fiddles at all. She was thinking about the bright red cotton material that she would buy, to make up the curtains for the windows.

They had just got to that stretch of street where North Main Street merges with Main Street itself when another wagon passed .

This was the wagon of a peddler. It was a closed-in affair, and perched upon the single seat sat a plump and balding man is his middle fifties. He wore round spectacles, and as he neared the three, he clucked to his horses to slow them down. Sarah thought at first that this was out of courtesy so they wouldn't get such a shower of dirt from the wheels, until she realized that he was literally walking the horses right along beside her and her younger brothers. "Like a ride, Missey?"

She never really knew if it was the sound of his voice, or the baleful way that he was looking at her that made her stop in her tracks and look sharply at him. He had two little pig-eyes that seemed not to see her siblings at all. No, these dead-eyes were only for her and on her and they were intensely watching, and for once in her life Sarah was glad that she was wearing many undergarments in the tradition of the White woman, for this man would have a harder time trying to see what interested him. She also knew that if Aunt Nel's massive bulk was treading along beside them, he would have gone on his way and never slowed down his wagon. "Cowards were so obvious," she thought.

Sarah faced him then and when he brought the team to a complete stop and lifted his hat she said "No, we want no ride, thank you." And at that moment Sarah tried to look as matronly as she could at seventeen years.

The man's face picked up color and his apparent anger was visible by the tight set of his thin lips, and the frown that formed on his close-knitted brow and only his dead man's eyes seemed not to notice the rejection of his generous offer.

"Snippy one, eh?" he said, and then doffed his hat, and made a harder cut of his buggy whip than was necessary. He laid another lash across the backs of the horses and as they bolted ahead, he called back "Perhaps another time, Missey." And now the Jackson family had stopped and were looking after the strange peddler and his spirited team as it disappeared in a cloud of dust and kicked-up dirt, down the street ahead of them.

Dennis was thirteen, but not ever missing much, commented "Funny man! I don't like him. Where do you suppose he comes from?"

"Hell is where he comes from and Hell is where that one will be going," Sarah answered his question and then said "He reeks of dirt — the kind you can never wash off. He dirties many paths. Don't ever go near one like that who carries in his head the eyes of the dead-already."

They watched the sharp looking wagon until it disappeared out of sight and then they walked on in silence and stopped at the first shop they came to and there Sarah sold five baskets. With the money she purchased some molasses.

At the insistence of Dennis they went to the corner, the cross streets that lay just before crossing the Siwooganock (Israel's River) to a unique little what-not shop with a friendly proprietor that seemed to have everything from soup to nuts, but the only thing that Dennis wanted Sarah to look at was that second-hand fiddle that was hanging on the wall.

"Good morning sir, would you care to buy or swap for some sweetgrass baskets today," Sarah asked.

The owner of the shop was a thin and sparse-haired man in his late thirties, but he had good eyes and a pleasant smile.

He thought Sarah was a graceful young woman, and obviously one that had been taught good manners, which was more than he say for that queer acting old goat that had just left in that peddler's wagon.

"Well young lady, I think that I could use a couple of these baskets. Now what did you say they are made of?"

"Two from ash— most from sweetgrass, but they are all well made and very strong." Sarah commented. Her smile charmed him. The fellow bought not two but in fact four of Sarah's baskets, and she was pleased because now she had enough money to purchase that red cotton cloth that she wanted for the curtains.

The merchant asked her "Now, you say the little fancy ones are jewelry boxes and the big ones are sewing baskets, right?"

Sarah nodded her head and after a long moment she finally asked the question that Dennis had been waiting to hear all day, "Would you please tell me sir what are you asking for the fiddle up there on the wall?"

He smiled. The thought of an Indian playing a violin had never occurred to him at the time. "Oh, do you play the violin?" he asked, and Sarah shook her head no, but it was obvious that she still desired to hear the price of the instrument.

After thinking a moment, the merchant said "I'd probably sell it for four dollars Ma'am, if you don't think that too high a price." Her face showed almost no emotion until she smiled and said "I do think it is too high a price, I'll give you two dollars," she said and then held up two fingers. This proprietor loved to dicker and he quickly said, "three" but Sarah was already shaking her head no.

A long minute later she said "two— with another small basket or that fiddle, it stays on the wall."

Here Dennis looked at the floor,"there goes my fiddle," he thought.

He knew how stubborn and uncompromising that his sister Sarah could be. The shop keeper scratched his head and said "Well, it is second hand but it is still in good condition." Sarah countered, "The basket is new and it has no flaws," and this brought a snicker out of the merchant and he said "Ok, I'll do it, two dollars and another small basket."

And so the deed was done and Sarah left one more basket with the merchant and paid him two dollars of the money that he had just paid her.

As she and Dennis left, Dennis carried the fiddle and the man who had sold it, called after Sarah, "I sure hope I can sell all these baskets." She turned and met his gaze squarely and said, "Sir you can always sell a basket. It is harder to sell a fiddle." "But you wanted one," the man said with a grin on his face and Sarah made one too and quipped, "I did not, but I knew a man that did." And here she looked at Dennis and they left the little shop.

The smiling owner was standing there with both of his arms full of sweetgrass baskets, made by Abenaki Indians who went out carrying a violin which was made by a White Man. And yes, the world was changing and because of that, both cultures merged here in the far reaches of the Connecticut River Valley, where ladies in fine houses in Lancaster would keep their jewelry and sewing in Indian baskets and the Indians would play fiddles, so that both races could dance to the universal sound of music.

It was exactly half past three when Sarah and her brothers finished their business in downtown Lancaster. The very last basket had been sold and the red cotton cloth had been purchased, and the three were making their way up Main Street to a where the Weeks Memorial Library now sits. Then a wagon, open and clanging with empty milk cans in the back of it, pulled up beside them.

The friendly voice of Mrs. Valley from South Guildhall called to them, "You yungans want a ride across the river?" The three exchanged quick smiles and climbed aboard the back of the wagon like three monkeys scaling a banana tree.

Mrs. Valley was a big and matronly woman who wore her hair in a tight pug at the back of her head, but she had kind eyes and her pleasant bulk was a welcome sight to see for these basketmakers.

"Thank you, Mrs. Valley, we sure would like a ride!" exclaimed Sarah as Dennis helped his sister up amid the grain bags and milk jugs, but Mrs. Valley, seeing Sarah's pretty blouse, shook her head no, and said "Nope, Sari Girl, you be too big now to sit back there. You climb right up here beside me and Frank and we can visit on the way." Sarah was very proud to be let sit in the front of the wagon, and she wasn't long scampering to her outside position on the old wooden seat. But at least she had a seat, and she was not bouncing around between grain bags and milk cans and sitting in damp sawdust.

The Valley's lived on a large farm on the Vermont side of the river, and Sarah knew that her next run of baskets would be up that side of the Connecticut, all the way to Guildhall and then down the New Hampshire side.

"Good to see you back, Sari. How is Peter and Nel?" asked the driver, Frank Valley and Sarah replied, "Both well, except Aunt Nel's lameness. She has good days and bad ones, but we are staying all winter this time."

"We'd heard that from the neighbors to the south of us, Sari, and we was mighty glad to hear that too," said Mrs. Valley. She was remembering that only last summer, Frank Charles, her youngest son, was stricken with a debilitating diarrhea condition which lasted for several weeks and it weakened him so that he was unable to help with the haying or do very much farm work at all. Aunt Nel had been consulted and she had sent Sarah to the Valley farm, carrying a bottle that contained a mixture of strained blackberries and God only knew what else, but anyhow, that sick boy, Charles took one tablespoon every six hours and in less than a week his bowels were back to normal. When he got his strength back he was as good as ever, thanks to Nelemano Jackson.

"Your father stops in to visit us once in a great while on his way back from Guildhall or Maidstone," Mrs. Valley said.

Sarah listened but she said nothing. Peter had friends up in both those little hamlets and he went up there and they hunted, fished and got drunk together, but if Mrs. Valley did not know this already, Sarah would let someone else tell her. "Dennis is carrying a fiddle, ain't he?" Frank Valley wanted to know, and Sarah nodded and said "Yes. he is eager to learn to play it." Now the Valleys had heard Dennis playing his guitar at various kitchen junkets and even once at a barn raising, and they had no doubt that a lad as musically inclined as he was would learn.

"Twon't be long before he learns, If I know Dennis," Mrs. Valley stated and she was exactly right.

By the time the new red curtains hung in the Jackson's kitchen window, Dennis was playing simple songs on his fiddle. As a matter of fact, he could shut his eyes and taste the high and trembling notes that this instrument made, in the roof of he mouth. He told his family that, one evening as he finished a haunting ballad on the new violin.

Dennis in later years hardly ever touched the guitar, but he played his fiddle every chance he could and he even carried it in his duffle bag when he left for the Civil War and he carried it back home to Vermont with him at the end of that war and for many years he played for dances at the old town hall's in Lunenburg and Guildhall and many neighboring towns.

As the snows of November fell that year the Jackson root cellar was full, and the house rang with music provided by Dennis on the fiddle and brother John on the guitar. By the time the Christmas season approached, Dennis was playing old familiar Carols, and Sarah would hum along with him.

Brother John, added rhythm guitar and Peter joined in with the flute. Winona played the spoons and these were good family times. The house was warm and they had plenty to eat. Even if the north wind howled and threatened outside, inside sitting around their wood burning stove, the Jacksons spent good winter evenings with their repeated legends, and the music which all of them loved.

This Native American family had learned to enjoy the fruits of the Yuletide, the giving and the good will of it, the peacefulness it proclaimed, and the best side that it seemed to bring out in most men and the change in their spirits — for the better. In fact, Sarah had more than once thought, "If the White race celebrated Christmas all year, every day, what a good-hearted and good-living people they would be."

Peter Sr., was not planning on bringing in a Christmas tree, but when he returned from a visit to Maidstone, three days prior to Christmas Eve, he found one sitting already in the sparsely furnished living room. This evergreen was well shaped and decorated with strings of popped corn and cranberries, and Aunt Nel had made stars out of quilting material, and the tree not only looked festive, but it smelled wonderful.

Upon entering the room and seeing the tree, Peter felt that pang that he always felt when he saw his very own family, so readily adopting the customs of another culture.

"Why the tree, Nel?" he asked his stoic sister, who sat calmly darning a stocking. With a shrug Nel replied, "Why not a tree, Peter?"

Peter knew that he could start a long argument with Nel, but he was tired, he had been drinking a little, and his head already ached. He also knew that if he got too demanding and made them carry the tree out, that Nel would not make his favorite upside down maple cake, nor the hard candy or fudge either. That's the way Nel was and they had had this fight before, and with Aunt Nel it was either celebrate Christmas, with giving some small gifts to each other, eating more than one should, having a decorated tree in the house, or being a sourpuss—and not having a decorated tree in the house or any of the other things either!

Peter glowered. She drove a hard bargain, that Nelemano did. Sometimes he liked to think that his life would have been happier if she had run off with that Mohawk from St. Regis (that one who saw only good in Nel and wanted her to go and live with him and become a Catholic, like he was). But, No, Nel she would not do that, but she would keep the traditions of Christmas in her brother's house and against his wishes. "She would have made a good Christian," Peter thought,"Yes, a good Catholic," and he knew damned well she would have made a good Mohawk! Nel was stubborn and mean and bossy enough to be one. Sometimes he wondered?

Peter was on his way upstairs to bed, but feeling his power rapidly being undermined by Nelemano, he spoke to his sister crisply "You are such a good White woman, Nel, may as well have married and turned Mohawk!"

Fire flashed in Nel's dark eyes, and although she knew it was the booze that loosened her brother's biting tongue, she snapped "May as well," and then laying her sewing in her lap, she folded her arms across her massive chest and continued, "May as well turn to a Mohawk as turn to a drunk, Peter!" and here her brother could not face the contempt and yes, the stark truth of her words—hateful, hurting and truthful words.

Peter stumbled and half-staggered up the narrow stairway. His heart lay in his chest like a lead weight. His humiliation was complete now, for here in front of the most important people in the world, his children, Nel had looked him in the eyes and called him a drunk, and she had called it just right!

Peter felt suddenly like stopping in his tracks and screaming back at all of them "Merry Christmas— you White hearts!" But he did not, this unhappy man just went on up the stairs and straight to bed.

The little family sat in silence. "Why is Father always such a grouch at Christmas?" asked John and Sarah was already shaking her head no, for him to say nothing, but Nelemano answered "Because he is unhappy. The liquor clouds his mind and he wants nobody else to be happy. Christmas is a happy time."

Sarah had a question for Aunt Nel. She had never known before this night that her beloved aunt-mother, had once had a chance to get married and to have a life or perhaps even a family of her own, even if it was with another kind of Indian.

"Aunt Nel, have you ever been sorry that you did not go away and marry the Mohawk and live you own life?"

Nelemano smiled and said "No, never, not even once."

"Why?" Sarah asked flatly.

Aunt Nel had resumed her sewing, and as John placed another stick of wood in the big stove she answered, "For good reasons I never regretted my choice."

As the hissing fire blazed higher, Sarah asked "What good reasons? And, Nel smiled tenderly at her niece and listed them in the correct order, "Sarah, Peter Jr., Dennis, John and Winona— five very good reasons" smiled Nelemano, and she meant every word.

On the Eve of Christmas Sarah hung stockings, and these were mysteriously filled with candy and small tools and trinkets in the morning, but no one knew who did it. Now, there were none in this old farmhouse that actually believed in Santa Claus, but every one of them believed in the spirit of giving. To celebrate the birthday of the Great Spirit was a good thing, kind of like the feasts of old, and so they did celebrate and this included the wonderful taste of a roast goose on Christmas Day, plus music and carols and even Peter Senior finally mellowed and at last did join in with the rest of the family because — it was Christmas.

The house was banked high with evergreen boughs covered with snow, and the snow was half way up the bottom part of the window panes. Blustery days when icicles hung from the eaves of this house, gave way to the January thaw.

The sun peeked through the grey sky of winter, and the icicles dripped and melted. Some snow left, and for almost a week it seemed that there was a glimmer of hope that this world of ice and snow would sometime melt and turn to fields of green, come spring.

Then suddenly, winter was back upon them like it was on all those other hardy residents of the upper Connecticut River Valley. The temperatures dropped to below zero in early February and stayed there for the first two weeks of that unpredictable month. All through the valley, fires blazed higher and woodpiles got lower.

In the days of Peter's boyhood the Moose Hunt always took place in late February or early March. It was the biggest event of the season up in the Village of St. Francis, but now there were too few moose to hold a hunt. And there were too few Indians who could have organized one.

Peter brought down an occasional deer, and this got the family through the winter. Supplies and firewood were getting low, but in a month or two there would be fiddlehead and dandelion greens to eat, and until then Peter and his three sons settled for drilling holes in the ice on the Connecticut River, and beside these cavities they patiently sat and watched their fishing lines and they were able to help sustain their dwindling food stock, with fish they caught during this cold and yet rewarding ordeal called "ice fishing."

Peter had also set some traps for fur-bearing animals, and Dennis and John checked his traplines every day on snowshoes, and like all youths they frolicked in the heavy Green Mountain snows and indeed made the very best of the very worst that winter could throw at them.

Under Peter's watchful eye, John and Dennis had been taught to mend a snowshoe, for it was something a man should know. Peter knew that working with "babiche" or rawhide was a necessity to a hunter's survival.

Untanned hide, was perhaps the all-important material to the Indian, and Peter showed his sons how to take the "green" hide of an animal and stretch it out on a wooden frame, where all the flesh was scraped away. After scraping, the hides had set or dried for three days. These hides were then removed from wooden frames and submerged in a stream of running water, or sprinkled with hardwood ashes (on the hair side) and buried in the ground for four or five days. The process changed "green" hide to rawhide.

Once a hide had been properly softened it was often cut into strings or thongs and used as lacings for nets, bags and also for making or mending snowshoes. The "babiche" (Micmac Indian word meaning cord or thread) was carried by most all the Algonquian Indian peoples and many early trappers.

Some of this "green" hide was left untreated, and unlike rawhide it would shrink. It became very hard and was known as Red Man's iron, and for that reason was used for tools and durable handles for clubs, and in earlier times, was what Indian drumheads were made of.

Dennis and John each carried a whistle made from the wing bone of a turkey. The sound escaping from the bone whistles, was exactly like the plaintive cry of a wild turkey. This was their signal to their father when they hunted.

Peter himself carried a whistle made from the wing bone of an eagle that had belonged to his own father, and it was perhaps, save the bearclaw necklace, his most prized possession.

Peter like most Abenakis, only believed in killing the bear when it was necessary, for the bear was their clan totem, and some Indians were so superstitious about this animal, that they were reluctant ever to harm it. If it was one's animal helper, then that particular hunter could not kill the bear. But when the bear was killed, its fur provided wonderfully warm robes, and good hide for making moccasins, and it also provided the grease that was used to preserve other hides. Bear grease was wonderful to keep human hair healthy and shiny. With the teeth and the claws always in demand for jewelry, there was almost no part of that big animal that got wasted.

Second to the bear, the beaver was a very much respected animal, and the Indian thought him brave, industrious and very intelligent, and often praised him in songs and legends.

The beaver's teeth that could fall mighty trees were prized highly by most Native American tribes and the fact that brother beaver always lived in colonies ruled over by a chief and lived by their own laws, made him very man-like to the Indian, a true brother.

Sarah always hated the smell of horns or antlers being softened, but she could dislike and be darned because the offensive aroma could be detected often around the Jackson home. Horn was easier to work with than antler, because when it hardened, it could be molded easily with another piece of horn. Antler, which is bone and not horn, also had to be heated and although they were harder to work with, these made beautiful knives, buttons and other small and useful tools. John had a bow made with a set of antlers.

Peter seemed to enjoy this winter here in the north, for he was teaching his sons to do the things he had been taught to do himself and it was a very important thing to do.

Sometimes Peter would be gone for three days at a time, but when he returned he tried to be sober for his family. He seemed driven lately to tell his sons old stories long remembered and to show them the skills that he himself had almost forgotten.

When Peter's hands would shake as he helped John or Dennis to mend a snowshoe, he would stop and then go on. His dreams were always frightening and frequent but he still had the patience that was needed to do the job that should be done— to teach. And, Peter could not understand why he felt the need to rush so lately, he only knew, he did.

He had to admit that to stay that first winter of 1841 had for Nelemano been a very good move. Her rheumatism seemed better in this dry northern climate, even in the snows of winter, than it was in the dampness of the Massachusetts coastline.

When Nel felt better, she was easier to get along with, like Peter himself was.

Nel's big hands were always mending, sewing or creating baskets for sale in the summer months. She helped Sarah with all the medicinal business, the mixing of the various potions and the measuring, and then she carefully instructed in the administration. She was a very active force now in the old farmhouse. While Peter grew weak, Nelemano grew stronger.

When she made molasses cookies Peter could smell their aroma all over the house. He would request that she make his favorite meal of all — something Nel called "Connecticut River Shad." She would get her old wood cookstove cranked up, and then after her brother had cleaned a side of fresh shad Nel would wash it in cold water and gently pat it dry with a cheesecloth. It was then placed skin-side-down in a deep pan and she would lay half-inch strips of bacon across the fish. It was sprinkled with salt then and with lots of pepper and after twenty minutes in a hot oven, the dish was ready, and usually Peter beat the fish to the pine table. "Yes, of course, Nel, she was okay sometimes— cooktimes mostly," thought Peter.

In other places and parts of the country where this family had traveled and lived, Aunt Nelemano had also baked the shad, but Peter and his children always swore that the Connecticut River shad was the best of all, unspoiled and delicious.

The Jackson family learned more White ways with each day they lived. They called one full day a sleep. They used the White Man's calendar but still managed to live their lives around Abenaki time in which one year was called a winter. Each month was referred to as a moon and always began with a new moon. An Indian day wasn't divided up into increments of minutes or hours, but it constituted four time periods—sunrise, noon, sunset and midnight. Most Indians thought the White race had been running around like scared rabbits ever since the invention of the clock. Still, the Jacksons had used clocks, and timepieces since the missionaries had arrived at Odanak, or St. Francis. They used the standard calendar too, except for the seasons. Each season was for the Indian determined by the budding or leafing of plants, the spawning of fish or the rutting time for animals. Each season was a special time to do what had to be done.

From Tarritine country all the way back to Catbow Swamp it was the moon to make sweet food medicine, and so when the juice or sap was running in the maple trees it was time to make maple syrup and sugar.

The sap was gathered in wooden buckets, after carefully tapping a spigot or a sap-spout into a maple tree to catch the liquid gold, drop by drop. This was later boiled in a large evaporator to a deeper and richer state called maple syrup. This was a delicacy then and it is a delicacy now. It tops our pancakes and French toast, and we crave it, but the early Native Americans used it scarcely because they believed that it was a medicine that cleansed the blood and soothed the lungs, and that the sap itself, when consumed in its natural unboiled state, was a sure-fire cure for constipation. They ate it, but made sure that their small children and their old ones had more than any of the younger people who actually had the toil of making this good medicine. Every precious drop was used, and not any of it wasted. The Indians gave us maple syrup and popcorn and Sarah used to laugh and say, "That shows we have good taste."

For two years more this Abenaki family lived like Indians at home and White men out in public. They were making adjustments to live normal and productive lives in this new culture, all but Peter, that is. But none of them except Peter was the chosen leader and chief of a family band, a band that was reduced now to his immediate family. No matter how many strides he made, no matter what challenges Peter overcame during these tumultuous times of constant change, he felt that he had always lost. He believed that he had given and been denied...so much more than he had ever won—his heritage.

His dependency upon alcohol increased and he felt lost and burdened with a heavy sense of despair, for although he was not homeless there were times when he felt indeed hopeless, with no cause at all. To loose control of your destiny is a frightening thing to face up to, and for Peter in the year of 1843, which was to be the last winter of his life, the reality of not being able to control his lot, simply overwhelmed him. This new civilization required so many skills to succeed and lead his people on a good course. He felt so inadequate. He could and did live with the ignorance of not knowing many things, and after years of trying hard this ignorance was replaced by a deader feeling, called apathy, because he didn't care anymore. When this final apathy consumed his being, liquor was his escape from reality as it had always been. The once proud heart that beat in the once powerful chest seemed to break, in a quiet and almost unnoticed surrender of heart and mind and spirit.

In sober moments, he would often think of the much repeated words of the great Pennacook Chief Passaconnaway, that wise old leader who had warned his people, "Peace; Peace is your only hope." Well, this struggling chief of another generation had heeded those words. He had lived in peace and he had lost all hope. Peter was sure that his culture and heritage were at an end.

He could not lead a people when he had no place to take them except into more changes forever. He had led them into great changes already and they had changed admirably and survived against all odds. But, in the process of survival, they had paid a mighty price, for in winning their future his Dawnland People —had lost their past.

But Peter, Polani-Taxos-Kohla-Cost, my great-great grandfather was wrong, because thanks to an Indian's memory and a White Man's pencil a people long silent have been heard. The flame on the candle of heritage never did die out, it only flickered low.

"Cold nights and sunny days are what it takes to make good maple syrup," thought Sarah as she stood and watched the great kettle boiling on the woodstove. This batch was nearing the crossover point, and as she dipped her long wooden spoon into the steaming caldron, she could tell that it would not be a very long time before she had to fight down the bubbling froth with a piece of salt pork on a fork. Sometimes she used cream for this but today she used what she had available, a piece of salt pork.

She was tired. Her father had awakened the entire household last night, with another of his bad dreams. All day he had not felt well, and in fact, he had stayed in bed most of the day because the willow bark mixture, would not ease the pain in his throbbing head.

Aunt Nel and Sarah were staying up nights on shifts, in order to boil the syrup. The season of making sugar was one that would not wait. When the sap was running you had better be there to gather it and when you boiled it, you had better stay with it— until the job was done.

Sarah was thinking as she stood there, in the early hours of the morning, that it took such a lot of sap to make a quart of maple syrup and it took such a lot of work too, but the wonderful taste it added to food, and its medicinal properties alone, were worth all the hard and time-consuming work. This year Dennis turned sixteen and John would be turning thirteen and they had worked like beavers to gather this bubbling sap on snowshoes. "Fun work," they had said.

Sarah knew that it was not good to mention the name of any deceased person, for that might disturb the spirit of the dead. But every now and then curiosity would prevail and she would question her Aunt Mother about her natural mother, whom she remembered nothing about.

Sarah knew that her mother's name was Dancel but she would not say that name, she would just ask about this woman in the context of her mother; and she stopped her stirring at one point, wiped the perspiration from her smooth brow, and asked, Nelemano "Aunt Nel, what was our mother like?" Nel gave Sarah a sharp and penetrating glance. Sarah was fishing again, Nel realized quickly. Now had Sarah actually used her mother's name, she would have gotten no answer but now, at nineteen, Sarah knew how to find out things that were often hard to find out.

Nel, seated at the table, pushed her half-constructed basket out in front of her and answered. "She was some like you Sarah, very quiet. But, not so tall, and physically she did not look strong, but mentally she was, and also very stubborn. And she could be a force to deal with, that one."

"Do I look like her?" Sarah quizzed her Aunt, and once more Aunt Nel thought a moment and then she replied "Some. When you smile you look like her, when you are angry you show more the Taxos (wolf) blood. You look some like her—some like me too, and now I go to bed. That Peter and his dreams, they make me crazy!" Aunt Nel, got up out of her chair and began to pick up her basketry that was spread in disarray around the table and hoping to let Sarah see, that she had fished enough for one night, because Nelemano wasn't biting. "It makes Father crazy too, Aunt Nel. Do you think if we built him a wickiup of boughs, a private place for a sweat bath, it would help to clear his mind and chase the evil spirits out of his dreams?"

"No," said Aunt Nel, as she moved her heavy bulk towards the stairway,"No, child. He has nothing to sweat now— but rum. I cannot help my brother. I have tried, but his demons are strong." She shrugged her shoulders and then departed up the stairway with a step so light, her niece did not even hear it, for when Sarah looked up from her kettle again, Aunt Nel was gone and she was alone, to worry about her father, his dreams and his drunkenness.

For a long time Sarah thought about Peter Jackson, now as compared to the one she had known as a child. As a little girl, Sarah was closer to Peter than Peter had been to his three sons. She was his favorite and she knew it. From puberty on there hadn't been the closeness she had once shared with her father, for his time was spent teaching the boys to hunt and fish and trap. She spent her time with Aunt Nel as a constant companion. This was the Indian way, but still she missed the old Peter, the one who helped her mend a bird's broken leg, or who carved her a special toy. Time changes every person, and for Sarah it was that as she grew up and her father grew old, there was a gulf between them, and her companion and playmate in the games of childhood was no more, and in his place stood an introverted and sad-faced man whom she called —Father.

Sarah recalled only two weeks prior to this night, when he had somehow managed to get home. John and Peter had to drag him up the stairs and literally put him in bed. He had looked at Sarah and lowered his dark eyes and mumbled, "I'm sorry I'm drunk," and at that time, he had not called her by name but instead had shaken his head and said clearer this time, "Sorry Dancel." He, in his inebriated state, had thought that she was her mother! Perhaps she did look like her mother.
Who knew? Only one thing was Sarah sure of, and that was that her father was a dying man— only when?

Gradually the snows of winter melted and the north wind didn't howl quite as loud as it had a few days past. Spring was making its presence felt all across northern New England, and gradually even the little hamlets of Guildhall and Lunenburg had to thaw out.

Last spring Sarah and her brothers had planted corn, and they had so enjoyed it in the later part of August. Peter and Nel had said that in the old days a great feast with dancing was held at the time the corn was planted. Another feat with dancing was held when the fruit of that labor was ready for harvest. This was a thank you celebration, and again there was dancing and feasting. But now the Jacksons just planted their maize, and when it was ripe they sat down and ate it with great relish, only now they were forgetting to be thankful for the gift of the corn crop. This was not their way, they were changing rapidly.

This spring Aunt Nel was teasing for some hens, and Peter had stamped his foot and made the "cut off" sign with his left hand and bellowed "No. Nelemano! Not by a damned sight. I am not plucking a stinking chicken. If you get these and bring them home, I say to you like you say about my rabbits, "You got it— You clean it!"

Nel's bottom lip shot out in a pout and Sarah sighed, for she knew darned well who would be dipping the headless chickens in a pail of boiling water to loosen the feathers.... she would, that's who.

"Well, we can always talk the feathers off them," stated Winona, and all at once Peter and Nel both began to grin. These two who so loved to laugh just couldn't help it. Leave it to that Winona, to find some humor in any situation.

Last summer and this one also Peter Jr. would stay home to help get the next winter's firewood in. Dennis and John, both would work for the local farmers in the barns and hayfields to help support the family. Sarah and Nel would make and sell their baskets, and Peter Senior would watch the weather signs closely and would head for the nearest brook when it was time to go fishing. "Well, someone has to take care of you people!" he was heard to say one day as he headed down the road with his fishpole over his shoulder. Sarah roared with laughter.

Only the dead didn't know when spring had sprung in the upper Connecticut Valley. The smell of sugar on show was soon replaced by the aroma of mud, and tiny springs of water poured out of the ground and ran in many directions. All things were new and fresh and turning green. It was the growing season, and even before the ice had melted in the streams and the mighty Connecticut River itself some greens and shoots had been gathered and eaten.

The raw cold winds of winter were not biting anymore but the fish were, and that alone was proof of a good life ahead; and when the scent of apple blossoms filled the air, summer was not coming, it was here. Sarah had gone down to the root cellar and taken an inventory of the remaining food stock, and though not entirely depleted it was getting mighty low, she remarked as she climbed up the ladder that led down there.

Aunt Nel shook her head. This coming winter would be a hard one! The spring had been too dry. Spring rain is as important to the thirsty things under the ground as heavy snow cover is in the winter.

The maple harvest was stored away and it had been a bounteous one. Aunt Nel realized that all the rain that fell later in July and early August wouldn't help the struggling berries. They would be small and few in number and not as sweet and succulent as they should be. Oh well, somehow they would make do, they always did.

There was a large pantry off the kitchen, and this was a food reservoir for the family. In the kitchen itself was a closet with rows and rows of shelves, and these were filled with baskets, baskets of all sizes and all kinds. The large ones were fireplace baskets used to carry in wood, and the very largest baskets of all were used for laundry containers, and were stored in the ramshackle shed.

Much of the wonderful sweetgrass of Tarritine Ledge country and all along the Connecticut River had been gathered and by now had been combed and dried, separated and dyed different colors and had already been made into useful containers. The first gift from Mother Earth was the sweetgrass itself, and the second gift was the baskets woven from that sweetgrass that would last a lifetime.

Sarah, in her contact with the White world, knew enough about the Bible to know that "The work of the hands was always blessed."

In mid-May just after the high water, began the first annual trek into Lancaster, on down to Dalton, and then back to Fitzdale or Gilman, and up the River Road to Lunenburg Village and all its outlying farms. Yes, the Moon of Trading was upon them.

The stockpile of baskets would be divided into thirds, and the first sales trip would make it possible to get many of the supplies the family was low on. "Funny," thought Sarah, "even before you had the baskets sold, you were already, in your own mind—spending the money." She knew that they bought things now, like spices and salt and some articles of clothing, that they didn't really badly need, but they liked what they were buying. This family had grown used to these things, and the "Save, and hurry up and hord up" attitude of brother squirrel was rapidly being replaced by the desires and the gambles offered by a free-enterprise system. Indeed, these Dawnland People were changing.

One thing Sarah wanted this year was a new dress. Summer was closing in upon them and she would be invited to the usual kitchen junkets and local goings-on. She was nineteen winters old now, and had become quite conscious of her appearance. She wanted to look like the other young ladies near her age in this valley.

Some of them had such beautiful golden tresses that actually swirled and curled, others had fine hair, as fine as a new born infant's fuzzy crown. There were those whose hair was the color of a fox's tail, but all of them wore their locks in different styles. They could do so many thing with their hair, that Sarah could not do with her own, which was coarse and black and as straight as a string. She remembered the time a friend of her's had tried to change that by wetting Sarah's tresses and rolling them in soft rags, that were supposed to turn into ringlets. But when the rags were removed, the end result had been disastrous! Her thick and resistant mop did not "take a curl and turn to ringlets," what it did was rise up in the air and stick right out on both sides of her head, and the younger children had laughed and laughed and this hurt Sarah's feelings until she finally had to laugh herself, because she thought she looked just like a Raggedy-Ann doll that Winona had been given for Christmas. In fact her hair looked like it had just come out of a whirlwind, and Sarah eventually had to wash it out, let it dry and comb it back into the French twist at the back of her head. That might not be pretty but at least it wasn't laughable.

Oh well, some special dance or get-together she decided that she would buy a fancy comb, or even let her hair flow loose, cascading down her back and she could buy some pretty ribbons to put in it.

What she wouldn't do, she wouldn't cut it! Years ago, when there was a death in the family, all the women cut their hair in mourning, but this was not done anymore and Sarah was glad, because she would not do it! She believed that hair was a growing thing, to cherish and keep clean and to let grow.

Whenever a group of local musicians set up to play in Guildhall or Lunenburg, Dennis that accomplished young fiddler, was always part of the band. And to these get-togethers the entire Jackson family went, and they all danced too except Aunt Nel. Still, she went and sat along the sidelines and clapped her arthritic hands in time with the music. Sarah was a beautiful dancer, light on her feet and as graceful as a willow. She and Winona had been taught to dance as young children, and Sarah was a fine clog dancer too. The art had been taught to her by one of her cousins by the name of Dana Capineau, who made his living dancing professionally with the Aaron Turner Circus.

Sarah enjoyed these box parties, that were then so popular and prominent in rural America where young women come to the dance carrying baskets or box-lunches, and all the men would bid for the box lunch of their favorite young woman. It was suspenseful and light-hearted fun, and if an old friend didn't wind up with your box, a new friend would.

This is why Sarah wanted a new dress. She could not wear pretty ringlets in her hair, but she could wear a new dress as well as the next one, and by gosh she was going to save some of the basket money and buy some cloth and make herself a new dress.

She smiled as she pursued the normal routine household chores. This was indeed the most exciting time of her life! She was restless and independent and longing to be carefree. Sarah was just like all the little plants and flowers that were poking their heads up out of the rich black dirt of this valley. Even the worry over her father's increased depression and drinking, paled before the glory of this coming season. Yes Sarah the child was gone with last winter's snow, and Sarah the woman was here now, and unbeknownst to her, she was as free and lovely as those apple blossoms that she loved.

Early summer always made the heart light, but somehow Sarah knew that this summer something very good and very special was going to happen in her life.

The last two weeks of May were wet ones and by the time the wild flowers bloomed in early June, Sarah had saved up enough basket money so that she could have that new dress.

She found the right material in a shop in Lancaster, and as her quick eyes flew across the many bolts of cloth, at last she saw it. The minute her dark eyes fell upon that particular cloth, Sarah could visualize her first new dress, right down to the last detail.

The fabric was a fine cotton-muslin, with a bone or cream colored background, and embroidered with clusters of tiny clover leaves in the color of jade green. These seemed to lift off the very cloth itself and almost looked alive. "It is so beautiful," she thought and she could close her eyes and picture how the dress would look with long tapered sleeves, trimmed with bone-colored lace at the cuffs and along the jewel neckline. She envisioned that it would have a fitted bodice and a long and full-flowing skirt, as was the fashion. The final touch would be a complimentary sash made of wide jade-green ribbon, to fit around her small waist and to tie into a pretty bow in the back. That was it. All she needed now was a narrow jade-green ribbon to tie back her hair, and this she had to find at another shop, but Sarah was not dissuaded until all the cloth, the ribbon and lace were in her carrying sack and ready to go home.

She couldn't wait to get back with the supplies Aunt Nel had ordered. Her excitement was short-lived however, because in her quest to hurry home with the makings for her new dress she had overlooked one of the most important items on Nel's grocery list, and that was molasses, for the baked beans that she had planned to make for supper on Saturday night.

As a rule, Sarah was not one that had a history of forgetting anything. She apologized to Aunt Nel who was quick to read her shame, and said lightly, "Don't fret Sarah, I use more maple syrup than molasses, anyhow— and molasses just give beans a good color." Nelemano had made very light of the matter because she herself had been nineteen once, and then like Sarah now, had her own thoughts and hopes and dreams and Nel knew that many times her mind also had been more on how she looked than on molasses.

With much of her enthusiasm gone, Sarah showed Nelemano her material, and she could tell by Aunt Nel's eyes that she liked it too. "Very nice Sarah!" Nel exclaimed and then with a big grin she continued, "glad that you did something right today." Then she and Sarah laughed together over Sarah's mistake.

Sarah never did go through a "boy crazy" phase, but she was noticing the opposite sex now, certain ones that is, and unbeknownst to her many of them were also noticing her. Aunt Nel saw this because she always saw everything. She especially noticed that her niece-daughter Sarah had grown into a lovely young woman.

As Sarah tied a long white apron around her middle, and began helping her Aunt with the evening meal, Nel asked her mischievously, "Who you want to look so pretty for, Sarah?" Her niece only smiled and answered, "For me, just for Me." And that was a good answer, thought Nelemano, because she knew if one was not pleased with themselves that they would never be pleased with or pleasing to others.

Early June was a special herb and root gathering time, but Sarah and Nel still found time in the evening hours to work on that new garment.

The dance would be held up at Guildhall, and another musician who played in the band would be picking up Sarah and Dennis. John was off on a fishing trip with his father and Peter Jr., and Nel had decided that she would not go to this dance. "After all, Dennis was there to watch over his sister, and Sarah was certainly able to take care of herself," thought her Aunt.

The evening of the Box Party finally came, and Sarah, stood in front of the mirror, turning this way and that as she appraised her reflection. She was pleased with all that she saw, the dress and herself.

She touched the folds of that new garment, almost as if to reassure herself that this was her, here in the old looking glass and wearing such a pretty dress.

She tied the wide jade-green sash tightly around her small waist and then carefully adjusted the bow in the back.

From the shadows, Winona said "Oh Sarah, you look just like a Princess!" And Sarah smiled at her younger sibling because that is what she felt like, a real Princess —on her way to the ball.

Pocahontas, was the daughter of an Indian chief, and she was called a princess. Well Sarah was also the daughter of an Indian Chief but she did not feel like Pocahontas. At the very last minute, full of girlish fears and apprehension, she actually felt like "Cinderella" about to take her place in society, the society of the young.

Aunt Nel called from the bottom of the stairs, "Sarah, Dennis, he says the wagon comes soon." Sarah finished placing the jade-green ribbon over the top of her shiny black hair. Her hair was so thick that it had taken three combs to keep it in place, free-flowing as it was. And without further ado, she came down the stars and climbed into the wagon with her brother and his friend and two other young ladies. This was a big night for these five young people, because they were going to a dance —unchaperoned.

The red haired girl called "Sally" by the others asked, "Where is John? Isn't he going, Sarah?" and when Sarah explained that he had chosen to go fishing, she was immediately sorry, for she could see by this young woman's face, that for her, this dance had already lost its magic.

The Guild Hall loomed up ahead of them, and as the wagon jolted along, the women adjusted their clothing. They all agreed that Sarah, had the prettiest dress of them all, and they even told her that her hair as it cascaded down her straight back, should be worn free more often.

The musicians started to play and some began to waltz, and many of the young were already out on the floor, circling and whirling in time with the soft and haunting strains of the violin. The first dance of the evening, Sarah stepped lightly around the floor with a local boy, but when the second waltz started a young man whom she had never seen before, appeared before her and asked for the pleasure of the next dance. He was tall, over six feet. Sarah noted that he was fully as tall as her brother Dennis, but his bones were finer, his shoulders not so wide. She was aware of sandy-blond hair, and skin that was not only tanned by the sun but was the actual bronze tone of her own. He smiled down at her with grey-blue eyes and with his dark skin, it indeed seemed as though his eyes had been stolen from somebody else.

As they whirled, Sarah felt herself melt into his strong arms, and he spoke. "What do they call you?" She looked up and said "I am called Sarah, Sarah Jackson. And You?"

"John Somers" he said. " I work at one of the logging camps in Victory Bog country. Do you know where that is?" She shook her head yes, and continued to enjoy the sensation of not really dancing anymore but simply gliding because this stranger, called John Somers, was as graceful as a ballet dancer, and they whirled and glided and dipped and then whirled again around the floor. And as they did this, Sarah would have "bet the fox a chicken," that this handsome dashing-rake of a man, at least a handful of winters older than she was—was the beginning of that "something good," that she had anticipated was coming into her life.

John had no idea what Sarah's box looked like, and she gave him no clues, and he wound up eating the lunch of another young lady, and Sarah ate hers with a local boy. However, John Somers never took his eyes off Sarah, and after politely dancing with the other young woman, he turned up again in front of Sarah, and with a teasing grin, asked again that she dance with him.

A square dance came, "The Lady of the Lake" and they danced and whirled and curtsied low and "doe-see-doed" with all the rest, caught up in the music and the moment. For one dance they sat down, and after John found out that Sarah was a basket maker he confided in her: "One of my grandmothers made sweetgrass and white ash baskets." This was not a craft practiced by very many White people. Sarah smiled at him, and now she knew what she had suspected, that he had not stolen his eyes from someone else, that they were indeed his own. John somers was apparently of some Indian extraction, a mixed-blood with a sense of adventure about him. He was very handsome and he knew it and he would bear watching, this one.

John came from Maine originally, and had migrated to Vermont with a cousin of his to work in the lumber camps. Sarah found out that John was, of all things, a cook! He had the lean and agile physic of a woodsman and the confidence of a log driver, but he claimed to be a cook—and a darn good one.

"I thought men didn't like to cook?" she remarked, and John Somers responded "I like to, especially when it's forty below outside!" and they laughed in unison.

As he led her to the dance floor again for a waltz, John asked, "Sarah are you Passamaquoddy or Mic-Mac?" She looked him squarely in the eye and answered, "I am Abenaki, St. Francis Abenaki." John made a fake grimace and said, "Oh, Oh, the Bad Ones!" And Sarah thought a minute and then looked up at him and said, "Can't we all be Bad Ones, John Somers?" He smiled down at her, thinking that she was as smart as she was pretty, and she was one to stay away from. She bore a lot of watching, because her kind of woman was very dangerous to a free man if he planned to stay one.

As they danced again, and the haunting notes of the fiddle engulfed them, John asked, "Sarah, you pretty girl, how come you are not married?" And Sarah, lost in the music and the magic of his grey-blue eyes answered with a question of her own "How come you aren't married John Somers — or are you?"

"No, I'm not married." He laughed and then went on "Never will be either. I'm too busy lookin' and I'm born to be free." Sarah looked up at him and said "Me too." And he laughed and then whirled this woman across the floor as he had so many others. But, Sarah Jackson knew that always when they said they were not ready, that when they met the right one, all men— were ready.

"Do you ever plan to marry, Sarah?" he questioned as the music stopped and he walked her back to the benches than lined the floor and she said, "I don't think about this ....who knows?" And she was silently amused, thinking to herself, "I hope he's a better cook than a fisherman!"

John said to her than, "I don't think about it either, Sarah Jackson." And, Sarah knew that this was not true, because if he wasn't thinking about marriage, why was he always talking about it?

John saw the knowing smile on her full lips and he said, "What's so funny?" And in mocked fun, Sarah quipped, "You John Somers, you. Those who don't think of marriage — don't talk about marriage."

He tipped his handsome head back and laughed, she was even smarter than he thought. No other words were spoken between these two this night as they danced in silence and the floor under their feet felt like it was not there at all, but instead the clouds were. The roof, which rang to the very rafters with sweet music was not there either. Only they were there, John and Sarah, dancing for the first time really, on their way to the stars.

As the dew settled, the night stars looked down on the wagon as it headed for home in South Guildhall, in those early morning hours. The dance was over and the dancers and musicians too, were tired. There was a subdued hush over all the passengers. The one called "Sally," said she had a headache. Dennis spoke to Sarah like a brother and like a friend. "That Somers you danced with. I've seen him before. He usually drinks instead of dances. Most times, he listens, standing by the door."

Without a turn of her head Sarah said, "Tonight, he danced," and Dennis said no more. She knew that this was Dennis's way of warning her about the stranger that had taken so much of her time this evening, but her mind was on another kind of warning, cold and frightening, for she had gazed up towards the stars, and seen what she hated most to see, a flaming star. This was a very bad omen, for the "Kitsia" or the old ones claimed that it usually bespoke of the death of a loved one. Sarah sucked in her breath with a start, and Dennis said, "I saw it too. Perhaps it means nothing, Sarah," but both he and his sister knew exactly what it meant.

The wind picked up on the way home, and Sarah reached to touch the ribbon that along with the combs, helped secure her hair in place, and found to her surprise that the ribbon was not there. That was funny, it must have come loose in one of the square dances, she thought. She smiled softly as she reflected about the man named John Somers, but then the superstitious side of her nature came to the fore, and she forgot the dashing stranger. She dismissed him along with the ribbon that she would never see again.

The next day, as she and Nel combed the fields for sweetgrass and early strawberry leaves, Sarah told Aunt Nel about meeting a stranger and then about seeing the flaming star, and she could read the silent alarm in her Aunt's eyes, although Nel's stoic face remained calm and impassive.

A cloudy and overcast sky settled in the first week of July and lingered until nearly the middle of that month. About every other day there was either a day of rain or a thunderstorm. "April weather, all summer we have this April weather," Aunt Nel was heard to remark.

Peter and his sons had returned and John had gone to work immediately for the same farmer that Dennis worked for. Upon hearing that a certain, "Sally," had been interested in his absence from the dance, he simply said, "Her. She is a chaser," and quite frankly Sarah was surprised because she had never seen this girl do anything out of the way, but Aunt Nel had long before observed her interest in John, and she said so.

Sarah decided this was a sad thing. Yes, it would be better to be alone and unloved in this world, like the traditional "old maid" of White society, than to ever have it be said that you were — a chaser.

July stayed in fits of good and bad weather, with the family taking advantage of the good days, to garden, food gather or go on foot selling their baskets.

August came with wild strawberries, not many, but some. The weather was sweltering that first week, and the farmers were racing to get their hay crop in. It was a poor year for hay and for farmers in general.

Peter Sr., had gone off to Maidstone to visit his friends, and the family knew that he would not return until he had drunk and caroused to his heart's content.

Sarah watched him walk down the thin ribbon of a road, and a cold and foreboding feeling came all over her. She was just returning from pulling weeds in the vegetable garden, when she saw him striding away. He had not said goodbye. This was not like her father. She felt the little mounds of gooseflesh rising on her bare arms. He had not said goodbye to any of them, but she had this terrible feeling that it was goodbye, and for just a minute she shut her eyes up tight and could see that flaming star with its fiery tail streaking across the heavens, as clearly as if she had just seen it now and not a few weeks past.

That night she and Nelemano sat out on the ramshackle porch and Sarah spoke of this. Nelemano said nothing and they listened to the sounds of the night until, from far off, the eerie cry of a loon was detected. This was a very bad sound both women knew. The old ones always cancelled battle plans if a loon was heard calling on the eve of any confrontation. Many said it was the spirit of a departed friend or relative coming to warn of an impending disaster. Sarah looked at Nelemano and decided, seeing the dismay on her face, that she must not tell her she had even had another sign. Sarah had seen the silver wolf, that one who stands on a hill and wails into the night to tell one to beware. No, there was no need to say a word. Nelemano was upset enough and what good would that do? What would happen—would happen.

That very night a severe thunderstorm rolled in and lightening destroyed the Valley Farm barn. The sky was crimson-red until daybreak. Men came from everywhere to fight the fire and many head of cattle were lost.

Sarah had seen the red of the sky when she had awakened to the sound of a wolf crying. The dream had been so real. She sat up in bed with a sick feeling in the pit of her stomach. For a few minutes, she thought that the wolf was standing at the foot of her and Winona's bed. Sarah saw his pale and glittering eyes, and knew that he had come again to prepare her for bad news. How strange, to see compassion in his eyes.

That was when she saw the red against the skyline. She thought of blood and of fire and especially of her father. She shivered.

For days the thick smoke and ashes hung low over the Connecticut River, and all the neighbors along both sides shared in the loss that the Valley family had sustained. There would be a barn-raising before the snow fell, because these people helped each other when in need.

As for Peter Jackson, he did not know about the fire until it had been over for two days. He had started out on a fishing trip deep into Granby territory. He and three friends of his who used to enjoy fishing as hard as they could, drinking as much as they could, and staying away from civilization as long as they could, only coming into town for some card playing or even a good friendly fistfight among friends where nobody ever held a grudge or could seldom remember what the fight was about.

By the time Peter himself had heard the loon call, Sarah had dreamed for the third time of the silver wolf. This spectrum did not slink, he stood majestic.

And on the last Saturday in August, 1843 Peter had gotten very angry at his cohorts in a poker game and he had headed for home, very intoxicated and in a simply foul mood.

It had been threatening rain all day and now the rain was closing in fast. He came through the woods from Granby to Guildhall Hill and at the turn at the old Canfield Place, he decided that he would go down the Guildhall side. He might stop at Guildhall and try another hand of cards and drink some more and that is exactly what he did. But, Peter lost this game of cards too.

He was getting tired of this. He should sleep, but if he did, he would only dream about the screaming whirlwind, so why bother. He would just drink the last of the rum in his flask and then walk down the railroad tracks toward home.

As he staggered along in the evening mists, he was feeling extremely agitated by the raindrops that trickled down his nose. He drank the last few drops in the flask and then with a curse, slung the empty vessel to the ground and the sound of the shattering glass made him more angry still, at himself and at the night and especially this miserable rain.

His head ached dully at first, and then much harder as he struggled on, his balance more off center with each unsteady step. A cold wind came up sighing.

He hurried on, but he didn't really know why he was hurrying so. Peter was almost running home and he knew that there was no need for that. Sarah was constantly studying and gathering her herbal medicines and Nel was either harping at him over his drinking or spending all of her time attempting to make Winona into a lady. The boys were gone more than they were home, so what in hell was his hurry to get to a place where no one needed him? "I'm an old bear," he thought, "An old bear with no teeth!"

Suddenly up ahead of him, out of the cold rain and mist, he saw a wolf. It was tremendous, the powerful chest wide, and its eyes were not baleful but glittered in the night. Peter stopped dead in his tracks. He had no gun, he had nothing.

The wolf stood there and appraised the man like he was a piece of steak to be cooked on a stick. He cocked his head as if expecting to see fear on the aging chief's face, but he would see none.

Then Peter saw the bright light directly ahead of him, felt the ground tremble beneath his feet, and he knew that he had come face-to-face with his nightmare—the "Whirlwind Menace." Peter let out a war cry and attacked the bright light. It was roaring and bellowing at him, spitting fire as it did, but Peter was not afraid, he was crazy drunk and mad. "You die, Whirlwind—I'll beat you — I'll beat you and your God Damned wolf!"

He could smell the smoke and cinders. He could feel the heat of this hellish monster that had deviled him for years and he should be afraid like he was in his nightmares, but he was not. He was a warrior and he thirsted for this fight.

As a young man, Peter had fasted and had witnessed a vision of an eagle, a noble and huge white-headed bird that circled high above his head, soaring so gracefully and then sweeping so low to the ground that the youth could hear the thunder of the powerful wings. From that time on, Peter Jackson had considered the bald eagle to be his personal Animal Helper, but in his many hundreds of nightmares and dreams before, he had called out in vain to his protecting eagle, because that magnificent bird never did come to help. But this was no dream, this was real, and just as Peter yelled his blood-curdling war cry, and charged this hot and roaring whirlwind enemy of old, he had heard a fearsome and unearthly scream, and then soaring high above his head, Peter saw his eagle! He was here, at last he was here!

Suddenly Peter felt more powerful than he had ever felt in all of his life before. He had the eagle's strength now, and he shook his head to clear his vision, for he would also inherit the extraordinary powers of vision, possessed by this "chief of all the birds."

Peter's nostrils flared with the smell of hot coals and cinders, as the mighty Whirlwind Demon spit fire and bellowed at him, drawing him into its core of light and wind and fire and smoke. Peter sobered as he braced himself just before hurling his body directly in front of this hateful adversary. And, then that specter wolf, that Demon's friend, appeared again out of nowhere, his mouth red, his great fangs flashing white, and he snarled as he dove nipping and biting and tearing at Peter's legs. Then Peter heard his eagle helper, saw that mighty bird coming out of the rain and mist, diving low with great speed and deadly accuracy, and its beak was red with blood, as its menacing talons reached for that specter wolf, driving him off Peter and to the side.

Peter's fists were bared in anger at the hissing, braking, locomotive. He charged through the fog and mist and lunged into that bright light, as his tired spirit joined with that of the eagle and they soared away on wings of thunder, toward eternity, over all the mountains of the moon, past all sorrows and that train and forever past all earthly cares.

Part II

Moccasins, Clowns and Sawdust

Part II

Moccasins, Clowns and Sawdust

Peter Jackson's remains would never be moved very far from trackside, for they were too few. And he was interred, by strangers mostly, in the black dirt of Vermont, not far from the very spot his life ended. When the engineer and one other trainman came out of their immediate state of shock following the accident, they summoned help as soon as they could, but for this troubled chief his time had come and passed already, in this the fifty-eighth summer of his paradoxical life.

Long before the wagon was within hearing distance of the house, Sarah somehow knew that it was coming. When the wolf woke her this final time he had stood and looked at her, his broad head proud. He only howled once, and then with baleful eyes he stood quietly and stared at her. He was not a skulker nor a slinker, he was a messenger doing his duty, and in the cobwebs of her ghostly dream Sarah had been fascinated with the glittering eyes and dumbfounded when she realized that tears slid from them! The thick fur at his neck was silver-flecked and standing upright. He lifted his head and whimpered once before he loped away into the mists.

She was sitting in the kitchen by herself. With trembling hands, Sarah put some wood in the woodstove and put the tea kettle on to boil. It was chilly here. Her hands were working mechanically on a basket when the knock came on the door. She walked toward the door like a sleep walker and opened it, and her sharp eyes strained against the dawn shadows to see the face of the man who brought her the bad news.

He stepped inside, removed a rain soaked hat, and even before he spoke she read the pain in the man's eyes, just as she had read it earlier this night in the eyes of Grandfather Wolf. He cleared his throat to give her this message of death, a message that some part of her already knew.

"I'm so sorry Ma'am. I truly am. Two miles out of Guildhall, Mr. Peter Jackson, he was killed tonight by the Midnight Train." The messenger crushed the hat in his hands, and then he forged on, "I'm told they tried to stop, Ma'am, they slid and tried to stop so bad that they almost derailed the train but he, he just up and — well, Mr. Jackson, he just attacked that train, Ma'am."

She did hear the words and she did not her the words, because it suddenly became so clear to Sarah what Peter's warnings had been about. The train! Of course — the train, the fire, the steam, the squeal of the brakes, the bright light. Oh God, why until now couldn't she have figured out that the only possible thing the "Whirlwind Menace" could have been, was a train! "I should have known, I should have known," she mumbled, and the stranger did not understand. Why should he? Peter himself did not understand, and until now neither had she.

Her father's true enemy was progress and change — she had believed this for a few years now. His depression was triggered by all the things in life that he felt he was losing control over, most especially his own destiny.

Sarah's mind was having a hard time adjusting to the enormity of the fact that Peter was gone. She pressed her hand to her trembling lips to suppress the cry that was rising in her throat. She knew she would be hearing bad news, and that her father was dead, but she had not anticipated the horror and violence of his death. Her father was gone forever with no goodbyes, and even as he had walked away this last time, she had known this.

Sarah could hear the rest of the family getting up and scurrying about, and she listened in shocked horror to the story again as the stranger repeated it for them. She walked over to the table suddenly and sat down hard, because she felt her knees begin to wobble. She felt quite numb, but she willed the tears that filled her dark eyes to stay put, at least until this man was gone. There was a time for tears.

With an inner strength and calmness that she didn't realize she possessed, Sarah returned to confront the man in the doorway, and she controlled the sob in her voice as she spoke. "Thank you for coming this distance to tell us. My father was probably drinking. Drink made him crazy."

His deadly message delivered, the rain-soaked stranger closed the door and went out into the storm. He climbed into his wagon and clucked to the horses, and the squeaking wagon wheels were the only sound in the night. He drove away feeling especially sad because he had not one article or possession that had been on Peter Jackson's person to give them. There was just nothing left. Of course there was that unusually large brown feather with the white tips found at the scene, which some had claimed was an eagle feather. Perhaps an Indian would have carried this, but they had left it where they found it, deciding that it probably wasn't his anyhow.

What no one could figure out, even years after the tragedy, was the strange dog. The witnesses had seen a tremendous wolf-like dog emerge from the forest, and it ran up and down trackside and seemed to be trying to pull Peter out of the path of the train. The driving rain and the heavy fog had made the engineer and the fireman both question that they had seen this ghostly sight, for when the locomotive came to a stop the dog was nowhere to be seen. With their lanterns, though, they saw his tracks as big as a man's hand, and he had run off to the deep woods from which he came.

The phantom animal's part not mentioned, the family didn't hear about this until afterwards, because the messenger dismissed it as some sort of hysteria on the part of the trainmen, as the steady downpour had destroyed all evidence of the great paw prints, by the time others had been summoned to the death scene.

Still, driving off into the misty night, it haunted this man. Perhaps he should have said something, but no, he guessed that he had done the right thing.

As the family he had left behind this night clung together in their shock and grief, Aunt Nel hugged them to her large bosom and said "Oh, my Children, your father has fought his last battle. At last he can rest now for he has gone to his Long Sleep."

Tears slid down Nelemano's broad face in a rapid and blinding procession, and in all honesty she herself did not know how they would go on, she only knew that they would.

As the "strange wild dog" part of the story was reiterated to the family a few days later, bewildered and yet knowing glances were exchanged. That evening, looking out at those twinkling night stars, Sarah whispered to a wily carnivore friend of hers "Thank you, Grandfather."

She knew that he had heard her. The very tears she had seen in his glittering eyes were in her own eyes now. She knew his heart, he shared her pain.

Sarah sobbed quietly against her pillow and then she consoled herself with the fact that one day when she walked that pathway to eternity, the Milky Way, she would meet her father and her mother there on the other side. She would meet old friends, those that she had known and loved, even those she had only known about through stories and legends at the nightfires of her childhood. And yes, he would be there also, that "Grandfather Wolf," because he had always lived there in the land beyond the stars.

True to the nature of the inhabitants of the upper Connecticut River valley, neighbors and friends alike visited the Jacksons during their time of grief and loss. They came bringing food and condolences and never stayed long, just long enough to let the family know that they too had lost a friend. They were sympathetic to Peter's children who wept openly once in a while, and they paid no attention to the fact that Aunt Nel, to show her grief, had cut her long braided hair off close to her ears. Since childhood this was how her family had displayed their grief, and so she did this. It was their way.

Two weeks after Peter's demise, Sarah read aloud to her whole family a letter that had been addressed to Aunt Nelemano, at Nel's request. This letter came from Peter's nephew, Jack Capineau, who along with his family travelled the country with the Aaron Turner Circus. He was coming here for a visit before his family left for the winter quarters of the circus in Florida. Jack was seven years older than Sarah, but he had spent his early years with Peter Jackson's family band on Territine Ledge.

Nelemano was excited, Sarah was curious, and Winona was almost wild eyed. She was still determined to run off with the circus, and now as she was nearing her early teens the bird in her nature never did fly off, indeed it became more restless. She would learn the flying trapeze acts, yes she would!

All the family began to speak at once but Aunt Nel made the cut-off sign and they became silent. "We must talk, but one at a time!" Nel exclaimed. She motioned these, her children now, toward the kitchen table saying "My Children, you sit. We Powwow today. We go on now but how we do that is up to each one of us...to all of us."

Sarah folded the letter and handed it to her Aunt Nel and sat down as Nel began, "My Children you are now grown, with minds and dreams of your own. Together we must decide what to do. We can stay here in this valley, and I'm sure we will survive, for it is home to us, but is this the choice we want to make? We do not own this house, we rent this house and land. This plot of earth has been our friend but there is friendly earth in many places, many plots. What are your ideas about your future?"

Sarah smiled. She knew her Aunt was shrewd and direct, but she was not aware until now that Nelemano knew that at least two of these family members did not wish to be farmers themselves, or worse than that, day laborers for other farmers. Her eyes fell on the faces of John and Winona. John was the first to speak. "I want to walk the skyline too, like Winona, but not on a highwire. I think I will write to our uncle in Billy in Boston and see if he needs another man to work putting in those elevators. Once he said, 'When you are big, John, get in touch.' Well, I am big now and I am going to get in touch with him." They all looked at him but said nothing, and then Winona spoke. "I am going with the circus! That has always been my dream and I shall have my dream!" Aunt Nel grunted and then she asked, "Sarah, what do you think? Winona cannot go with the circus all alone. Are you happy here?" "Yes I am, Aunt-mother," Sarah said, "but I do know Winona doesn't want to make baskets. She has a thirst for this nomad life. I would stay if you cannot travel, but I have no ties here. I will go with Winona and you if you decide that." Nelemano smiled. There was a big world out there to see, and apparently Sarah, like her, had a desire to see all of it that she could.

Sarah looked at Dennis, and said "What say you, my brother?" He was silent for a long minute and then he answered "I am a farmer and a fiddler. I don't like to climb, but I throw knives well. I am strong and I'd like to try circus life myself."

Nelemano was the last to speak. "Life is good here but in a minute that could change. Let us talk with your uncle when he arrives. It seems the time in our lives has come that we should change again. I say, we go. I can cook and sew, who knows?" Here she made a humorous grin and said, "I might run off with a wealthy clown!"

Three weeks after that family powwow Sarah was walking toward Lunenburg. It was late August now, and cool. She wore a long grey coat, and in her right hand pocket she carried a tiny sweetgrass basket. She had designed it with delicate curlicues on the bottom and matching ones on the cover of the basket. It was a jewelry box, and she was walking this day to the home of a friend, the red-headed girl called "Sally," and Sarah was going to give the young woman this basket as a farewell gift.

The leaves on the maple trees were getting crimson and the ash and beech were now bright gold or withered brown. The girl's mother welcomed Sarah warmly into their huge farmhouse kitchen, and then said for her to go into the living room where Sally was entertaining a friend. Sarah, a little reluctant to intrude, walked into the spacious room and there on the couch sat her friend and Mr. John Somers.

He stood up when Sarah entered the room and she smiled. She had not seen him since that dance in June. She never expected to see him here, or she would have walked right by. She was no chaser!

"Sarah, Come in. John may go to work for my father." Sally explained as she hugged the tall young woman in the long grey coat. "Hello, Sarah," the young man said, and Sarah smiled warmly at him and then turned her attention to her business. "I came to bring you something, Sally," Sarah said and she gave Sally the small basket. "Oh Sarah!" the girl exclaimed, "Thank you. It's so beautiful. Just like you."

Then something sad in Sarah's dark eyes caused Sally to ask, "What's wrong Sarah? Why did you bring me this gift?"

"It is a goodbye present, Sally, we are moving away very soon and I wanted you to have this from me."

Sally was on her feet, tears starting in her pale blue eyes. "No, Sarah," she said.

"Yes, we are going far away. We will travel with the circus. They are always looking for farm boys, strong and not afraid of animals, and more and more women are finding work there all the time. I'm some sad, but still I am very excited."

Sally looked Sarah in the eyes and plaintively asked, "Are you all going?... Is John going?" Sarah smiled. "No, he goes in another direction — Boston way, with another uncle. He will work installing something new in tall buildings. They call them 'elevators.'" Sarah added quickly "Dennis goes with us," but she knew that Sally really didn't care what Dennis did.

John Somer's handsome face darkened. He got up and said "And I thought we were going to be neighbors." "No, I guess we are not." smiled Sarah. John had heard about Sarah's father but said nothing. If he had known Sarah was coming to visit, he would not have been caught laughing and so casual and free with Sally. Sarah didn't seem to mind at all, though, and this bothered his ego some, and at the same time he couldn't understand why.

Sarah visited a few minutes more and then left. It was raining out and the wind had picked up, and Sarah suddenly felt very sad to be leaving her friend Sally and also sad over something else, but she wasn't sure just what it was. The rain mingled with her tears as she faced the elements of late summer, and headed home before dark.

What was it about this beautiful valley that she hated to leave it so? She was descended from nomads and people who followed the herds and the rivers and whose home was where their next meal could be found, but saying goodbye to the soils on and around Tarritine Ledge was a very hard thing to do.

She walked on in the rain, and just as she turned up the narrow ribbon that was the road on which she lived she heard a noise behind her, but before she could turn to investigate there directly in her path, not more than fifty feet ahead of her, stood a mountain lion, looking languidly at her. He was wet and tired, and so he stopped and they stared at each other in silence. A breeze whipped the treetops, and the big cat switched his tail but did not move.

Sarah faced him squarely and never stopped walking. As her light steps drew nearer he again began to whip the great yellow tail, and now she spoke to him, low and soothingly. "Say Grandfather, we have no quarrel, you and I."

What would have happened is hard to say, but suddenly she felt a hand on her shoulder, and someone spun her around and pushed her to the side. He was then flailing his hands and making motions of throwing rocks in the direction of that eastern cougar.

Sarah was aware that John Somers was slapping his hands together and making barking sounds at the huge tawny feline, which undoubtedly had decided that the woman was perhaps all right but this man was a complete lunatic, and in two great bounds it was gone into the underbrush at the side of the road, and Sarah was laughing unabashed at the antics of her protective rescuer.

When she faced him she saw beads of perspiration mixed with rain drops on his nose, and his breathing was uneven. It angered him that she should take this incident so lightly, and in a crisp voice he asked her "Are you crazy, Sarah?" She shook her head no, still laughing, and he asked "Do you always walk up and start talking to panthers?"

"Only the ones I'm not afraid of," she replied, and she saw John's handsome face darken with anger.

Now Sarah stopped laughing. She did not know what this man was doing here, but if he was making himself her champion it was his own decision, for she had not asked him to.

"Have you ever seen what a cougar can do in a field of young stock?" John demanded. Yes, Sarah knew and she had seen the aftermath of the slaughter in a sheep pen. She well knew the blood and gore that the mighty claws and teeth of a mountain lion were capable of. She also knew that this big mountain cat always ate the head of his prey first, but that was just the nature of a feline on down through to the common house cat that eats the head of the mouse, rips and mutilates its victim and then leaves it to go and find other game. Not always so, she realized, for the cougar was totally dependent on his own food supply and would return to his kill for a second or third feeding. Sarah knew that Tarritine Ledge in South Guildhall, was a crossing place for the eastern cougar, for he loved the steep ledges where he could sit up high and look down on the Connecticut River valley below him. In her grandfather's day, when the Abenakis travelled at night, they wore strapped to their shoulders a rack made of hide straps and topped with sharpened cedar poles, pointing up toward the sky, to greet the "Indian Devil" or catamount, when he pounced upon the shoulders of these evening venturers.

Her grandfather, Old Jack Taxos, bore a savage scar that he took to his long sleep from an encounter with a cougar. The big cat had ripped his shoulder so deep that the muscles were hanging loose and torn, making his left arm hang at a curious angle for the rest of his life. That animal had lived to run away, but her grandfather had lived through this ordeal also and Sarah decided that the fight was even.

The more these things crowded into her mind the less she liked this lesson in wild life that she was about to get from a stranger.

The rain had for the most part subsided, and now Sarah faced John Somers and asked crisply "What are you doing here?" Taken back some by the cool anger he could see rising on her face, he simply said "I have something of yours. I found it outside the Guild Hall after the dance. I've been planning to bring it to you and I guess it is a good thing, I did, since you like to play games with wild beasts!" He handed her at that moment the wrinkled jade ribbon, that she had missed for several weeks. It did not change her frame of mind or her train of thought. Without a flinch she reached for the ribbon that he held out to her, and said "John Somers, I do not play games—with men or with beasts!"

John placed his hands upon her shoulders and said "When I came up behind you, Sarah, you were walking towards that cougar, talking to him!" She shook off his hands and stiffened facing him, and her anger at his interference in her business was visible in the set of her full lips and in the crispness with which she reproached him. "We had no quarrel, Grandfather and I. He did not scare me and he knew this. When he was ready he would have left, I know this thing." There was a look of mysticism and truth in her eyes.

Sensing his dismissal, John replied "I thought you were a smart woman, Sarah!"

Sarah looked at him, and with her dark eyes never wavering she retorted, "You did not think, John Somers! His kind was here before mine or yours. He had the right to cross my path, but not you, not you!"

"I was just concerned for your health and safety," he insisted, and Sarah said shortly, "Well don't be. I do not need your protection or your lecture either, so I go now!" With her left hand she made the cut-off sign.

She walked away from him then, not realizing, as she did this, that each footfall made a thump upon the wet earth below, because she was not Nelemano Jackson's niece for nothing. Aunt Nel never walked away from a fight in her whole life, but often, she was seen to stomp away; and this is what Sarah did because she had nothing more to say to this man at this time. What was it about men, that they thought all women were helpless and dim-witted? "When I need a hero, I'll call," she thought.

John Somers watched her as she stomped on up the road, and then he made a couple of running steps behind her. "Stop, Sarah," he commanded, and then as she turned to look sharply at him he said "You, didn't even thank me!"

Sarah looked at him with a level gaze and quipped "For What?" The young man almost squirmed under that stare, and then he said, almost in a muffled tone, "Well, I thought I was helping you, is all."

"Making a fool of yourself is helping me? No, I think not, John!" she said, and when she turned to go he stood there without a word, for he knew that stoic Sarah had thought he was over-reacting. Perhaps he was. He could feel again the cold fear that had gripped his stomach when he saw her walking steadily toward the cougar, and now he realized that perhaps she was right. Why should a peaceful mountain lion in its right mind go out and pick a fight with any creature as ugly and unreasonable as this young woman called Sarah Ann Jackson.

John walked off in the other direction, thinking "Why should she turn out for a cougar? Her father would not even turn out for a God Damned train." And then he laughed softly to himself, for there was little else to do. "Blood tells," his grandmother used to remind him. He turned once and looked in the direction Sarah had gone, but she was not in sight. Now if he could only get her out of his mind...

Sarah made her way along the narrow dirt road, and the more distance she covered the lighter were her footsteps. She was walking normally now, and she thought back to the cougar incident and recalled the glorious tawny fur, and she was well aware that the cougar's skin was highly prized among the Algonquian tribes, because it made such wonderful quivers for hunting arrows, but that lion was not a "quiver to be," it was indeed one of the Grandfathers.

No one used arrows any more, so the big cat was relatively safe, and somehow Sarah knew that she was safe with that cougar. She knew his heart because animals never have ulterior motives, which was more than she could say for John Somers!

Her smooth brows knit together as she accepted the fact that if he had wanted to return her hair-ribbon, he had all summer to do it. He apparently couldn't find the time, but he could find the time to sit and chat with other young women. Well, her time was precious also. She would not waste it.

As she turned up the rocky driveway, she knew that this was actually what he had come to tell her, but she did not want to hear it. No, she did not care to hear anything John Somers had to say, because he never really spoke his mind.

Her good humor was returning as she climbed the rickety steps that led up to her doorway. "Saving me!" she thought, as a wry grin tugged at the corners of her mouth. "Sorry, John Somers, but I'm safer with the cougar!"

Inside Sarah doffed her coat, and went to the pump in the sink and began washing her hands to help serve the family's supper. Then she looked at Aunt Nel and said "I know what I will be at the circus."

"What?" cried Aunt Nel and Winona in unison.

Sarah's eyes crinkled at the corners as she set a pan of steaming biscuits on the table and laughingly said "A lion tamer!"

The first week in September, any supplies that the Jacksons could not take with them on their journey they distributed around the little hamlets of South Guildhall and Lunenburg, to friends that had been there for them.

Jack Capineau and his family came and stayed four days with them. He told them all that he could about circus life, and was sure that they could get employment. Yes, it was a good life, if you liked to be free of the law except for the laws of the circus itself. He had explained that the wanderer in his blood agreed with the way circus people lived, and so for him and his, this life was what they chose.

The Peter Jackson family would go part of the way by wagons, and after Boston they would travel by train. A train would take them to Sarasota, Florida, if Uncle Jack could get the okay that there was a place for them all. He left, and said that as soon as it was a sure thing they would hear from him, and so they prepared to leave sweetgrass country for a new venture in the process of change called living.

As the family prepared for this trek there was a sense of excitement and anticipation, and yet great sadness, because this time when they left the Connecticut River valley Peter Jackson's bones would be lying there behind them.

John would stop off at Boston, and Aunt Nel and Peter, Winona, Dennis and Sarah would head for the winter quarters of a new world for them.... a world called "circus."

On the last Saturday in September, as Nel's big hands worked on some mending and Sarah trimmed a new basket, there came a knock upon the door.

"Who could this be after dark?" Aunt Nelemano wondered. Sarah went to the door and opened it, and looked squarely into the face of her friend John Somers.

Realizing who it was, Sarah unconsciously smoothed her hair back and thought "What now?" All she said however was "Hello John, won't you come in?" He did so, carrying his hat in his hands, and the aroma of freshly made gingerbread filled his nostrils, and he thought it smelled almost as good as Sarah looked.

Standing there as they looked straight at each other, a pleased and knowing smile softened John's handsome face. Sarah momentarily flushed, because she was dressed in old clothes and was all dust from packing boxes. Smiling at him, she asked "What brings you here, John" He met her direct gaze and replied "I came to say goodbye, Sarah." She flashed a fleeting smile at him and answered, "I thought we had already done that, John." He looked deeply into her dark eyes and held his ground, and simply said "We did...your way. I have come this night to say it my way." Sarah's eyes crinkled, and the tender smile that formed on her lips was lovely to behold. At last she had draged a simple and honest answer out of this rake, she thought to herself.

Sarah introduced him to Aunt Nel, who had her chopped-off-hair tied back with a folded bandanna across her high forehead. She did not look pretty, but she did look like a picture on a cigar box that John had once seen. She nodded and went back to her work.

"This is my sister Winona, the trapeze artist," Sarah said lightly, and the younger girl blushed and curtsied to John.

John and Peter were not at home, but Dennis was upstairs practicing some new songs on the violin, and the music drifted down to those seated around the table.

For a long minute no one spoke, and then Nelemano rose and said that she thought her eyes were too tired to sew any more. "I think it is my bedtime, Sarah," she said, knowing that Sarah needed her privacy with this young man—John Somers.

Before Aunt Nel ascended the stairs she spoke softly to Winona, saying "Bird Child, you need your rest to look beautiful for your future life." This was telling the younger daughter that she could stay up only a little longer and listen in on this conversation.

They sat facing one another, this young man and this young woman, and talked of everyday things. Sarah rose and put the tea kettle on to boil, and asked if John or Winona would care for a slice of Aunt Nel's gingerbread and they both said yes. As they ate the tasty cake and sipped the hot tea, John asked Sarah "What will you do at the circus, Sarah?"

Remembering Sarah's remark a few days past Winona beamed "She's going to have a whip and a chair and make the lions dance!" John Somers began to laugh and wound up choking on his food. When he could speak he said to Winona, who was placing her empty plate in the sink, "Well if anyone can do it, she can!" And now it was Sarah who laughed involuntarily and was forced to spit out cake crumbs to keep from choking.

Winona left them and Sarah refilled the tea cups again, and as they saw Winona's slim frame disappear up the stairway John spoke again. "Really, what will you do at the circus?" Sarah shrugged and replied "I'm not sure. My uncle said everyone there has two or three jobs. I might clog-dance, or just be a part of an act like knife throwing. The circus places you where you best fit, sometimes entertaining, sometimes mending canvas, it depends."

"I've thought sometimes of doing that, but I never really knew any people who belonged to the circus. I suppose they hire cooks." Sarah took a long sip of her tea and nodded yes, I would suppose they do." There were several long minutes when only the ticking of the clock on the wall could be heard.

"Will you be working here in the valley?" Sarah asked, and he said "No. I guess now I'll be heading back for Maine. Big job coming up in Parmacheenee."

When the clock indicated eleven, John rose to his feet suddenly and said "I know you believe in goodbye gifts, since I saw you give one, so I have brought one for you."

Sarah looked at him with her eyebrows raised. She had not expected a gift from him. He smiled and reached into his pocket and brought out a mall box. He handed it to her and she was at first reluctant to take it, but finally she reached for the present.

Upon opening it she saw a small wooden cross hanging on a slender cord. It had been carved out of oak. Sarah looked at it startled, and wondered why he had given her this?

Taking the slender string, John looped it about her neck and the dark cross stood out against the white cloth of her apron.

He knew she did not understand, and so he explained, "Sarah, this is the most powerful weapon against all bad things. It is the symbol of the Great Spirit. It is one kind of adornment that no one ever laughs at! When you wear this sign you will be respected as one who lives a good life, which I know that you do."

She thanked him. This was the same as giving her the "protection medals" that the Black Robes, or Roman Catholic Priests, used to give her people. John had carved this with his own hands, and Sarah was touched and speechless, for she thought now that her father was not here, no one would ever carve anything for her again.

She tried to blink away the tears, but they spilled out in spite of her, and he simply said "Don't cry Sarah. I thought that you might like to wear this now or take it with you." Sarah touched the well-made wooden cross with trembling fingers and replied "I will do that. Thank you, John. I will never forget this — or where it came from."

John's face lit up with a broad smile, and he was about to take his leave when from down the stairs came the haunting strains of the song "Beautiful Ohio." Dennis was still playing the violin upstairs. Sarah was suddenly embarrassed and she spoke openly of it. "I'm sorry, John, but I have nothing to give you in return."

Her color was high now with dismay followed so soon after the unexpected tears, and John thought that in this flustered state she was more lovely that he had ever imagined. A lazy grin played around the corners of his mouth. It was good to see her vulnerable and feminine qualities once in a while, since she seemed to be in control and a tower of womanly strength most of the time. This was good, but not too good.

He faced her there in the shadows of the flickering oil lamps. Taking her hand, he said "Sarah, would you do me the honor of a goodbye waltz?" She smiled. This she could give him, and so she nodded, and there in the confines of that small farmhouse kitchen, cluttered with packing boxes, she went into his arms. They whirled and dipped and swayed to the music with the moonlight shining through the windows on them. And the wooden floor below their feet once more became the clouds.

Sarah's head lay close to John's heart. It was their last waltz, their goodbye song, and yet it was a waltz that Sarah knew would never end. Muted shadows of lamplight cast ghostly silhouettes upon the wall, as John's arms tightened around her and he bent his head and kissed her. There was no sound at all except the haunting violin above, and the hearts that beat below.

With that one kiss and no other word, John Somers went out into the night. He did not tell Sarah that she was very special to him or that he hoped that they would meet again, or that he wished she would often think of him. She waved a long goodbye and stood in silence looking after him, until his graceful shadow disappeared out of sight in the moonlight. Sarah did not tell him that he was the one, or that she hoped they would one day meet again, for they were descended from a proud and self-disciplined race who did not make commitments or promises about things they didn't know about.... their destiny.

As she snuffed the lamps low and started up the familiar stairway, Sarah's young heart was full. She was pleased with how this day had ended. Once more she had danced upon the clouds. If there had been things between her and John left unsaid it did not matter, because important things are not said by the lips, they can only be spoken by the heart. And then Sarah knew that the very dearest things never even have to be heard, they are known.

SARASOTA FLORIDA — Late November, 1847. This was the fourth consecutive year that the Jackson family had spent the month of November in these, the winter quarters of the circus.

In that time Sarah had seen her brother John, who was still erecting elevator's in Boston, only twice. Once when the "Great Asiatic Caravan" was playing in Boston, and the second time was in Hartford, Connecticut. John Jackson had grown broader and looked very much now like their father, the late Peter Jackson. Winona had said of him that "he was a pompous, surly man," and he had said of her that "she was the same spoiled kid he remembered." Sarah had been forced to laugh.

Dennis was now a strapping young giant of a man, looking older than his eighteen years, and although he enjoyed circus life, he was saving his money now to go home to the upper Connecticut River valley and buy a farm of his own. The circus had been good to Dennis but he was older now and wanted to settle down.

Aunt Nel was "on the other side," having left them only two winter's past. When her arthritic condition allowed her to move at all she ruled the roost. She had been a stoic and vital example, right to the end.

Aunt Nel's demise left Sarah to rein as family matriarch, and she and Winona had their own closed-in sleeping wagon. Brother Peter was still with the show, but he and Dennis slept in one of the many bunkhouse wagons. Peter was also a big man, strong and he worked hard, always eager for a kind word. He got many kind words because this circus family was good to him.

Winona had just turned sixteen, and she was very pretty and seemed to be destined for stardom.

Sarah had changed less then any of them. She was still very quiet and she was always in the background, a quiet force that kept Winona in line.

Every spare minute Sarah combed the earth for herbs and roots. She was always the "Medawanna" Medicine Woman, learning and studying and healing.

Sometimes Sarah thought that later, when Winona got married (if any man dared ask her), she might go back to Vermont herself. But she faced the fact that life would not be as she once knew it, for the old ones were gone. She stopped her work for a minute and swallowed hard. Funny, how the thought of sweetgrass and a little place called Tarritine Ledge could be so close and yet so far away.

Sarah was still a clog-dance and she also helped to design and make the costumes for the acrobats, including Winona.

Winona was shorter in stature than Sarah. She was finer featured, with raven-colored hair, a doll-like face and flashing eyes that narrowed often with rage. She had a very bad temper. Winona could be a clown, but she was vain, and the more she began to emerge as a trapeze star and tight-wire walker, the more stormy and demanding she became. She was so particular about her costumes that one day she threw such a tantrum that Sarah had actually threatened to leave. This ended Winona's rebellion, because one of the unwritten codes of the circus at that time was that no unchaperoned young women were allowed to work there. Many times in the last year Sarah had wished that she had that "whip and chair" her sister had talked about so long ago. Indeed, she could use these tools. It was not easy making the young lioness Winona Jackson dance.

As the Jackson family made their debut with the circus, the circuses of the world were themselves caught up in change and upheaval. The mud shows and menageries were eaten up and combined with side shows or rare sights and curiosities called "freak shows."

Like their uncle's family, the Jackson's were first employed by one Aaron Turner. This show was bought lock stock and barrel by an enterprising young man who once sold tickets for Turner, called Phineas Taylor Barnum. He had vision and gall and he loved to make a buck. P.T. Barnum had made his mark upon the circus world at the corner of Broadway and Ann Streets in New York City on New Year's Day, 1841. At that time, he opened a new world of public entertainment called "Barnum's American Museum." Here wholesome and yet awesome attractions could be seen for twenty-five cents for adults and half price for children. This revolutionized the entertainment world, and Barnum prospered.

In the coming years, P.T. Barnum started a travelling (over the road) circus using horse drawn carts and wagons. "The Great Asiatic Caravan," was owned by Barnum and now employed the Jackson family. It was a collection of sideshows, clowns, musicians, dancers, high-wire artists, equestrians, caged animals and a herd of ten elephants. In the years ahead this circus would be the forerunner of the merge with showman James Bailey's travelling show, which became "The Greatest Show on Earth."

Phineas Taylor Barnum paid his employees regularly and provided for them living conditions that were average. Sarah respected P.T. Barnum and went to her own grave never knowing he got his real start in show business, when he purchased an old Negress named Joyce Heath, who had been a slave and claimed to be at least a century old. And it was rumored that she had been George Washington's nurse. P.T. Barnum bought Joyce Heath and exhibited the multi-wrinkled old soul, along with a twenty-five-inch-tall dwarf named Charles Stratton, who was called "Tom Thumb." And between these two exhibits alone, Barnum made a fortune.

It was ironic that Sarah, who hated slavery with all of her heart, would work for a man who got his start in life by buying a former slave and exploiting her for profit.

As she sewed, Sarah recalled how Dennis had gotten his third job. Dennis was a musician, a clog-dancer and now he had a new job which was throwing knives.

Dennis had tried to speak with the fellow in charge of that act and talk him into letting the youth try out, but he was a very jealous man of Polish descent, and he would never let Dennis do this. Sarah smiled as she thought of how she just happened to walk by them one day as Dennis asked once again to try out as a knife-thrower. The man said "Okay, but you use my knives, and not my girl. She trusts only me. Get your own target."

"I'd rather use my knives," said Dennis, but the older man was firm. "No! You use my knives and get your own damned target, boy!"

Her first thought was to walk right past them, but her second one would not allow her younger brother to be dismissed so easily. Dennis could use anybody's knives. Dennis was good! Upon hearing this ultimatum, Sarah stopped and became angry and she set the two water buckets she was carrying down with such a thud that water slopped all over her feet. She walked unnoticed up to where the two men stood and said "Give Dennis the knives. I am his target!"

Dennis looked at her quite obviously startled. Sarah's expression had not changed, and the three of them walked through the damp sawdust-covered earth to where the knife-thrower always practiced his art.

Sarah took her place before the huge canvas-covered board that was already dotted with knife holes. She stood straight and took a long breath and spread her arms out wide. She did not know what her brother was thinking, but she trusted him. She had seen him throw knives at targets. At twelve he could throw a knife and knock an old pipe out of her father's mouth, and she had even seen him pin the head of a black snake to the ground many, many yards ahead of him.

Dennis had never thrown knives around a human target before, and Sarah had not joined the circus to become a target, but Dennis wanted to be a knife thrower and he needed her help to do that, it would seem.

Dennis stepped up to meet this challenge, and in doing so picked up the first knife and it whizzed by Sarah's head and then he began to draw the outline of her body with the knives. They hissed and made a zinging sound as they cartwheeled by her head and neck and arms, and Sarah shut her eyes but did not flinch or move. If Dennis was to follow his dreams, she must remain calm and still. "He can trust me," she thought. She already trusted him with her life.

As the last knife was thrown, Sarah knew that Dennis now had his third job.

"That was good, boy, damned good!" the older man said. And, Sarah straightened her rumpled clothing and walked off. Dennis soon followed her and he was beaming all over. "Sarah, you don't know how scared I was!" he laughed. She smiled up at him and said, "Brother, that made two of us!" They laughed out loud together, and Dennis put his arm around his sister and life was good and another star was born.

"Here today and gone tomorrow" was a phrase often used by the old ones, meaning the "cycle of life," and the realistic uncertainty of it. After being on the road for years with the circus, Sarah Jackson had come to understand that in every sense, this was the code by which the circus existed.

She reflected a minute or two on this. Ah, the circus, that strange intermingling of clowns and acrobats, showmen and animals, which indeed was the very last place,it seemed, that an Indian could stay an Indian.

Concise mobility was the actual lifeline of that nomadic entity. When the circus came to town, with all its grandeur, magic and fanfare, the circus had to be "here today and gone tomorrow," or for that institution there would be no tomorrow. The ability to tear down, perform, and move on to do the same thing the very next day kept the circus alive, and those old time "Dog and Pony Shows" did very well. They adapted to all the new surroundings and were able to move quickly and precisely, even in those noisy wagons on the main roads as well as the back roads of America.

The first tent up in the morning was the cookhouse, and it was also the very first tent dismantled, after the matinee and supper. The dining department was taken apart and sent off in wagons just as soon as the evening show was underway. Already a silent army of men and women had begun to dismantle this show, so that this circus could be in a new place, doing the same thing tomorrow. And like an army of ants, they worked together....and achieved.

The side shows and those caged animals not featured in the acts were often called the "Menagerie," and these were always moved out and gone by the end of the last performance of the day. And it was again part of this silent kind of magic, because the audience kept its eyes riveted on the center ring, and no one seemed to notice this nightly ritual as that silent army of seasoned professionals proceeded with the tear-down of the existing circus. It was packed up one unit at a time, and the wagons were sent on their way. The animal trainers and trapeze artists, as soon as their acts were completed, went hurriedly to the dressing room. This was a huge tent where all the performers changed into and out of costumes. This tent was separated down the middle with a large canvas that made it impossible to see what the other sex was doing. This was usually a frenzied place, Sarah remembered. Since most of the acrobats and performers had two or three jobs, when an act was finished the splendidly adorned acrobats and trainers alike quickly changed into working clothes and immediately took their place in the "silent army" of men and women as they helped load animals, disassemble tents and rigging, and often actually drove the wagons themselves. This was done with such precise expertise that by the time the show was over, there was usually nothing remaining but the big top tent itself.

As the last of the audience straggled out the front door, the rings, rigging and even the empty seats were already being dismantled and loaded for shipment to a new destination, which had to have a new cookhouse tent set up for five thirty sharp the next morning.

Sarah smiled as she thought about the cook tent. She helped out there often. Especially during winter quarters, the cookhouse was often the only collective gathering place.

In those early days of the circus, men and women were not allowed to speak or to be caught talking to each other, only at the cook tent was this allowed.

Sarah used to think of the cook tent as being the biggest kitchen table in the world. People came together at the cooktent to eat and converse with one another in the only homey atmosphere the circus had to offer. Yes, the circus family, like any other, gathered at the kitchen table.

In bigger cities the circus frequently stayed two days at least, and always a gigantic parade was held. This enjoyable spectacle portrayed the circus in the light most people see it, as a wonderful place where magic was everywhere and where men and animals were beautifully arrayed in splendor and glitter. This display never gave a hint of all the hard work and self-discipline it took to make it all work.

For the crowd, the circus was a wonderful two or three hour escape from the normal hum-drum existence of everyday living, and there was for many a personal yearning from the spectators to be a part of this easy and free lifestyle of the performers that they watched. Often they secretly envied these circus people, because they did not know what personal and team commitment it took to keep the show on the road.

There were few pampered celebrities in those days, and who would have believed that the lady who rode in on the head of a huge bull elephant was also the lady that had to bring his water and shovel his dung. If the big expensive animals were sick, their trainers often bedded down in the straw with them.

Very early on, Sarah realized that if ever there was a place where teamwork and cooperation were first and foremost, it was indeed this biggest and quite possibly the most diverse of all families, the circus. Just like your own family, when you were hurting they felt your pain and when you needed them they were there.

There was a great amount of respect that circus people gave to one another, because everyone depended upon someone else for something, and therefore every person was an important one. After all, the most highly paid aerialist, knew that his life depended not only on his own balance and timing, but on the attention to detail and the judgment and safety measures and precautions taken by the ground crews that took care of each act's apparatus. When you trust your life to a man, you do not believe inside that he is a "no account" or a nobody. He is a friend and a respected confidant, and a member of the team which worked so hard to make all the little successes a total big success.

Another feature about the circus that so appealed to the Indian side of Sarah, was the privacy it offered to those who took their place within its open arms. A man or a woman could be as open or as closed about their lives ad they desired, and no one ever pried into another's life, because they valued and respected their own privacy so very much. Sarah felt that this was good. If you talked, someone would listen. If you did not talk, no one cared. Your life was none of their business, and visa versa.

Unwritten codes were lived. There was no police protection needed, for it was said "The circus took care of its own."

If a man went wrong and unjustly harmed another member of the circus family, just like in old Indian society, friends of the victim would settle with the criminal. Some called it "an eye for an eye," and it was a swift though sometimes unmerciful justice; yet it was the deterrent that truly worked, because sympathy was on the side of the person abused rather than the abuser.

Lonely people, homeless people, and people of different colored skins, all of these had a family and a home within the circumference of the world of the circus.

To the Indian, the circle was a sacred thing. Life was not a road to nowhere, it was a circle, a wide circle, beginning at life, ending in death to life as previously known, and continuing on in life hereafter — there "on the other side." The great circle of life is never completed until that circle of life has met itself in death. The circus itself revolved around a circle. Its entertainment was performed in circles or rings, and no matter where it travelled it always returned to where it began, home or winter quarters, and from there it would begin again.

The pride of all circus performers and laborers, was to do whatever thing they did as well as they could. This was done to please themselves as much as it was to please onlookers.

The life lived within a circle, whether it was a family circle or the entire circus family sphere, was a life in which family ties were all-important. The bonds of comradeship were strong, because a circle does not have sides. Circus people were all on the same side, that of living together in harmony, for the good of this their chosen livelihood.

Sarah had made acquaintances, both male and female, of people from many different heritages and many different parts of the world, and yet there was nothing too different about any of them. They were all human beings who laughed and cried, struggled and failed and tried again. The more she met natives from other countries, the more sure she became that they were close enough to be brothers all. "Just another tribe, like Brother Fox," thought Sarah.

The Indian lifestyle could easily identify with circus life. No matter what religious beliefs, the very nomadic and spiritual nature of the Indian, believing in a Happy Hunting Ground, as he did, drew him to the dangers and the thrill of circus life. This often placed men and women in life and death situations daily. The day-to-day realities of admitting that their destinies were not so much in their own hands as in those of a higher power made believers out of many. If you lived well you could die well.

Sarah often said "In my years travelling with those Dog and Pony Shows, no one ever congregated or even went to church, but I never met a man there who did not believe in a power far greater than himself."

She thought of Winona, hot tempered, ambitious, and sometimes contrary. She wished Winona would stop flying through life, and walk slower and see the wondrous beauty of it all — now, while her eyes and heart were young.

It had not taken Sarah long to understand that as long as the Jackson family stayed with the circus, they would never be outside the circle — indeed, they would be a crucial part of it.

No matter where they were appearing, when the last act was finished Sarah always felt that this somber "goodbye" was just another reminder to all men that nothing on this earth is ever permanent. In fact, all on earth is indeed very temporary, even this wondrous world of man and animal and magic called the circus.

Setting up the "Dog and Pony shows," as Sarah called them, was always a time marked with anticipation and high excitement, but that evening, tearing it down in the shadow of torches, lanterns and always the night stars, was indeed a sober and rather melancholy time, brightened only by the thought of a new and gasping audience, in a different place.

The morning after the circus left a vacant lot, the sounds of silence could be deafening. That vibrant world of glitter and daring stood stripped and void of sounds and smells.

The mood was somber in this lonely place now, and the wind seemed to whisper "The circus is dead!" But indeed the circus was not dead, it was alive and well and setting up right now in the next town down the line.

JANUARY 7TH, 1848 — On a return trip from the outer limits of Sarasota, where she had been selling baskets, Sarah was pleasantly surprised to see the huge shadow of her brother John from Boston. He was standing in front of the doorway of her and Winona's traveling wagon. It was almost dark when he arrived, and Sarah was just about to go out and poke up the coals in her nightfire. "John!" she exclaimed, and Winona heard this and came running.

Winona went to find Dennis and Peter, and not long after, the Jackson family were gathered around this little bed of coals and talking about old times.

The elevator business was growing up in the Commonwealth of Massachusetts. John was a hiring boss now and he was in Florida for a vacation. He was interested in seeing if his brothers Dennis or Peter would consider going back up north and working in the building trades. The construction business was booming, and John was doing very well. For just a flash, Sarah wondered if Peter would be able to go? He needed patience and guidance with directions. Her brother John read this in her eyes and he said "Sarah, I'm getting married in April. I have a friend who runs a good boarding house. Dennis and Peter can both stay there. We will take care of Peter." Sarah had her answer.

Dennis scratched his head. The offer sounded very tempting. He liked the circus life, but he did want to go back to the Lunenburg, Vermont area and buy himself that farm he had dreamed about. The wages John was offering were excellent, and if Dennis took this job he could have his farm sooner.

John explained to Peter that it was hard work, but in all actuality, it was probably not as hard as he worked here. Peter with a little help could follow instructions and he did not have a lazy bone in his body. He was strong and strong backs were what John Jackson was looking for. He left just one week later, and he had five of them — both of his brothers, one cousin and two young men who had up to this point been circus Strong Men.

The fact that they were travelling alone now across this land with no men to look out for them, did not stop or even worry Sarah and Winona. They had lives totally independent of their brothers, and they would go on with those lives.

Sarah smiled as she thought of the third party who lived with them now in winter quarters. Winona had come back from tight-wire practice, running and crying hysterically and begging Sarah to come quick! And Sarah had run to meet her sister, who had gathered in her arms the bloody and abused carcass of a young male kitten. He had been at war with something and he had lost. His left hind paw was hanging by a piece of skin and there were deep scratches across his hips. Upon closer inspection Sarah could see that this poor little animal had been castrated by the same claws or teeth of whatever had cut his paw off.

Winona sobbed and begged her older sister. "Sarah, he's only a baby kitty and he's gonna die!" Sarah at first glance believed this also, but then in her calm way she simply said "Hush Winona, let me see him." The little cat, in shock, allowed himself to be handed over to Sarah and she took her clean white apron off and wrapped him in it, and stepped up into their little wagon home.

"Winona, get my bag," she said, and when it had been handed to her

Sarah took her surgical scissors from it and cut with one swift stroke the skin that held the dangling paw, and it fell from the cat's leg and lay on the bed between the cat and Sarah. That little cat had flinched but he did not cry out. Sarah never got over the fact that animals can tell when you are trying to help them.

"It's all right, Old Man," she soothed, and stroked his head. "I've got some medicine. It won't hurt you, and it will work faster than just licking your wounds yourself."

The stump of a leg was bleeding badly, but Sarah wrapped white cotton around it, disinfected it and put a powder on it. The cat lay, staring up at her with eyes bright but not glazed in death.

"Oh Sarah, he's going to die, isn't he?" Winona sobbed, and Sarah said "No Winona. He is young and strong and he won't be good for much but housework, but he will not die — he will live, I think."

All his cuts Sarah cleaned, but the only one she bandaged was that stump of a leg and that only until the blood clotted.

"Where did you find this cat?" Sarah wanted to know, and Winona replied "I heard him crying when I got off the tight wire, he just came crawling in from the roadside."

"All right now stop crying. We will warm him some milk and see if he wants to live. It is up to him now, Winona."

That was almost five years ago, and "Kino" had chosen to overcome his wounds and his castration and to live with Sarah and Winona in their little house on wheels. And Winona had smiled broadly and said "Welcome home Kino, we need a man around the house!"

The irony of it all was, however, that even though it was Sarah to he whom Kino actually owed his life, it was Winona that Kino chose to be his mistress. He sang her to sleep at night, he lay in her lap when she and Sarah sat before their nightfire. He followed Winona to practice and waited under the trapeze and high wires, for her to come down, and as a reward he rode on Winona's shoulder back to the little boxed-in wagon she called home. The cat tolerated and perhaps even liked Sarah, but he worshipped Winona.

Sarah used to think sometimes how much alike this cat and this young woman were; fiercely independent, willful but still soft and charming in a vain sort of way. From each of these two creatures of God, one line projected "Love me or Lump It." The only thing was, Kino was willing to adopt Winona and let her be his master but Winona, no one would ever be her master.

The days of February whirled by in rapid succession. The show was getting ready for the road. Acts were polished, just as equipment and rigging were made ready for this new season.

At seventeen, Winona was a star. Her balance was uncanny and she had no fear of height. She was always pushing herself to try harder and do one somersault or one cartwheel more. It was her nature to strive for perfection. She practiced harder and longer hours than any of them because she loved her work.

Often at the end of a hard day of practicing, when the older members of the act wanted to pack it in, Winona would protest and beg to stay just a few minutes longer. "Please, just watch me do this once more!"

And then this "bird child" started doing something very dangerous. She began getting up in the morning and going to the high-wire apparatus and ascending it and practicing her routine alone, with no one around to act as catcher if she fell, except Kino.

When this was noticed she was scolded, threatened and told that she meant more to the act alive than she did dead. Winona snapped back, "Let me fly! You are all smothering me. I will worry about falling, not you. Now you leave me be and let me fly!" But, the other acrobats had all stuck to their guns, and Winona was not allowed to practice alone anymore.

You could feel it in the air, this time approaching when the circus would take to the road. There was excitement everywhere. The acts were honed and sharpened to perfection as the acrobats and artists strived to turn their crafts into refined entertainment.

Even with three jobs, practicing clog-dancing routines, sewing costumes and helping out in the cookhouse tent, Sarah always found time to create her baskets, and at least once every other week she found time to slip into town and to sell these creations of her hands; her baskets, woven this time from the native barks and grasses of Florida.

This basket money was kept in a stocking under her mattress, for life was uncertain, and one never knew when an unforeseen circumstance could crop up and a person might need that sock full of money.

Sarah looked at her time-piece. It was nearing supper time and Winona would be coming in soon from practice. She smiled as she thought how proud her father would be if he knew that his youngest daughter had emerged to top billing now in one of the aerial acts. She was not called Winona but "Little Daring Eagle," and she was introduced that way.

Sarah worked some grasses she was dying through her fingers, and she smiled to herself when she remembered, during that very first year that they had travelled with the caravan, how Winona had shocked them all.

At the beginning of the show, "Princess Kahn," a former acrobat now married to the elephant trainer, always rode in perched cross-legged on the head of a huge bull elephant named Brutus. She was always beautifully attired, in East Indian silks and bangles.

Brutus was an extraordinarily large elephant with tremendous tusks protruding from his massive head. The audience always gasped at the drumroll when Princess Kahn and Brutus made their grand entrance around the center ring of the Big Top.

Sarah always liked to watch the elephant show. The ungainly looking animals were the force that moved all heavy objects in setting up and tearing down the circus. They were treated well and respected for the intelligent, agile performers that they were.

On this particular night they were in Maryland, and she and Dennis were dressed in their clog-dancing costumes and waiting for their act to come on. When Brutus ambled into the arena, all eyes were upon him. At a second glace Sarah could see that Princes Kahn looked different tonight.

They did not know that only minutes before, Princess Kahn was supposed to allow Brutus to help her climb aboard his mighty trunk, she had slipped and fell to the ground. She twisted her ankle in such a way that it was broken, with the bone actually protruding through the skin. She had been running late and had fallen in the wet sawdust, and now she lay helpless on the ground in front of Brutus. He lowered his trunk and waited.

As she lay there writhing in pain on the damp earth, Princess Kahn, suddenly realized, that she had no understudy. It had been suggested, but she had been adamant that this was her job.

"Get a rider, get a rider!" someone yelled, but who, at a moment's notice, would step up on to Brutus's great trunk and be elevated to the top of his head? Well, only one, it seemed.

As the years flashed before her, Sarah recalled how she and Dennis both had stood transfixed, their mouths open with surprise when they recognized the slender form of their baby sister, then only fourteen years old, dressed as Princess Kahn and perched comfortably atop the head of mighty Brutus.

Coming out of his shock, in a voice tinged with anger, Dennis spat, "How in hell did Winona get up there?" as he gazed at the form of the gigantic pachyderm now minding his sister's commands.

With a wry smile Sarah answered her disgusted brother, "Perhaps she soared over from the trapeze, Dennis." And "Umm," was all that Dennis had to say.

As for her part, Winona had carefully watched every move that Princess Kahn made. She knew the points at which she waved to the crowd as they passed around the Big Top tent, and she knew the hand signal from the elephant's trainer once inside the center ring, telling her it was time to descend. Winona performed the routine to perfection.

The crowd last night knew Princess Kahn as a blonde but this audience assembled here today readily accepted a dark-eyed, raven haired Princess Kahn, and Winona, had a magnetic quality about her anyhow, and this audience liked her very much.

Well, she wasn't an East Indian princess, but she was a Native American Princess, so Winona reasoned that was close enough!

Winona was a heroine and she stayed as the replacement for Princess Kahn, until her ankle healed enough so that she could descend to Brutus's back once more.

The recovering Princess Kahn's husband was the elephant trainer. He was much impressed with the beauty and grace and especially, the spirit of this new and younger woman. Over his wife's protestations he offered Winona a job with the elephant act, coming to her one evening and saying "Winona, you are a natural! Brave and good with the elephants, too. We can find a place for you in our act permanently, if you are willing."

Sarah saw the flash of Winona's dark eyes and with no hesitation she shook her head from side to side and said firmly "No. I thank you and I like the elephants, but I'm not carrying their water and cleaning their dung. That is not what I want to do. I want to walk on the high-wires and fly on the trapeze."

The trainer, a proud man, twisted his mustache and said "Winona, it could pay far more than the high-wires."

Sarah never forgot the way her sister looked at this man and said "It is not the money. I would do these high-flying acts that I do for no money at all, but for your elephants, well, I only went along for the ride." Winona smiled as she said this but the trainer read it as a way of belittling his act. His anger was quite visible as red color crept across his face. As he turned to leave he abruptly turned to Winona and said "My wife, she said you were self-serving!"

Winona's eyes were narrow slits now, and she took a step towards the departing man and remarked "And your wife should know! I never took one dime of her money all those weeks that I did her job and I don't have to take your insults now, so I think you should go!"

After his rapid departure, Sarah said "There has been friction between you three?" Winona picked up a hairbrush and began to stroke her long hair, and she said "No, Sarah. She is a jealous woman! He would be more than an acquaintance of any younger woman, but I stayed out of his way! The best heart in their act belongs to Brutus." This was good to hear. Sarah had been afraid that the older man, always the star as he was, would somehow appeal to her sister, but he had not succeeded.

Sarah was diverted from her reminiscing as Winona stepped up into their coach-home.

"The wind was bad out there today. We had to stop early, Sarah!" And as Sarah put the basket down, Kino got up from where he lay sleeping and went over and rubbed himself against Winona's legs until she picked him up and told him that he was lovely, and that they would be on the road soon.

Winona poured water from the pitcher into the big porcelain wash basin, and proceeded to wash the sweat from her hands and face and neck. Sarah smiled and said "Winona, you have a letter here," and she handed it to the younger woman. Winona left it on the table and began changing her clothes. Then she smoothed her hair and opened the letter and read it in silence.

Sarah knew the handwriting. It was from a young man who had joined the circus and stayed only eighteen months. He had left and gone to Kansas, but before he left he had asked Winona to marry him. She did not say this. He himself had told Dennis.

Winona folded the letter and said "He says it is wild country out there. He is homesteading." Her young face softened, and then she said "He still loves me Sarah, but I don't love him."

There was a sadness in Winona's face, and Sarah said "He will find one who will love him some day." And then Winona said something that intrigued her older sister. "Sarah, he said that they are having bad Indian trouble out there. Hostile Indians, that scalp and burn and kill, just like we from St. Francis did."

Sarah had not thought about her history in years. But now, knowing that many thousands of Native Americans were still fighting and dying and trying to hang on to their heritage and Hunting Grounds, made Sarah very sad. All the eastern tribes now conquered once had done this. She found a voice from inside that she never knew could speak until now. "We did what we had to then, and they do what they have to do now. They fight a battle for survival of a people, but they like us before them, cannot win. They can die and they can change, but they cannot win!" Tears filled Sarah's proud dark eyes, and she went on "They will turn that red blood pink and finally white."

Winona not expecting this emotional outburst from her older sister, went on light-heartedly. "Sarah, they haven't turned us pink and they will never turn us white! We are St. Francis Abenaki. We will always be outside the White circle, and you know that!"

Sarah pulled a fringed grey shawl over her shoulders, and she and Winona started for the cookhouse tent.

"Well, I wonder who we will chat with tonight?" asked Winona and then an impish smile spread across Winona's face and she said "Sister, I know why we have never really seen the "Tallest Man in the World," only when he parades around the Big Top." Sarah cocked her head. "Why?"

Winona, wanting to get Sarah into a different frame of mind, poked her gently in the ribs as they strode along, and said "Because he is actually those three dwarfs that sell popcorn."

"No! Winona, is that so?" Sarah laughed, and Winona made the cross your heart sign and insisted "Yes, it is true, Sarah. The tall man, he is just three midgets standing on each other's shoulders! It is a hoax, a plain old White Man's trick, Sarah!" Winona chuckled.

"Sometimes I think all of life is," said Sarah, as they entered the cookhouse tent.

In the four years encompassing their induction into circus life, Winona Jackson had grown into a beautiful, even if willful young woman. She had changed and even this new name "Little Daring Eagle" bespoke those changes.

Sarah too had grown and changed. She was a very independent woman, sure of herself in all that she did, and she knew that without the aid of her sister, her three brothers or any other person, that she could survive in this world and take care of herself. She marched to her own drum, and she answered to no one except her own conscience and a deeply rooted sense of righteousness.

As a matter of fact, Sarah was making a sacrifice. She was staying with the circus so that Winona could attain her dream. However, this could only be done if Sarah stayed to chaperon her, for regardless of Winona's aerial talents, single women, under twenty-one did not travel alone with these dog and pony shows.

It made the older sister's heart glad to see little Winona, so happily achieving her goals and so Sarah's own dreams were put on hold.

Sarah's first love was always other people. She still gathered her herbs, and it was soon recognized here that this young woman who dabbled in herbal medicine did have healing in her strong young hands.

In the southern states, Sarah was not nearly as proficient or sure of herself in the science of herb and root gathering because so many of the native plants in this section of the country were foreign to her. But, she observed and studied and often even compared their worth with those northern medicinal herbs that had been familiar to her since childhood.

She had another quality that set her apart from many people, and this was that children absolutely adored her. In her calm and gentle way she touched their hearts. Sarah was never one to scold or preach; instead she was a listener. When she did speak children felt the honesty that radiated from her soul, and they trusted in her words. Sarah never expected a child to think or to act like an adult, and yet she respected them much for being what they were, at this time in their young lives. And children, always eager to be loved and to learn, empathized with this theory.

When the circus was stationary in winter quarters, Sarah combed the nearby fields for berries and roots, and she always had company because the offspring of the circus performers were always close to her heals.

She truly was a Pied Piper of that carnival, and in her day-to-day nursing of insect bites, scratches and other childhood scars, Sarah the Doctor had inherited a new name from her sibling friends. "Aunt Sarah," they started calling her, and then so did their parents, and this name followed her all the remaining days of her long and service-oriented life. And as for Sarah, she felt that to be adopted regardless of skin-color or beliefs was indeed an honor. Now she knew why her beloved "Aunt Nel," often smiled softly when relatively unknown people referred to her as their Aunt. The Great Spirit is the ultimate chooser of all blood aunts, but to be made an aunt out of love was a very good thing. In fact, one could have many more relatives that way than by blood.

Winona would burst out laughing when a rap come on the door and a group of little urchins stood there, and one brave spokesman, with blue eyes and hundreds of freckles, would step forward and ask "Please Ma'am, càn Aunt Sarah come out and play with us today?"

Aunt Sarah, always had time to go and to frolic with the children. She believed in that old Indian commandment,"Have time for your children when they are young, and they will have time for you in your old age."

"Time spent with children is the most important time in an adult's life," Sarah is reported to have often said. She taught the children the good herbs that she knew, and she warned them of the bad, and how to tell the difference. When she learned something new, she shared it with her little following and they digested this new knowledge together. Sarah played in their games of stick ball or whatever, and always stressed the importance of good sportsmanship.

"A game is only a game," she said, but the teamwork we learn there will be an important part of living for all the rest of our days." And so, the children who trusted Sarah, listened, and always these little ones turned up at her nightly campfires to listen some more to their Aunt Sarah.

The story hour was where the children heard about Azeban, the Trickster Raccoon, and the heroic deeds of the Great Bear, and always the Legend of the Crow. Sarah also told them the authentic version of the noble chieftain Hiawatha, which had passed from nightfire to nightfire, handed on from father to son, from the Tortoise Clan of the Mohawk to the Bear Clan of the Abenaki. Her father had first heard it from his grandmother in the Village of St. Francis, Canada, in the year 1791, when he was five and the family matriarch who told him this story was nearing her 100th winter. The real Hiawatha was a reformer and a statesman, and he was an advocate of peace. He presented new ideas to his Native American brethren, for he sought to banish murder among mankind and to abolish the practice of eating the flesh of the enemy, as was the custom of the Mohawks.

Hiawatha proclaimed that when a man was killed in a blood feud, his relatives would receive three strings of wampum, each the length of the forearm, and so he actually placed a value on human life.

This man of peace, Sarah always connected as being Christ-like in his ideology, and his convictions were so strong that he was banished from the Mohawk tribe at first, because these foreign concepts of enemy tribes living in peace and brotherly love, were considered unacceptably radical, during the time in which he lived which was the sixteenth century.

Banishment did not stop Hiawatha, and he went all up and down the Mohawk Valley in New York and continued preaching peace and brotherly love, and finally they listened; and this great reformer and able statesman is credited with being the true founder of the League of the Iroquois, or "The Five Nations."

Sarah did not know at this time, that in 1855, Henry Wardsworth Longfellow would rock the literary world with his story of a Chippewa deity, as he set to poetry "The Song of Hiawatha." Longfellow is said to have become interested in this tale, taken from Indian legends as it was, but he was a trifle confused because Hiawatha was neither a Chippewa or a divine being. Thus in this year of 1848, Sarah told the children who gathered about her nightfire, the correct story of the real-life man called Hiawatha. And she told this story just as it had been told to her, staring at the glowing coals and speaking with a straight tongue, exactly as her great-great grandmother had passed this legend down to her.

She truly did not know if this meant that she could possibly have Mohawk roots as well as Abenaki, but she did know that Hiawatha was a Mohawk. And so, Sarah shared her time and her heritage with all the circus youth.

The children loved the stories, and enjoyed the trip back in time and making the acquaintance of generations of Native Americans gone before, but apparently never forgotten.

If there was indeed any of "Sarah the child" left in Aunt Sarah, the children brought it to the fore. They loved to see the dimples at the corners of Sarah's mouth, when she laughed and these little men and women made her do that often.

For her part, Sarah could never understand why the White people misguidedly adhered to that old adage, "Children should be seen and not heard." She disagreed whole-heartedly with this biased philosophy. Children should be seen and heard too, for they often saw into the heart of a matter, with the clearest eyes of all. She believed this because the vision of a child was never clouded by politics or compromised by self-serving influences.

How could a child grow to a whole person, if he was stifled in his ability to express what he thought about life as he knew it, in these the most important and informative years of life, childhood?

Life did not begin at sixteen, it began at conception and took on reality at birth, and by the time a child was old enough to have his own thoughts and ideas about a thing, he should be allowed to express them, and be given the dignity of having someone listen.

"Aunt Sarah, how come you're so smart?" was a question often asked to Sarah by the children, and their Aunt Sarah would reply gently "I watch the animals and I listen to the children. And if her captive audience didn't understand this line it really didn't matter, because they knew that they could believe it, because their Aunt Sarah said so!

Now that the show was in its final preparation stage before taking it on the road, Sarah and the children saw less and less of each other, unless a worried mother brought a child for her to do some mending on from time to time.

Sarah always remembered one little black-skinned boy called Josh, who said to her one day "Aunt Sarah, I wish you really was my Aunt!" And Sarah, finished bandaging his scraped knee, cupped his little black chin in her own copper hand, and said "Then it is so Josh, for wishes are very important." Thus Aunt Sarah had inherited another relative on the road of life, and it was long and there would be many.

Another day, while she was scratching the flat blade of a sharp knife across the arm of young Ben Klien to remove a wasp stinger, the little boy asked, "Aunt Sarah, what would the world be like if it was the kids who ran it?" Sarah smiled. She knew Ben to be a very smart little man, and without looking up from her work she said, "Peaceful, Ben, it would be peaceful." The ten year old looked up at her quizzically and said "Peaceful? Are you sure, Aunt Sarah?"

Now Aunt Sarah could understand why the boy questioned her. Since time began there had been no peace on earth. Well, perhaps that was because the adults had always run it, and so she answered him in this way:

"Men can make war, Ben, children cannot. They have to grow up to be men and learn to hate, and then they can make war."

Benjamin Klien, looked up at her with big dark Hebrew eyes, and he thoughtfully asked her this time, "Okay Aunt Sarah, what if the animals ran the world ... would it still be peaceful?"

Sarah nodded her head as the flat blade of the knife rubbed back and forth across the swelled flesh and finally popped out the hateful stinger of the wasp, and she answered him. "Yes, I believe so Ben. It would be peaceful until the animals learned to talk and told their secrets to man."

Benjamin smiled at her and said "Thank you Aunt Sarah, my arm feels better, but I'd sure like to know how come you are so smart?"

Sarah gave him a hug and replied "Because I watch the animals, Ben, and I listen to the children." And, all her long life, she did.

On the fifteenth day of March, the circus wagons rolled. Sarah was by now an accomplished driver, and sitting beside her on the leather seat of their over-the-road vehicle was Winona, with Kino the three-legged cat, perched nonchalantly upon her lap.

Winona was like a bird being set free from a winter of confinement because winter quarters for her was always a slow punishment.

The wistful look on Sarah Jackson's attractive face this morning, caused the younger sister to ask, "Sarah, where is your mind today?" They hit a rut head-on and got jostled around in the seat. Sarah clucked to the horses and replied "They are making maple syrup up in Vermont this time of year. It is not my mind that wanders, Sister, it is my heart." In her dreams last night she had been there, back home in the Green Mountain state, gathering maple sap that soon would be boiled into syrup.

Winona looked sharply at the driver. The younger girl liked Vermont, and when she died, her bones would no doubt rest under the rich, black dirt of that quaint place, but she was not dead yet, and living for her was on the road with the circus. She did not argue with Sarah, there was no point, neither mind would change.

Seven days into the season, just outside of Macon, Georgia, Sarah rushed off to the cooktent shortly before five in the morning, to help to set up tables and serve the first meal of the day. She could smell the bacon and eggs frying as she made her way along briskly, in the semi-dawn light. "Coffee!" she thought, "How could anything that tastes so bad, smell so good?"

Tearing off her shawl, she made her way to the high counter from where the cook gave and received orders.

"I'm here Sam!" she said, and a strange and yet familiar deja vu feeling swept all over her.

"Sam, I'm here! she repeated, and then she heard a strange voice answer "I am too, but I'm not Sam. My name is John."

Sarah looked up and across the rough wall of boards and canvas that separated the dining area from the kitchen, and at the same time looked into the handsomely chiselled profile of a man in his early thirties. He had medium brown hair, skin as dark as her own and the most remarkable blue-gray eyes, that did indeed look stolen, in that copper-colored face. She could not see, in the lantern light, the greying streaks in his hair, but she recognized the tenderness of his smile and she knew him as the one that danced off with her heart, a man called John Somers. Sarah stood erect and met his eyes squarely. His smile broadened, and as she tied her apron strings around her slender waist and began rolling up her sleeves, he spoke again.

"Sarah! I finally found you! I've been five years and three circuses trying to track you down!"

When Sarah spoke her voice was controlled, and she smiled and replied. "Either I hide good John, or you track bad!" He tipped his head back and laughed. He had found Sarah!

Around the tables she went, setting up places, delivering coffee and as the first rays of daylight spread silently inside the cooktent, the dining area rapidly filled with hungry men and women.

As Sarah delivered the orders, she noticed how big they were. "Oh well, he's used to feeding lumberjacks!" she thought. And he was, but he was a good cook, not afraid to use garlic and onion in his dishes, and when the circus workers tasted his cooking and found out that an ailing old Sam, over seventy, needed help, they readily accepted John.

John and the older cook, liked each other immediately, and there was never any mean spirit or professional competitiveness between the two.

Things rushed through Sarah's mind. She had simply smoothed her hair back into its twist, not even touching a comb to it. She didn't even know if her blouse matched her skirt, because until this very minute she hadn't really cared.

Then she was disgusted with the girlishness of her confusion. Half the population of the world were men, so why did this one have the ability to fluster her so? She told herself, "You are not nineteen, now Sarah."

John Somers, for his part, thought that Sarah looked altogether fine. Hers was not a beautiful face, but there was a proud look to the set of her smooth jaw, and that quiet dignity that was inherent in her.

She moved about swiftly and silently doing her work. John would steal a minute from his cooking and look up from his work and stare into the face of this young woman. Her face was not really stunning, but it was the face that had haunted his dreams for over five years now. "Strange!" he thought.

Three times each table was refilled with steaming bowls of fried potatoes, ham, sausage, bacon, and even pan cakes, and Sarah ate at the last setting as she always did, and she had not been seated long before the newly hired cook was seating himself.

"Sarah! I'm so glad to see you. You look lovely!" he exclaimed, because it was true and he was elated to see her. And to him she did look lovely. His deep-set eyes swept over Sarah's face. Her face was one that flushed mightily under the intensity of his gaze.

Surveying her now, John thought that Sarah looked smaller than he had imagined her to be, but this was because he himself had filled out. She was not a small woman — he was a big man.

Sarah sipped the coffee and then she remarked "you're the last person that I ever expected to see here." She still hadn't figured out his greeting to her. Had he actually been trying to find her? No, he was a smooth one, probably married already, or married and divorced. He'd not play heart games with her again, she vowed.

John knew that this was the one place that he could talk to her, and he didn't waste his time.

"Sarah, are you married yet?" he questioned, but this time she was in no hurry to let him know her business — he hunted too slow!

Rising and preparing to leave the table, Sarah smiled and teased him. "And what would you say John Somers if I said I was!"

In acknowledgment that a lady was leaving his presence, John stood out of respect, and then with a lazy grin playing around the corners of his mouth he said "I'd say I'm sorry for your husband. I did not come all this way for nothing, woman."

Sarah stared up at him open mouthed, and then she snatched up her shawl and walked briskly from the cooktent, muttering "Ummmph."

For one brief moment she wished that she was married. He looked so smug and sure of himself, and not only that, but he was bold in his questions. Her life was none of his business. His type only married when they had to. Well, no man would ever have to marry her, she vowed, especially —that one.

Sarah in her haste, had somehow managed to wrap a corn muffin in a napkin and once home she shook Winona awake and gave her the only breakfast that the younger girl would have this day. But Winona often missed her breakfast, she was usually not an early riser.

The morning was spent in a rush as the Big-Top tent was put up, and when Sarah and Winona entered the cooktent for their mid-day meal, Winona still did not know that John Somers was now employed as the cook.

Sarah worked breakfast and supper as a waitress, but at lunch she sat and enjoyed her meal. After the supper meal, however, she was one of the dishwashers for the cook would have no part of this.

As they sat down, nodding to familiar faces, Winona looked up and saw the newest addition to circus life. With a jerk of her head she said "Sarah, isn't that...Yes Sarah, that is John Somers!"

"Ummph," is all that Sarah Jackson said, eating her rolls and soup. This was the way Peter Jackson, and three generations of Indians before him, had dismissed any subject that they wished not to discuss. Winona grinned suspiciously. She knew that Sarah was not in a good mood, but until now she did not know why.

"Soup is Good, Sister!...That Somer's, he can cook!" and again Sarah answered "Ummph."

John and Winona exchanged nods to one another, and he was amazed to see what a beautiful young woman this Winona had become. They carried their dishes to the huge washing tubs, and Sarah was careful not to look in Mr. Somers direction, but Winona did and came along and touched Sarah on the shoulder and said "Sarah, I hate to tell you this, but "Ummph," over there wants to talk to you."

He came out of the kitchen to sit and eat, and he bid them to take a minute and sit with him and they did.

"Winona," he smiled, "I had to look twice, I couldn't believe it was really you." She smiled back at him and then John turned his attention to the other sister. "Sarah, I wish there was some place other than here that we could talk." And Sarah said, "Well, there is not." And then with a look of mischief and merriment, Winona, sensing her dismissal, got up from the table and announced that she was late for practice and that Kino would be mad.

Thus, they were left alone across the table and the silence grew.

Then Sarah came directly to the point. "Why did you come here, John?" she said, and the man across from her answered, "To find you!" Sarah flushed darkly under her bronze-colored skin.

She looked him squarely in the eye and questioned "Why would you do a thing like that?"

He met her steady gaze and said "Because I should not have let you leave Vermont," he said with a visible sense of regret in his voice.

"And how could you have stopped me?" was what Sarah wanted to know. "Well, I could have tried," he said. And upon hearing that Sarah spoke, emotion rising as she did so. "We hardly knew one another, John. You wanted to be free. You should stay free, because things designed to be free die in captivity. I'm sure that you in your long search for me, did enjoy your freedom."

John put his coffee cup down and looked hard at her. "I did," he said and then went on "I almost once had to get married, and when it was not necessary to do so, I decided that I had better smarten up and go and find the daughter of an Indian chief. Marriage to this woman would not be captivity, it would be good."

Sarah's eyes opened wide. She had not expected a proposal, but now that it had come, she felt a warm glow pass over her whole being.

She met his direct gaze and said, "I must think about this. It is not good unless I say it is good, and I have not said that."

With his face very serious, John touched her hand lightly and asked "Is there another? Have you made a commitment to someone else?" and Sarah shook her head no and replied "Only to myself, John, that I would not pursue this way of life once Winona marries. I am a very independent woman and I like my freedom, perhaps more than you." John never forgot the dark eyes that were boring holes into his own, or the fierce and yet quiet determination displayed on her face. She rested her case: "If and when I give up my freedom, I will not have to do so. It will be the choice of my mind and my heart because no other way is acceptable."

Sarah smiled softly and then calmly turned and walked away. A frown crossed the young man's face. Damn, he wished there was a better place for them to talk. When he had first become interested in Sarah some few years ago, he had seen the promise of great beauty and great strength, but now he was seeing the fulfillment of those promises, highlighted by an air or independence that he found disturbing. He was here, at last he had caught up with her and it seemed that she really did not care. And John found this fact even more disconcerting.

He refilled his coffee mug and sat back down at the rough wooden table to be alone with his thoughts, but old Sam shuffled out of the kitchen and seated himself across from the younger man.

"Glad you chose Sarah! Most are attracted to that younger sister, but she can be mean! Now that little Sarah is one fine and virtuous lady, smartern' a whip too! Course she's mighty strong willed though," Sam finished.

John Somers turned his steady gaze on the straight back of Sarah Jackson as she walked out of sight and then he looked at Sam and said "Ummph."

The towns and cities went by one by one as the caravan made its way up the eastern seaboard.

In the haste of the road trips, the matinees and a new town each day, Sarah and John saw each other only at the cooktent, and even there they had little opportunity to talk.

Winona could feel the strain between them even during the brief encounters. One evening she questioned her older sister, "Sarah, I did think you really liked that John Somers. Now, I don't think that you do. He must love you! You said he proposed."

Sarah answered, "Yes, now at thirty-four, tired of his free living and carousing, he is ready to settle down. Well, I have never in my life been free. I have things to do and things to see my way. He needed time to grow, Winona, and so do I. No, I will not marry John Somers."

At the end of the third week of the season, a knock came on the door just after the matinee. Winona, with Kino wrapped around her neck like a scarf, answered it to find John standing there with his hat in his hands.

"Please, Winona, may I speak to Sarah?" he asked. With a wry grin Winona called to Sarah, who was napping. Get up Sarah, "Ummph," is here."

Sarah arose with a start. She pressed her hands against her eyes still gently swollen with sleep. "Come outside, John," she said. "We can not talk in here. It is not permitted!"

Once outside he said "That's one of the reasons I'm leaving this damned place! Insane rules! Can't speak to a woman unless it is daylight in the cooktent!"

There were two little chairs of sorts, close beside the darkened embers of what had been Sarah's outside fire a few hours earlier. She sat down, and John stood nervously before her, but when he spoke his voice was low and controlled. There was something to be said between them.

"Sarah, I think our courtship is one of good love and bad timing." She raised her eyebrows quizzically up to where he towered. Then John spoke again. "I thought there was a special thing between us. I guess I read much into it that was not there. I knew back in Vermont that you were the one, but I drank a lot, brawled a lot. I found love, but I was not ready. Now you are the one who is not ready! You have changed, Sarah, and there is someone between us, someone I do not know."

Without a blink of an eye Sarah said "I am between us John, me, Sarah, the one you never tried to know. The girl of nineteen winters that you danced with is a woman now, with her own dreams to follow. She did love you back then, and to go from her father's house into the arms of a husband, seemed right, but now it is not right. I like this feeling of being dependent on no one but Sarah, the now Sarah."

"I told you the truth, Sarah. Do you think less of me because I said I was careless and almost had to marry another?" She studied his grey-blue eyes for a long minute and then she answered softly, "No. It is good that you are a responsible man and would have done the decent thing, John." A faint smile crossed his otherwise grim face. And then he took both of her hands and pulled her to her feet. "Someday, Sarah Jackson, I may track you down again and ask you one more time," and as a beautiful smile made its way across her face, this "Now Sarah" replied, "And I may be fully grown, my freedom sated and I might even say Yes, John Somers."

She was in his muscular arms, and as their mouths caressed there was an urgency in his kisses, made even more so by the inexperience of her lips. The blood sang in Sarah's ears. Pressed hard against every line of this lean and powerfully built young man, Sarah, in her innocence, had no idea of the primal instincts that this gentle giant was battling.

She stood on the tips of her toes, reaching upward for his kisses as he kissed her again, and again, until he felt the tide of passion mounting and he suddenly stopped abruptly and pushed her away. He forced a laugh, and in a voice that did not sound like his he whispered, "I am a patient tracker, Sarah, but I always get my prized game. Our paths will cross again, little one, I promise."

There was a strange look in his eye, and Sarah's breathing was uneven and her heart still hammering with this new excitement of love. She took an involuntary step backwards herself, and then she laughed and reminded him, "Stalking cougars do not frighten me, John. I can talk to them, remember? And, I still have my chair and whip!"

He turned then and walked away from her, a slow smile playing on his lips. She was not one to forget, he noted, but then neither was he.

And he knew with every step he took away from her that indeed whatever was between them was not over, not today, not tomorrow and for as long as the grass grew green and the rivers flowed to the sea.

Another young man came to work with old Sam, and replaced John Somers in the kitchen but not in Sarah's heart. However, about John, she decided that it was a good feeling to be loved, but there was no hurry about it. This had been very soothing to the older sister's ego though. At least now she had one proposal to Winona's three!

In August of that year, up around Syracuse, New York, a young man of Scottish heritage who played the bagpipes beautifully, hired on with the circus. He was in his early twenties, but had been the sole support of his widowed mother and two younger sisters since the death of his father. He was strong as a bull, and because of the responsibilities laid upon him so early in life, he was not only well adjusted, he was also mature for his age. Before she even met him, Winona heard his tryout song, "Amazing Grace," and as she and Sarah poked the coals of their outside fire, she said wistfully, "Oh, Sarah! That is the most beautiful and sad sound, I've ever heard!"

Two days later at the cooktent Winona was introduced to the light-haired, blue-eyed young man named Ian MacWain, and when her dark eyes met his blue ones, they both felt a twinge of their heartstrings.

Ian came from a long line of Scottish Highlanders and wore his kilt with pride and dignity. Sarah thought that after meeting Ian and hearing about his heritage, and the bond that kept the clans of Scotland together, that this was one tribe of White Men, that was very proud and clannish.

Extending a sunburned hand to a blushing Winona, Ian had introduced himself, "I'm Ian MacWain, of the O'Donnell Clan." Winona exchanged a half-curtsy, accepted his hand and replied, "I'm Winona Jackson of the Bear Clan." Sarah had to smother a laugh. She didn't know which of these two youngsters were smitten the most, or which one was actually the proudest of their clans.

Sarah simply walked away from the breakfast table and let these descendants of two clans of man, become acquainted. With a slight "burr" in his speech, Ian asked quickly, "Be you the lass called Little Daring Eagle, on the trapeze?" and Winona said that she was. Then she added something else. "And it is you that plays my beautiful song, Amazing Grace?" He colored a little. "Aye, I play it on me sticks," he said and when Winona said it was her favorite song, their friendship had begun.

Thus as one sister's love had walked out of her life, for the younger girl, true love for the first time really had walked in.

With the turning of the wagon wheels and the changing of the seasons, the Jackson women, were exposed to many different facets of life and their experiences differed greatly. Three years ago, a man with a long british face, nearing fifty, had joined the circus. He had been a sharpshooter with the Wild Bill Hickock Show. Age and liquor together had not dimmed his eagle eye and his target was a lovely young woman, his daughter. Her name was Brynn Ellingwood, and her mother had been Irish. Brynn was attractive, fair of skin and hair, with that rosy cheeked look, that so many English women possess. She was slender and as tall as Sarah, and there was an honesty about her that shown plainly through her sea-green eyes. Brynn was Sarah's best friend and in her secret heart, Sarah wished many times that Dennis could meet Brynn, so trustworthy and good.

Winona for several months now also had made a new best friend. Her name was Janele Tremane, and that French girl, had a sly, sheepish look about her. Sarah was sorry for Winona. She had made a poor choice, for this young woman would never be anyone's best friend, except her own sneaky self. She was a coward and a schemer and Sarah knew that instinctively. This sly one followed Winona around, but Sarah knew that someday Winona would turn her back and Janele would bury a knife in it! The older sister felt this to her very bones, and she knew that she was far more fortunate than Winona, for she had placed her trust and friendship in a young woman, half-blood Irish, half-blood English, but even so, Brynn Ellingwood was three times more the woman than Janele Tremane would ever be.

Sarah was saddened by what she sensed. In her family for generations the oldest grandmother had said, "The Great Spirit chooses our relatives. We can choose our friends," and Sarah believed this, and all her life she chose them very carefully, just as the Great Spirit had done with her relatives.

Janele followed Winona to practice and watched her performance on the high wires. She was shorter than Winona and squarely built, like many women of French blood are. She was also part of the clog dancing group which Sarah belonged to.

Winona sensed her sister's dislike of her best friend and she said accusingly, "I know you don't like her Sarah. You're just jealous because I have such a good friend!" Sarah looked up from her mending and retorted, "You need no enemies with that hypocrite as your friend, Winona!"

"She knows that you don't like her, Sarah!" Winona said, and Sarah answered shortly "Good! Then she will stay out of my way!"

"You are too jealous!" Winona raged, and the older sister laughed and said "Be serious, Winona. If I'm ever jealous of another woman, it will be a whole woman!" Winona didn't answer Sarah, it was well not to do that when good-natured Sarah was angry.

Well out of harm's way, on her way out the door, Winona challenged, "At least Janele goes to church!" "She needs to!" the older sister answered back.

Winona went to perfect her act, and Sarah had to reflect on whether she was swayed in her opinion because from childhood, she had heard Aunt Nel and other Indian women say, "You can trust a French man, but you can never trust a French woman."

Sarah did not want to think that she was unfair or biased. But then Winona would bring that girl over and she would act so sweet and pious, and sooner or later Sarah would see and feel the hypocracy and the cunningness behind her smile, and she would know that she was not unjust in her opinion of Winona's best friend. She was being blatantly honest.

On a Sunday night, a particular Sunday that the circus was not playing, but instead was resting to repair equipment and give everyone a much-needed break, Sarah and Winona sat by their outside fire. They drank tea and watched the stars above and Winona talked. "Sarah, did Aunt Nel ever say what she, my mother, was like?" Sarah looked up at her momentarily startled, for Winona never seemed to care about the past, only the future that she raced to. It was good that Winona felt the need to fish, thought Sarah.

Being careful not mention the name of "Alwildia," Sarah said to her younger sister, "Aunt Nel never spoke of her, except to say that you had her deadly temper!" Then Sarah's face softened and she went on "You know she was killed by a wounded bear! Well, father said that she was very brave, Winona, and that she died that way." For the most part this seemed to be enough.

Then from the swamp behind where they were camped, came the cry of a loon. Its call tore the night sky, and Sarah felt a chill run along her shoulders. This went back to her early childhood years, when everybody heeded the call of the loon. He only spoke when warning of death or an impending disaster.

"I like to hear the loons," Winona said, and Sarah said "Ummph." The younger sister would not let go of this subject and said "Sarah, those loon warnings and wolf spottings and owls screaming are nothing but old foolish tales. They were just fireside stories that frightened children and I don't believe in any of them!"

Sarah said nothing for she knew that Winona did not share the closeness of the land or to her brothers, the animals, that she herself did. And yet a smile crossed her lips when she realized, why should Winona understand fear? After all, no eagle did. Sarah had enjoyed the peacefulness of this surrounding night and then from out of the darkness came the beautiful notes of a lone bagpipe, and the song "Amazing Grace" broke the spell of silence.

Winona, eyes sparkling, clasped her small hands across her heart and whispered, "Hear that Sarah? Ian's playing it just for me!" Sarah's heart was happy to at last have her sister interested in something other than death-defying stunts on a high wire.

"So, this Ian is special, Winona?" Sarah asked and Winona nodded her head and confessed, "No Sarah, he is the one!" And even if she had not said this thing, Sarah would have known it.

These words had hardly escaped from Winona's lips, when Ian MacWain loomed before their nightfire. The flames in the fire flickered and even in that poor lighting, anger was clearly written on his face.

Why did Sarah have a gut feeling that the ugly snake of treachery and deceit was about to show its head?

She got up to go inside and give these two some privacy, offering Ian her chair, but he motioned that she stay, he didn't care who heard what he had to say.

Rising to her feet, Sarah answered, "I care. I have no desire to know my sister's private business," and she went inside and Ian was quick to apologize and then he turned his anger toward the younger sister. Winona had risen to her feet and stood with her mouth open in shock and surprise.

"I'm so disappointed in you, lass!" he said, and then he went on, "I couldn't believe that you were that kind of woman! 'Meet me in the woods tonight! I'll show you what a real woman is!' That's what this damned paper says. I thought you were a real lady, Winona!" There was such rage and pain in his voice, and Winona, now realizing that she was being dragged into something that she knew nothing about, became rigid; and hot anger forced her to clench her teeth. She actually had to bite her words as she snapped "I am a lady— you fool!" Winona had stomped over to where he stood, and Ian raged, "You are no lady, and I am a fool all right!"

From his pocket he took out a folded paper and exclaimed, "Look at this Winona, would a lady write such a thing? No, a harlot would! And here is your name —here, look at it!" Winona snatched the note from his hands. She stared at it, and even in the glow of the nightfire coals she could clearly see that the name neatly written on the bottom was Winona Jackson.

Winona looked up at Ian and there were tears spilling from her eyes and her hands shook with rage and anger when she realized that in addition to knowing that it was not her signature, she recognized the writing. It was that of Janele Tremane — Winona's best friend. The dagger Sarah had warned her about was plunged.

For a minute she could not speak. Ian blurted out, "An I'll be tellin' ye another thing, Winona, I'd never have picked ye for a harlot, least of all a damned cowardly one to boot." Winona stopped her sobbing long enough to shake her head no and try to say that word, but Ian cried out "I heard the rap on me wagon door, but I opened it up and found only this note. And then I saw your sly-fox friend, runnin' away as fast as she could. Ye' couldn't even do your own dirty work, Winona!"

Winona hardly heard what more he said. She came up off the ground about a foot and slapped him full across the face with a force that rocked his head from side to side and seemed to knock some sense into him.

"I did not write this note, Ian! I did not send it! If you want to call names, you better take your anger to Janele. I'm innocent of this whole affair!"

In a instant his whole manner changed. Winona's words hit him like a blow to the pit of his stomach. He had accused an innocent person and suddenly, Ian was filled with self-disgust.

Looking down into her upturned face, he saw eyes that were not lying. "Oh my God, Winona — I'm so sorry!" Ian cried. He tried to put his arms around her but Winona was not having any of this. Her hurt had been replaced with anger and she shook off his comforting arms. She reached down suddenly and came up with the heavy iron poker that they used to poke their nightfire. She swung it high over Ian's head and hissed "You Ian, you take one more step towards me or you say one more lying word to me and I'll stave your God damned skull in!"

This brought Sarah flying out the door. She ran up behind Winona and from that vantage point, she succeeded in wrestling the weapon away from her sister. "Ian, You go now. You Go!" she cried and Sarah flung the heavy poker to the ground. He turned on his heal to leave and Winona screamed after him "You go to Hell, Ian MacWain....and you take that hypocrite Janele Tremane with you!"

As the shrieks broke the early evening stillness, heads were popping out of doors and Ian in his agony and confusion, with the imprint of Winona's left hand rising red and livid on his face, cursed under his breath and strode off into the night.

She had God Damned him! She had called him a fool! Ian knew that she was right about the fool.

An old Biblical phrase came into his head. "Oh Ye of Little Faith." Ian knew if he had used his reason he would have known that the fiery, and yet funny girl that he played "Amazing Grace" for, would never have been a party to such a devious plot. What was the matter with him? Why, he loved that girl and in his heart she was above all things... all things except suspicion, it would seem.

Once inside the little wagon, the younger sister, her anger spent, sobbed on Sarah's shoulder. "Don't say it Sarah! Don't say it! You warned me, but please don't say 'I told you so'"

"I'll never speak to that man again!" Winona raged, but Sarah spoke out in defense of love. "Winona, Ian came here because he cared so, not because he didn't. He confronted you and not many in his moccasins would have done that. When he learned the truth he was sorry, that young man. I saw his face. Don't let the treachery of that "back-stabbing coward come between you and the man you love."

"Don't say 'Love' to me, Sarah. I hate them both!"

Sarah poured hot tea into two cups, and encouraged Winona to drink of it and let its calming additives have some effect on her.

"Hating Ian is like shooting the messenger, Winona. Janele's treachery has made a victim out of him as well as you. Right now, little sister, you do not hate Ian, as much as he hates himself," said Sarah.

Winona drank the tea, wiped her watering eyes and blew her nose. Eventually she did stop sobbing and just before she closed her eyes in sleep Sarah said, "Winona, you are the daughter of the eagle, brave and noble, and no scavenger bird was ever made that could soar as high as you...could make you less than what you are....could make your brave heart small."

It was very late when Sarah closed her own eyes. Her sleep was a troubled one, for she had dreamed of being back in South Guildhall, Vermont, root-gathering on top of Tarritine Ledge, and below her the blue Connecticut River drifted along on a serpentine course. It was getting dark and loons were calling. In this restless sleep she woke up tossing, and finally returned again to slumber only to be awakened once again. In this dream too she had returned to Vermont, the town of Lunenburg actually, and she was within the dampened mists and walking upon the wetlands of a place called Catbow Swamp. The frogs, the birds and the crickets, all these forms of life she saw and heard, there in this familiar dead-tree-forest. Then from out of the mists she saw him clearly, that hard to see Grandfather Owl.

Long before daybreak Sarah was awake. This was very common. What was not common was the fact that Winona was not only up, but her bed was empty.

"Oh No!" Sarah thought. "She didn't get up this early to eat! She's gone to fight that Frenchie!"

Sarah dressed hastily, half tying, half buttoning her clothing and running her hands through her hair but taking no time for the comb. She ran out into a steady downpour. She hadn't noticed that it was raining, and now without her shawl she felt the damp chill. She had to stop Winona, and she ran faster.

Sarah headed for the cooktent as fast as her legs would carry her, but even as ran, Winona was walking past where Janele sat eating corn meal gruel. The guilt in her soul was reflected in her face when she saw Winona standing there.

Ignoring the others, Winona leaned over and said "Good Morning!" The sly one turned her head and looked into Winona's dark eyes, and knew already that it was going to be anything but a good morning!

Wasting no time, Winona said, "I have a note here. It came from you." She held the note out for the girl to see it, but she would not raise her eyes to look at it and said sheepishly, "If my name isn't on it, it's not mine." The Indian girl snapped "My name is on it, but it is your hand that put it there." Janele felt safe, she was in the company of her three midget uncles and she asked slowly, "Well, what are you going to do about it?"

With one swift and almost cat-like motion, Winona Jackson crumbled the note up and then actually proceeded to stuff it into Janele's gruel-filled mouth. "I'm going to make you eat it, liar!" was what Winona said, and then without mercy she grabbed the girl by the hair and forced her face, note and all, down into the bowl of mushy gruel. "Grueling Task, Eh?" asked Winona with no mirth.

The blond culprit sat beside her protecting uncles Claudio, Georgio and Antonio, who when piled three high, made up the three components of the "Tallest Man in the World." Surveying this family, it was evident to Winona that the men all tended to be dwarfs and the women to be treacherous. "Pitiful," she thought.

Janele screamed wildly and spit out the note crying "Help! Help! I'm being attacked!" This is when Claudio jumped up and pointed his breakfast fork at Winona, and when she wouldn't relinquish her hold on Janele's neck, Claudio tried to stick the fork into Winona's arm. She sidestepped, and as she did, her captive struggled from her vise-like grip.

Antonio now joined in. He ran up behind Winona and tried to grab her arms, but Winona slung back a vicious elbow and Antonio staggered backwards. She raised her foot and kicked at Claudio, who was coming at her again, but he ducked away. Winona did place one swift kick squarely in Janele's fat behind, as she made her getaway. Janele landed outside the cooktent door, sprawling face down in the sawdust, mud and rain.

Winona shrieked after Janele "You were attacked from behind girl, the way you like to fight!" Suddenly as she stood there dusting her hands off, the sight of that unhappy girl crawling away seemed indeed hilarious to Winona. She laughed heartily only a moment before she was set upon by Janele's three little uncles in retaliation for her seemingly unprovoked abuse of their niece.

Claudio, the most militant one of the bunch, jumped up on a wooden bench beside Winona and attempted to restrain her, but she shook him off and he screamed and tried to bite her. And for that attempt Winona, with a curse, kicked the bench out from under the bow-legged rascal and he crashed to the sawdust-covered floor.

Brynn Ellingwood came out of the kitchen, carrying an empty lard pail which she intended to use to catch the rains drops that were tapping on the tin dishes. She hadn't seen what caused the trouble, but what she did see was Sarah's younger sister in a three-against-one battle, and quickly she handed the lard bucket to Winona. It wasn't a tomahawk, but as a weapon it would be fine, especially, with the handle that Winona wrapped her fingers quickly around. She swung the pail high and in a circular motion, and then she fiercely connected with two of her assailants and both Georgio and Antonio were knocked to the floor. But, Claudio was back. He was cursing and leaping at Winona and in the flash of an eye she slammed the bucket over his large head and he went sprawling flat on his back, kicking his short, crooked legs and looking like a dying fly. "Help, Antonio! I can't see! Get that Squaw, Georgio!" he raged, and Georgio, in a green vest-coat and looking like a swamp frog, charged like a raging bull. With a well-placed knee right between his bulging eyes, Georgio went down, roaring "God Damned miserable Squaw!" And, Winona yelled back "That Squaw is a match for you, Frog Face!"

In all of her life Brynn Ellingwood had never seen anything like this! She put her hands on her shapely hips and laughed out loud. Brynn looked down at Claudio, rolling and kicking on the floor, trying to get the bucket off his big head, and without a sound Winona placed her foot upon the bucket, pinning Claudio to the ground.

"Damn!" thought Brynn, "I wish Sarah could see this. Talk about a circus! This is a circus!" But Sarah was there by then and had surveyed the battle, and decided that one St. Francis Indian, especially armed with a lard bucket, was indeed a match for three small palefaces.

Sarah was laughing to the point where she had to lean against a tent pole to stay standing. "It was combat at its very best!" she thought, but Old Sam the cook, whose stovetop was full of bacon trying to burn, was bellowing like a bull. "Hey Rube, Hey Rube!" That signal brought people from all sides as they attempted to put a stop to this fracas.

Ian MacWain made his way to the inside of the cooktent from out of the hammering rain. As he did this he met Janele Tremane, covered with cornmeal gruel and mud, crawling away on her hands and knees. He was even more surprised to see Winona Jackson in a knock-down dragout fight with three mud-covered midgets. "Stop this!" Ian bellowed and he was a big fellow, and Claudio, who was already a captive of the bucket over his head, and the foot on top of it, stopped kicking his crooked legs and lay still.

Antonio and Georgio wouldn't quit though. What they lacked in size they made up for in determination. If it was the last thing they ever did, they would get a good swing at that damned squaw. Georgio made another jump off the ground and took a punch at Winona, but she brought her knee up and took him under the chin and he hit the sawdust again.

Antonio saw that he was too short to hit her, so he ran up on her left side and tried to mule-kick her in the leg. Now, Ian came roaring in with "Get away from that girl or I'll break your damned neck!" He pushed Antonio back, and on second thought, picked him up by the scruff of the neck and the seat of the pants and threw him like a rubber ball, out the door of the cooktent. Next, Ian grabbed Georgio and tossed him after his brother.

Poor Claudio was picked up and tossed out into the torrential rain, bucket and all. Claudio was in the dark as he flew through the air, but before he hit the ground he landed squarely in the arms of Boris the surly Russian Strong Man. Boris was not amused. He uttered a startled grunt, held Claudio out in front of his powerful chest, examined him a minute in disgust, then drove Claudio bucket-first down to the wet earth below. From that day forth, Claudio, was called "Little Bucket Head" by his circus friends.

An angry Ian, asked a disheveled Winona, "Are you hurt?"

"No," she raged "but you're going to be if you don't keep your damned nose out of my business, Ian!" Ian took Winona by the shoulders firmly but gently which was a mistake, and she shook herself out of his grip. He was heard to emit a terrible curse and then he picked up Winona and threw her over his shoulder like a sack of grain, and carried her out of the cooktent into the rain. "If you won't shut your mouth and stop fightin' lass, I'll take ya away from the bloody fight!" he said. And he did.

Everyone who had enjoyed the skirmish joined in to help clean up the dining area, Sarah included. None of those involved in this fight ever got fired because of it.

The long-term good thing was that Ian and Winona did become best friends again.

Janele Tremane and her stout-hearted little uncles remained with the circus for a long time after this altercation, but the four of them stayed as far away from Winona Jackson as they possibly could.

And, Winona that "eagle child," in regards to Janele Tremane, never spoke of her or to her, ever again.

"The sad thing about making any Jackson your enemy, is that you had lost such a good friend!" thought Sarah.

As the years passed, this was always one of Aunt Sarah's most often repeated tales of the circus.

In her slow and deliberate speech, accentuated by an almost poetic rhythm that so many Native Americans possess, Sarah's bright, bird-like eyes would crinkle at the corners. And with a soft laugh in her voice she would say, " And, except for one scheming she creature ... and three angry little men ... there in that leaky cooktent ... a good time was had by all.... while raindrops danced on tin dishes.... and the bacon burned."

Ironic as it was, however, Sarah's humorous story didn't really end there; and yet it did, but she was careful never to connect the sad ending.

Almost one hundred winters later, Aunt Sarah could remember well the chain of events that followed that infamous cooktent battle.

You see, on that very night Sarah had dreamed again of Grandfather Owl, only this was not a dream. Indeed it was a nightmare. Grandfather Owl, had looked at Sarah, but he called — Winona's name.

Sarah pondered the precariousness of her disturbing dreams of late. She decided that sometimes it would be less stressful on her if, like Winona, she did not believe in any of the old ways; but this was very hard to do for Sarah, as she had seen enough to believe, and believed enough to give credence to warnings and omens, good and bad.

Torrential rains had followed the circus that spring as it ventured up the eastern coast of the United States. The show animals were irritable and unpredictable, and the trainers often worse than that. Tempers flared, for when equipment was wet even a simple trick was hard to do, especially when you performed high in the air as Winona did.

Sarah reflected on how beautiful and graceful Winona was to watch as she walked the tight wire. She had mastered the trapeze as well, but no matter what she accomplished she was driven to do one more somersault or one back-flip more, and always she strived to do this at greater and more dangerous heights. "Be careful, Eagle!" was the prayer on Sarah's lips.

Ian still played "Amazing Grace" for Winona every night, and it filled the air with its haunting sound. Ian, for his part, was indeed a fine musician and played all his songs well, but when he played this one particular tune one could tell his heart was truly in it.

"He is playing it just for me!" Winona would say as she patted Kino, who lay purring in her lap.

Looking up from her basketry, Sarah would smile, for it was good to see the soft look of young love on the younger woman's face.

"Indeed, he is playing it just for you!" Sarah said.

One rainy day turned into another, and then came the night of a performance, the one Sarah would never forget. She hurriedly changed from her clog-dancing costume and was rushing to get into her work clothes. She would take a minute or two tonight and go and watch Winona, because she was trying for the first time a new acrobatic trick on the high wire. Winona was ready and she was eager to attempt it, and Sarah knew that as the "Eagle" cartwheeled high in the air and landed cat-like on the wire, she would somersault to the ground as the drums rolled, and then the gasping audience would erupt with a thunderous outburst of applause.

Sarah heard the lead-in music, and a strange prickling feeling came over her. Something was wrong!

She ran barefooted, racing over wet sawdust. She had to stop that drum roll! But, even as she ran she heard it and momentarily she froze, because she heard the gasp and roar of the crowd but then she heard a deadly silence that she should not have been hearing had the newly perfected trick have gone as planned.

Terror added wings to Sarah's feet as she entered the center ring. She saw other people, tight-rope walkers, crewman, performers, and they were all running. Concerned, fellow trapeze artists were descending down the ropes like monkeys, and then Sarah broke thorough the crowd and saw her sister Winona. She lay face-down on the ground. She was very pale and still, and her head was turned or twisted somehow at an awkward angle.

Hands reached for Sarah and tried to pull her away but they were not quick enough or strong enough, and Sarah ran to Winona's side, touched her face and one of her hands, then fell to her knees and rubbed a tear-stained cheek against Winona's face. But her sister did not move, her eyes were wide open, and Sarah knew immediately that her neck was broken. Winona was dead.

Tears clouded her vision as she was dragged away, and she stood like one in a trance, and watched that lifeless body being loaded onto a stretcher. The announcer was assuring people that Little Daring Eagle would be just fine. In her most secret heart Sarah knew that this was true. Winona had crossed over to the other side now, and she would be fine, but it was still a sad thing that in order to be fine forever one had also to be dead.

Visions of flaming stars and crying wolves and screaming owl's flashed before Aunt Sarah's eyes. She thought about her father and Aunt Nel, gone forever, but not all gone, because she carried them with her all the time within her heart. Their blood ran in her veins as did Winona's. And now Winona also would be carried in Sarah's heart. For one fleeting second Sarah found some comfort in thinking that at last her sister's free-spirit was really free. She was remembering her own words, spoken to Winona's trainer, Zachary. "She knows no fear. She only knows to fly," and somehow at this very minute, in another place, the older sister liked to think that Winona's Eagle's Spirit was soaring high, and answering only to the wind beneath her wings.

There was a span of hours that Sarah never could remember much about. She recalled faces, many, many compassionate and familiar ones, wet with tears and strained with grief and shock, as was her own.

The circus made an unscheduled stop and rested. Winona's untimely passing had been hard on all these people who had been her family for nearly five years now. Even that mighty wrestling tag-team Claudio, Georgio and Antonio, and Boris the strong man broke down and wept with all the rest.

These friends grieved for Winona, for they had lost their "Eagle Child, one who loved life and yet gambled with it every day as so many of these circus people did. In their kindness they rallied around Sarah, and Brynn wrote a letter to Sarah's brother in Boston, and Sarah thought "I'll be there before the letter will." For just as Winona's work was done here with the circus, so also was Aunt Sarah's.

Winona's remains were taken by wagon to the nearest town that had an undertaker, and they were sent home to Vermont on a train. In a cemetery lot in Guildhall, Vermont the Jackson family had a resting place for their sister, and her Long Sleep continues there today in the shadow of old Stone Mountain, beneath the rich, black-dirt of Vermont.

Many of her circus family hypothesized that it was no doubt wet wires that caused Winona to slip and fall to her death, but why that agile and powerful man employed to catch any falling acrobats had missed by slipping and falling himself, was known only to Grandfather Owl, I guess.

In her preparations to leave, Sarah sold the wagon, some baskets and some of her clothing. She would be traveling light, and heading North.

All of Winona's jewelry was buried with her, for these were personal things that she loved. Sarah kept not one of Winona's things, only Kino the cat, and she cradled him in her arms and wondered how she could tell him that he was alone now.

From a wardrobe attendant Sarah asked for and was brought a large lady's hat box. She cut holes in the sides and cover and sprinkled some catnip in the bottom, and Kino rolled in this and took it for a new bed, and Sarah knew that when she left, Kino would go with her. Her sister would have wanted this.

The second afternoon after her demise, a memorial service was held for Winona and this little group of friends tried in every way to give comfort and sympathy to Sarah.

Chairs were set up in a good-sized tent and the people tried to have Aunt Sarah sit up front, but she would not. Funerals were very uncomfortable to her.

Sarah realized that this was Winona's friends way of showing respect to her and to Winona's spirit, and she was very appreciative of how hard they tried to ease her pain, but they could not, either hers or theirs.

Ian MacWain, that big strong man, was a broken one, and Sarah wept each time she attempted to look into his swollen and red-streaked eyes. She knew that her sister loved Ian — she had even said, "He is the one," and Sarah had anticipated her sister someday leaving circus life to walk the "Marriage Trail" with Ian, but now that young man would walk it with another.

One by one, fellow artists spoke eloquently about Winona that day. In fact, they eulogized her to the point where Sarah felt like looking around her and seeing who they were talking about?

Sarah knew that Winona was a free spirit, some good, some bad, an animal lover, but not a saint by any stretch of the imagination. She was just a young eagle trapped in a woman's body, and that young woman loved life and lived it to the fullest.

If someone had spoken these words about Winona, Sarah would have felt that they really knew her sister better, but no one did.

When the eulogy was accomplished, some praying was done and they all felt sure that Winona's spirit was in Heaven.

Sarah got up quietly. She carried a small valise in one hand and Kino, drunk on catnip, in his traveling-hat-box, in the other. And she slipped away from that memorial service and this circus life, as silent as a shadow.

The sun was setting as she walked along that narrow road, and she could hear in the background broken strains of Ian MacWain's bagpipe, as bits and pieces of "Amazing Grace" filled the cooling air. Fresh tears smarted Sarah's eyes, but she blinked them away.

The wind picked up and whipped her face and made a crying sound, but then a soft and girlish voice too familiar to be the wind, was heard to say "Sarah, he is playing it just for me!" Sarah answered the voice of the crying wind. And, she spoke out loud these words. "Yes, he is playing it just for you!"

She never did look back but kept on walking straight ahead to where her own future lay.

The night stars would be twinkling soon, "and there will be another one up there tonight," she thought. In the distance she could see the lights of a town, and as she walked toward these beacons, the words of the memorial service played heavily on her mind.

It was hard to be torn between the belief of two worlds, and Sarah wondered if Winona's restless spirit really was in heaven? Heaven, like the Happy Hunting Grounds was on the other side, or was it really — the Other Side? But, the question that Sarah's heart had asked, was "Where do Eagle's go?"

This time it was the wind that answered, "Over the Mountains of the Moon.... to the Land Beyond the Stars."

Sarah could smell the smoke and cinders quite some time before she actually approached the railroad station. She had freed Kino from his cage, and while she rested on the roadside, he had scampered away to do his chores.

Sarah ate an apple that she had stashed in her pocket and then called to the cat, and he came running back as fast as his three legs would allow, and she stooped and attached a slim cord to his collar and he reluctantly followed along.

As the station loomed ahead of them, Sarah picked up Kino, removed his tether and placed him back inside the box. She entered the railroad station under the cover of darkness and the flickering light from lamps and lanterns on the inside of that building, was a warm and welcome sight to her. It was a little place, one men's facility, one lady's facility, and an office. Benches lined the tiny waiting room, and Sarah thought that it would be good to sink down on one and sleep for a long time.

She approached the window where a man with little horn-rimmed spectacles, looked at her. He was not used to seeing lone women passengers, this time of night, but all he said was "Where to, Ma'am?" and Sarah answered "Boston, Massachusetts ... your next train, please." The clerk said "You got a four-hour wait or you can put up at the hotel. It's about half a mile from here. You can leave at ten tomorrow morning." Sarah listened and then she replied, "No, I'll go tonight," and taking some money from her purse she asked "How much?"

Once her traveling arrangements were made she took Kino to the lady's room, and there he drank cold water from her cupped hands. Then from her pocket she gave him a piece of cheese, which Kino loved, and when it was gone she took him outside for his toilet. With this done, Sarah put Kino back in his traveling box, returned to the ladies room and washed her hands and freshened up as much as she could.

She was glad no other travelers were here. Returning to the wooden benches Sarah sit down on one. The hat box was beside her and through the holes in the sides she started stuffing more of the hard cheese into Kino's unusual cage. He was hungry and when he had sated his hunger, he settled down and purred himself to sleep. Sarah tried to sit very straight as she waited. Once she tapped on the box because Kino had momentarily woke up and was purring so loud that Sarah was afraid the man in the ticket box would hear him!

The purring stopped and the cat eventually went back to sleep and Sarah, with her feet and her heart both aching, stretched out on the hard bench and did the same thing.

A door shut somewhere and Sarah was instantly awake. She looked around and after a few seconds knew where she was. The station agent had gone out with a lantern to check something.

Sarah opened her valise, took out a shawl, and then closed the valise and placed it up on the bench where she could settle back and rest her head and shoulders on it. She stretched her long legs once again out on that uncomfortable bench and she did not hear the station agent when he came back in, because she was warm and even though this bench was not very comfortable, her body was terribly tired and this wooden bed was fine.

Sometime almost four hours later, a hand touched her shoulder and a man's voice spoke. "Wake up, Ma'am, trains a comin'." And she could not believe that she had spent four hours here until she tried to move, and then with pains in her neck, shoulders and legs she realized she must have.

The train whistled and belched as it came into the station where Sarah and Kino waited. She was wide awake now and so was the cat, and Sarah was hoping that he would be too scared to be any trouble, and he was.

Swinging a lantern, the conductor helped her onto the train and a porter took her valise. She insisted on carrying the hat box herself and he let her. "Women and their foolish Hats!" the porter thought. "Women and their foolish Cats!" is what Sarah was thinking. But she wasn't doing this for herself she was doing it for Winona.

There were very few people on this train, for most of the passengers were in the sleeping car. Sarah contemplated whether she should take a chance on this with the cat, and then decided just to sit down in the comfortable seats with the hat box on her lap. This she did, and in a few short miles, Kino got used to the rumble and sway of the train. He, was after all, used to traveling in a wagon. This train was just a little nosier but the jolting did not cause him too much concern, for he went to sleep again, full of cheese and catnip. He purred softly and then was soon fast asleep and so was his Aunt Sarah, and through the dark night they flew across the land on ribbons of steel. Many hours later they were disembarking at the old South Station in Boston, and Sarah was glad, for this was where her closest family lived and she needed to share her grief and heartbreak with them and to feel their strength at this time. Home was the high bluffs of the upper Connecticut River valley, but today family was in some of the blinking yellow lights, radiating from the buildings gaunt and tall that overlooked the Atlantic Ocean.

Sarah had not seen her brothers in two years, and she wondered how they had changed? And they would have changed, just as she had, for all that was alive was in a constant state of change. Only the dead did not, and when Sarah thought of this, she also thought of Winona, and again tears smarted her eyes.

It was after seven o'clock in the evening when Sarah and Kino hired a surrey to take them in the direction of her brother John's house which was located on a narrow street in Boston's Back Bay section.

On a slip of paper in her purse, Sarah had the address of that house. The driver of the surrey knew this city well and could have taken her directly to the very door, but Sarah was not ready yet, to see her brothers or to see John's wife of two years that she knew only as Lou Ann. No, when she met her family she would not be weary and travel-stained, she would be rested and bathed and presentable.

As they drove past the guest houses and small hotels Sarah told the driver that she would like to spend the night at a decent hotel, not too big or too expensive, but reputable and clean. The driver pulled to the curb and said, "This one is reputable, Ma'am, and reasonable and very clean. My Aunt owns it."

Sarah and Kino got out. She paid the driver and tipped him, and then with the valise in one hand and the hat box or cat box in the other, she started walking towards the hotel in front of her.

As they went along, Sarah was digesting the sounds and sights of this big city by the sea, and she was almost repelled by the odor of it. She knew that the ocean itself has a strange smell to one who comes from the mountains, but this was a rank scent. Boston did what Winona used to say it did — stunk.

As the scent of raw sewerage, decay and sickness intermingled with the natural smells of salt and seaweed, Sarah was glad that her stomach was empty. "Of course! It is their refuse!" she was thinking. What was it about this White race, so smart to invent and downright genius to construct, and so lax as to let their own filth, rot the good earth and all that they have created away? "Smart in books and dumb outside," she thought.

Sarah thought it very sad to see the ruination of another water supply. It was true, the ocean was not a body of water to drink from, but it should be respected, protected and kept clean because it was the Grandfather of all the waters. And if this horrendous outpouring of human and industrial wastes dumped into the ocean was not curbed, then not only fish life but all life that ate of these polluted fish, be it bird or animal or man — was doomed.

Sarah passed people scurrying home, or somewhere. Wagons rattled by her, and none but she seemed to notice the unpleasant smell.

She looked ahead up at the granite steps and then entered the hotel, and when the door closed behind her she was pleased to get inside, out of this unclean air.

As Sarah entered the lobby it seemed somewhat austere at first glance, for the lobby was plain white, softened only by green velvet drapes and a few hanging plants. The stairway was a winding one with a green and gold carpet, and the carpet was well worn but it was clean.

Off to the right-hand side of the lobby were wide open doors leading to a dining room where food was being served, and it smelled very good. Sarah suddenly recognized the aroma of steak sizzling, and she realized that she was famished. Travel and intrigue were taking their toll on her.

Walking to the desk, she asked if she might have a room for the night, and the man at the desk didn't look twice at the hat box, just gave her a book to sign and politely called a stately colored gentlemen to carry her bags up to the third floor.

He, like the train porter, tried to get his paws on her hat box, but

Sarah hung on to this with such a vengeance that the colored man was suspicious, especially, when a loud "MEEEOOOWW" was clearly emitted from the box, when the man was in the process of opening the door for Sarah.

"Oh No!" she thought, but she gave no outward sign. As the white-haired old gentleman helped her inside, with a wide grin on his face he said "What kind of a hat have you got in that box, Ma'am?" Sarah, met his gaze and answered, "A furry one." The man looked down at Sarah and with a straight face asked, "Don't s'pose I did hear that hat Meow!"

"Don't s'pose you did," Sarah countered.

With that the man stepped back and she entered. He sat the valise down and left, his shoulders shaking with laughter. "Whew! Good thing that man likes furry hats, Kino," Sarah said out loud as she looked around the room.

The floor had scatter rugs and there were roses on the papered walls. There was a bureau, a wash stand, and even a tin bathtub in a little alcove that served as the bathroom.

Stepping to the window Sarah could look out over the ocean and see the twinkling lights reflecting on the boundless sea below.

"If they try to throw us out of here tonight," she thought, "they are in for one hell of a fight!"

Sarah freed Kino from his confinement and he scampered out, even more lame than he usually was, but he recovered quickly and landed up on the bed to check things out.

Kicking off her shoes, Sarah unloaded the valise and hung her clothing on hangers and hooks in the closet. Then she found to her complete delight that by simply turning a knob both cold and hot water ran in a swift clear stream into the bathtub. "It looks clean. It smells clean. I'm getting in!" she thought.

Sarah lost no time in climbing into the tub and soaking, and she scrubbed herself with soap, thinking that she had never felt so pampered.

After the bath she smoothed her hair back into its French twist secured by a shell comb, and put on a change of fresh clothing and made her way downstairs to the dining room.

She sat alone and enjoyed her meal. She then felt eyes upon her back and turned to hear a woman say "Charles, I wonder how long she's been in this country? Look at that, more foreigners every day. She is probably a Gypsy."

And Sarah suddenly realized that "she" was the foreigner, but she took no offense. She did not come here to fight, she came to eat and she knew that this poor woman didn't know an original American when she saw one.

Returning to her room, Sarah fed Kino some scraps of meat and ordered a pot of tea, some cookies and a glass of warm milk, these to be delivered to her later that evening.

She turned down the bed covers. Then she opened the widow, and tested the sturdiness of the window box outside. It seemed very strong but the flowers inside were wilted. Sarah picked up the cat and set him in the window box so that he could relieve himself outside in the dirt and also help the flowers grow.

When the tea and cookies arrived Sarah enjoyed them, and she poured most of the warm milk into the saucer of her teacup and put it on the floor for Kino. He lapped the warm milk with slurping sounds. She did not worry about giving this cat soft bowels, for she had plied him with so much catnip and cheese on the way that he was probably plugged tighter than a ward of tobacco.

With the close of this day Sarah climbed into bed, and she fell asleep with the sights and smells of Boston whirling through her head, especially the sound of horses' hoofbeats as they clopped along those streets of cobblestone.

It had rained over night, and Sarah's hard-soled shoes contacted with the cobblestones beneath her feet with a muted sound. With Kino in the hat box, in her left hand and the valise in the right, she made her way along the street that lead to her brother John's home. She passed people on the way, most of them dressed in their Sunday best and on their way to church. They smiled and nodded to Sarah as she passed them and most of the men doffed their tall hats, and Sarah nodded and smiled in a gesture of politeness, thinking "Boston has some good things too!"

Sarah noticed that every woman she passed was wearing a hat. She supposed she should have put one on, but perhaps many of them would think that she was carrying a hat in the hat box — it was a far more likely prospect that a cat.

Toward the end of the street, she saw the house. It was large and needed a fresh coat of paint, but it had a tower than ran up three floors and Sarah thought that it looked like and old enchanted castle.

She knocked on the door and it was opened by a young woman as tall as Sarah herself, with dark brown hair and amber-colored eyes. This must be John's wife, Lou Ann, but before Sarah could speak, the woman said to her. "You must be Sarah! Come in, Sarah, I'm Lou Ann." And Sarah stepped inside, and in the hall light, she could see that John had chosen a very pretty woman to marry. Sarah liked her immediately for her eyes were full of warmth and kindness and she had a lovely smile. She was hospitable and gracious, and this was very good.

"So good to meet you, Lou Ann," Sarah smiled, but then she added, "I have a lazy good-for-nothing friend with me. I could not leave him, she loved that useless rascal so." Already the woman's amber eyes had seen the holes in the cat box, and she gave Sarah a reassuring hug and said, "Of course you couldn't! Bring the bugger in!"

Lou Ann beckoned her guest to follow her, and now Sarah could see that she was not plump at all, she was very pregnant.

"I'll call John and your brothers. On Sunday, I get up and go to church, but they sleep late, you know."

Yes, Sarah knew. Her brothers, like herself, had not been brought up in a religion where people congregated; and perhaps they, much like she, had a hard time remembering very much about early religious teachings at all. And the more the years rolled by, the more this Dawnland Woman came to believe that the God of the Abenakis and the God of the White Man were the same one. After all, there were many trails up the mountain.

Sarah's brother John came down the stairs, and one look at his face told her that he had gotten Brynn Ellingwood's letter, and knew that Winona was gone.

"I'm so sorry, Sarah!" he said, and then he came forward to hug her. "Dennis and Peter will be right down." he said.

Sarah stood back and surveyed her youngest brother. John was a giant of a man. And then she heard Dennis and Peter as they came rushing down the stairs to welcome her.

Sarah lay her head on Dennis's shoulder and he asked her, "Sarah, did she suffer?"

"No." Sarah said and then Dennis asked her "Are you all right Sarah?" and she answered that she was, and then realized that Dennis had grown even taller than John. Sarah was crying then and Peter was hugging her, and poor Peter, he was sobbing openly and Sarah hugged him tight and through her own tears she said "It is all right Peter. She is fine." And Sarah was careful not to use Winona's name so that her spirit would not be disturbed.

"Peter, him not fine, Sister. Peter him want to go home!" was what her slow brother said, and Sarah could see by his eyes that he was not fine, he was terribly unhappy.

"You don't like Boston, Peter?" she wanted to know, and Peter shook his head and said that he did not.

"I work Sarah. I never hunt no more. Peter him don't fish. Ocean him stink. Water dirty and stink and fish don't swim, him float dead on top of water."

And now with tears for Peter, still-the-child as well as for her sister, Sarah spoke. "It is all right, Peter. I'm going home and when I'm settled, I'll send for you. Hear me brother. Sarah promises... Peter will go home."

Dennis always in tune with Sarah's own heart said "I'll take you back with me Peter. We can fish the rivers all the way," and Peter wiped his eyes. He knew that Sarah and Dennis would keep their word, he was going home.

Sarah noted that Dennis was a handsome young man now, and she wondered why some woman had not set her cap for him.

Lou Ann had a chicken in the oven and it smelled very good. At the supper table that night, John and Dennis spoke about their work. Then thinking about Winona, John said, "I feel bad. The last time I saw her she said that I was pompous and surly, and I said that she was spoiled rotten." Sarah looked up and said, "Well Brother, neither one of you was lying!"

And then this little family began to laugh and in good conscience too. In fact, if she had been there no one would have laughed any harder than Winona herself.

It was good, they were eating together as a family and they had cried together and laughed together and accepted truth together, just as they had accepted this life of constant change and conversion, trying to be something that they never would — part of the great White circle.

This was not a sad thing, it was the way things were. And these remnants of the Bear Clan, these People of the Dawnland -Abenakis like their father, and his father and all the grandfathers before that, knew whose moccasins had roamed and whose tongues had named, the rivers and mountains and the valleys of New England, long before the White Man came to see — and change it for all time.

The two-day visit in Boston had turned into a full three-week stay for Sarah, because on the second evening following her arrival Lou Ann went into a lengthy labor.

A doctor had been called and he promptly appeared on the scene, but he had checked Lou Ann over and said it would be a long labor, and then he was content to sit with his feet propped up in front of the fireplace and let nature take its course.

Sarah agreed to help the doctor, and it was she and not he who stayed at the bedside, and lent her support to the mother-to-be.

Sarah was not unaccustomed to birthing, but she never got used to the way a woman was usually at the mercy of a man-doctor, who hadn't any idea of what she was going through. Not only that, but the woman was always laid out in bed, flat on her back, where she couldn't help herself at all to do what should have been the natural thing, give birth. Often Sarah wondered whether it was harder on the mother or on the baby.

Lou Ann was very brave and John remained calm, and the doctor would leave the fireside once in a while and go and check the patient. He ordered Sarah to boil water, three large kettles full, and so she did his bidding and the top of the stove was full of large pots of boiling water and the kitchen was full of steam. Sarah was thinking that this doctor was full of something else! She had acted many times as a nurse and midwife, but not for a man of medicine that she really did not like. His detached attitude had Sarah boiling harder than the water after about four hours of Lou Ann's suffering, with no change in sight.

Lou Ann's hair was wet and perspiration ran in drops down her face, and she bit her lips to keep from crying and they were swollen and bled some. As the labor increased Sarah realized that this woman should be working with her pains, but the doctor felt that she had a ways to go yet. He plunked himself back down in front of the hearth again to wait a little longer.

Sarah remembered a thick black syrup that Aunt Nel carried when she was mid-wifing. This was administered carefully and given only in the case of a difficult delivery. An effective medication (only snakes blood and water) it was commonly taken in earlier times by Indian mothers prior to birth. And it usually ensured an easy delivery. Right now Sarah wished that she had some of that tonic to give to her sister-in-law, since her attending physician had nothing helpful to offer.

Squeezing Sarah's hands with a force that left them aching and numb, Lou Ann cried, "Help me Sarah!" and Sarah answered, "I'm going to Lou, right now!" And heading toward the window, Sarah tore off a sturdy cord that held back the lower tier of the curtain. Sarah looped it over the foot of the bed, and instructed Lou Ann to pull on the cord as hard as she could and to push at the same time with every contraction. Brave Lou Ann began to do this, stopping in between pains to rest and to breathe. And by the time the doctor next stuck his head into the room, the baby was nearly out in the world. Seeing the head in sight, the doctor went right to work, and as the mother-to-be worked the cord and pulled and pushed, in short order the doctor handed Sarah a red and screaming female baby.

"Is it a boy, Sarah? John wants a boy!" an exhausted young mother wanted to know, and Sarah, taking the new life away to be cleaned and wrapped in soft blankets, only smiled and whispered, "No! It's better than that! This is a raven-haired girl child, pretty as a rosebud."

As he finished attending to Lou Ann, the doctor seemed to notice the cord attached to the foot of the bed for the first time. "What in hell is this?" he asked.

"It is a birthing rope. It helps a baby to be born sooner." Sarah said. The doctor snorted, but gave no other answer as Aunt Sarah placed the tiny pink woman-child upon its mother's breast. Sarah smiled at the little Rosebud, her first-born blood niece. She was really an Aunt now, really.

Daylight was breaking as the doctor departed. John came into the bedroom and looked into the face of his daughter, and suddenly he forgot that he had ever desired a boy. She not only was his daughter, but she beautiful and perfect in every way.

Later, as Lou Ann slept, John and Sarah went down to the kitchen were many of the pots on the stove were still bubbling.

"What in hell will we do with all this boiling water?" her brother asked, and Sarah looked at him for a long minute and then with a mischievous grin tugging at the corners of her lips answered, "Well, John...I can make us some tea!"

They laughed together and Sarah made the tea, and they sat down to relax and enjoy it. "Thank you for being here, Sarah," he said, "I know that you did not like the doctor."

She sipped her tea and replied, "I never trust a guy with a woodchuck face, John." Her brother snorted with humor. She was so like Dennis, who was always describing people as looking like animals or other things, like that man "Fish Face Jones" they worked with or "Hog Chops Hansen," another acquaintance. The awful reality of these nicknames was that Jones had a Fish Face and Hansen had Hog Chops, and come to think of it that useless damned doctor did resemble a Woodchuck!" "Indian Names!" John thought.

That afternoon, John and Lou Ann named their woman child, Ivy Rose, because she was as fresh as spring ivy and she was as pretty as a rosebud.

This day had been a long one, but it was so good to be needed. And it was more than good to be an Aunt.

Sarah lay down on the bed in the tower bed room and she didn't even turn the covers down.

She closed her eyes and the face of her younger sister drifted in the mist before her and Sarah's tired eyes once more filled with tears. She thought she had no more to shed, but she was wrong.

Then Winona's beautiful face was replaced by another beautiful face....by the face of little Ivy Rose. And the Jackson family circle had not ended, it had grown bigger.

Why was it that so often within a family, a death would be immediately followed by a birth?

Like phantom ghosts the faces whirled above Sarah's head, and then like wisps of smoke from a wood fire rising, these apparitions faded slowly into nothingness, only to reappear again and again until exhaustion and a gentle sleep finally overtook her.

In these last minutes of consciousness, Sarah remembered as she lay there, an ancient family saying. So many times, Aunt Nelemano had repeated it to Sarah, "In life it happens...One comes....One goes."

As Lou Ann recovered from Ivy Rose's birth, a strong and lasting respect and friendship formed between her and Sarah.

The new mother tried to teach Sarah some fancy sewing stitches, and Sarah promised to help Lou Ann construct a basket. Lou Ann was up and walking at the end of the first week. She was an accomplished seamstress, and in her gentle way, she made Sarah aware that her years of circus life had played havoc with her wardrobe.

"Sarah, you are so pretty, we have got to get you a new dress!" Lou Ann had insisted. John had tried to pay Sarah for staying on as a nurse for mother and baby, but she refused. Lou Ann, however, explained that if Sarah wouldn't let her buy her a new dress for all her hard work that Lou Ann would feel very hurt, and so Sarah agreed.

At the end of Sarah's third and final week in Boston, Lou Ann left John in charge of the baby for a little while and she and Sarah went by carriage to a dress shop not too far from home.

It was not until she walked inside that Sarah realized just how far out of style she was. Lou Ann had impeccable taste and showed Sarah several dresses that would look good on her, and Sarah was pleased, for she had never before had a friend to ask about women's things. Of course she had her best friend Brynn, but Brynn was just as ignorant about being "in style" as Sarah herself was.

Not since Aunt Nel, had Sarah found another female that she trusted enough to ask for "womanly advice" until she met Lou Ann.

The styles of the dresses were varied and the colors were beautiful, but Sarah saw one dress that seemed to speak to her. It was bone-colored and made almost of solid lace. The collar was medium high with small seed pearls and mutton-leg styled sleeves that tapered to fit the wrists, which were also studded with tiny seed pearls. It had a tight-fitting bodice and nipped in at the waist, then fell flat again over the hips and was complete with a bustle in the back. And tiers of lace had been used to make up the front of this beautiful garment.

"This is it!" thought Sarah, and then she wondered if Lou Ann would approve? She was about to point this dress out to Lou Ann, who was looking through racks of dresses and gowns, but suddenly, she fished this dress out and held it up and asked "Sarah, what about this one?"

"It is beautiful," whispered Sarah."

"This dress is elegant, Sarah. In fact, it is so nice that it could be used as a wedding dress, with the proper head piece." And as she said this, Lou Ann with her head full of knowledge about fabrics that only a seamstress has, examined the dress with her eyes and her hands.

"What kind of head piece?" Sarah asked and at the questioning look in Sarah's eyes Lou Ann smiled and said, "It needs a hat dear, with wide lace ties, for it is too fancy to wear without one."

This almost spoiled the dress because Sarah the child who loathed hats was now Sarah the woman that still hated to wear one. As her face dropped Lou Ann quickly said "Well Sarah you can always take the hat off," and then these two began to laugh.

Sarah took the dress and headed for the changing room. It was the only one they had, so if it didn't fit that was it; but it did. She stared at her reflection in the mirror and she was pleased at what she saw. The slender young woman looking back at her was a pretty one and she looked as though she belonged in this fancy dress.

Before she could remove the garment, the clerk came and tapped on the dressing room door, explaining that the lady with her wished that she try on this hat, along with the dress. Sarah opened the door and the pale young woman handed her a huge hat, complete with wide lace ties, and when she stood with it on her head, she did remind herself of a bride but more so of a fine lady, who lived in a house with a tower that overlooked the sea.

Once outside the new dress, Sarah complained to Lou Ann that the hat and the dress added up to a price that she considered ridiculous and said she could not accept such a gift from John and Lou Ann.

Lou smiled at her and said, "It is from Ivy! She was making a tough entrance into this world, Sarah and you made her work and her mother's work easier. And besides I have a special discount because I do alterations in my home for this shop. All things considered it is a very affordable price." Lou commented.

Sarah felt that it was still too expensive a gift, but Lou Ann reminded her that "it wouldn't seem right to turn down a gift from her first-born niece, and with that, Sarah agreed to it, and went happily home with her sister-in-law.

That evening as they visited by the fire Sarah smiled and said, "I'll save that dress for my wedding, Lou Ann."

Lou Ann looked up from her sewing and remarked, "Good, dear. I found the right dress, now you find the right man, or have you one in mind already?"

Sarah had not heard Dennis walk into the room and so with a girlish giggle she said "Well, I got asked, but I turned him down. John, his name was John." Sarah was visibly blushing and Lou Ann was beaming, and then from behind Sarah a voice said, "Well, if his last name was Somers, I'm damned glad that you did." Sarah and Lou Ann both looked up startled, and anger flashed suddenly across Sarah's crimson face. This was out of character for Dennis, not with brother John, but surely for Dennis.

She turned a cool eye upon him as he stood there and she simply said "You never did like John Somers, Dennis. Why do you dislike that man so?" Dennis took his place in an overstuffed chair, stretched his long legs and said, "He is a no account, Sarah! You can do better than that!" And now Sarah was very angry. It was none of her brother's business who she selected for friends or husbands.

"Dennis, he is always a gentleman in my presence, sober and very respectful. I said 'No,' this time but when I say 'Yes,' to him or to anyone else, it will be because of what I think they are, not what you think they are, Dennis."

As the sparks of tension filled the air Lou Ann stood abruptly and said she would check on Ivy and she departed from the room.

Dennis looked hard at Sarah, and he would not change his mind but he did say, "Sarah, it is not that I think so little of him, it is because I think so much of you. And no, I do not like him."

Sarah understood. Dennis was telling the truth and Dennis was entitled to his opinion and that was that in his mind's eye: John Somers was not good enough for her. She faced Dennis squarely and asked, "Dennis, is it because he is a half-breed that you don't like him?" Her brother shook his head sadly and replied, "No Sarah, it is because he is half drunk most of the time and that is why I don't like him." Don't settle for a drunk, Sarah!"

She did not answer Dennis. His mind was made up. Sarah felt tears stinging her eyes. She wanted to tell her brother that he was wrong about this man John, because with all of his faults, she felt that John Somers was not a "no account"—for her he was right.

John and Lou Ann Jackson made their entrance into the living room and Dennis and Sarah dropped the subject.

The next evening Sarah announced to her family that Sunday she was heading for Vermont. She would stop and see her cousin Nancee, whom she had not seen for years, and she wanted to make that stop before she returned home to Lunenburg, Vermont.

Lou Ann questioned, "Sarah, what is up there, dear? You could make your baskets and sell them to the shops and stores here. Boston is really a good place to live. Why don't you stay with us. We have the room and we would love to have you."

Sarah smiled and thanked them and then something rolled from her lips, that she had not intended, but was true in every sense.

"Thank you, I appreciate that generous offer, but I am like Peter, I guess. The Connecticut River valley is my home. It calls out to me and I want to go there," said Sarah. Dennis spoke then, "I have been making payments on a farm in Lunenburg for some time now. In less than a year it will be mine and I will also be going home."

Sarah nodded her head and said," We are brothers of the salmon, Dennis. And the salmon always go home." Then she added, "This salmon goes home Sunday and when she is settled, she will send for Peter."

As Peter sat quietly in the shadows he smiled broadly. He could almost taste a freshwater trout now, and speaking of salmon, the Connecticut River around Guildhall, Vermont was probably still full of them.

The Saturday night before she left, John announced that he had made plans to take them all out that evening to a Chinese restaurant. Sarah looked at him with a smile on her face. She loved to try new food, in fact she loved most any food... that she didn't have to cook.

Lou Ann's sister had offered to stay with Ivy Rose, so that John and Lou Ann could have this family evening out and so the gala feast approached. And this Native American family went out to dine on the cuisine of a Chinese American family, and from the moment they entered the establishment, Sarah thought that it was not only decorated beautifully with dragons and hand-painted lamps, but it smelled wonderful! The scent of garlic and ginger from the kitchen, mixed with other wonderful and enticing aromas, set the water running in her mouth. She never knew that food could smell this good.

Lou Ann, however, did not share her eager appetite. The English roots of John Jackson's wife made her a selective eater. She was slow to try new cooking ideas and she had heard bad stories about Chinese cooking, and not knowing any Chinese people, she was quite suspicious.

The tea arrived and all partook of that, and then one by one the dishes began arriving, some flaming and others covered with silver domes, and Sarah tried each and every dish. And looking over to where Lou Ann sat picking at a chicken wing, Sarah questioned "Lou, do you mean you do not like this food?"

"No. Some is very good. It is just that I heard that they use cats in it," said Lou Ann almost in a hushed whisper.

Dennis snorted out to keep from laughing and Peter put down a fork full of food.

John watched Sarah as she was greedily eating and then he said, "Now, tell me Sarah, you have heard what Lou was told... do you in fact, think that you are eating a cat?"

Chewing her food and relishing it, Sarah gave John a long look and said "Well, If I am....they got it fixed good!"

Dennis and Peter had bought Sarah a larger valise, one that would hold all of her clothing, including the new outfit, all but the hat, and that had to be carried in its own hat box. Now Sarah was carrying two hat boxes, one with a hat, and one with a cat, inside. She had chosen not to leave Kino in Boston. Her family had been good to the animal. They had fed him well and let him in and out of the house at will, but he had not taken to any of them. And he searched each stranger's face for that of Winona's. That was the real reason that Sarah carried the beast along with her. She laughingly told her family that "if she left him there, he might wind up in a chow mein," but that was not the real reason.

Sarah boarded a train headed inland for Springfield across the state, and the first town over the Massachusetts and Vermont border was where she was headed.

Her cousin Nancee was married to a man named George Mc....something. Sarah could not remember, but she knew that in her letters Nancee had called him a kind Irishman, and asked if she ever ventured her way to please stop. Sarah was pleased that Nancee had been taught to write.

It was going on the first week of April, as Sarah walked down that country road. She could see wisps of wood smoke rising from the chimney of the sugar house up ahead. There were patches of snow and chunks of ice and mud all along the sides of the narrow, dirt road. She had passed a couple of farms where the smell of manure was rank, but that is how home was supposed to smell in the early spring, if your home was a farm in the Green Mountain state.

At the second farmhouse she rested and drank some water from the dipper at the well. Her larger valise was heavier and the two large hat boxes were cumbersome and hard to carry. Sarah was pleased when she was told by the farmer's wife that George and Nancee McKosh, lived just about a half a mile ahead. That was good, her feet were getting tired and Kino was starting to cause trouble in the box. Sarah couldn't blame the cat, he'd been a hat too long.

It was nearly supper time when Sarah walked up the driveway leading to a small white house. She rapped on the door and as she waited, she gazed at the red barn, a chicken coop and some fertile pastures beyond. And then soundlessly the door opened and Sarah stepped back, not quite prepared for what she saw.

There in the doorway looking directly at her was Nancee, only it was like looking into the face of Winona.

Nancee pushed a strand of greying hair back from her face and then she smiled broadly and in a voice that even sounded like Winona Jackson's she cried "Oh Sarah...It is You!" And then Nancee hugged her cousin Sarah and helped her get her luggage inside.

Sarah entered under an air of deja vu, for Nancee's walk and talk and appearance was that of a woman that Sarah knew was dead. "I have a cat with me. It was my sister's. Will I leave him outside, Nancee?"

"No, bring him in. I like all animals and so does George," the hostess answered, and so Sarah entered and then opened up the hat box and Kino jumped out. He too had noticed the sound of that voice, and he walked up to Nancee and began to rub around her legs, singing loudly.

When she and Sarah sat down, Kino made a leap and landed squarely in Nancee's lap, and she laughed and gave him a hug. "Oh, what a friendly kitty," she said, but Sarah knew much better. He was a stand-offish cuss.

Kino sat contentedly and let Nancee pat him and then he climbed up and draped himself around her shoulders. She laughed and said, "It is good I haven't got a cat!" and Sarah was thinking "You do now."

Once inside, Sarah discovered that the house was much larger than it had first appeared when she had walked down the driveway lined with sugar maples, each one wearing a sap bucket.

The sink had a pump that could be primed into spouting a good-sized stream of cold water. This could soon be heated in the reservoir on the side of the huge wood-burning stove in the kitchen.

The ceilings were high and the furnishings were simple, nothing like the houses in Boston, but it was the kind of house that Sarah was very comfortable in because it was Vermont-like and homey.

Nancee helped Sarah to carry her valise and the other hat box up the stairs to the one guest room. From the small window panes they could look across a field and see a maple orchard, and from somewhere hidden in the middle of it, a stream of white steam rose silently into the sky.

"George, he is boiling. Little Georgianne, she is five, and she goes wherever her father goes," the young mother smiled.

When they returned downstairs, Nancee made tea for them and Sarah was aware of a wonderful smell coming from the oven of the stove. "Is that apple pie?" she asked and Nancee said "Yes, it is George's favorite." She removed it from the oven and it was a golden pie, very high and smelling of sweet cinnamon.

From a pantry off to the right of the kitchen, Nancee came back carrying a baking dish filled with chicken and gravy. She let this get hot on the woodstove, and then added fresh biscuits to the top of the chicken and gravy mixture. And just before she put it into the already hot oven, she took from a jar some spearmint leaves, crushed them in her hands and then sprinkled them over the biscuits that topped this chicken pie. Sarah had not seen anyone do that since Aunt Nel, and when she spoke of this, saying that most cooks used poultry seasoning, Nancee said "It is Aunt Nel's recipe."

This warmed Sarah's heart. It was good to see that all of the old ways were not gone, for this one and many other good recipes were well worth keeping; some for cooking and some for medicine.

As Nancee worked preparing supper, Sarah went to the sink and washed her hands and helped to wash the potatoes that were put into the oven to bake.

She was still having a hard time to fathom just how much Nancee was like Winona. She had the same quick movements, and when she laughed Sarah had to look sharply at her, for the overall resemblance was uncanny. And yet it was not such a bad feeling either.

Whatever this strange likeness was, Kino the cat sensed it too, because he followed Nancee around the kitchen and Sarah knew that he at last had adopted a new owner. In Nancee's overall likeness Kino had found another Winona.

"Poor thing. He is probably hungry," said Nancee as she poured the cat a dish of milk.

While the biscuits browned, Nancee explained to Sarah that she and George were married over ten years before they had the one girl child, Georgianne. "She is willful, Sarah! I told her recently about the Swamp Creature, so as to discipline her, and she said to me, "He don't scare me! If he comes after me Ma', I'll whip his ugly butt!" And both women had to laugh.

Nancee went on, "George, he loves her dearly, but she has a wild streak in her, and not from him either. Not from me, Sarah. I don't know where it comes from?" "I do!" thought Sarah but she smiled and said nothing, for it seemed that even if Nancee had Winona's looks, it was Georgianne that had her defiant spirit.

As the teakettle sang, Sarah thought this was an orderly and a happy house. "George is good to you then, Nancee?" asked Sarah. And her cousin answered "George is the best, Sarah! His mother did not want him to marry an... Indian, but when she met me she changed her mind. It was either accept me or —loose George."

When supper was ready, the two women wrapped it in heavy dishes and towels and placed it in a basket. Then they walked toward the thin column of steam pouring up from the sugar orchard.

"We will eat down there, with George. And Sarah you will like him. And you may even like our Georgianne, if she is in a decent mood," Nancee said, and Sarah again thought, "Yes, I know the type" but she said nothing.

As they walked along, Sarah was so pleased that she was back in Vermont, at least for the end of sugar season. They passed a stand of evergreens and Sarah inhaled that fragrant air. And as they neared the little grey building, which was the sugar house, the smell of sap boiling was a wonderful one.

"George taught me to read and to write." Nancee laughed, and then she said in a hush, "He said, 'You are a fine Lady, Nan, and you are going to know how to read and to write,' and that George, he always keeps his word."

A warm smile crossed Sarah's face. Her own heart was very glad that Nancee had such a fine man for a husband. She remembered the days of her early childhood and that Council Meeting, where Nancee's first husband skulked away just before he got his throat cut.

"It was good that Nancee had a real-man now and not one who 'dirtied her path.'" Sarah was thinking.

As they entered the small steam-filled building, George came forward and extended a big, hard-working hand to Sarah. He was tall and lanky, with a long English upper lip and a fine Irish smile that told Sarah that she was indeed welcome.

"Nice to meet you Sarah. We don't see many of Nan's relatives! Hope you like maple syrup!" And Sarah explained that she did and that it was nice to meet him also.

Georgianne, looked more like an elf than a child, was what Sarah's initial thought was. She was tiny, with coal black hair and an upturned nose, that shouldn't be on the descendant of a Taxos, (Wolf) but neither should those flashing eyes of her's that were as violet as could be! "What an Imp!" thought Sarah, and then she sat down at a make-shift board table, across from the child's father and ate from a tin plate. She could see that George also had those violet eyes. Georgianne was not deja vu, she was like spring, a future promise.

"Georgianne, this is your Aunt Sarah," the Elf's mother said, and then she went on, "She has been with the circus!" With this, little Georgianne stopped eating on her biscuit and asked, "Was you a clown?" And when she could stop her laughing Sarah answered, "Well, I tried sometimes, but no, I really wasn't a clown." And her cousin was very embarrassed, but Sarah being Sarah, and loving to see why children thought what they thought, pursued the matter good-naturedly, "What made you think I was a clown? I'll bet it was my hair or my clothes!" And the child flashed a grin at her Aunt Sarah and answered "Nope! You have crinkly eyes at the corners. All clowns have crinkly eyes." And as the adults at the table laughed again, Nancee served the apple pie and tried to change the subject. And once again Aunt Sarah marvelled because children saw so clearly.

George went up toward the barn with a lantern to do the evening chores, and Sarah and Nancee replaced him and tended the boiling sap. It would bubble up and froth and one of them would put a dash of cream into it and it would go back down into the evaporator, and by the time George returned, Georgianne was asleep on a bench, and Sarah would soon be helping to strain the fresh-poured maple syrup. It was late before this task was done. George stayed at the sugar house and Sarah and Nancee and Georgianne went back to the farm house.

Sarah had not been so happy with the sounds and smells of life around her for a long, long time. Aunt Nel used to boil sap outside, but being in a real sugar house was a special thing, and Sarah was so glad that she had made this stop.

Once the Elf was in bed, Sarah and Nancee had some tea and visited a while. "You have a good life, Nancee, I am glad for you." Sarah spoke these words from the heart, and Nancee smiled and said "Forgetting my heritage at first was hard. I felt dumb in George's world, but now I can't really remember anything else." "I know," said Sarah, "the only way to go is forward, and when you do, you have to leave the past behind, leave what you are behind. And, I do most of the time, but once in a while something comes back to me. I remember enough of the old ways to know that some of that life was good, very good and it should not all be forgotten."

Nancee nodded and then rose to put more wood in the fireplace. She had asked Sarah to stay for a week, but Sarah had said "three days."

Sarah carried the lamp up the stairs to where she would sleep, and she poured water from the wash basin and washed the sweat and steam from her face and neck and hands. It was late and she was tired, but she felt somehow renewed and determined to go ahead on her own, even more so now. She walked an unknown trail, but she had no fear of that path. And she knew that she would walk it well.

She called to Kino, but the cat would not come up to bed. He was going to follow Nancee to bed, and Sarah smiled. This was the first night since her sister's departure from this earth, that Sarah had not cried herself to sleep, and this was good. Winona's most beloved earthly-possession had found himself a home of his own choosing. And Sarah knew that she herself, must do the same. Aunt Sarah smiled and felt at peace.

She was not lost, she was going where her heart had always been. And the sweetgrass of the Connecticut River valley was calling her back home.

Sarah rested her back against the seat, and the locomotive rumbled along in a northerly direction. George, Nancee and Georgianne (that elf) were the last three figures to be seen as the train departed from the station. These people became smaller and smaller still, until they diminished into dots and then could no longer be seen at all.

Looking around her, Sarah noted that some of the travelers in this passenger car looked tired and others seemed either to be nervous or perhaps were bored to be going to a destination that they did not wish to go to. In Sarah's case this was not so, for when the train whistled and rolled on toward the way of the Northern Lights, her young heart soared.

The train was now not awfully far from White River Junction, and the railroad tracks ran high along the ridge of steep and rocky bluffs overlooking the rugged terrain below. The Connecticut River and the White River raced and roared along, each a swirling mass of thunderous foam, that splashed high against the ledge-lined banks. A little further along these two rival waters would clash head on. "A powerful hand had carved this valley," Sarah thought.

As a small child, Sarah had camped with her family along both these rivers, but she could not remember this, only what she had been told — that here the fish were fat and plentiful and there were many different species. However, the sweetgrass was more bountiful and better suited to the soil farther on up the valley.

The windows were misting from the cold. And raw raindrops spattered against the outside panes this April day. But inside, steam was building on the glass, and it was warm and would have been a pleasant journey if not for the fat and balding man a few seats ahead who reeked of cigars. The aroma of tobacco especially when mixed with sumac, was not unpleasant to Sarah, and the Great Spirit received his messages on wings of smoke, but the frazzled and nauseating stub protruding from the obese fellow's drooping mouth smelled so bad that it would have run a skunk off the trail! It would take him a few minutes to stink up the dining car, Sarah reasoned and she headed for it at a gallop. It was strange that people who puffed those odorous "Headache Makers" didn't realize that they themselves smelled of these all the time, whether smoking or not, because that disgusting aroma adhered itself to the hair and the clothing of the cigar smoker. She decided if that man sat down beside her that she would ask him to please move. If he refused, she would be less polite and more firm. The more severe her headache became the more Sarah thought about staging an Elf attack, "Whipping his ugly butt, and throwing him and his cigar off the damned train!"

As she moved toward the dining car, Sarah saw that the cause of her headache and discomfort was sitting with his head down on his chest, apparently asleep. "No such luck that he'd be dead!" said a voice inside her head.

Aunt Nel used to say, "The Indian smokes at evening ceremonies, but the White Man never stops, he puffs day and night blowing hot air to the wind!" Sarah smiled. Her Aunt Nel on this subject was very prejudiced, and also very right.

It was another change the world had lived through, for smoking was now a big part of the White culture, and it was not ceremonial, it was debilitating. It was another pollutant of clean air. Sarah sighed. Could she expect any less from a carefree race that polluted the water and the earth....why not the air too? It was sad to think, however, that as brilliant and scholarly as this White race was, these people were not smart enough to know that their abusive treatment of their own bodies and of nature, made them a threat to themselves and to all other living things.

"Waste not...want not," so said their text books, and it was true, for there was nothing that they did not want, or nothing that they would not waste — to attain their many wants.

Sitting alone at a table, Sarah gently massaged her throbbing temples and decided that she would stop trying to make sense out of the world of either the White or the Red Man. She was not a philosopher, she was a simple woman who made baskets and healed the sick when she could. And she also thanked a higher order every day of her life that she was able to do that.

A soft masculine voice beside her shoulder said "Would you mind if I shared your table, Miss?" Shaken from her thoughts, Sarah surveyed his yellow hair which was the color of corn silk. He was tall and a bit on the thin side, with pale blue eyes deeply set in a kind and honest face.

Sarah agreed, and as he seated himself he spoke " I am Dr. Stephen J.

Brayden. I'm from Massachusetts and I am on my way to White River Junction, Vermont, to open a new practice."

Sarah smiled. He didn't look old enough to be a Medicine Man, but he was carrying a black bag. "I am Sarah Jackson. I'm going home."

With this introduction done, Sarah's eyes flew to the menu, and that bill of fare had many inviting things to tempt the palate.

Perhaps if she ate something her headache would stop. It was already too late to enjoy the meal of pot roast, she was contemplating, because "Old Stinky" waddled past her table and he had to walk sideways so that his huge belly did not rub against it. He was like a big ugly roll of tobacco on the move.

The young man sitting with her went on to say. "I saw you get on the train. Is this area the home you speak of or is your home a long ways from here?"

Sarah cocked her head at him and replied, "Yes, I am on my way to northern Vermont. I have been away a long time. I am an herbalist and a basket maker."

The personable doctor thought that this was a rare trade, but then this confident young woman with poise and grace was also rare, and somehow special.

The young man ate a minute and then said, "My wife died. My mother lives alone in White River Junction. The house is big, it will be a fresh start for me."

And now Sarah could see in his face the sadness that she had felt about him, even as he sat down. He was also going to a new life and taking each step in sorrow.

Sarah nodded her head but said nothing. He liked this, liked the idea of having someone to talk to, but someone who wasn't full of questions for him about why his wife died, how she died and so on. This woman was a very good listener, and at this point in his life, Dr. Brayden could appreciate this. His mother, when he arrived, would expect to know every last detail, and he dreaded this.

"A doctor is always welcome anywhere," Sarah commented, and the young man smiled and replied, "Except for that strange lot who don't believe in them."

Sarah met his eyes squarely and said, "Most believe. My Grandmother was a Shaman, a Medicine Woman, and my Aunt was a fine herbalist. I dabble in this field some because I know so many gifts of medicine are waiting for us in the earth."

The young doctor smiled and Sarah noted that it was a nice smile, easy and gentle. "I'm pleased to know you, Miss Sarah," he said, and then continued, "I'm fascinated by herbal science."

This subject broke the ice between them, and they remained across the table and visited long after their plates were empty. "I wish you were going to be staying in the White River area," he told Sarah, and she was sure that he was speaking what he felt, but Sarah planned only a one-night stop in that railroad town, and she politely excused herself. He rose to his feet in a gesture of respect when she made her exit. Stephen looked after her. She had caught his eye the minute she had boarded the train. Her hair, the color of a crow's wing, was beautiful. She however, was not beautiful, but she was pretty and wholesome, with those lady-like qualities that all men like to be readily seen, in a lady of their choosing. "She is pretty, almost regal," he mused.

She was an Indian. Stephen knew this, but she was intelligent and sitting across from her he had enjoyed not only the sight of her and the sounds of her but also the very smell of her, because she was bare of the scent of perfume. This woman would always smell of hay and clover and sweetgrass and he found this somehow intoxicating.

White River Junction loomed up ahead. In the dark of early evening they would be disembarking at the station.

Sarah retrieved her luggage, and walked straight ahead for the hotel. "Sarah, can I help you with that?" she heard him ask and then this young physician took up her luggage as well as his own. She thought he was very kind — the type of man that should be a doctor.

He walked Sarah to the hotel, and then left for his mother's home. Sarah could tell that he liked her, really liked her, and she also liked him, but there was no magic between them.

The next morning her Aunt Belle Capineau would pick her up with a horse and buggy and she would stay at the Capineau farm for one day and night and then continue her journey north.

Ironically she and Aunt Belle, who was really a second cousin, were just leaving the general store, when the door opened and a young man emerged. He was helping a frail and noisy, elderly woman down the steps. As they walked past the wagon where Sarah and Aunt Belle sat, the young man said "Mother this is Sarah, the basket maker and herbalist, that I spoke of." Then with a wide smile on his face he said "Mother, this is my friend Sarah Jackson."

This young man was obviously smitten with young Sarah, but his mother, a stern-faced woman with a long thin neck, was squinting her bird-like eyes and surveying the young woman in the wagon. And she was seeing things that she liked and things that she did not. "Hello Miss Jackson," she said, and Sarah nodded to her, her own eyes never wavering. The older woman liked the looks of the girl. She liked the proud face in general and the way Sarah held her head and she approved of the stubborn chin, but when she spoke, it was only of what was unacceptable to her, the skin color. And Sarah heard the biting sting of prejudice in the woman's voice as she gently reproached her son, with a disdainful sigh that finished, "Stephen, she is an Indian!"

Her appraisal complete, the old matriarch had to her way of thinking, seen it all and heard it all and said all that was necessary to say to her son. She turned away, and he helped her to her waiting carriage.

Sarah could not hear what the young man said, but she knew that he was arguing in her defense and she knew that he was angry. Walking back to where she sat, he was red faced and he spoke very nervously, "Sarah, please don't mind Mother."

Sarah smiled warmly at him and replied "I don't. You tell her she is right, Dr. Stephen... I am an Indian ..... and I'm very proud of it."

Aunt Belle, two-hundred and fifty pounds of solid ugly, grunted to the horses and they started, driving out of town and out of the lives of a very nice young man and his worried mother.

For a long time neither woman said anything, and then Aunt Belle declared, "Sarah, a doctor is a good catch!"

With no change of expression Sarah said, "For someone. Not for Sarah."

Then she looked at her Aunt Belle and said "This Indian Sarah....just threw him back to his Mama!"

Aunt Belle and Sarah laughed together now, for they both knew that White women were notorious for being overly protective as well as strict disciplinarians of their little boys, so as to make them better men. And they also had a reputation of never letting them go! The price of manhood, no doubt.

The ride from White River Junction to St. Johnsbury, Vermont had been a good one, and Sarah did not mind the constant movement of the locomotive. It sure beat a circus wagon.

From the windows of that train, she could see that it was definitely an April landscape on both sides of her. The rivers were high, some open and some still laden with chunks of solid ice and unmelted snow. The grass had not yet turned green, it still looked golden-brown, the color it was after the moon of harvest.

The mountains rose high above her, and there was something strong and vital about them that said, "I am strong, a survivor of wind and rain and snow. I will always be here."

These mountains displayed the color green in very direction. They were heavy with evergreen trees, which had given Vermont the name, "The Green Mountain State," but long before that time, her people called it Abenakis — "Dawnland."

Gazing up the sides of the natural elevations, toward their summits she could see the maple and the beechnut and the mountain ash trees, all still standing bare of leaves, for it was just a tad too soon for these to dawn their early robes of lime green.

This was the moon when the sap was running, and after that moon would come the Leafing Season. This was spring, and it was the best time of the year, Sarah thought, for there was nothing under your feet, nor on all sides of you, that was not already growing and getting bigger.

Walking along with her valise and her huge hat box, Sarah looked around at St. Johnsbury, and it had changed. She had not imagined that it would be this size! The last time she saw it she was a child, and just as she had grown so had this pretty town, circled by rolling hills. There were new streets and houses under construction. Sarah heard dogs barking, and her eyes were drawn to the tall church spires and steeples. These would not change. They were like the mountains, tall and proud with a quiet and enduring strength, just like the people who worshipped therein.

Here and there as she made her way along, shifting her load, Sarah could see small dandelions, not yet as big as the palm of her hand, but they were already trying to poke their curious heads out of the rich, black dirt of Vermont.

Sarah chuckled. She was glad to see them, and she didn't even like them. She was glad to smell sap in the air and even the stench of spring mud beneath her feet.

Now outside and closer to mountains rising in the background, she could see that the poplar trees were already starting to fill out, and these were the first of all the trees to leap into this time called ... spring.

She carried the hat box until she came to a narrow street, and then she put it on top of her head and carried it just like she did her baskets on the way to market.

Once in a while a stranger would pass her by and give her a strange look but that was all. They went their way and she went hers, and that was another thing she always liked about Vermont. "Live and Let Live."

Sarah did not realize how late it was in the afternoon, until a group of school children romped past her on their way home. They carried books, books that would teach them many things that Sarah would never know, and perhaps even some things that she would not care to.

She had wanted to come into the South Lancaster, New Hampshire train station by daylight, but now it looked for sure that the night would be overseeing her walk across the foot bridge that crossed the Connecticut River. She had friends in South Guildhall, and had they known that she was coming, they would have sent a wagon after her, but since they did not, Sarah would just have to walk in and surprise them.

Removing the hat box from her head, Sarah headed down the Main Street. She was hungry and wanted a place to rest for a minute and to eat a hot meal, for tonight she would have a long, long walk.

With this on her mind, she entered a small tavern and went inside to a clean table, covered with a red and white checkered table cloth.

She was glad that she had chosen this spot, for she could smell tomato sauce, and she knew that in this clean and homey atmosphere she would refresh her spirit along with her appetite.

By seven o'clock, Sarah had her hunger sated and was climbing aboard the train that would take her home. There were only half a dozen passengers going this far north, and she mused to herself, were they smart or dumb?

Just before the locomotive pulled out, two men took their places in seats a couple of rows ahead of her. One was a short, red headed fellow with a bull-neck and a bushy beard.

Sarah eyed the unkept whiskers and shuddered. How men could eat with a face haired out like a Quilly Pig, she would never know. She smiled to herself. It was little wonder that the old ones had called the first White Men they ever saw, "Dog Faces," because so many of them were. But, the bearded man in the seat ahead of Sarah did not look like a dog. He looked like porccupine.

Sarah could not see the face of the second man. He was tall with wide shoulders, and she watched as he took off the slouch hat that he had been wearing.

The train started up with a good natured jolt and then chugged off, and as it did the tallest of the two strangers in front of Sarah turned to look around and his gaze fell squarely on Sarah's face, but she was looking at the hat box which had taken a tumble when the train started. She picked the box up and put it in her lap. When she next looked up, she was staring into the face of John Somers.

She sucked in her breath when she saw him, and he looked at her with his unflinching stolen eyes; "stolen" because they were so blue compared to his copper skin. Then he smiled and said something to the Quilly Pig man and got up and walked back to where Sarah sat.

"Sarah, may I sit with you a minute?" he wanted to know, and she moved the hat box from her lap to the floor and told him that he could.

John appraised her face, and this did not make her mad, it made the flush of crimson color her cheeks, and she was glad that the lighting in this coach was not very good.

"It is good to see you, girl! You are looking wonderful!" John said, and Sarah smiled.

"Thank you...John Somers," was what she said. He always knew just what to say to make a woman feel fine. Then she warned herself, "Of course, it wouldn't be him, if he wasn't smooth as cream."

"What are you doing up here Sarah?" John asked her and she answered "I'm going home."

He didn't understand and his next question was "That pretty little Winona finally found someone brave enough to marry her, Huh?" And Sarah knew that he was going to say this, and that the tears would fill her eyes, when once he had, but there was nothing she could do, but to fight for composure and hope that since he couldn't see the blush that neither could he see the tears.

"No, Winona, she is dead." Sarah said, and the pain was obvious in her strained voice. It was still hard for her to talk about her sister, but at least she could do it now with a semblance of control.

She saw compassion and shock both spreading across John's handsome face, and it was he who had the red face now.

"Oh, Sarah, I didn't realize! I'm so sorry! God, I can't believe that she is ...gone.

"A high wire accident. The catcher missed her. No net. It was an instant thing....but sometimes even I still cant believe it either."

In spite of herself, the tears welled up in Sarah's eyes and spilled down over her high cheekbones and John saw this, and took from his pocket a clean handkerchief and dabbed at her overflowing eyes.

"Here, Here, Sarah....don't cry.... please, don't cry?" And he thought the sound of his own voice was strange to his own ears because at thirty-four years old, he could not remember ever begging a woman for anything.

Sarah sniffed, and regained control and in an effort to change the subject, she asked "Where are you going, John?" Before he could answer, the conductor having seen the young lady board this train alone, asked if it was alright with her that this man was sitting there."

"Yes, he is an old friend," Sarah explained and when the concerned man departed, John answered her question, "New Hampshire. There is a big job starting up over in Androscoggin country, and Whiskers and I are going."

Sarah nodded. Whiskers had to be that haired-out Quilly Pig that John boarded the train with.

John ran a hand through his thick hair. "Gosh, you are the last person that I ever expected to see." John said.

"Me too!" said Sarah and then as the wheels whined under them these two rode along in silence. John got up and went up to where "Whiskers" sat and talked a few minutes and then he came back and sat beside Sarah again.

As the outside light faded, Sarah was thinking that although she had never heard it, apparently, trains were good places to meet young men. She chuckled to herself. By White standards, she was already on her way to becoming an Old Maid. She was twenty-four years old and unmarried. She was glad that she did not adhere to this way of thinking because she believed as her grandmother had, that a person got married, when it was right, because there was no time limit on love.

She had seen a couple of young women take men as their husbands and the single strong emotion in these women's hearts was fear, fear that they would not get any husband. And in Sarah's mind, this was not choosing a mate, this was grabbing at what ever was going by, so as not to be an... Old Maid.

Darkness came outside and as the coach-lights brightened the interior of the car, Sarah could see John's face better. "It was such a fine face," she had always thought, as though sculptured by an artist. And his features were manly and rugged and yet softly handsome too.

When once he turned his head, she could see an angry white scar that ran down the left side of his neck. She had never seen this before. This scar was not there when last she saw this man and it was not an old one, it was quite new.

"What happened to your neck, John?" she asked.

He looked away and then lowered his head and said "Oh I just got into a row in a bar. We went outside to settle it,"... John laughed then, a sardonic laugh and then continued, "I was carrying my hat here. The other guy was carrying a knife. I did not know he had a weapon." Sarah knew enough about doctoring to realize that a scar like this one was certainly a life-threatening thing. It made her a trifle angry that he would make so light of it.

"Next time...maybe you should run!" she quipped. Sarah could remember that her brother Dennis had told her that his man was a heavy drinker and a brawler too, but she remembered more vividly that he had called John Somers a "no account"

"Old Whiskers over there, he and another guy got the knife away from my adversary and then a doctor sewed me all up. It wasn't but a scratch," he lied.

John looked at her and he could see by the set of her mouth that she did not like this story. "I suppose you think I shouldn't drink!" he said defensively and she answered sharply "Either that or start carrying a knife! A hat is a poor match for a knife." John Somers had to smother a laugh. Under that calm exterior was a fiery female with a biting tongue. He would bet right now that her dark eyes were blazing. Damn! wish he could see them, he thought.

Through the night the train traveled on, and finally around eleven-thirty it came to a grinding halt at the lonely and dimly lit little railroad station in South Lancaster, New Hampshire.

"You are walking to a farm on the Vermont side this time of night?" John asked her, and Sarah said "Yes, It is across the bridge, but up the road a ways."

He did not like the idea of this. These were times when a young woman traveling alone should not go on foot under the cover of darkness. There were a lot of men out there a whole lot worse than him, John thought.

He was supposed to continue his journey on and get off at the railroad station in Gorham, New Hampshire, but when Sarah stepped down off the locomotive, John had taken her luggage. "Come on," he said, "I'll walk with you. I'll come back and sleep here in the station, and take the morning train and join the crew in Berlin tomorrow."

Whiskers grinned. He had never seen John so caring or apparently so unstrung over a female.

Sarah walked along beside him into the darkness and she was surprised to say the least. It disgusted Sarah some, to think that he had appointed himself her bodyguard, but still, to have a personal protector on a dark and misty evening, was not such a bad thing. Sarah was glad to have his company as the shadow of the Mount Orne Bridge loomed ominously up ahead. And hidden somewhere in the dense fog of this April night was that narrow dirt road leading Aunt Sarah back to where she came from.

This was just another spring pilgrimage for part of the Jackson family. And like knots on a counting rope, each mile and each step of this journey brought Aunt Sarah closer to "The Place Where the Sweetgrass Grows," a place her heart called — home.

Through the mist they walked side by side carefully and silently. It was a damp night and a quiet one, the only sound being the slapping sounds from the Connecticut River, rolling along in front of them. The peepers were not ready to peep yet, and about the only sound emitted from the river's edge was the rustle of the night wind and the pitter-patter of icy raindrops falling on the wet earth below their feet.

Life would never cease to amaze Sarah. Ironically it had happened that just the day that she would be returning to the valley, she would be destined to meet John Somers on a northbound train. One more day either way and he would not have been here walking beside her.

There had been no conversation between them since they discussed his drinking. Sarah was by nature not a talker, and it used to amuse her to think that she was attracted to this man, John.... who could talk a rock to death.

The silent journey continued until John broke it by chiding "You don't talk much, do you Sarah?" For a long minute she said nothing and then he got his answer. "I do when I have something that needs to be said." He made a half laugh and they walked on until they started across that span of boards, called the Mount Orne Bridge, which would connect them with the Vermont shoreline. The clatter of their hard-sole shoes seemed to drown out even the murmur of the water beneath them. "Clip clop, clip clop," was the sound that drummed in Sarah's ears as they stepped across those boards, through a fog so thick that they could not see but a few feet ahead.

After crossing the bridge they took a right hand turn up a slight hill and continued walking on up the Vermont side.

"How far?" he asked Sarah, and she said "Only about a mile or so." John stopped in his tracks. "You said just across the bridge, up the road a ways."

"It is" she exclaimed, and then added, "I wouldn't call a mile or so a long walk, would you, John?"

With an air of disgust clearly visible in his voice, her protector said, "Oh, now it's a mile of so!" Sarah kept walking ahead and replied, "Ummmph." It would have ended there if he would have dropped it, but no, egotistical man that he was, he just kept talking, "Well probably have to walk all night!" he growled, and Sarah, wet and cold and tired of his whining, spat back, "We...we don't have to walk another step, John Somers! I did not ask you to escort me, and if you want to go back right no...fine with me!"

"Real smart, Sarah," he said, and continued "Anywhere that civilization runs near a railroad track, there are drunks and no accounts following along behind! This is no time of night to be walking alone, my sweet young lady, and you know it."

His chivalry galled Sarah but he probably was right. Yet in her heart she felt like telling him that there were some who would think that she was walking with a drunk and a no account. She did not tell him that, but instead began planting her feet a little harder on the earth below, until she was traveling at full stomp.

Ahead of them, just as they rounded a sharp bend, they saw a lurching shadow looming. John stopped, and placing a hand on Sarah's arm he whispered, "Did you see something?" She nodded, and they kept walking straight ahead to see what lay there waiting for them up ahead in the darkness. It was too big to be a fisher cat, perhaps it was a large dog, but whatever it was, it had departed for the cover of some sparse bushes at the side of the narrow road.

In silence they pressed on, and then John took three quick steps toward a thrashing noise in the underbrush. When he rose up, he had a man by the throat, and he stood him up with a jerk. "Who in hell are you," John growled at a pathetic creature, reeking of unwashed clothes, stale whiskey and even the stench of vomit and urine.

"What are you hiding in the bushes for?" was the next question John asked the man he had collared. "I don' know...jes wanna sleep is all," the poor man answered in a voice that was on the verge of crying.

John let go of him and the frightened wretch fell to the ground, because he was too intoxicated to stand alone. "He had drunk his dignity away," thought Sarah.

John turned to her and picked up her valise and hat box, and then as they started off up the road he said, "Just a drunk. At the crawling stage, he won't harm anyone but himself."

"Most drunks do!" Sarah came back with, and under the cover of darkness she could not see the red that crept into John's face, because another night, another bridge, this could have been him.

"I hope he didn't frighten you," he said to Sarah, and she replied "No, what frightens me John, is that he could have been you."

Damn! It made John mad. How did she know what he was thinking? "Look Sarah, I drink. Not so bad that I cannot work and hold a steady job, but on weekends, or when I'm not working, I drink and that is how it is!"

She stopped now and looked up at him. "Do you drink because you like to be out of your mind, or perhaps now...because you have to, John?"

Denial of course was the first thing from his mouth. "Of course I don't have to! Why'd you ask me such a damned stupid thing?"

"The question is not stupid, John Somers, what is stupid is drinking until you are drunk. My father used to get drunk, for peace from his nightmares. He found peace all right, peace forever there....on the other side."

"There is a difference! I can stop drinking any time I want to!" John said crisply, and Sarah challenged, "Oh, I doubt that, John! You don't drink in short periods, you are sober in short periods. That is why you have no home, no family ...just your good friend —the bottle."

In a way John could have kicked himself. At first she wouldn't talk and then he had to go and goad her into a row, and now she wouldn't shut up! She spoke with a soft voice but she had a scathing tongue.

"Someday I will have a family. Then I won't drink anymore, but I am not ready to quit now," John finally said.

"Ummmph," was Sarah's answer.

Suddenly through the dense fog, the dim lights of a farmhouse could be seen. Sarah's heart leaped. The Gees were home and their lights were still on.

John stopped then. He supposed this was as good a time as any to break up this relationship. Well, of course there really wasn't any relationship and there never would be, because Sarah Jackson had to have a damned saint, not a man.

He turned her to face him and spoke softly. "I'm glad I was here this night to walk with you, Sarah. I think when the job ends over Berlin way, I'll head south for the winter. You are a lovely woman, but you are too idealistic for my blood. You don't want a man like me!"

And Sarah looked up at him and said the words that had been nagging at her heart. "What I don't want is a no account drunk!...That is what I don't want! We just left a man in the ditch...one who lets rum control his life. He is weak! No, I don't want a man like you John Somers, if you are that weak!"

He could smell the sweetness of her. He touched her face with his hand and said, "You said one day if I asked you....you might say yes."

"Well, don't ask me now! If you do, I will certainly say no!"

John's lips brushed over hers and he said, "Sarah, if you loved me... you would love me as I am."

She shook off his tender kisses, and stepped back angry. "Then I don't love you John, not like you are!" Now a strange and bitter laugh escaped her full lips, and she continued, "You are not ready. I am not ready! In truth, we will never be ready. We are like the tree and the rock....living but never moving on with life." Her voice was old and sad sounding.

A dog came running up the road to meet them and it was barking and growling, but John and Sarah talked to it and convinced it that they meant no harm.

As they approached the long driveway, faces appeared in the windows, and in a way John was relieved that they were at their destination and that whatever strange bond there was between him and this hard-headed woman, was no more.

As the Gee family warmly embraced her, Sarah's chaperon, placed her luggage inside and then whirled to head out of the driveway. Sarah watched him walking proudly off into the night and she felt a pang of lonesomeness of some sort, that was indeed, spoiling her homecoming.

She went from the house and called to him and he turned to look back at her and she stammered, "Thank you, John Somers, for walking with me this night...My heart is glad you did."

"Mine too," he answered with a smile that the darkness prevented her from seeing, and for the first time this evening, those tight little stress lines disappeared from the corners of his mouth.

"Sarah,...when I'm with you, I cannot think straight." He ventured on, "I won't change, woman, and as I am...you won't have me, so goodbye, Sarah." And he walked away from her again, knowing in his heart, they loved each other. However, their love according to Sarah, was caught between a tree — and a rock.

Blinking away her tears, Sarah started back to the spacious farm house kitchen, where Aunt Nel had saved young Robert Gees life, a few years back. "That big old room, it had not changed. It would never change; like the mountains and the ledges, like ....me and him," she thought, "Too proud to change."

Once again out in the dampness of the foggy night, John Somers made his way through the rain and mist. When he passed by where the inebriated fellow lay, in a still unconscious state, John felt a swell of pity rising up within himself and only seconds later, he felt nothing but contempt for this man. This hopeless wretch was, like so many times in his life he had been and would most likely be again. He was disgusted.

He took a flask from his coat pocket. He carried it with him most of the time now. And then he wondered, was this because he enjoyed rum so much, or was it that he needed it....because he was so weak? No, that Sarah made him crazy!

John removed the cork from the bottle and had every intention of taking a drink of the golden liquid contained therein, but suddenly a face flashed before his eyes. It was Sarah's calm and gentle face and she was looking at him with pity and also with contempt!

John had always felt that Sarah Jackson's eyes never looked at you, they looked through you and..... they saw your heart.

He never did put his lips to the flask but instead he cursed and then threw the bottle as far as he could into the woods. "There, Sarah!" he said through clenched teeth, "Saint John, will someday have you!"

About the time that this was actually happening, Sarah was starting up the stairway of her new home, her new life.

At last Sarah Jackson was home. Her young heart was light and yet it was not; and she could not help but wonder why she felt so sad and empty because a "no account" had walked out of her life, even if at times he was a chivalrous one.

"Welcome home, Sarah!" a wistful voice whispered from deep inside her head — or was it from her heart?

Part III

The Medicine Woman

Part III

The Medicine Woman

In the middle of the night Sarah awoke, and she listened to the sound of rain on the tin roof above her head. For a minute or two she was not sure where she was, and then she remembered the walk to the Gee Farm in South Guildhall, and this brought the realization that she was snuggled on a feather-tick mattress, covered with heavy hand-made quilts. She was warm and dry. This "salmon" had completed her journey, and from here she would go on.

She listened for a while, as the raindrops danced, and then their fury was driven by a wind and the rain became torrential. Sarah did not mind this sound, in fact it was one of her most favorite ones. Her father used to tell her that the rain was telling her a story, and as a child she would often go to sleep listening to the rain and trying to imagine what each drop was saying. Tonight, she was content just to enjoy the special sound of this spring rain. It pleased her heart to know how much good the water was doing for all the little new, green things struggling to grow. She went back to sleep again and she was glad that she had two good ears so that she might always listen to this beautiful song of rain.

Before daybreak she woke up again and this was to the sound of a rooster crowing. She smiled softly to herself. She had not heard a rooster crow for so long that she couldn't remember when, but this was the official wake-up sound in rural Vermont.

Not long after the rooster sounded, the clock on the wall told her that it was time to get up. "The rooster has no clock and he usually beats the clock," she thought. How does he know these things? Rising up and getting dressed, Sarah decided that this was one of the things only birds and animals could understand, like what the rain really said.

She poured water into the pitcher and washed her face and combed her hair back into its twist at the back of her head.

Looking out the window, she could see that the sun was trying ever so hard to show itself.

She would go down and help with breakfast, but first she would go and stand on the porch and inhale this pungent air and look across the valley toward Lancaster, New Hampshire and especially just to stand and listen to the murmur of the Connecticut River below her.

A smile crossed her face as she stood there, because she knew that by June, the sweetgrass that lined the meadows all along this valley would be thick. When it was ready for harvest the wonderful aroma of sweetgrass could be detected way up here on higher ground.

Sarah saw some chickens and a rooster eating in front of the barn that was badly in need of paint. Going back to the kitchen, she found that Mrs. Gee was already there and the smell of coffee was strong and good. On the back of the big wood-burning stove, oat meal was simmering in a large black kettle. The bacon snapped and fresh eggs would soon be cooking in that excess bacon grease. These farmers worked hard and like the people who traveled with the circus, they ate hard and hearty.

Grandpa Gee had gone to the other side. Grammy Gee was still present and when seated in her rocker, there was not too much that she missed in the operation of that old farm.

Mrs. Gee, Margaret, her daughter-in-law, was a hard worker and two of her older children were married and gone, but she still had six at home. Sarah remembered the older two, but the younger ones had to be introduced to her. Ben and Joe worked out in the fields with Fred, their father, and they were fourteen and sixteen years. Polly, Nadine and Anna were between twelve and six years, and Jacinta was just a toddler and it was easy to see that Margaret Gee had a handful...with this houseful.

Sarah enjoyed her first breakfast with this family and after that delicious meal, she helped to pack school lunch pails for the children and then there were the dishes to be washed.

As the day wore on, a pot of cottage cheese was simmering on the back of the cook stove. "Curds and whey," thought Sarah, "on a farm everyone eats what Miss Muffet did, but they did not sit on their "tuffets" very long. There was too much work to do."

Sarah always liked the smell of cheese cooking, but the smell of high bush cranberries simmering was one that took some getting used to.

As Sarah thumped away on the butter churn she watched Margaret mixing up a batch of bread. It smelled good, even as it rose. "Even if I was blindfolded, I'd know that I was in the kitchen of a Vermont farmhouse," thought Sarah, because of the aromas emitted from basic food stuff, basic in Vermont, that is.

As the rest of the family scattered, Sarah accompanied Margaret up the stairs to Fred's mother's room. Grammy, as they called her, slept late now, in the eighty-seventh winter of her life. Margaret carried a tray of hot, steaming oat meal topped with crab-apple sauce, because it was the elderly woman's favorite.

Propped up in her bed with high pillows supporting her back, Grammy Gee squinted to look at Sarah.

"Good Morning Mother Gee," said Margaret, and the elderly matriarch, with snow-white hair, nodded. Her eyes were covered with a milky blue-grey film. She suffered from a condition we know today as cataracts. She recognized people now only by their voice, but when asked if she remembered Aunt Nelemano Jackson, this grandmother said she did.

"Aunt Nel helped me when my babies were born and when they were young and sick, also," said Margaret, adding "This is Sarah, that little girl who followed her Aunt everywhere. She is all grown up now, and an Aunt herself."

Sarah stepped nearer to the bed. She leaned down close to the elderly woman who studied her face and traced the contour of one of Sarah's high cheekbones with a frail finger. "Yes, I remember Aunt Nel. Welcome to the valley, Sarah."

Sarah smiled. Although the old woman's vision was impaired to the extent that she only saw shadows, apparently Grammy Gee's mind was still clear. "Thank you Mrs.Gee," said Sarah.

"How old are you now, Sarah?" this grandmother asked as Sarah set baby Jacinta down and then poured some tea. "I am old enough to be called Aunt Sarah, myself, Mrs. Gee." Sarah said. This made the older woman chuckle and she said, "Good answer Aunt Sarah, but for me, two Mrs. Gees in one house are too many. Please call me Elizabeth."

Sarah agreed, and Margaret said they would come back for the tray later and then she and Sarah and Jacinta left the room so the elderly lady could eat.

"She is smart," Sarah mused and then asked, "Is her appetite always this good?"

"Land sakes yes, Sarah. She will eat anything that don't try to eat her first!" Margaret said and Sarah laughed.

At the foot of the stairs they were met by Fred, and he was in a hurry. "Quick Maggie," he said to his wife, "I need some clean cloths. Got a ewe out there bleedin' bad! Had two little ones, but one's dead. Tuther, I'd like to save."

Without a word, his wife went off hurriedly and came back with an assortment of clean, white towels and cloths.

"Damn! I hate bleedin'," said Fred, and his face was strained.

"Let me help you, Fred," said Sarah, and even while he was agreeing she was pumping water at the sink to wash her hands.

Sarah followed Fred to the barn, and she saw the downed ewe. She knew that for hemorrhaging, often there was little that could be done, but one could always try. And besides that, if they lost the mother maybe the baby could be saved.

Fred, a small man in stature, dropped to his knees and examined the quiet mother sheep "Oh, it's stopped up a little. By Gum, we might pull her through, Sarah." he said.

Sarah knelt down and looked at the ewe. "Oh, not Bad! The afterbirth is normal. Looks like a couple of really bad tears is all, Fred." Sarah diagnosed. Behind them, Margaret came carrying a pail of warm water in one hand and toting the baby with the other.

"Good Margaret!" said Fred, and he poured some of the tepid water over the clean cloths and bathed the exposed part of the ewe. Fred was gentle but the new mother jumped, her little feet flailing the barn floor. Sarah got up and ran quickly into the house. In her haste she had forgotten her medicine box. It did not take her long to find it and she tore down the stairs and ran back to the barn.

Once inside she said breathlessly, "Fred, you watch her feet and I'll take a few stitches, just three or four. It will be quick. She should heal up then with less chance of infection."

Before she began to stitch up the animal, Sarah went in front of her and patted her head and placed something in her mouth. The ewe seemed to bite onto it and then her head began to drop.

As the ewe's body relaxed, Fred said, "Guess we're too late Sarah, seems to me she's dying!"

"No, she is going to sleep Fred. I gave her something," Sarah said, and before Fred could raise his questioning eyebrows, Sarah was already in kneeling position and her dexterous fingers flew in rapid procession until five well-placed stitches had been sewn. The ewe raised her head, but didn't begin to thrash until Sarah was shaking a strange smelling grey powder on the bloodied area.

"If she licks this, it won't hurt her. She will be fine, Fred." This done, Sarah turned her attention to the newly born baby sheep. He was standing up now on his unsteady little legs and trying to get to his Mama.

Fred started to pull him away. "Better not let him drink, Sarah, 'cause you just gave that ewe a drug or some kind of medicine to keep her quiet." Sarah smiled. "Let him go to her and eat, Fred. It was not a drug, just a root to soothe and calm her. A pain killer would hurt this fellow, but not what I gave her. She needs him too. Let him eat, Fred."

Fred Gee trusted Sarah, and while he took the carcass of the dead sheep out to bury it Sarah sat beside the hungry baby and let him eat a little.

The ewe was already trying to clean him off, and her bleeding had completely stopped now with the stitching. Sarah went and stood in front of her and knelt down and scratched her head. "Close one for you, Miss. You will do better next time." The ewe stopped cleaning her baby and licked Sarah's hand, "I know, you thank me, and your boy he thanks me too!" Sarah laughed.

Just then Sarah heard Fred calling to her. She headed in the direction of his voice. And there stood Fred, holding the dead sheep, with a strange look on his face, "I was diggin' his grave and he moved Sarah! I can't bury the little critter 'til he's really dead!" Fred exclaimed.

"Put him down, Fred," Sarah said, and then she went on. "Maybe we can revive him." And then she took the small new born animal and flipped it onto its back and pumped its little legs. She reached inside its small mouth and removed great gobs of phlegm and mucus, much more than usual for a newborn. Sarah massaged his little chest and talked with him, "Come on little Brother! You don't want to die! You just got here, too soon to go back now! Come on, breathe!....You breathe for your Aunt Sarah and I'll fix you a bottle and feed you breakfast myself."

Fred and Margaret stood and listened and could almost not believe it when the little lamb began to wiggle first his tail, then one foot and then the other and he finally opened his eyes. Sarah never stopped working on the lamb. She kept massaging him, turning him, patting his back and she removed more mucus from his mouth, and with this last effort, his breathing became even and grew stronger.

"Good! Little Brother... you breathe, and tonight, Aunt Sarah will take you to your Mama and your little brother."

For a long time Sarah stayed with that small lamb. At last on his wobbly legs he attempted to stand, and she praised him and the next time, he did stand.

Sarah's face was beaming and now, she wrapped this little fellow in a blanket and headed for the house with him.

"Where are you going with him?" Fred asked her and Aunt Sarah said, "I promised this man breakfast. I keep my word."

Fred smiled and watched her go. Margaret would probably have something to say about a sheep in her kitchen, but Margaret fixed the bottle and warmed it, when Sarah requested it. Fred was amazed.

Then Sarah sat down and fed the squirming lamb, which pulled and tugged at the nipple. "He is strong. I can take him to his family tonight, I believe." And this Aunt Sarah did.

At first his mother wasn't sure if she wanted him or not, but Sarah insisted that if they went away and left the lamb and its mother alone, she would accept her baby. And like all the other things that Aunt Sarah had said today, this too was true.

"Damn!" thought Fred, "Sure wish she'd been around last fall when that mare died of colic."

"Sarah," smiled Margaret, when Sarah had bathed and changed into clean clothes, "You saved him, so you name that little cuss." Sarah thought a moment and then she said, "Okay, I will call that little brother, Ramsy."

That was another thing Sarah liked about Vermont, everybody on a farm had the dignity of having a name, even a sheep.

On the eve of her first full day here, Sarah again lay in her bed and once more listened as another April rain made gentle tapping sounds on the roof above her head.

She tried to remember all the sounds and smells of this first day back in the valley, like crab apples in a sauce that topped steaming oat meal. She remembered too the smell of blood as she stitched up the ewe. But most of all she remembered the new-life smell of Ramsy the lamb as she cuddled him in her arms and observed him making a pig out of himself as he glutted away his first meal. She remembered her father holding in his then-powerful arms a spotted fawn that had been abandoned. This little baby had also eaten in a gluttonous fashion, and Peter was forced to keep withdrawing the bottle from the mouth of the yearling, as Sarah had to remove the bottle from the greedy, black mouth of this little ram today.

But then, Sarah remembered Peter Jackson telling the spotted fawn to be patient and grow strong. "You must go and climb the mountains, little brother, and roam the swamps, before I eat you. You must be a highland deer, fat and robust and taste of beechnuts when I eat you brother." At six, Sarah had asked, "Father, will you eat him later?" With love and compassion showing in her father's dark eyes, he said, "Only if I fail to recognize him, Sarah. This deer and I will know each other, I think."

To the tears building in her eyes he said, "I would never kill a friend I knew. You know that, don't you Sarah?"

Sarah smiled her tears away then, for she knew that her father's words were ones that he would keep. It was their way.

Peter had then given her the bottle and she herself had fed that spotted fawn, and it too had that strange and clean aroma, only present at a birthing. It was as if this new life had not been here long enough to pick up any unpleasant earthy scent.

Tomorrow was Saturday and there was a full day ahead for her, but on Sunday, Sarah was going to take a walk along the river bank and she might even go and visit Tarritine Ledge, to see what green gifts were and were not growing well this Leafing Season.

Right now, she would shut her eyes and thank the one who made it all, that she was in the right place this morning and that she was able to help a couple of His little creatures, her brothers, to survive and participate in this life; which was most times good like this, the tap, tap, tapping sound of spring rain on a tin roof.

"Where do they go...the little raindrops, Father?" In the seventh winter of her young life she asked, and he had thought for a while and answered, "To Mother Earth they fall child... to rise again as flowers and green life-giving things."

And to the tempo of these dancing raindrops, Sarah could almost mouth the words that they were saying,

"We are raindrops only passing; We will fall and rise and be;
Gifts of flowers, roots and berries;
Care for what we give to thee; tap, tap,
tap, tap... tap, tap."

Saturday morning arrived with the sounds of the rooster outside and shortly after that the sounds that half a dozen healthy children make inside. This day started with the smell of coffee boiling and the aroma of slowly baking soldier beans in a heavy pot swinging from an open hearth. The beans bubbled softly and a piece of salt pork floated around amid the sauce which smelled of maple syrup, mustard, onions and molasses.

Sarah had decided at about twelve years old that if you didn't like home baked beans, you could probably go to bed hungry on any given Saturday night, if you lived in Vermont.

Shortly after the breakfast chores, she donned an old frock and a pair of barn boots that were too big for her. Then Sarah walked over to the barn to check on Ramsy and his mother who's name was Elsbeth.

The ewe was looking much better as Sarah knelt down and examined the stitches. Everything looked fine. When she turned her attention to Elsbeth's two sons, Sarah had to laugh because they were cavorting around the sheep pen, prancing and dancing and in all honesty, she was not really sure which little ram....was Ramsy.

This was shopping day and Fred hitched up the wagon and then Margaret took the reins firmly and with baby Jacinta perched on Aunt Sarah's lap, Margaret clucked to the horses. In the back sat Polly, Nadine and Anna, who amused themselves with children's games, as the wagon groaned and creaked over the bumpy road.

"Has Lancaster changed?" Sarah wanted to know, and her chauffeur replied, "Not too much. Has a lot of people around in the summer. They leave in the fall." "Duck Chasers," thought Sarah.

"Just like the geese," Sarah said, and then added, "of course, they always come back."

"So do the summer people, snooty bunch!" said Margaret, and she and Sarah chuckled at the truth of this statement.

Sarah and Margaret were women born to farm life, country women used to hard work and a no-frills lifestyle. Indeed, they had no time or inclination to be "snooty."

As they passed the farms along the road, Margaret told Sarah the names of all the farmers. Some of these names she recognized, and then some were names of people that she had never heard of.

As they passed the flat meadows that lay adjacent to Tarritine Ledge, many sections of the meadows were under water with this springs melting ice and snow. On these shallow pools were wild ducks swimming. This was their mating season and the black ducks were pairing up and staking out their nesting territories.

"I want some tame ducks. Nothin' like duck eggs to cook with," Margaret Gee said, and Sarah nodded, because Aunt Nel had claimed this also.

From the back of the wagon, Nadine, the second from the oldest, asked "Aunt Sarah, when we get home tonight, would you please tell us a story?" Sarah smiled. She hoped they would be home before tonight, but who knew? She answered, "If it is fine with your Mother, I will tell you a story about the rabbit who caused a stew."

The little girls giggled and then were quiet, and as they passed more farms, Margaret had something nice to say about all of her neighbors along the river, but one. She, being a Christian, had nothing good to say about that farmer, so she said nothing at all. At that moment, Sarah's attention was drawn to some manure covered cows, standing near a barn. "What a dirty farmer," said Sarah, and Margaret, still reluctant to criticize, condescended, "Dirty is right!"

Instinctively, Sarah realized that since Margaret was no gossip, the farmer of whom she spoke was in her opinion, dirty...but, with an inside dirt that could not be washed off.

As they rode along surveying the landscape, it was apparent to Sarah that here in the upper Connecticut River valley, was much evidence of hard work and yet, it was not growing very fast and it did not seem to be a very prosperous place. The buildings, even the better kept ones, looked bad this time of year, but in another month things would be looking better.

Her dark eyes surveyed the ruggedness of the terrain with granite ledges protruding here and there from towering mountains on all sides and stoic pines rising high. Mighty elms and oak trees, too, lined the banks of the river below. Sarah decided that it took a people with the strength of the mountains to live here. It was a backward place with few comforts, short growing seasons, long bleak winters and no great halls or institutions of learning anywhere to be seen. If you needed a soft and easy life, you would never find it tilling the soils of these verdant meadows.

As the wagon moved along North Main Street in Lancaster, Sarah could see the stately elms that lined both sides of that wide road which ran through this town. Lancaster hadn't changed too much in the half a dozen years she had been gone.

In the stores were many old and many new faces, but by August, she would know them better because her basket market would be growing by that time. At least that was her hope.

Her initial plan was to stay two weeks at the Gee residence, but Fred and Margaret were trying hard to persuade Sarah to say on with them indefinitely. She could not. She needed time to make her baskets and also to secure a market for them.

"Sarah," Margaret offered, "how about just working a Monday through Friday work week? The weekends are your own, to do your basketry or whatever. We could use the help, Sarah."

Before Sarah could answer, Margaret had explained that they could provide her with room and board and two dollars a month.

That was not a bad deal, Sarah decided. It would cut into the time she usually spent making baskets, but since she had no place of her own to live, it would take a lot of baskets to pay room and board someplace else. The money Sarah had brought with her from the circus was still in a long wool sock. This had been carried in the valise and now it was tucked into one of the dresser drawers, in the room that she had been given.

Her basket money she could add to this, and someday, well, who knew what might happen? She knew that she would only spend this saved security, her sock money, when she or one of her family or friends was in extremely bad circumstances. Sarah thought that it was good to save. Keep what you have in case something worse happens, was her motto. It was a pessimistic and cynical theory but her salvation fund was alive and well and had been in that old wool sock for over six years now.

Margaret Gee had purchased flour, a barrel of tripe, some lard and other staples that the farm itself did not furnish. While Sarah rode in silence, counting her future pennies, Margaret was hoping that someone, Fred or one of the boys, would notice that the beans might need some water.

As they unloaded the supplies, Sarah was noticing that the dandelion greens were now a little bigger than the palm of her hand and in less than a week, they would be ready to be dug.

Margaret saw Sarah examining the dandelions and she said, "Next

Sunday, we will all go digging greens on the meadow." And Sarah smiled, because it sounded like fun.

"We'll dig all we can, eat all we can and preserve the rest." said Margaret and then she chuckled "Course my Fred now, he don't care a whit for dandelions and says they are a weed and they ain't good for nothin'."

Sarah thought and replied, "They are very good for constipation," and she and Margaret laughed.

All that day the sun had gone in and out of the clouds, and when it was out you had to take your jacket off, but when it went back in, you had to put it back on, and Sarah hoped that tomorrow as she reacquainted herself with the land, the sun would come out and stay out.

Margaret was relieved to see that the beans had not cooked dry. She had gotten home just in time.

That evening as the family gathered around the table for their supper, Sarah smelled the aroma of baked beans, ham and hot rolls. She knew that to eat like this for seven days a week and work only five, to pay for the luxury of such wonderful food, was a heck of a deal!

And when would she find time to gather the materials to make her sweetgrass baskets? Well, Saturdays and Sundays and on weekdays after supper, of course....if she hadn't eaten so much that she couldn't walk, that is.

In the huge living room the family gathered after their evening meal. Grammy Gee, said she liked beans, but ate them only sparingly, for they gave her stomach gas.

"Fennel seeds are very good to aid the stomach juices," Sarah said. She did not go on to say that over-weight people had been known to use larger doses of the seeds of the fennel plant to help them decrease a big appetite.

Now that her mind was momentarily on her medicine box, Sarah remembered that she needed some black cohosh root. Her supply was low, and it was the effective relaxant that she had administered to the ewe yesterday. The powder that she had applied after the stitching episode was made from the ground up root of a plant named comfrey.

When Elizabeth Gee had asked Sarah later,"Is there something I can eat a lot of that might aid my digestion, Aunt Sarah?"

Sarah had thought and then said, "Yes, We will fill you with juniper berries, this summer, they are wonderful for any gastric disorder."

The elderly woman's amusement was visible to all. "All right Aunt Sarah, if it is what your Aunt Nel said." "It is what she said," was Sarah's answer.

The evening wore on and these people all decided, one by one, that the day had made them sleepy.

Grammy was the first to express that she would like to retire, and the two oldest little girls guided her to her bedroom. "It is good," thought Sarah, "to see young ones caring for older ones."

Before she went to sleep this evening, Sarah kept her word and told the story about the rabbit that caused the stew, and the little girls laughed and giggled at what one pesky rabbit could do. Of course, he was not the usual and timid rabbit, but instead a long-eared hopper, that flitted around the forest and was always stewing about something.

His exploits were colorful and many, but the rabbit was never invited to the fox's den or to the beaver's lodge, because he complained and stewed so much about his sad and dreary existence.

Then one day the stewing hare met a wise shaman. The shaman was very tired, for he had worked hard for three days and nights trying to save the leg of a black bear that was nearly severed by a trap. The shaman was very angry with the rabbit's self-centered tale of woe.

"I'd like you to hear how sorry and bleak my life is," cried the stewing rabbit, as he jumped up on a hollow stump and sat there feeling ever so sorry for himself.

"It could be much worse!" the Shaman said. "Oh, no. There is no forest creature could be in such a sad state of affairs as me," the rabbit insisted.

Suddenly the shaman touched the stump with one of his feet, and it became a deep bowl and grew very hollow. With a flick of his hand, the shaman filled the stump with rain water and then as thunder rumbled overhead, he brought a bolt of lightening down from the sky and it hit the stump with a hiss and set the stump on fire. The rain water around where the depressed rabbit sat, began to bubble and boil and as the heat intensified, the water smelled to the rabbit like—rabbit broth! He began to jump up and down in the stump-pot, simmering like the stew that he was finally in! "Let me out!" he cried. "I won't complain any more. I'll never cause a stew again, please let me out!" That rabbit had learned to accept life as it was and the shaman, being a wise and a compassionate man, turned the pot back into a stump and the broth disappeared, and from that day forward, the rabbit stopped complaining.

At this point in the story Aunt Sarah smiled and dimples appeared at the corners of her mouth and her laughing eyes looked very crinkly, and she said, "That rabbit learned a lot that day. He never, ever again stewed in his own juice....and neither should we!" As Sarah finished the story her young and captive audience clapped their hands.

"But why is the rabbit so timid, Aunt Sarah?" the children asked her, and she replied, "Oh, that is another story, for another time."

Later in her room, Sarah became too warm and she crawled from beneath the quilts and walked to the window to open it. And when she did, the sound she heard was a wonderful one, because the peepers were singing in a chorus that was almost deafening as each one tried to tell his own story to the night.

Sarah returned to her comfortable bed, but left the window open just a bit so that she could lay there for a while and listen to this latest proof that spring was here. And at last, the upper Connecticut River valley was thawing out.

Aunt Nel always said that the peepers forecasted warm weather. She also had another saying which was very true, "All is right with the world....when the peepers are singing."

Bright and early Sunday morning, Sarah was up and dressed in an old frock and a pair of ancient hand-made buckskin moccasins with high tops. They were worn and battered, but they were just what she needed, because she would not walk on the road. Aunt Sarah would follow the river and comb the banks for medicine.

She was pleased that she had been asked to join the Gee family at church services, but she had graciously declined, saying that she would go another time. Sarah was a believer, just not one who congregated. As a Dawnland woman she actually gave thanks many times during a week for her blessings, because she was born of a heart and a heritage that loved and respected the earth and all its creatures. The Great Spirit's presence was recognized daily in her life, not just for one hour on Sunday.

The rain clouds were gone and the sky was high and blue as Sarah bent to examine the precious "green things," for more than gifts to people these were life, as hundreds of roots and herbs sprouted skyward out of that rich, black dirt of Vermont, a place her people knew as "Dawnland."

Sarah headed in a northerly direction. She started down the high bluff overlooking the water-spotted meadows below. She picked her steps with care, keeping to the dry ground as she zig-zagged her way across the soggy meadows toward the river bank ahead. As she did this, ducks swimming there were startled and took flight, only to return shortly when they sensed she would not hurt them.

The moon when the fish would be jumping, was fast approaching and she was glad, because Sarah was a fisherman of trout, and shad and pickerel. And she actually hankered for the sweet taste of hornpout! Her whole family used to go at night and build a fire and catch these. As a child, she was told the hornpout came to listen to the stories being told around the nightfire. That was really what attracted them and not those leaping flames. "But Father, fish have no ears! How can they hear?" Sarah the child had asked her father and he had smiled and said, "That is why we catch them so easily, Sarah....you see they have to come close... to listen."

Now that she was older, Sarah felt sure that it was the fire that brought the hornpout, and yet if she could understand the murmur of the raindrops, perhaps these fin-bearing brothers, could understand what men said. Who but that Great Spirit (God) knew such things as this?

Her dark eyes traveled across this familiar valley. There was much snow left on the towering slopes of the Agiachook, Mt. Washington Range. The Starr King Range had no snow cover left, and once the Crystal Hills were stripped bare of their snowy coat, the Connecticut River valley would truly come alive. But until this thing happened, no matter how warm the sun beat on your face, an icy wind would bite at your backside. Yet, this cold wind would help to melt the snows of winter in that high place. Aunt Nel always called this wind the "little Chinook."

Bending to the floor of those damp meadows, Sarah examined many stems and roots and tiny blades of grass. She was particularly interested in the pipsissewa weed. The root of this, when boiled and pulverized became a liquid known as pipsi water that was taken to induce sweating, which was said to drive evil spirits from the body. In the wrong hands or the wrong dosage, the pipsissewa was an extremely dangerous medicine.

Sarah found dandelion roots, for the blood, and noticed that in one section at the bow of the Connecticut River, that two kinds of black snake root were growing side by side. The one called cohosh was taken by mouth, by those who suffered with respiratory problems. The second kind, the senega, was less commonly used and was considered by Aunt Nel to be a poison that should be avoided.

As Sarah touched the little green plants she remembered a special salve Aunt Nel used to apply externally to swollen and blistered limbs. This salve was made from the poisonous pipsissewa weed which seemed to be very scarce here, whereas the cohosh was everywhere. That was no problem. Sarah knew that the wet marshes and the swamps like Cat Bow, in Lunenburg, had all she needed. The Whites gave little importance to the swamps, not realizing that these were actually the places where many of the very best medicinal herbs and roots, grew most abundantly.

On another Sunday, Sarah would take a trip to Cat Bow Swamp, and in that soggy wetland, she would find the scarce pipsissewa, and the wonderful cattails too. Walking closer to the river bank, Sarah was pleased to see the pokeweed growing fast and there were many of these. She grinned. Pokeweed root was also a poison and it would kill a horse, but parts of that root when carefully mixed with certain berries, could be made into wonderful poultices for rheumatic symptoms or even a nagging cough.

The sun beat down and Sarah was pleased again to find the juniper root and berries doing so well this year. The juniper root and the berries were used to cure kidney related problems, but Sarah herself, considered the leaves of the wintergreen, when crushed and steeped, to be just as effective as the bitter juniper berries. Then she would think what Aunt Nel had told her about sugar or sweet things; "What is sweet to the taste is bitter to the stomach. What is bitter to the taste is sweet to the stomach."

All along that winding bank, the river sang melodiously to her. She looked across to the New Hampshire shore. At some times of year, you could wade across, but spring was not one. Then too, you had to know the right place, for this now swollen river that sang in the sunlight, was also famous for dropoffs and whirlpools, and a deadly under current.

Around her waist, Sarah had tied a small doeskin bag, one she used to jokingly say, "Is as old as Me," and once in a while she would find an herb or a plant that was already big enough to be effectively used in her medicinal supply stock.

"Leafing season or the beginning of life as we know it," Sarah thought, as she followed the river, and watched several ducks cruising along on the back of that waterway. They were in no hurry and they appeared to be visiting with each other, just as she and another person might.

There was one birch tree standing near two elms, and all of them looked so bare, not yet having any leaves. Then Sarah's eyes fell upon a young otter on the opposite bank. He had seen her first, but he gave no sign. For just a second, that little medicine bag of long ago with the otter tails hanging from it was on her mind. Sarah sat down lightly upon a rock at the base of the birch tree and whispered to the otter, "Pay no attention, little brother." She smiled as she watched him slide down the bank and scurry away on his little webbed feet. She would have loved to see that otter play, for they were all marvelous swimmers, able to use their long somewhat flat tails as a rudder. He was a fisher and he was also a comedian when he was not startled. But this one seemed nervous and did not stay to perform his normal otter antics, like slithering and sliding and scampering in and out of the water. "His world is changing too," Sarah thought.

He was suddenly gone, and Sarah said "I hope to see you again, brother." And her face looked wistfully sad, because his kind was scarce now ....like hers.

She rested here a short while and then made her way along up the river. Sarah saw loons swimming on the river and they ignored her presence and seemed also to be talking to one another as they glided past where she stood watching them in silence. "Spirit Ducks," Sarah thought.

She was nearing the point where Cat Bow Brook emptied into the Connecticut River, and the swirling water was roaring and the current was swift here.

Across from Sarah the Agiachook, those Crystal Hills were still an awesome and impressive looking mountain range. Ahead of her, Tarritine Ledge would soon be looming. Sarah was bending again and examining the new and fragile blades of grass, especially the sweetgrass and she was smiling, because it was thick, like it always was at this place. When it got a little bit bigger she would pick some, dry it and burn it in a small dish in her room for there was no smell so rare and sweet as this.

She would also weave a fine necklace of it so as to always have it near her, because there was magic in the sweetgrass. Prayers were sent to the Father on its fragrant smoke and in earlier times, this smoke was actually blown into the ears and eyes and mouth of sick people to heal them. And it usually did. There was more to sweetgrass than baskets.

As Sarah approached the exact place where Cat Bow Brook and the Long River met, she climbed up the embankment and headed toward the road, because the ground was very wet here and there was water everywhere.

She heard a wagon approaching from behind and turned to see a man with a woman and a child as passengers. He stared at Sarah with blue eyes, that somehow seemed more strange looking than they were blue.

The man stopped the wagon and smiled at Sarah. "Like a ride, Missy?" Instinctively she did not like him, his stubble of a beard, his dirty face or even his voice.

"No thank you," she replied and her eyes swept across the woman who was small, with a pinched face and dowcast eyes. There was a huge purple bruise along her jawline. The child sat like a stick, saying nothing.

"We live on the next farm," the driver said all smiles. And Sarah thought, "You are the dirty man, who owns the dirty cows."

She walked at a faster pace now, but he was trotting the horses and they clopped right beside her, and his yap ran on, asking this time, "You live 'round here?" "No," she said, and faced him and there was a contemptuous look on her face that would have discouraged a less drunken man. Sarah was quite a ways now from where she had started out this morning and she did not want this "dirty man," to know where she lived. He licked his red lips when he spoke to her and his voice was so sweet that Sarah had the desire to vomit. This man was "bad news," and her dislike for him was instantaneous. Sarah knew that if he persisted in making a pest of himself that the whole upper Connecticut River valley was not big enough for both of them.

He could see, even in the inebriated state that he was in, that she did not wish to carry on a conversation with him, but still he insisted, "This be my wife, Mae....a sickly soul and this be my step-daughter Molly." Sarah looked at the two women in the wagon and nodded her head to them.

The frail sickly woman nodded back and her bruised face was very tight and drawn. The woman looked like a scared rabbit and the child sat rigid.

"They are both frightened to death of that man!" thought Sarah, and she made a quick turn into the driveway of a farm that they were passing. "Good Day," she said, and he laid the reins hard upon the back of the horses, angry over his dismissal. He looked back at Sarah and she could see him wetting his lips with his tongue and it made Sarah feel somehow "dirty" herself to be leered at by his greedy rum-glazed eyes.

The woman said something to him and he bellowed at her and lashed the horses. Sarah thought, "Slaves...two slaves held by chains of fear!" And this was a strange thought, because somehow Sarah had always connected a slave with the Black race and not the White.

The child was sobbing now, and the disgusting man was growling at the woman, bellowing, "You Dumb Ass!....Ifn' you'd knowed 'nuff to ask her to git in, she would of!" The man raised his hand and Sarah could not hear the slap, but she saw the little woman's head rock from side to side with the force of that blow.

Sarah stopped dead in her tracks and anger boiled up in her throat so strong that she felt like throwing a rock after this yellow-bellied coward.

Then the wagon went around the bend and out of sight with the women slumped forward and Sarah thought, "You damned old goat....someday you will raise your hand and hit the wrong woman!"

From deep inside her head a warning voice said, "It could be you Sarah Jackson."

"It hadn't better be," she thought.

Sarah wandered up that winding road. She decided not to walk back down to the meadows below, because her feet were very wet now. There was one more place and one more thing to be checked out today. Leaving the dirt road she took a climbing shortcut and headed in the direction of Tarritine Ledge, but she had no intention of going to the top of that precipice today. Instead, she combed the low ground there, looking for something special, the moccasin flower, more commonly known as the "lady's slipper." They grew scarce here, but there were always some. It was plain, they were not ready. The internal use of this flower is deadly, but the stem could be ground with other ingredients and it did have some healing properties. What Sarah really wanted was a handful of these delicate little pink and white "moccasins" to pick and put in a vase in her room. When she was a child the softness and the design of this flower fascinated her and it still did.

She passed pussy willows and they were at their prime, so Sarah gathered these and headed back home. Later there would be sweet lilacs to gather and not long after that, the landscape would be decked in the pink and white splendor of fragrant apple blossoms. And for one short time during the leafing season, they would claim this beautiful valley for their own.

The sun was still bright, but it had been hard for Sarah to keep her mind on new things growing, when she was aware that in spite of all the good things in this valley, there were bad things too, like women and children living a life terror and slavery.

Long after the wagon rolled out of sight, Sarah could hear the sobs of the child and in her mind's eye she could see the pinched and bruised face of that woman Mae, no matter where she looked.

"I wonder if she has a family.....this woman, Mae?" Sarah wondered. She instinctively realized that if she did, they would surely help to rescue her and the child called Molly, from the abuse of that dirty man.

It suddenly occurred to Sarah that the man had not told her what his name was, but this really did not matter. He was not a nice man. And, to her way of thinking, Sarah Jackson had already named him.....and it was not a nice name.

Returning to the farm she found the children playing games and the three adults sitting on the long open porch enjoying this fine spring day.

Sarah joined them there and was glad to rest a spell and to take in the sounds and smells of the valley around her.

As the afternoon wore on, Margaret went inside to prepare the evening meal for her family and Sarah, even on one of her days off, went gladly to help, because she liked to do for people who were good to her, to her and to everyone else.

As Margaret checked the roast, Sarah told her what had happened in the wagon that passed her today.

Margaret stuck a two-tine fork into the meat, and said, "So, Old Jed, is at it again, abusing Mae."

"She wears bruises on her face and the child....sits like a stick and cries." said Sarah.

Margaret put the long handled fork down with a thud on the counter top. "He is the meanest man in this valley!" she snapped, and Sarah was quick to ask, "Has she — the wife no family to turn to? She must free her child and herself from that life."

"Don't know much about them," said Margaret and then she went on, "he came here with her and the girl Molly, a few years back. Mae his wife, she is a right sickly woman and she don't mix with others much, but Old Jed, he and his rum bottle, they show up at all neighborly get-togethers, unfortunately!" Sarah looked straight into Margaret's kind eyes and said, "Years ago,... I found a slave woman. She was on the run, hiding out with her two sons, one wounded and one deaf. They were fleeing from their master."

Margaret raised her eyebrows and sucked in her breath and said, "What happened, Sarah?"

Sarah busied herself peeling potatoes and she never looked up but answered "I brought them home. We fed them, treated the wounded boy and then we gave these refugees shelter and packed food to go with them on their long journey to freedom in Canada."

"That was very Christian and good Sarah," said Margaret and then she added, "you would like to help Mae and little Molly too, wouldn't you Sarah?"

"Yes, I would," Sarah stated flatly. Margaret Gee looked at her then and said wistfully, "We all would Sarah. All her neighbors would like to help Mae, but you can lead a horse to water, girl, but you can't make it drink."

Sarah knew that ultimately what the older woman said was, you can't help a person if they won't help themselves and are not willing to take part in the fight. Sarah was sorry for Mae, but not as sorry as she was for the child called Molly.

Margaret wiped her wet hands on a clean towel and reminisced "My Dad always said "only a cowardly man strikes a woman."

Sarah met her eyes squarely and said "My father said that a man who strikes a woman or a child was not brave enough to strike a man." Margaret smiled at Sarah then. "Well Sarah, I guess there are some things that a Vermont farmer and an Indian Chief, had similar thoughts about." Sarah smiled. "The coward's mark...it is the same."

The two women were silent and then from back in her mind, Sarah was recalling the proud black face of that wrinkled and freedom-seeking slave, Eunice Mae. The defiance and determination to be free was a noticeable thing that shined through her eyes. But this courage and strong will was totally lacking on the part of the dirty man's wife.

"She is the worst slave of all," thought Sarah, "One who isn't smart enough to know that she is." But, she was not well, Margaret and her husband had both said this. Perhaps, she did not have the physical strength to stand up against her domineering spouse. "Even so," thought Sarah "there should be at least a spark of resentment in this woman's eyes, but there was none.

Then Sarah heard the words of her father, Peter Jackson, saying "A man's body can be driven into slavery, but not his soul, for the soul is of the Spirit World....and spirits are born free." And Sarah realized sadly, that Peter didn't realize, in his later years that he himself was a slave....to his rum bottle.

When Sarah spoke again she said, "I wish that women knew that all human beings should be accorded their dignity. It is the greatest of all gifts, either to give or to receive." And Sarah knew that this was true, because the old ones said so.

In her dreams that night strange scenes and images clouded her mind. She was back at the circus, but she was not a performer, only a spectator and in the center ring she recognized the whisker-stubbled face of Jed, that dirty man. He danced around the ring, snapping a whip and cracking it over the head of his wife, Mae. She ran in fear and cowered from him and he lashed at her with his whip and his tongue. He was making his wife jump through hoops of fire and she went through them at breakneck speed.

Suddenly at the edge of the ring a real lion pounced and Jed then turned his concentration and his snapping whip upon the lion, which was not a lion at all, but instead a lioness. The lioness snarled at Jed and he dropped the whip and ran away in fear. The lioness did not run after him, but his wife Mae did.

She ran after him because she cared and feared for him, instead of making her own escape to freedom.

The lioness watched, swishing her long golden tail as she did this and then into the ring came the dirty man again, but he had no whip this time. He raised his fist to the lioness, but she was no longer there. And, in her place stood Sarah herself, cold with anger.

Jed bellowed hateful, hurting words that were not true, at Sarah, and she could smell the liquor strong upon his feted breath. His face began to change then and he turned into another man; a taller, far more handsome one in fact, and this man smelled good, like hay and clover. Then suddenly the dirty man had changed into the person of John Somers.

Sarah gasped, and then she heard John's voice as he bellowed obscene accusations at her and flung out a powerful hand to hit her across the face, but Sarah was gone and that lioness was back, standing where Sarah had been. John saw this thing and he was frightened, but he still slapped at the lioness. But, it was Sarah who felt the sting of that slap and then Sarah was no more and it was the lioness that roared at him and her great, sharp claws reached for him, desiring to tear the flesh from his bones. Her teeth were hungry to rip his throat out and with a terrible scream that lioness lunged at her adversary.

This lioness could talk, however, and did, and Sarah woke in a cold sweat and a murderous rage, threatening, "I'll kill you!" Her voice rang out in the stillness of the night.

She sat up in bed and was thankful to see that she was herself and... not an eastern cougar. She examined her hands and saw short, hardworking nails at the ends of her slender fingers. This was a relief, because for a few seconds, Sarah expected to see bloody claws.

Her strong even teeth were those of a human and not the fangs of a great mountain cat. As she became more fully awake Sarah was forced to smother a laugh, because this strange dream had been so real that when she felt the sting of the slap on her face, her rage had been like white coals within. Sarah decided that maybe she should look down and check and make sure that although her upper body was still her own, indeed she did not have a long golden tail, slapping and swishing there under the warm quilts.

In twenty-four years of her life spent among the Indians and including the time she traveled with the circus, Sarah never had a hand laid on her in anger, until this unsettling nightmare.

lying there in the dark and thinking about it, she decided that one part of the dream was a confirmation of her suspicions that only Mae herself could help Mae.

The matter of John Somers appearance was probably because he, like Jed, was controlled by the bottle. And still, deep in her heart, Sarah trusted that John (even a drunken John) would never raise his hand to a woman, especially not to her, to Sarah, who was first named "Gentle Spirit."

The hardest part of the confusing scenes played out in her subconscious mind was to decipher why a woman who possessed such a gentle spirit, had werewolf traits.

Sarah smiled sleepily and solved the puzzle humorously by thinking "that's it....at first blood, Gentle Spirit becomes a bad cat!"

Outside her window, somewhere in the night a loon cried and it was an ominous sound, shattering the darkness, but Sarah did not hear it. She had fallen back to sleep and was deep in dreamland, dancing with John Somers and just like when she was awake and danced with him, the clouds were under their feet.

Sarah's head lay on John's broad chest and encircled by his arms, she could see all of Mother Earth below. And, it was green, and good and part of them — and they were part of it.

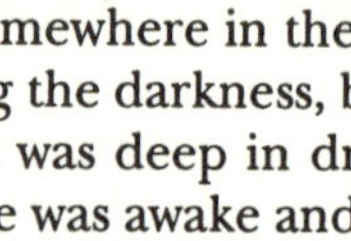

June was here and the peepers sang nightly and around the second week of that month the monotonous whine of the June bugs could also be heard. The lilacs were a little late this spring, but at last, they were prevalent on both sides of the Connecticut River. They varied in shades of light pinkish-purple, orchid, and lastly a deep plum-purple. Sarah had a favorite place to gather lilacs and that was on the Dalton, New Hampshire side of the river, near the old railroad bed. These lilacs were pure white.

Life and work on the farm had fallen pretty much into a routine. Every morning Sarah was up early, ahead of everyone else, making sure that she was bathed and dressed before the rest of this household was awake, because she desired the privacy of the woods to do her morning toilet.

The leaning "old-three-holer," had a well-worn path to its door, but her tracks never led there. To Sarah's way of thinking, this communal comfort station was an abomination. It was a loathsome thing. She had an aversion to that foul-smelling, fly-infested place. In her mind she considered this little building as a health hazard that could never be made clean by the very nature of its existence. "Stink holes spread sickness," Aunt Nel had always said.

Verbally Sarah had never refused to patronize the outhouse, but if this family ever found out that she did not, that she instead had chosen the "old ways," they might think that she was dirty.

She often thought, "Dirty," what could be more dirty than an outhouse?"

Sarah realized that the Gees would not understand this way of thinking, because they were used to "piling it up," which in reality was not as abhorrent a practice, as that of piping it directly into the rivers and streams, and even the ocean.

Sarah wondered if ever there would be a time when the White race would come to understand what was clean and what was dirty? If they progressed to that point of discerning the difference, then many of their strange and communicable diseases would cease to be.

"They will stop someday...or they will die," Aunt Sarah thought.

From her bedroom window then she heard the outside sounds of birds singing and the wonderful aroma of lilacs filled the air. It was impossible to inhale the fragrance of lilacs and think about pollutants like an old-three-holer unless, you sadly realized that, if they did not learn, if they did not stop polluting, then they indeed would die in their own filth... by their own volition.

This was not fair to the lilacs or to the birds who would also die....because these things had no choice.

Sarah's most favorite flower was the apple blossom. She never found any fragrance that so appealed to her as did these blossoms when the trees were dressed in pink and white. This short and beautiful time also passed away and with the entrance of July came a letter from Dennis. He and Peter would be home during August and Peter would stay in the Connecticut Valley, but Dennis, his farm not paid for, was not sure what he would do.

Sarah's heart was light. It would be good to see her brothers again. It was something to look forward too, she thought, as she rubbed the clothes up and down the soapy washboard. Monday was the official wash day and the tub was set outside. A second tub, one heated with a fire underneath it, was used as a scalding tub to take germs off handkerchiefs and the like. "That backhouse needs a darn good boiling," Sarah thought. She continued to scrub the clothes and the harsh soap dried her hands, but that wouldn't cause a fuss, for in her medicine box she had a salve that would undo any damage that the soap hand done.

This was a large family and it took all day to do the washing and half of another day to do the ironing. These were two of Sarah's tasks, but she minded neither one.

In the long summer evenings she gathered sweetgrass for her baskets and when she finally did get the time to sit down and weave the baskets, her dexterous fingers worked fast and with great skill. Sarah seldom had to look at her hands, because she knew what they were doing as each basket took shape and form.

The bottom part of one of the two closets in her bedroom was half full of sweetgrass baskets that would last Sarah's own lifetime and another one besides that.

In the second week of July the hot and humid air changed and a cold wet spell set in which spent itself in torrential rains that left the ground soggy and the small streams swollen.

More seasonable temperatures had not returned before Sarah was awakened in the middle of the night, not by raindrops falling on the roof, but by Margaret Gee, tapping on her door and saying, "Sarah, Aunt Sarah, get up quick!"

Sarah was on her feet and dressed in minutes and she went flying out the door to see what the problem was.

"Old Jed is here, Sarah. I didn't hear the wagon come into the driveway for the rain, but he came to get help. Molly has bad croup and Mae thinks she's dyin'!"

Sarah threw on a heavy shawl and she and Margaret went out into the wet night and climbed into the wagon beside the dirty man called Jed. In the darkness, they could not see the stubble of beard on his unwashed face, but they could smell the stench of stale rum on his person.

Sarah was glad that she had renewed her supply of skunk cabbage, for unpleasant as it was to inhale or eat, it still was a great cure for bronchitis and whooping cough. It was especially effective for croup even if the root itself was extremely poisonous.

Jed lashed the horses and the wagon took off against a hail of wind and rain. Up the road that wagon flew and by the time they arrived at Molly's bedside Sarah and Margaret looked like drowned rats.

Mae had Molly propped up with pillows and she was about frantic.

Molly struggled for each breath and the sound of her breathing was shallow and raspy.

Sarah leaned over and touched the child's forehead and it was hot. She had a very high fever.

Sarah would administer some spirea or meadowsweet in a spoon as soon as Molly stopped coughing and choking so she could. It would help reduce the fever. Sarah mixed this carefully with honey so that the child would not object to the taste. She knew that the honey would help the rawness in her little patient's throat.

This was a bad case of croup. Sarah had only seen one other as bad as this. Aunt Nel had inserted a hollow tube into the trachea of a smothering child in order to let the air pass from the larynx through the bronchial tubes. But that child had no fever and this one did, a raging one. "complicated croup," thought Sarah. Frightened at seeing strangers by her bedside, the little girl began to cry and shake. Sarah smoothed her brow. "Molly, be calm. It is your Aunt Sarah, and I have come to help you." To that gentle voice the sick young one responded.

Sarah helped lift Molly's head up and gave her a spoonful of the meadowsweet mixture. Margaret and Mae stood back and Margaret asked, "What do you think, Sarah?"

Moving out of hearing distance of the little girl, Sarah asked that the child be moved to the kitchen. "Move her to the kitchen?" Margaret questioned and Sarah answered, "Yes, I think I can save her there, but not here. Make a bed for her on the table and get water boiling. We need steam, all the steam that we can get, hurry!"

Jed came in and carried the child, blankets and all, to the table and Mae and Margaret sat kettles of water to boil on top of the big wood-burning stove. Luckily there was already water steaming in the reservoir on the side of that stove, and Sarah had the kitchen table dragged very close beside that reservoir. Next blankets were arranged tent-like over Molly's head and over the steaming reservoir so that when the child breathed, steam went into her nose and throat via this "steam tent."

Sarah asked for dry mustard, to which she measured and added turnip root, pokeweed root, and horseradish root. This was mixed in a dish, water was added and then it was applied to the child's chest. This concoction was strong and stung the nose and the eyes, but within an hour the cough seemed looser and the child's breathing was easier, less labored, and Sarah knew that was a very good sign.

Often she touched Molly's forehead and was pleased to see that the fever was going down also. Sarah soothed the little girl when she fussed, saying, "Molly, see how the 'steam wigwam' helps you."

As the congestion subsided, Sarah asked a more alert Molly, "Is your throat sore?" The child shook her head yes, and Sarah made her a promise saying, "We'll stop that too, Molly."

Sarah asked for some tea with sugar and to this she added "yellow plant," or gold thread in carefully measured amounts. She held up the cup and Molly drank from it.

At about four in the morning, the fever broke and the croup let go of its little victim. Sarah smiled thinking, "We won... this time we won!"

The tent-affair between the table and the stove had been taken down, but still the whole kitchen was bathed in a cloud of steam. That did not matter, for Molly could breathe now and was out of the woods. That poisonous yellow plant also seemed to be working.

Just before daybreak Molly was carried back to her own bed and there she slept peacefully, while Sarah maintained a silent watch at bedside.

Jed hitched up the wagon and took Margaret home to begin her morning chores and Sarah decided to stay until she felt sure that Molly was out of danger of a relapse.

Going to the child's bedside again and again throughout the day, Sarah realized that Molly had a breathing problem. She spoke of this to her mother. "Has a doctor ever told you that Molly suffers from asthma?"

Mae sipped her tea and nodded that one had. "It comes and goes, especially if she gets nervous or if she gets a cold like now. Then that croup sets in."

Sarah sat across the table from Mae and met her eyes squarely. "Colds can be helped and a resistance can be built up against them, but the nervousness.... that is a harder problem to deal with. If it is Molly's nature to be timid, when she is under stress the asthma will always rear its ugly head. Sarah was also aware that nerves alone could trigger asthma.

Sarah was fishing. She was thinking that with such a mean man around as Jed, perhaps he was the reason the child was nervous.

Mae sipped her tea and stated flatly, "Jed, he's always a roarin' and a rantin' and drinkin' too much. Guess that bothers little Molly."

"I guess it does," Sarah said and then she went on, "People, especially children, can die from an attack of asthma. I did not cure it, I only arrested it for this night. If this little girl is not kept calm, this could happen again and it could be fatal."

Mae's drawn face looked worn and tired and now filling with fear she cried, "God forbid that to happen!"

"Yes, God forbid that, and until then...you should forbid your husband from keeping the child in a tense and worried state."

Tears crept into Mae's eyes and her thin lips trembled as she confessed, "Me forbid! Jed would never do what I forbid! He'd just laugh or else he'd up an hit me or both of us!"

Sarah looked at Mae and felt compassion for her, because she could see the hopelessness in her eyes and hear the anguish in her voice, and even in the droop of her bony shoulders.

Sarah spoke then, "I will talk to him when he gets back."

"Oh, Lord God, No, Aunt Sarah, when he gets to drinkin,' he won't listen to anyone. He'd just as soon hit you as us two, for buttin' into his affairs. He's fearsome when he's boozin' Aunt Sarah....he is a devil!"

"Ummmmph." was all that Sarah said, but when Jed opened the door to come inside for his breakfast, Sarah sat down across from him.

"Your drinking and bellowing is killing your child!" she stated flatly.

Jed finished cutting up the slice of ham on his plate and then he made a snarling face, "Don't need no damned Injun tellin' me 'bout my own kin!" he said.

Sarah levelled a gaze at him that would have frightened a sober man and snapped coolly, "You need someone to tell you this. Unless you mend your ways, your young one will not see next summer. She has constriction of the breathing tubes caused by fear...fear of you, I think."

Jed stopped eating and glared at Sarah and retaliated, "Too damned bad what you think! You go git inta' that God damned wagon and I'm takin' you home Missey, right now!"

Sarah stood up from the table and faced him. "Mr. Jed," she said, "Molly needs more medicine. I will stay and give it to her. She may be afraid of you, but I am not, Mr Jed. She is my patient....not yours."

Anger flooded Jed's face. The nerve of that Indian Witch Doctor, to come into his own house and accuse him of making Molly sick.

"If'n I say to git out—you'd best be goin' Missey," he threatened and Aunt Sarah met his cold gaze and answered, "If I go from this house this way, with my work not done, for the rest of your life Mr. Jed, never call me for a sickness of you or any of yours." Sarah's stare was very intimidating to her adversary.

Mae had been standing back, wringing her hands and noticing that Sarah didn't seem to be afraid of Jed. Now she half cried and half yelled, "Damn you Jed! That's my baby...my flesh and blood in there. You leave Aunt Sarah alone, you drunken old fool. She saved my Molly last night and she's a goin' when I say she's a goin' which is when she thinks its safe to leave Molly!"

One woman Jed could beat up, but two, no way. Besides, that damned squaw had a look in her eye that said she could kill a man as quick as she could look it him. Jed was not so drunk but what he could see that. He got up and laughing a bitter laugh, he departed from the kitchen.

Sarah did not leave until after dark that night. Molly was much better now, and she left two kinds of herbal medicine for Mae to give to the little girl; a gargle of sumac, and some balsam-honey cough syrup.

Jed had been quiet during the supper hour and when he saw that Sarah was about to leave, he got up and announced that he had brought her here and that he would take her home.

"I wish to walk, thank you." Sarah said, and this made Jed very angry. He supposed she thought she was too damned good to ride with the likes of him anyhow. Mae looked perplexed when Jed snarled, "I could drag you out of here to that wagon!"

Sarah turned and replied coolly, "Mr. Jed.... you hadn't better try that," and with a harsh glance into his eyes, Jed looked away.

Aunt Sarah made a final check on her patient. "Molly, Aunt Sarah is going home now, but if you need me, I will be here in no time."

Thank you Aunt Sarah," the young one said, and then Sarah touched Molly's face to make sure that the fever had not returned and she said, "Molly, would you do something for yourself and also for Aunt Sarah?" The little girl nodded, and Sarah continued, "Molly, sometimes there are situations that we can not get out of or away from. When we are trapped in a place or a circumstance and we cannot help the situation we become a victim of it." Then Sarah went on, "Molly, sometimes when we can't escape from an unpleasant thing, our bodies tighten up, our lips and our throat and suddenly we can't breath." Now Aunt Sarah fished deeply and she asked, "Has this ever happened to you, Molly?"

Before the child confirmed her suspicions, Sarah knew what had to be done.

"Molly, I think if you will do something for me and for you, you might not be sick so much. You want to know what that is?"

"Yes," the child replied, her hand's twisting compulsively on the yarn hair of a rag doll.

Aunt Sarah smiled and continued, "It is simple, Molly, and it works! When we can't remove our body from what is making us upset and sick, we put it out of our minds and that is our escape route. Do you understand, Molly?" and feeling that the child understood this in its simplistic form, Aunt Sarah went on, "From now on Molly, when your father is... not himself, when he is drunk, I want you to not think about him or your mother either. You think about happy things, like a picnic with friends. But mostly, you shut your eyes and think of a beautiful mountain stream and crystal water slowly, slowly slapping against the shoreline. And in your mind's eye Molly, you think of fish slowly swimming and watching you back."

Molly smiled and Sarah said, "Slow water Molly, very slow crystal water and then you can imagine all the beautiful animals that come to drink of that clear water, the deer and the fox and the great bear, and so....Molly, you have escaped your fathers bad times. And you have made your escape to a peaceful place with birds and animals and fish. Since your mind is away from trouble and stress, your throat will not constrict and I think you will be able to breathe much, much better."

Molly promised that she would try this, and Sarah left her then, saying that she would be back tomorrow and tell Molly a real Indian story and the little girl was delighted. They each promised, "Honest Injun" and Aunt Sarah left the room.

Sarah went over the medicine dosage with Mae again and then she headed out into the night, hoping that little Molly would be able to find her escape from the stress of her life in that house.

It was misting outside and Sarah's slender shadow drifted into that black nothingness called night. She walked along the narrow dirt road and was glad that she was away from that house that held such sadness, Mr. Jed's.

She ventured along and about a half mile from home she could see the flicker of lightening in the distance. Suddenly up ahead of her, Sarah heard a sound, and as she moved toward that sound, the silhouette of a large dog could be distinguished. She knew it was a dog, being able to tell this by its gate, and moments lager she knew who the dog was.

Old Moses, the Gee family pet walked silently up to her and Sarah bent and scratched his ears and as she neared him, she could smell the slightly unpleasant aroma of his coat. She felt that this was a small price to pay for such good company. She was glad to have the fellowship of this trusted friend on this wet and dreary night. Moses licked Sarah's outstretched hand and they walked on together, getting wetter with each step toward home.

"Ah Moses, old friend! You came to meet me. Next time your nose is full of porcupine quills, I will not forget this and I will snip the ends of those quills so that they will come out easier." She chuckled to herself after she spoke this and Moses wagged his tail good naturedly and instinctively knew that Aunt Sarah would have done this good deed even if he had not come to meet her.

Sarah knew that Moses understood that he was one of her brothers and she said, "Friend Moses, I wish there were more around like you....than like him," as she compared the faithful sheep dog's good heart and trustworthy qualities with those of that drunken bully, the "dirty man" called Jed.

As they neared the homestead, the flickering lamps could be detected through the windows and they looked warm and welcome to Sarah and to Moses.

"Moses needs a bath, but at least his dirt is on the outside and will wash off," thought Sarah.

And that man Jed, for his part, had sat in the corner of the kitchen and glowered as Sarah ignored him and made her silent exit from his home, in her own time, and in the manner of her own choosing. The very thought of this angered and disgusted him, but he decided not to follow her.

Outside the nightbird softly wobbled and that feathered creature, so in tune with all of nature, could have told that dirty man, that he had made a wise decision...very wise indeed.

A season of rain came and lasted until the second week into July, and ended as abruptly as it had begun. There was within that span of days one eventful evening. A marauding "awasos," black bear made a middle-of-the-night raid on the sheep pen, and killed two ewes and mauled a third so badly that Fred had to shoot it out of mercy.

Moses had driven the bear off and Fred got up, and in the confusion of the animal sounds and the surrounding darkness he had gotten a shot off after the bear, but he had cleanly missed.

The light of day clearly showed that the bear was more intent on tearing the milk bags off the ewes and getting the milk than he was in devouring the meat of the sheep, but regardless, the youngest lambs had to be bottle fed now and Sarah and the two oldest boys did this.

Fred began an all-night vigil, sitting in the dark with his rifle across his lap and waiting for the bear to return. The sheep pen itself was guarded with torch light, and looking out her window toward the flickering light, so bright orange against the dark sky, Sarah found it strange that a bear would be so bold unless it was very hungry. She decided this probably was the case, as every time land was cleared by a logging operation, more of the natural habitat and food supply for her animal brothers was lost. It seemed, that those that had been stolen from would in turn also steal to exist.

The smell of drying sweetgrass and strawberry shortcake filled the air today, and Old Moses got his bath, but not before a skunk had gotten him—and good! Thus, in a state of disgrace the dog had been thoroughly sprayed, but because this had happened to him as he was attempting to drive a skunk away from the chicken coop, Moses was considered a hero. "An unfortunate and stinking one," Sarah thought, but only said, "Oh no, Moses!" as the big family pet pawed at his tearing eyes and rolled in the dirt unsuccessfully to rid himself of the stench of skunk scent.

In a kettle, home made stewed tomatoes were mashed into a juice and then this was rubbed all over Moses. Then he had a vinegar bath, and his final bath found him standing in a tub of luke-warm water while Sarah scrubbed him down with homemade soap and added ground mint leaves to the rinse water.

"Whew Moses!" laughed Sarah, "Next time, you give him the chickens and any fresh eggs too!"

When the indignities of his first public bath were over Moses was towel dried, and then Sarah had cut apples in half and the younger Gee children rubbed the meat of the apples all over the dog's coat. Between the tomato juice, the vinegar and the mint, Moses emerged smelling like a dog, almost. The pectin of the apples did more to restore his natural scent than anything else.

Sarah had her arms down in the water, and by the time the dog was considered as smelling better, she decided that she wasn't any apple blossom herself. He smelled like a dog and she smelled like a skunk wearing mint perfume.

"Ah, Moses, Who is the "stinking hero" now?" grinned Sarah.

As the children took over and began rubbing the apples into the dog's fur, Sarah said, "He has learned one very valuable lesson, this one." She turned her steady gaze toward the dog, as the children asked," What did her learn, Aunt Sarah?" Aunt Sarah grinned, "To confront a skunk, no matter how noble....is to lose big!"

With a clean bar of soap and a fresh change of clothing, Sarah slipped away and walked along the riverbank to a secluded spot that was sat off by some small bushes and alders. Here she stripped and went into the water and rubbed her body vigorously with soap. She put her arm up and could still smell the skunk scent and so she scrubbed her arms again, and then she rubbed sand all over her body, for this was a better cleaner than any soap. It left no perfume or false order. It cleaned skin and never dried it out as soaps did.

When this was done, Sarah just swam there in the sunlight, in that pure blue water. She returned then to the bank and dried her body on towels and proceeded to get dressed.

She combed her wet hair and it was long and silky. Even now, in the middle of summer, she could see already that the sun was starting to fade the blue-black of her hair color. The ends of the tresses were becoming that reddish-black shade that her father so detested, but that would have to be, for Sarah had no bear grease unless, that bear came back and Fred got lucky and shot him, she grinned wryly.

It had been a long day and Sarah was tired when her bath began, but now the sand and the clear water had given her body a new surge of life, and she was suddenly full of energy and very hungry.

Walking back across the lawn toward the house, Sarah noticed a wagon parked in the drive, and who sat there inside the wagon, but Old Jed, Mae and little Molly.

They were engaged in a friendly conversation with Fred and Margaret, when Sarah, barefooted and carrying a basket of dirty clothing, made her way toward the porch.

"It's Aunt Sarah, Mother!" exclaimed Molly, and they called to Sarah, and she put the offensive basket down on the doorstep and made her way toward the wagon.

"Hello, Aunt Sarah!" the little girl beamed, and then went on, "See, Aunt Sarah, I'm all better and I came to say thank you!"

Sarah smiled warmly at the youngster, "Hello, Miss Molly," she said, and continued, "So glad that you are so fine today!"

Sarah saw gratitude reflect on Mae's thin and pinched face, and above his black stubble beard she could feel old Jed's eyes, and they were appraising Sarah like she was a piece of meat on a skewer.

"Well, if taint the Missey, herself," he said with mock sarcasm in his voice and Sarah avoided his beady little eyes and nodded her head politely. Mae spoke then. "Aunt Sarah, we came to bring you something for what you did for Molly here," and with that she handed Sarah a silver dollar. Sarah turned it over in her hand and then passed it back.

"Seeing her up and about, is good enough pay," Sarah said, but the mother and father, too, insisted that she take their money in pay for her services. Aunt Sarah thanked them and slipped the money into the pocket of the cotton dress she was wearing.

"You folks goin' up ta Guildhall Hill for that barn raisin' next Saturday?" The "dirty man," wanted to know, and Sarah, had until now been looking forward to going.

"Maggie and I and the kids, we may go, dependin' on if that bar comes back or if lightnin' strikes the backhouse." Fred joked, and all of them that were gathered around the wagon laughed. Aunt Sarah laughed the hardest of all because she hated that little backhouse, and it would be a funny sight if indeed lightening did strike it..., especially if that "dirty man" Jed....was in it!

While the two families were bidding goodbye to one another, Molly whispered to Sarah, "Aunt Sarah, it works! I tried it and I could breathe!" Sarah smiled, It was good that mind over matter had won until the little mite picked up a cold. But colds were nothing, stress now— was something.

Once inside, Sarah washed her hands and began helping Margaret with preparations for supper, and she chose to ignore Jed's parting comment. "You save a dance for me Aunt Sary!"

"Save a dance," she thought. If that old fool was going, then Sarah Jackson would not.

Long after the dishes were done and the children had been sated with their favorite stories, Sarah rocked in the big oak rocking chair in her bedroom. Her hands worked mechanically on a sweetgrass basket while her mind went over the prospect of seeing Dennis and Peter soon. It would be good to hear Dennis play the fiddle again.

Shortly before going to bed, Sarah took the silver dollar and put it into that wool stocking where she kept all of her money. She half smiled, because her savings were growing each month, and yet, she knew that if Mae ever got up the nerve to take Molly and run away from her husband, that she would give her all of the money in that stocking. And never expect a dime of it back. If this thing ever came to be, then once again she would have helped some more slaves to freedom.

Sarah hoped that the bear would not bother the sheep. The sound of the bleating and dying animals was a harsh one to wake up to. Outside her window all seemed calm and the catbird screamed from the forest floor, while inside the curtain swung with the night breeze. Against the glass, the flicker and glow of the firelight spitting from the torches that guarded the sheep pen below, looked orange and red. They were like flames leaping from a nightfire of long ago.

The crickets chirped and someone began to walk across the wide boards of the woodshed floor below, apparently headed for the outdoor privy. Then from another corner of the house a hinge creaked in the night, different from all the other sounds.

For just a minute, Sarah stood there almost mesmerized by those leaping lights that reflected on her window pane and she was sure that she was being drawn to them. But it was not now, it was a nightfire in another time. Sarah felt that if she stared at that fire real hard, she could see the gaunt shadows of her father and Aunt Nel, crouching before their fire, and also listening to all the valley sounds as daylight passes into darkness.

The hinge squeaked again, and this brought Sarah back from that childhood nightfire. She was fighting tears, as she left the past and listened to a new sound, which was old Moses answering the sharp bark of some neighboring dog.

Sarah's full lips curved into a soft smile, and just before retiring she thought, "Moses, friend....a skunk has also crossed my path... I will do what I told you— avoid him."

The weeds were growing faster than the corn in the garden where Sarah swung the hoe. The maize, as her family always called the corn, was doing well with a little help of the hoe now and then.

Sarah smiled as she worked at her task, bending every now and then to get rid of unwanted start-up weeds. Sweetgrass just grew, but corn and potatoes and carrots, these crops took some work.

As she worked the sun shone brightly on her upswept hair, and small drops of perspiration slid slowly down her face. Her skin was very copper-colored now, and her rosy cheeks bespoke of vitality and health.

Sarah watched the morning sun, and knew that it would soon be time to leave this job and start another one inside the house. It was baking day for Margaret and the day that Sarah churned the butter.

As Sarah entered the farm kitchen, Margaret handed her a letter, and as she took it she thought, "Two within two weeks...strange." Her next thought was disappointing, because she decided that it must be Dennis and Peter, with some complication arising in their lives. This might mean that possibly they were not coming after all.

Sarah reached for the letter and then dropped into a sturdy wooden chair and examined the envelope carefully.

This was not the hand-writing of her brother Dennis. She did not recognize it at all. Upon closer inspection she saw that the letter was postmarked, Berlin, New Hampshire. While opening the envelope she racked her brain, trying to think who she knew over there in Androscoggin Country, and then it hit her. It had to be from John Somers.

Sarah knew that this letter held very important news for her and in fact foretold, in a way, her destiny. She sensed this letter would be the permanent entrance of this young man into the life of Sarah Jackson, or else it would be the last time that she ever heard from him.

Sarah's hands trembled as she began to read the message scrawled inside and she was resigned to accept the news within, good or bad.

July 10, 1850

Dear Sarah:

I'm hoping this letter finds you well and happy. I thought of you when the apple blossoms were ripe because you like them. I have taken no alcohol since I last saw you, but I gambled more, so I have to save up some money now.

If you are interested in me, I will be back in August. If no other has claimed you, can I come courting when I get there?

I run my life now, not the bottle.

Please answer. If you say no, I'm out of your life forever. If you say yes, would you marry me?

Your friend,
John David Somers

Sarah's face broke into a bright smile and her heart was very glad. She folded up the letter and tucked it into her apron pocket, and after washing her grimy hands, took her place by the old butter churn.

Shortly after the noon meal, Sarah returned to her bedroom and sat down at the rickety desk-table and answered the letter that would change her life. With a steady hand and a loudly pounding heart, she answered John's letter.

July 17, 1850

Dear John,

I received your letter. It is with a glad heart that I answer your questions.

Yes.

Yes.

And it's about time.

Your friend,
Sarah Ann Jackson

Sarah was not a loquacious person and even less of a writer. But scanning her short message she decided that it said all that was necessary to say. After all, she was a basket maker by trade and not a writer. John knew that she was by nature quiet and besides she knew that he could talk a rock to death.

"It must be his White blood," thought Sarah.

Early the next day Sarah and Margaret and all the children went blackberrying. They filled buckets and pails and ate a lunch in the woods on the side of a dirt road in South Guildhall. The berries were plentiful and the pulp was sweet and juicy. Margaret had already promised the kids a blackberry cake for supper, and the thought of that palatable golden colored cake, dotted with black gems, made the water run in Sarah's mouth.

The family had been picking berries near a beaver pond, on the lower side of a marsh. They had seen the tracks of one moose and the children were fascinated by the distant beaver lodges. There were at least three different families of prime beaver living there and they worked the pond together well. Each time a flat beaver's tail slapped the water, the children would stop and watch and listen and Sarah was amazed that the young ones knew so little about the brother beaver.

In the northern corner toward the main part of the dam, a beaver stood on a mound of sticks and with its beaver-hands appeared to be rubbing its belly. "He is scratchin' fleas," said one of the older children, and Aunt Sarah's knowing smile, caused another voice to say, "Ain't that so, Aunt Sarah?"

"He is grooming himself, ridding himself of ticks and those blood-sucking leeches, and he is also removing twigs. He must do this when emerging from the water in the lodge."

"If he spends all day cleaning his coat, how can he get any work done?" someone questioned, and Aunt Sarah stopped her blueberry picking for a minute and said, "Grooming is a very important part of living to a beaver. Sometimes whole families help comb and groom one another. It is necessary to stimulate the oil glands in the sack on the beaver's belly in order to keep his pelt re-oiled. It is this precious oil that water-proofs the beaver's coat."

"Aunt Sarah, how come you're so smart?" Nadine wanted to know, and Sarah said, "Because I watch the animals and I listen to the children."

"Aunt Sarah, when are beaver born?" Sarah who seemed totally caught up in filling her pail with berries, took no time in replying. "Some kits are born in April, some in May. Right now, inside these lodges there are beaver kits, but their parents have them hid."

Margaret smiled and said to her children, "That is enough questions for Aunt Sarah today, now you youngens' get back to pickin' berries instead of Aunt Sarah's brain."

"It is all right, Margaret, I like to tell the children about the brother beaver. We will go one day just to watch and see the new kits, maybe."

Content in the knowledge that when she promised them something Sarah would deliver, these children did their mother's bidding and went back to the business of picking blackberries.

"It is good that they have such interest," thought Sarah, "for to know the living habits of a stranger somehow makes him no longer that."

Old Moses lay under a white pine out of the bright sunshine, just content to be a part of this expedition, but suddenly he rose, the fur rising high on his back, and he made a strange sound.

Sarah put up her hand and motioned to Margaret to come away, and she did. When the two women got to the bottom of the grade, Moses was slinking around, making little whimpers, and Sarah was very sure that the dog had caught the scent of a black bear. Dogs will act in just such a way, wanting to protect their own, but knowing with an inner canine instinct that avoiding contact with this animal was by far the most intelligent choice.

"What is it, Sarah?" Margaret whispered, not to alarm the children who were scattered about, and Sarah said "It is 'awasos,' the bear. Not the grandfather but the grandmother. We will gather the children and leave because she most likely has her cubs with her and the grandmothers are fiercely protective if they feel their young are threatened."

"I hope its not the one that's been killin' our sheep!" said Margaret in a hushed whisper, so that only Sarah heard.

"Come children, all of you come right now. It is late and we are going home." Margaret issued this command and they came one by one from the direction of the four winds, and Nadine was carrying little Jacinta.

"What is wrong, Ma?" the oldest boy wanted to know, and Margaret said. "Nothing is wrong. It is time to go back so that I can make that blackberry cake for supper." But she had said this too loud, with too much emotion, trying to hide her fear, and one by one the children sensed this and they came closer to where Sarah and Margaret stood, their berry pails nearly full.

Moses still whimpered and hung around Margaret's legs, and just then from the high ground above them came a snarl and a growl. It was not an attacking sound yet, Sarah knew. This was just a fair warning that they were intruding on the bear's turf. She turned and said to the others, "Just walk slowly away. She is just a greedy berry picker today," and then from the underbrush a streak of black crossed their path and Sarah bid that they all stop, and they did.

The cub came back in their direction. This could be a terrible situation, Sarah knew, and then Moses set to barking fiercely and backing away.

"Walk ahead slowly!" Sarah told the children, and they did and Moses followed along, but the cub stayed hidden now and the perturbed mother bear started lumbering along behind the family.

Somewhere in the distance a beaver slapped his tail and gave warning, and the bear stopped and stood up on her hind legs and sniffed the air.

Passing a jagged stump, Sarah stopped and dumped a pile of juicy berries out on top of it. "Here Grandmother! my gift to you today. I picked these just for you!" And with that she turned and followed after the worried Margaret and her brood, who now were almost up to the narrow dirt road.

Moses came back and walked beside Sarah, still making strange sounds and acting funny. Sarah scratched his ears and walked swiftly on. And by the time the family made its way onto that wonderful looking road, US Route 2, that old grandmother and not one, but two cubs were eagerly devouring the berries Sarah had left on the stump for them.

"Good thing you thought to bribe her, since we got no gun," Margaret said, and Sarah replied, "Well, we have much to eat and she has not." Margaret was again astounded by Sarah's always sympathetic heart toward those furry creatures she called "her brothers."

"I was gettin' worried about you back there, Aunt Sarah, I was afraid you would be treed or mauled."

Sarah chuckled, "Could have happened, but I figured she would swap me for a prepared meal!" and with this she and Margaret both laughed, with Margaret adding, "What ifn' she'd chosen you for the meal, Aunt Sarah?"

"I would be tough chewing and go down hard!" Sarah answered as the silo of the Gee barn rose up before them.

"Never got driven out of a berry patch before," Margaret remarked, and Sarah said, "Usually the 'awasos,' they run away before you know they are there, and if they don't run away Margaret....then you do, fast."

"Father will laugh when he hears this!" exclaimed Nadine, and her mother retorted, "If he wants any cake, he won't!"

Sarah laughed hard now, and she was thinking, "Margaret my good friend, your skin is different, but your heart is like my own." And then Aunt Sarah had another thought. "Our hides are not the same, but we all try to survive here, often taking from each other those things that we should share."

Well on this bright July day, Sarah Jackson of the Bear Clan had shared with her brother the bear, the berries that her hands had picked, and now her heart was full. She thought, "Good eating, Awasos!"

Margaret had called this gesture a bribe, but Sarah knew it was more than a peace offering. It was a simple matter of respecting another living creature and of sharing the bounty that the Great Spirit had put here to sustain us all, not just a few of us.

Three clotheslines stretched across one side of the bedroom that Sarah called her own, and upon these lines hung sweetgrass drying. It had been cleaned with Sarah's antique hardwood comb. Sarah had combed through the aromatic hanks of the "Holy Grass" to remove the roots and the spiderlets and weak culms. The special comb that Aunt Sarah worked with was a sweetgrass comb that had belonged to Aunt Nelemano. She had told Sarah many times that it had been carved out of wood by Aunt Nel's grandfather for her grandmother and was given to her as a wedding gift; and as rough looking as it may be with its six teeth, it was of course, very dear to Aunt Sarah. Now, one tooth was cracked and another showed signs of wear. It had been enthusiastically pulled through hanks of sweetgrass, trimming it and making it smooth and ready to braid, for two generations before Sarah's own hands had ever been trusted to touch it. "You are old but you serve me well," thought Sarah.

The small room smelled wonderful from the aroma of that sweetgrass. It was tied in bunches and then hung over the lines. When wet again, no matter how dry the grass, that wonderful inimitable fragrance of the sweetgrass would return. When Sarah's hands worked with it, shaping the silky smooth strands into cords, ropes and finally baskets, even on the darkest and dreariest day of the winter, when she wet the grass, the wonderful scent of summer and sweetgrass would surround her. This was very good, for to the Abenakis, sweetgrass was the smell of summer itself.

As long as the sweetgrass grew, Aunt Sarah would cling to the tradition of basket making, just as surely as the waxy stain from that "Holy Grass" would cling to her fingers, leaving them soft to the touch and fragrant to the smell.

Sweetgrass, being sacred and beloved by the Great Spirit, was much used by shamans as well as Native American herbalists, and Sarah believed with all of her heart in the magic and the mystery it possessed. She also felt that hands that worked with sweetgrass, were hands that had been blessed with a special gift of healing.

The end of July was fast approaching, and this was the time to gather the skunk cabbage roots and also the roots of the wild ginger.

Sarah collected her inner-bark medicine stock later in the fall, at the end of the growing season. But come spring, there were always flowers that must be gathered just before they opened, being free from dew or dampness. Flowering herbs had to be picked two days after a rain.

Seeds had to be collected when almost, but not quite ripe, just before the pods had opened and if she was not ready when these herbs and plants were ready, they were lost.

In addition to drying sweetgrass there was usually some flower or herb suspended, drying in the confines of Sarah's bedroom, and sometimes it looked messy to the outsider, but there was life-saving medicines drying here.

Some days were truly not long enough for all that Aunt Sarah had to do, but this was fine, because she was so busy that she had no time to grieve for the past. She also had very little time to sit around and think about the future, which was a good thing, since man had very little control of either the past or the future.

To survive and to live each present day was what Aunt Sarah's goal was, just like that of the grandmother bear that had eaten her berries, with no worry of tomorrow, only living well today; not too different from that sweetgrass waving in the swamp near Tarritine Ledge.

Sitting in front of the small desk, Sarah made a note for herself that would remind her to replenish some of her dyes for her baskets. She needed to steep some indigo roots and the longer she steeped these, the darker the color blue became. Sarah always made the color yellow from the root of the golden thread, and the color brown was made by steeping alder bark, but she had also made a durable dye from boiling the shell of the black butternut.

Her greenish-yellow shades were all but depleted, and for these she would use Aunt Nelemano's recipe of boiling together the bark of the elm with white cedar twigs. Checking her stock, Sarah was sure that she had enough red shades. These were the easiest ones to find as there were so many varieties of berries from which those red shades could be made.

She moved toward the window and seated herself in the rocking chair, and was about to begin construction of a new basket when a sharp rap on the door called her from this task.

Sarah went to the door and found Margaret standing there with Grammy Gee's breakfast tray, of which she had not eaten a morsel.

"Sarah," Margaret said, "I hate to bother you, but would you go in and take a look at Mother Gee? She won't eat because she says everything is either binding her up or giving her terrible gas."

Sarah nodded and followed Margaret back to the elderly woman's bedroom, where they found her sitting up in bed, her tiny birdlike eyes searching Sarah's face. "You do not feel well, Grandmother?" Sarah questioned, knowing this gastric condition or "state of flatulence," as once she heard a medical doctor call it, was a common complaint of the elderly.

"It don't matter what I eat, I'm tooting my horn in good fashion," the old lady snapped, and Sarah suppressed a smile. She liked a patient that told you what was wrong.

Sarah sat down on the bed beside Grammy, and said, "If you could walk more and get exercise this would not be, I think."

Sarah looked at a nearby chair and saw all the clothing that this grandmother had worn that day, and she wondered why this elderly woman had to wear a brassiere? At this ripe old age Grammy Gee was thin and shapeless. Sarah smiled and said, "Grandmother, you need comfort in your old age — not support." She talked a minute with the elderly matriarch and then said, "I will come back with some special tea and it will help you to digest your food, especially at night."

She went to the kitchen and Margaret watched with keen interest as Sarah brewed some dried leaves of peppermint together with a handful of seeds that Sarah knew as fleawort or psyllium. To this she added some rosemary herb and a tablespoon of honey.

It was not too bad-smelling, and Margaret followed Sarah back to where the elderly crone still sat propped up on her pillows.

"Here Grandmother," smiled Sarah, "this tea at night will do all the things that aid the digestive system, that your legs can no longer do. And it will help you to sleep better."

The small woman sipped the concoction and was surprised that it was indeed quite flavorful.

"Grandmother, during the day, when you are up, if you would not wear that....brassiere, I think you also would feel better and this would help the gastric condition." Now Grammy Gee took slight offense, as she clucked with her tongue and said, "Child, I have worn that under garment since I was a mere snip of a girl, I won't stop now!"

Sarah set her mouth, and Margaret hid a smile as Sarah stated simply, "Anything that binds you...is making your body work harder to do what it must do."

"You wear one!" said the older woman, and Sarah smiled and replied, "Because everyone else does! I hate them. For all their support, I feel they are trying to squeeze the life out of me. When I am older, I will never wear one!" Sarah's passion on the subject surprised them all.

"Why not, if you wear them now?" questioned Grandmother Gee, and Sarah said, "Because I can move about, but later when I will not be so active, I know that this will hurt me, and bother in the digestion of my food...most likely making me belch and hiccup and toot my horn in good fashion, too."

Now the grandmother was thinking about what the young woman said. She supposed this could be a reason that her food was always talking back to her, but she wasn't sure.

"I would like you to drink this tea, one half cup at noon before you eat and a full cup after supper and another at bedtime." The elderly woman agreed to do this and then she handed Sarah the empty cup and settled down against the pillows, and questioned the young herbalist with the copper-colored skin and the straight eyes. "Are you sure, it ain't necessary for me to wear a brassier, Aunt Sarah?" Aunt Sarah chuckled, "Grandmother, if you had no feet, would you need any shoes to wear?" Sarah's eyes crinkled at the corners and both women laughed.

And so it had finally happened: after seventy-nine years trapped inside the bra, Grammy Gee was liberated!

The Saturday morning chores were done as always, only today would be a little different than most Saturdays. There was going to be a barn-raising up on Guildhall Hill and the Gee family was going, all except Aunt Sarah, who had volunteered to stay home and keep an eye out for her patient.

As the wagon pulled out of the driveway, filled with tools for Fred to work with and food that Margaret had already prepared, Grandmother Gee picked at her breakfast and said, "I am feeing better, Aunt Sarah, but I'd still like to know what you put into that tea that I'm drinkin'?" Aunt Sarah answered, "Fleawort for constipation, rosemary and honey to help you to sleep, and peppermint to aid your gastric problem."

The elderly woman smiled at Sarah and said, "I just wanted to make sure it wasn't rattlesnakes blood or something." Aunt Sarah smiled and replied, "The ancient ones did use that, as a sure-cure for a hard birthing, but now we use raspberry leaves and partridge berries mixed together to ease labor in hard confinement cases."

"Sounds a lot more palatable to me" said the older woman, and Sarah had to agree with her.

Sarah was remembering how Aunt Nel always maintained that the leaves of the raspberry were excellent relaxants for the uterine muscles, and part of her black bottle mixture, contained these.

Thinking back to Sarah's Aunt Nel, Elizabeth Gee replied, "You know Sarah, in a baby case, your Aunt Nel was an angel!" Sarah smiled and said, "In any case...I always thought she was."

Then quickly, the elderly woman said, "Sarah, you didn't have to stay home with this old horse, you know!" Sarah said, "Yes, I know."

In actuality Aunt Sarah would have liked to have attended that barn-raising with the rest of the family, but then she just might run into that "dirty man," and she knew that the best way to stay out of trouble with that skunk was to stay clear of him. He was planning on dancing with her if she was there, but she would not be there.

Sarah had waved the fully loaded wagon away, and wished that she was going with the rest. At a barn-raising there was work to be done, and food to be shared and the sound of fiddle music to dance to at the end of the day. Sarah would have loved to have gone and danced. She had not danced since she left the circus, but the thought of dancing with Jed killed all desire to dance.

By not attending this function, she had done the right thing, because a confrontation with that skunk was something that she did not need. Now, if her brother Dennis was here and was playing the fiddle, she would go, and if John Somers was here she would go, for Jed would stay away from those two gentlemen, of this she was sure. And, as Sarah thought of John and Dennis, she was wondering how they would get along when both their trails led here next month. Then she smiled. John did not know about Dennis and there was no problem there, but Dennis had openly spoken that he did not like John. Sarah hoped that upon meeting a sober John, Dennis would find that the more he knew the man, the more he would come to respect and like him. If this was not to be the case...well, what would be— would be.

Up on Guildhall Hill, a barn was indeed being constructed and almost every family in the immediate area was represented as neighbor helped neighbor, and Sarah had guessed exactly right. Because, when that "dirty man" arrived; unshaven and sour smelling, he had driven up alone, claiming that Mae and Molly were down with a cold.

The disgust was apparent on Margaret's face when he made his way through the crowd and asked where Sarah was? Upon hearing that she was not there, disappointment and displeasure shown clearly on his surly face.

Jed pretended to work a little while with the rest of the men, but long before the other workers put down their saws and hammers to enjoy a well-earned supper, old Jed was gone, saying lamely that "Mae and Molly might be needin' him."

Back in the big farmhouse kitchen, Sarah prepared the final meal of the day for Elizabeth. Sarah's own day had been full, for she had again slipped away to the edge of the Connecticut River and bathed and washed her hair. Then she collected some flowering herbs, gathering them when they had no dew on them, and these were taken back to her room to be dried.

Saturday was a general house-cleaning day and though she was short handed, sarah did what she could.

The day was beautiful and the sky was blue and almost cloudless, and Sarah had helped Grammy over to her favorite rocking chair on the porch. She had sat down beside her while the old woman told of other times and people long since gone. Sarah listened quietly and her hands were moving constantly as she began the construction of a large round, sweetgrass basket. Sarah enjoyed this verbal history and she did not mind the elderly woman's memoirs of a past that she remembered with clarity and great attention to detail.

She told Sarah what her own Grandmother, who came from England, had told her about a life across the Atlantic Ocean. As Grammy talked about this British ancestor of hers, Sarah thought about Brynn Ellingwood. Sarah missed Brynn and how she wished that Brynn, that good English woman, could only be here now to meet a good Indian— her brother Dennis.

The hour spent in Elizabeth Gee's company on the veranda had been a good one, and Sarah had been a little reluctant to take the old woman inside and begin the task of fixing her an evening tray.

Now she carried this meal of dried beef and cream on toast, to the bedside chair where Grammy sat dozing.

Sarah sat and visited some more with Elizabeth while she ate and Sarah made sure that Grammy drank her herbal tea. When this was done Sarah returned to the kitchen with the tray. While the dishes soaked she ate some of the beef and cream mixture herself. This was hardly done when Sarah heard footsteps coming across the porch and Ben and Joseph, the two oldest boys, entered the house by way of the woodshed.

They had hitched a ride home with another farmer and had come back to do their father's night chores. Sarah fixed their supper and then followed them to the barn, where she helped to feed the sheep and milked one cow.

"You did not want to stay and dance?" Sarah asked, and Joseph said, "Nope, Aunt Sarah...Ben and I decided we'd rather go hornpoutin' instead." Sarah smiled. She didn't know as she blamed them. She had been wanting to sit by a hornpout fire herself for a long time now, and she would too, just as soon as her two brothers got here.

As Sarah changed from her barn frock and went to her room and washed up, the two young men, with Moses at their heels, were seen disappearing from the winding driveway. They had fish poles over their shoulders and they were armed with a small vial of citronella that Sarah had given them to rub on their skin and clothing to keep the no-see-ums and blackflies away.

As daylight turned to dusk, Sarah went to the sheep pen and ignited the torches that began blazing. These had up until this point, been doing a good job of keeping the bear away.

On her return to the porch, she seated herself and once again began work on the sweetgrass basket, that she had begun that afternoon. She was momentarily startled when a loon cried, and she said to herself, "I hope that means the boys startled him....and not that brother bear is coming tonight."

In the stillness of early evening, Sarah listened to all the night sounds so familiar to the upper Connecticut River valley. The birds had gone to nest and the cricket and the peeper friends set the tone of the forest now. As she watched the last rays of the once brilliant sun disappear into the blackness that was early night, she still sat in the darkness and waited to see the stars. She always wondered which ones were the people she once knew? How she wished she knew which one was her father, her Aunt Nel and Winona. Sometime, she would know this, but not until she had walked the long road to the stars herself. At this particular time in her life, Aunt Sarah had many grassy trails to walk before she descended the Milky Way, that trail to the spirit world. And yet, one should live her life in a way that she was always ready when the time was right, and this she did.

Sarah stood, stretched and walked to the end of the porch and looked in the direction of the Connecticut River, and sure enough, she could see the glow and flicker of the flame of the hornpout fire as Ben and Joe enjoyed this night of good company and good fishing. As she stood there Sarah could almost smell the beech and maple burning and she knew that sparks were hissing and flying into the air from that fire now, just like the hornpout fires of her childhood.

A smile crossed her face when she remembered one particular evening when the Jackson family had been fishing for hornpout at a favorite spot on a winding bank of the Connecticut River in Maidstone.

Peter had arrived late and he had been drinking. Nel was much irritated but kept the fire going and all the family fished there in its glow.

What happened this evening that she thought about now was that young Peter, never well coordinated, lost his footing and fell into the water with a great splash, and consequently nearly swallowed the Connecticut River.

Dennis and John had to stop their own fishing and jump into that black water and haul the slow boy out.

Peter had consumed just enough rum so that he thought the sight of his three sons floundering around in the mud and clay like beached whales looked funny. He did not offer to help the boys out, but instead stood on the bank and howled with laughter. His infuriated sister Nelemano had snuck up behind Peter and given him a swift kick in the rear that sent the big man sprawling headfirst into the Long River himself. Peter had stood up swearing and spitting, and from the shore Aunt Nel taunted, "Isn't that funny, Peter Jackson? Now the hornpout have all swum away for the night, but it is okay Peter, 'cause you look so funny!"

Before Peter could climb out of the water, insolent and intent on telling that saucy sister of his where to go, Winona, then about five years old, had decided that this was a fine game. It was more fun in fact than catching hornpout, and with a shrill scream that was her war cry, Winona jumped feet first into the black water. So unexpected was Winona's swift action that Sarah failed to move back and got drenched with spray as her younger sister hit the water.

"Winona!" Aunt Nel said harshly, high up her nose like Abenaki women often do in moments of stress. But, when Nel realized that she was the only one of the whole darn shooting match of them that was dry, Aunt Nel's massive shoulders began to shake and she laughed so hard that she sat down right where she stood. Aunt Nel hit the ground with a thud.

Peter was on the shore now, wringing out his shirt and when Nel fell down Peter said, "I hope you break your fat behind!"

When Aunt Nel could stop laughing, she said, "You know brother, without a shirt you are uglier than a hornpout!" and once again Nel roared with laughter and naturally all of Peter's children joined in to make his humiliation complete. But, it did not work out that way, for Peter Sr., had a wonderful sense of humor and he finally got to laughing with all the rest of his family. They were not laughing at each other, so much as with each other and Peter knew that.

Eventually all the wet ones sat wrapped blankets, while their clothing dried, propped up on sticks and rocks near the fire, and by the time Winona closed her eyes, the hornpout were back and many of them were caught.

Sarah had to wipe away a nostalgic tear that slid down over her high cheekbones. It was not a tear of sadness, but one of humor as she remembered the next day when Aunt Nel went to fill her teapot, and found a live hornpout swimming around in the water, compliments of Peter Jackson. Sarah was forced to smile again as she recalled that Aunt Nel had been so startled by the unexpected presence of a fish in her teapot that she had screamed like a screech owl and had made an involuntary leap into mid air, loosing one of her hair combs and dropping her teapot, fish and all.

Aunt Nel's fist was raised in anger and she scowered the area threatening, "Peter Taxos Jackson, you drunken lout. You'd better hide or I'll break your damned neck!" Nel looked everywhere for her brother Peter, but he was gone.

From a comfortable perch, off in the distance, Peter sat watching as his infuriated sister circled her outdoor cooking fire, calling him everything but a decent person. Peter chuckled and chuckled because this was such a funny sight. That Nel, she had no sense of humor— none at all, at least to Peter's way of thinking.

Sarah had to brush another tear away as she recalled these family times, for they were more than humorous—they were good.

Gazing up again toward the stars that were shining brightly she could only hope that the one who hung them there was careful to hang Winona's star between her father's and Aunt Nel's, or else the peace and tranquility of the heavens could be shaken!

Sarah knew that her father and her Aunt Nel never forgot a good deed or a kindness. And by the same token, they never forgot or forgave a wrongdoing or an injustice. They each of course had a good sense of humor, depending on who the joke was on — and that was the trouble.

A redtailed hawk let out a startled cry from the edge of a clearing, and Sarah said goodbye for now, to this world of bright and twinkling stars and to that unknown land beyond them.

August had arrived, hot and humid, and Sarah made her way across the narrow board and beam structure that was the early Mount Orne Bridge, separating the towns of Lunenburg, Vermont and South Lancaster, New Hampshire. Underneath her feet Sarah could hear the murmur of the Connecticut River as it rolled along on this lazy day.

She was on her way to the train station to meet her brothers, as

Dennis and Peter were due on the afternoon train. It would be interesting to hear all about John and Lou and little Ivy Rose.

Coming ashore on the New Hampshire side of that river, Sarah stopped and bent to more closely examine a new cluster of milkweed plants. She touched the small pods and knew that she would be eating some parts of this plant later in greens for a healthy vegetable, but more importantly, she needed the milk it contained. Sarah had a woman patient in Dalton, New Hampshire, who was expecting her seventh child, and she had confided in Sarah that she usually had a "milk" or lactation problem. Sarah knew that the milk from this weed would help that mother's milk.

Her attention was called to some small ferns, and she scratched her head and tried to think of the names of these and was disappointed that she could not, but it did not matter. The clue that told her what they were good for in medicinal terms was that they were small and thin and curly, just like the worms they would expel.

"You can forget the names, Sarah, but never the clue," Aunt Nel had told her, and she lived her life reading the signs that each green thing told about itself. These signs or clues told where to use them.

Sarah wondered why more physicians didn't study nature a little more closely. Those liver-like leaves of the liverwort were very useful for liver complaints, and as a matter of fact, even the flowers of the liverwort were used for this purpose.

Looking across the landscape her eyes rested on a stand of beech trees, and she thought quickly that she must go and collect those parasitical growths that form on the roots of the beech tree. This sticky red substance, when applied as a strong and cooled poultice to outside sores and ulcers, would heal them right up. This was one of the few healers that would actually arrest gangrene, and it was most effective in halting a bad sickness that doctors called erysipelas, which White children seemed very prone to contracting. Aunt Nel always saved this particular medicine for any outside ulcer or sore that she suspected of being "deadly," or cancerous. Today, science confirms that beech drops are often referred to as the cancer root, but the Indians called it broom rape plant. This adhering substance when mixed or diluted with proper amounts of water was taken internally to bind up severe cases of diarrhea or to heal a bleeding ulcer. Sarah smiled. She knew that it was a bitter and quite unpleasant tasting tea, but she knew that it also worked.

And yet when it came to ulcers, Aunt Nel always recommended that the patient eat raw cabbage, lots of it, and that always worked too. Sarah had been told very early in life that a diet of good green things and nuts and berries not only cured disease, but prevented disease in the first place.

Sarah and the faithful dog walked along, and she was thinking that she could have appreciated his presence the night of the barn raising.

The dog had gone fishing with the boys, and in the dusk of twilight old Jed's wagon pulled into the driveway quite unnoticed. He had crawled out of the wagon and half staggered out toward the torch-lit sheep pen. He had heard something about a problem with a bear. He hated bears! In fact, tonight he hated everything!

As the stranger leaned on the fence the sheep enclosed in the pen began to panic, and the more nervous they became the more they ran and the louder they bleated.

Jed bellowed at them and threw a pebble at them, ordering them to "shut up, you wooly bastards!" And this terrified the animals even more.

Sarah heard the sheep running and knew that something was bothering them. She thought instantly of the loon's warning, earlier that evening. Where was Moses? Then Sarah remembered that the dog had tagged along after the Gee boys when they went fishing.

Sarah opened up her bedroom window and listened now as hard as she could. This was not the screaming terror and pain that was noticeable in the bleat of the animals, nor in their frenzied running like when the bear was killing them, but something was out there bothering them just the same.

Probably that skunk that got Moses, most likely, was what Sarah was thinking and she was half right. A skunk was out there but it was a man-skunk and he was not the old dog's enemy, he was her's.

Sarah threw on her shawl and quickly lit a lantern, and decided that she had better go out and investigate the sheep pen.

She took the short cut from the porch through the woodshed and as a result never did see the wagon sitting in front of the house.

Sarah made her way cautiously toward the pen. The sheep were still bleating and snorting and running. Sarah held the lantern up above her head, and when she did this, she could see a shadow leaning up against the fence. She strained her eyes against the darkness and saw that it was not a bear, but the form of a man. The man seemed to be resting there and held a bottle in his hand from which he kept taking sips. Sarah slowed her steps. Already she could detect the smell of stale whiskey and unwashed clothing.

It was that human-skunk, old Jed, and yet she could not figure how he got there. Where was his wagon? She placed the lantern on the tailboard of a hayrack, and when she turned she could just see the outline of the back end of the man's wagon.

Sarah stopped when he tossed the empty bottle to the ground and turned to face her.

"What are you doing here, Mr. Jed?" she asked, and he answered, "I come to see you, lil' Missey! Old Jed, he wants to collect on that dance you owe him." He smiled at Sarah then, a menacing smile.

Sarah could feel anger building up within her. She faced him and said, "I owe you nothing!"

Even in the dim light furnished by a lantern and a few torches, the man could tell by her stance and by her tone that she did not like him, nor what he had chosen for words either. But, he didn't care because she thought she was too good for his kind anyway, the damned snooty squaw.

Jed turned then and took a faltering step toward the young woman, and she thought he smelled rank to the point that only a crow could be interested in him. "What a carrion!" thought Sarah.

"Say now, missey....don't go getting your pot boilin'. I just thought it would be nice if you an me had a moonlit night together, that's all!" His eyes looked pale yellow, like his teeth.

"I don't think so, Mr. Jed," said Sarah and there was a finality about her tone that would have been discerned by a less inebriated man.

Jed made a low and hateful laugh, way down in his throat that was more like a growl than a laugh and said, "Now you be alone here, snooty gal, and Old Jed, he ain't impressed cause you be a damned Indian! Now, I come to have a dance and you best be dancin' missey," he threatened, adding. "Now, I know the folks is all gone cept you and me and your wants...they don't count at all missey," and he started toward Sarah adding, "Tonight by God....it's my wants....all my wants!"

Sarah never flinched, and said crisply and yet controlled, Your wants....Mr. Jed....could kill you." And even as she said these words her hands had reached for the sturdy handle of a hayfork that someone had left standing in a propped up position, leaning against the hayrack. Sarah seized it with a vengeance and by the time Jed closed in and she could smell his fetid breath upon her face, he could feel the biting tines of that pitchfork pressing menacingly against his throat. Jed sucked in his breath for he had not seen her move, and he could see the dark and glittering eyes of a woman who was not afraid of him and then she said, "Touch me....put your hands on me...you're a dead man."

This cowardly man shook his head as if to clear it. This was not going the way he wished. She was in control here. He stopped and said, "What the hell? You little bitch! You'd soon as kill me!"

Sarah actually smiled and said, "No. Like the bear in this position, one hug, you kill yourself! Call me bitch again...I kill you!"

Jed could feel his anger rising. Why, he'd ought to kill her, but the way things looked here, she had the same idea about him.

He started to drop his hands and then he rasped, "I ought to slap your damned head off!"

"You try.....you die!" was Sarah's only answer.

As perspiration ran down Jed's florid face he cursed and said, "You'd like to kill a man, wouldn't you?"

Sarah shook her head and replied, "A man, no.....but whatever you are..yes," and she depressed the fork harder against his throat and neck, and he gasped and suddenly stepped back and lost his footing and fell down, only to find the pitchfork pressed hard against his belly. Thus he lay there flat on the ground and his rage was being replaced by another emotion, fear.

He didn't dare to move. This would be a slow and horrible death! And, indeed it might have been that, but at that very moment, the rumble of fast moving wagon wheels could be heard coming up the driveway, and Fred and Margaret jumped out of the wagon and came to old Jed's rescue. "You pick a fight with the wrong woman, Jed?" asked Margaret, her voice stinging with sarcasm. "You arn't abusing Mae now, old man," Margaret thought.

"Give me that hayfork, Sarah," Fred said calmly, and then he added, "I'll take care of him!" and with that, Sarah's face contorted with rage, "I can take care of him! Someone should!" Sarah exclaimed, and Margaret soothed, "We know you can Sarah, but he ain't even worth killin', now please dear, give Fred the pitchfork!"

Sarah raised the fork from Jed's soft and paunchy belly, and she could smell the added stench of the "coward's fear," along with the rest of the unpleasant scent of him as perspiration dripped from his face to his chest. "You ain't heard the last of this!" he warned and once more, found the fork tines pressed against his windpipe and Sarah said, "Neither have you! Next week my brother Dennis comes here. If he hears of this, he will carve his initials on the side of your face!"

Jed's eyes widened, and along with the sweat, little beads of blood ran down his chest. "You dirty my path!" Sarah told him and then she said, "You ever cross my path again....I will kill you," and with that she handed Fred the pitchfork and walked toward the house.

Fred helped an unsteady and shaken Jed to his feet and heard him say, "Jesus, is she ugly! Why, I was only funnin'... having fun is all!"

Margaret Gee spoke haughtily then, asking, "Is that what they call dyin' nowadays, Jed?"

That had happened over a week ago, and Sarah had not seen nor heard from Jed nor his family since the Gees had sent him packing. She was not surprised at the depth of her hostility and rage, for she was slow to anger, but when she did, there was a violent streak in Sarah. Her father always claimed that the good natured dog that seldom ever got mad, if he did get angry, was a bad animal to start a fight with.

"That is me, Moses, when I'm mad....I am mad clear to my bones," she chuckled to herself, and reached down and stroked the dog's head. "I tell you, friend Moses, that John Somers, he had better be reformed."

In the distance she could hear the whistle of a far off train, the very one in fact, she was coming to meet. She had better move along, that train was faster than she was, thought Sarah. Then she smiled when she thought how good it would be to see her family again, and it had been very good of Fred and Margaret to invite her brothers to stay a spell with their family. They would help with the chores and the haying and still would get some fishing in.

Sarah had planned three hornpouting trips and one canoe trip up the Connecticut River to Brunswick, Vermont. Today, this place is known as Brunswick springs. Her people called it "Nebsonbek," Mineral Water Place. The old ones said Mother Earth had given these waters to cure the afflictions of her children, and this was the Abenaki place of miracles. Now there was talk of building a resort there, and the resort came and the miracles stopped, for the old ones also said, "Bad luck would come to all who tried to profit from the healing waters," and so it did. The resorts burned, and the miracles were traded in for money.

Sarah pressed on, knowing she had so much to do, so many medicines to gather before the cold winds blew.

The train had already pulled into the station and the passengers were disembarking. For just a minute Sarah feared that Dennis and Peter were not on this train, but then she saw them. Dennis towered over most of the men and all of the women and Sarah was proud, for he was a fine figure of a man. Peter was not so tall and his carriage was not so erect as was Dennis's. Peter wore a child-like smile except when someone had hurt his feelings, but for the most part people were good to Peter, especially when he walked around with a man who looked and was as powerful as Dennis Jackson.

Sarah started running to meet them and the sound of her White lady's shoes made a thumping noise that irritated her. She had so much to ask Dennis about and so much to tell him. But she would never tell him about her confrontation with Jed, because Dennis would surely carve his initials on the side of Jed's face and probably would kill the man.

You see, Dennis was also one of those good-natured animals who, like good-natured old Moses, got mad right down to the very bone.

Sarah exchanged warm greetings with her brothers. Dennis carried one valise and in his left hand, of course, that violin that he called his "fiddle," which was the very one that Sarah had traded the baskets for a long time ago.

Peter, always emotional and always the child, had been forced to blink away the tears when his sister hugged him and told him how very glad she was to see him.

Then he beamed all over as he handed Sarah a small gift from Lou. It made Peter very proud to be trusted with the care of this token of Lou's affection for his sister. Sarah had held on to the gift while she hugged Dennis hello, and then as they walked off down the road, she opened the package.

"Oh! It is so lovely," said Sarah, and it was. Lou had decorated a hair comb for Sarah. This one was especially for a French twist, which was the way Sarah wore her hair. It was made of mother of pearl, and Lou had sewn soft seed pearls and fine lace and delicate silk ribbon to the comb, and it was a perfect complement to that ivory colored dress that was supposed to be her wedding dress. Good, thought Sarah, now I won't have to wear that hat, after all.

"Sarah, you and this place both look wonderful," smiled Dennis, as they made their way along. And Sarah could not wait to ask how John's family was, and Dennis said, "Well, but Lou has a lot of colds. I think the dampness of that ocean is not good for her."

Up until this time, Sarah had told no one that she had been asked to get married. She had not even told Margaret, for she felt that blood-family should be the first to know. And yet, Sarah knew or suspected that Margaret would welcome this news much better than Dennis would, when he found out who had asked her. Sarah glanced up at Dennis and said simply, "Brother, I have been asked to marry." Dennis looked down at her and smiled, "Well, it's about time!" Sarah made a grin and replied, "I said the same thing." This was a clue to her brother that this new love was not a new one but an old one, and he asked flatly, "Somers around here again?"

Dennis did not smile when he spoke of John Somers and this made Sarah feel bad, but Dennis said no more. He would not tell her ever again what he thought of the man, for once was enough. Sarah stopped in her tracks and placed both hands upon her hips and said, "Dennis Jackson, that man John, he has changed." Dennis said, "Ummmph," which is a sound that Sarah herself often made if she thought something not quite worthy of an argument. They began to walk again and Sarah spoke, "He walked me home in the dark from the station. He is a gentleman in my presence, Dennis, and he has stopped drinking. You only saw him brawling and drunk. You would like this man sober."

"I stopped a fight he was in one night," Dennis said. He probably wouldn't remember me, though. The other guy didn't, and I knew him well." This was very interesting to Sarah, and she asked, "Who was it brother?" And Dennis smiled and said, "It was our brother John," and both he and Sarah began to laugh.

It was a wonderful year for wild strawberries or "msk-ikoi-minsak," as the Abenakis called them. Sarah and her brothers entered the Gee kitchen, greeted by the wonderful aroma of strawberry shortcake. "Yum, Yum, smell fine," said Peter.

Margaret told her guests that the only price they had to pay for their supper was that after the evening chores were done, Dennis must play the fiddle for them all. Dennis inhaled the wonderful aroma of hot biscuits and fresh berries, and decided this was a very good deal.

When the supper dishes and the evening chores were done, the entire family, including Grammy Elizabeth, gathered in the spacious livingroom and Dennis played the violin to tunes like "The Campbells Are Coming," "The Fisher's Hornpipe," and the "St Anne's Reel." Sarah tapped her feet in time with the music.

Dennis Jackson always played the violin with his eyes closed and his fiddle tucked against his barrel of a chest. He was a left handed player and there were few of these, and he tapped one foot in time with the music. Margaret Gee thought he was the best fiddle player that she had ever heard. Many others also said this.

"Well, now we got ourselves a fiddler, Margaret, we best have a kitchen junket soon," stated Fred, but Margaret was already planning one.

In the wee hours of the morning, on the first evening of their visit, Dennis and Peter awoke to full-scale pandemonium. It had happened that in their delight of being able to hear a violin being played that evening, Fred and his sons forgot to ignite the torches that guarded the sheep pen. This was just what the pesky bear had been waiting for, and he was there now in the middle of the bleating and frenzied sheep, mauling and killing all that he could sink his deadly teeth and claws into. "Awasos! again," thought Sarah.

The family had stayed up late and sung and enjoyed this evening, and one-by-one they had given up and gone to bed, each one assuming that another one had checked on the torches.

Moses was driving the bear, ducking his swipes as the bear reached for the big animal. The sheep screamed and the bear also snarled and growled as he got under the fence and lit out across the back pasture.

Lamps came on from all over the house, and in every direction people were scurrying around in their night clothes. "Damnit, we forgot the torches," Fred muttered as he tore past Sarah and headed for the sheep pen. Margaret followed with a lantern that was smoking badly.

Dennis, his pants on, no shirt and bare foot to boot, passed Sarah in the woodshed. "What is it?" And his sister answered swiftly, "It is old Awasos again. Fred missed him last time and he killed nearly half of the ewes."

This time Fred didn't even get a chance to shoot at the bear, for he was too far away. Fred called Moses back and the old dog came, and the boys were lighting the torches again which revealed the slaughter and carnage in the sheep pen.

"Oh no," Fred said, "get the children in the house, Margaret!"

His wife was quick to understand and survey the situation. Fred would have to put some badly torn up animals out of their misery. He shook his head, for he didn't like to kill anything ever.

Sarah and Dennis went inside the pen and Dennis said, "Only two really need to go down, Sarah. We can fix up the rest, I know!"

And so only two of the animals were destroyed, and Sarah and Dennis spent the next several hours very carefully stitching and disinfecting great gashes and lacerations made by the bear's razor-like claws. "Dennis, I think if you could get him in your sights you'd bring him down," said Sarah, and Dennis replied, "He is bold, that bear. I know a sure way to stop him if Mr. Gee is willing."

The next day Dennis explained to Fred a thing that could be done to stop this marauding beast and Fred decided to give it a try. "If we wait for him, we do it on his terms," Dennis said, and then continued, "If we call him to us, he comes on our terms and the advantage is only with us."

Fred Gee was now looking at Dennis with an eyebrow raised. What was he talking about, "If we call him to us?" and, not understanding this, Fred replied, "We can call that bear to us?" Dennis smiled and shook his head yes. It was obvious to Dennis that Fred was not a hunting man.

"It is just another way to skin a cat—or get ourselves a bear," Dennis said.

And, then as Fred tamped his pipe down, listening carefully, Dennis outlined his plan. "We will hang some bait up in that apple tree just beyond the sheep pen, and then we will wait."

"Well, I'm a farmer first and a hunter second, but I'll give it a try. I missed that bugger the last time, though," Fred mused, and Dennis said, "I don't like to kill any animal, but when one becomes a threat, I am a good shot."

This would be the one time that Fred would get to delegate this unpleasant task to someone else, and he did it by saying, "I'd be much obliged if you would shoot that critter, Dennis!" And, Dennis, who now puffed on his own pipe (a newly acquired habit), said nothing but made the faintest of smiles and nodded his consent.

The next night the sheep pen was lit again with torches, which cast eerie shadows in the darkness, and that night the bear would not come. The next night every other torch was lit but it still gave enough light so that the bear would not come. But on the third night only one torch was ignited at the northern corner of the pen, and this flickered and burned, not giving much light and yet enough for Dennis to see to shoot by. Because this was the night the bear would come.

Inside the farmhouse life went on as usual, except that Moses was kept inside after supper and not let out so that he could catch scent of the troublesome bruin and go to barking and therefore drive him away.

From their position, a little to the left of the hay barn, Dennis and Fred sat quietly in the darkness, watching the moon peak in and out of heavy cloud cover. The one lonely torch didn't throw enough light to show anything much, only that what few sheep were left in the pen were pacing and nervous.

They sat there quietly for hours, and finally just before daybreak Fred was awakened by the sound of heavy walking. He had dropped off to sleep where he sat, leaned up against the side of the stone wall, but Dennis was wide awake and waiting.

Shortly before he had fallen asleep, Fred had begun to wonder if this trick was going to work anyhow. Dennis had carefully wrapped a smoked salmon in a fish net and hung it on the lower branches of the nearest apple tree, saying that, "the Awasos would soon forget about the sheep once he got a smell of that," and apparently Dennis had been right, because something was coming toward the tree and the men at this very moment.

The moon once more stuck its head out of the clouds above, and at that moment Fred could see the bear lumbering along, moving in a rolling gait and yet cautious at the same time, stopping and looking every few steps it took. It made low and grunting sounds and this started an all out frenzy in the sheep pen.

Dennis was up on one knee now with the rifle already pointing at the bear. At that precise moment the huge animal defecated and then rose on its hind feet and sniffed the air. His nose was long, and he turned his great head from side to side and sniffed the air in all directions. Then he dropped to all fours again and began his steady trek toward the apple tree that smelled so strong of smoked fish. He was heavy, and as he approached the tree, Fred could feel the ground around almost shake with each step the big animal took. Fred found himself praying that this Indian was the good shot that he claimed to be for both their sakes.

The bear, now directly in front of the two men, stood once more on his hind legs, his forepaws moving up and down, making grunting, hog-like sounds and he turned his wide head from side to side, sniffing the air while his small eyes searched. Then he reached for the salmon above his head, his massive claws outstretched and raking fiercely. He was hungry for salmon now, and impatient and salivating he tore at the net containing his prize.

As the bear was about to claim his fish, the moon once more appeared from behind a cloud, only for a few seconds, but it was enough for Dennis to take careful aim at that spot of white on the bear's chest. The rifle cracked in the darkness, and as the bullet hit its mark; the bear made a choking sound and spun completely around once, its small eyes literally rolling around in its head, and slowly it crumpled to the ground. It did not thrash, but lay very still as life left its body amid the scent of blood and excrement and the unmistakable stench of death.

Inside the house, Sarah and Margaret sat across the kitchen table sipping tea. "Oh no, one shot, he must have gotten away again," said Margaret. Sarah, however, knew that one was good and any more was anyone's guess. "Dennis is a good shot," Sarah replied calmly.

With shaking hands, Fred clumsily got the lantern lit and he and Dennis approached the bear. "Go slowly. Don't step in his dung!" Dennis said. "Don't you step in mine!" exclaimed Fred, and Dennis snorted out, "No! You didn't, did you?" "Nope, I was waitin' to see if ya missed," Fred remarked.

The lantern held high over the bear's head confirmed that it was dead, and now both Fred and Dennis were laughing heartily.

Leaning over and touching a spot on the chest of the dead bear, Dennis said, "Grandfather, you intruded here. I did not wish to take your life....I had to. Grandfather, give me your defiant heart and where you walk now, may there be many salmon for Awasos."

Fred had packed his pipe and listened, for this was the first time he had ever heard a hunting prayer, but he had heard many times in his life that Indians actually said prayers. "By gum it's true," he thought.

When Dennis stood, Fred reached to shake his hand and he said, "Thank you Dennis, and them sheep and lambs over there.....they thank you too. I ain't a killin' man...but comes a time."

Dennis accepted the hand extended in friendship and answered, "Yes, comes a time. Tonight old grandfather....his time had come." They made their way toward the house then, the White man at ease now, for he had lost an enemy, and the Indian just a little sad, for he had lost a brother.....a brother and a friend that the Abenakis called Awasos.

Dennis had destroyed by necessity a menace, which happened to be the symbol of the Bear Clan family of which he was a descendant. In the old days this would have been a taboo, but the old days were gone and now each man must do what he must do, to walk ahead and not look back or think about Awasos.

The carcass of the dead bear would be buried later. In other times, its hide would have been stripped away and a suitable rug made. But the Gees were not into such trivial things as saving teeth and skins and precious oils, so nothing was removed from this animal but one claw. Dennis gave this to Peter, who wanted to wear it around his neck on a string.

Sarah thought of all the useful things that would be buried with the bear and she felt very sad, for this magnificent creature should have meant more in the scheme of things than just a waste.

She read the sadness on her brother's face, but like him said nothing, for this was not their farm or their land or their bear.

News spread up and down the valley like wildfire, and before noon, four wagons belonging to local farmers made their way into the dooryard and enjoyed the sight of the bloody carcass before it was placed into that deep hole in the ground to rot.

One of the wagons that stopped carried cousins of Margaret Gee. They had a vain young woman with them by the name of Celia, and she was a second cousin of Margaret's. She had climbed out of that wagon and looked directly into Sarah's face, and the young woman just tossed her head and looked away contemptuously.

Her hair was the color of honey and she had deep blue eyes, and would have been pretty if her features had not been so sharp. Sarah looked down at her apron to make sure that her dress or she, was not dirty, but they were clean. It was not her clothing that this young woman did not like, it was her skin color.

Margaret sensed the snobbish air about the girl and said, "Celia, this is Sarah Jackson. Her brother killed the bear we're going to see."

The young woman called Celia was about Sarah's own age. She made a crisp smile but only with her mouth, because her eyes did not smile. Sarah had learned that there were two kinds of blue eyes; the warm and carefree, and the other kind that were more like the color of steel. These were still pretty and fascinating eyes, but they were also very cold ones.

To please Margaret, Celia nodded hastily to Sarah and had even pasted a smile on her lips when she had acknowledged her introduction. Margaret was not pleased because she hated her cousin's "airs and graces," as she called them. Sarah for her part, had risen to her full height and looked directly at Celia, and without so much as a blink of an eye, had turned and walked away.

Celia raised an eyebrow when Sarah dared do such a thing, her just hired help and an Indian to boot, but Margaret's face looked like a thundercloud about now, so Celia changed her strategy.

Sarah was emptying buckets of water into one of the big laundry tubs, and as she did this Dennis walked out of the barn carrying a bag of grain upon each shoulder. Sarah thought her brother was as strong as an ox, but Celia thought he was the handsomest man she had ever seen, and she quickly tapped Margaret's arm, inquiring who this newcomer was. Margaret called Dennis over and said, "Celia, this is Dennis, Sarah's brother who is from Boston." Dennis sat the grain down and shook Celia's outstretched hand, feeling rather awkward because he knew he smelled of barn. But this woman didn't seem to mind and she twittered, "Dennis, what a nice name! Hello Dennis," and she said that name like it was honey, the color of her hair.

Celia liked the looks of this man, even liked the shyness in his manner. The color of his skin did not matter, she could overlook that in this particular case. Why, she might even be able to tolerate that sister of his too, if she absolutely had to!

Dennis did not visit long, but picked up the grain bags with little effort, shouldered them and excused himself from the present company.

Celia's blue eyes trailed after him. "Margaret, is he married?" Margaret looked at her and said, "I don't think so. One brother is though, perhaps you'd better ask Sarah."

Sarah was bent over the washboard, and she looked up from her chores into the face of Celia. "Hello Sarah," the young woman smiled, and Sarah looked straight at her wondering, "What does she want?" Even though it was their first words, Sarah instinctively knew that this girl wanted something or else she would not be standing here trying to make conversation with her.

Sarah asked the question out loud now, "What do you want?" And just for a second Celia was taken aback, her face flushed and her blue eyes snapped. It chagrined Celia to be so obvious, but if that was what it took, well...and she went on, "Sarah, I just was wondering, is your brother staying in the Guildhall area long?" Sarah met her steady gaze and shrugged, "I do not know. He has not said." Celia was smiling now and she said, "As handsome as he is, I guess he is probably married with a wife on his hands, huh?" "No," was all that Sarah answered from where she labored, bent over the soapy board. She wished that she could have told the woman yes, because she now knew what this fishing trip on Celia's part was all about. Celia felt the coldness of Sarah's voice just as Sarah felt the coldness of Celia's icy blue eyes. Now Celia fished some more. "Well Sarah, do you know if he has a special girl stashed away somewhere?" "No," is all that Sarah said, and when Celia went on with, "Well, gee, I'd like to know," Sarah quickly cut her off by saying coolly, "You ask him."

Now blue eyes flashed and met calm dark ones looking back. Celia said, "Well, I thought if you and I were friends, that you could ask your brother for me, is all." Sarah shook her head and spoke softly, "No. It is his business," and she went back to work on the washboard again and was scrubbing with a vengeance. Celia pulled herself to her full height, which was about to Sarah's chin, and snapped, "Alright. It wasn't important, and besides, I'll find out. I have my ways!" And even as Celia tossed her honey colored hair and abruptly walked away, Sarah was thinking, "I'll bet you have, but you'll never use me as one of them."

Sarah watched silently as Celia approached Margaret to do some more fishing, no doubt, since Sarah would not take the bait. Celia smiled and chatted with Margaret and Sarah knew, even in this brief encounter, many things about Celia. She was direct and this was a good quality, but as Sarah watched Celia skillfully question Margaret, she realized that she was also a "pot stirrer," or carrier of tales from one to another, and undoubtedly what her people called a "crow woman."

Sarah wiped beads of perspiration from her forehead as she watched the unsuccessful manipulation of Margaret Gee, and as the calculating young woman climbed into the wagon to leave, Sarah knew that even if Dennis became the best of friends with Celia, she herself never would. People only got one shot to disparage or snub Sarah, and Celia had already had her shot.

Dennis walked out of the barn again as the wagon rolled from the driveway, and Celia turned and smiled and waved first at Margaret, then at Sarah and lastly at Dennis, who lifted his hand and waved back.

Margaret was waving good naturedly but Sarah had not waved, and was once more beating soapy clothes against the board.

Margaret smiled at Dennis and said, "I think you have an admirer, Dennis." Dennis smiled good naturedly and thought nothing about this, because as a fiddle player he was used to being the center of attraction to many young women. He went about his chores, knowing that he had only waved at the young woman with yellow hair out of courtesy, for she was not his type, too forward, too sweet, too sharp featured.

Sarah had looked up from her task in time to see Dennis smiling and waving back to Celia, and it was as though a cool wind passed through her.

The older sister thought sadly, "Brother, you have met a far more dangerous predator than that old Awasos you killed last night."

A robin hopped along the ground and knew that this was true. Sarah could sum all her thoughts up by saying, "He could do better," and ironically after supper the next evening when John Somers arrived at the Gee farm, asking to speak to Sarah, Dennis had sadly thought, "Sarah, you could do so much better."

As he walked along the narrow road that followed the Connecticut River, John Somers had been struck by the beauty and splendor of that winding serpentine ribbon of blue. It was as clear as a bell tonight, in fact so clear that a man could see his reflection as vividly as in a mirror. He wondered to himself what it was about this valley that kept calling people home. Sarah had told him once that she felt drawn to it by a strange magnetic force, and strangely enough he felt it himself. He inhaled the intoxicating aroma of sweetgrass and he smiled.

As he turned up the steep incline that was the Gee driveway, John could hear the sound of a fiddle playing. It was a good song, an old Canadian reel, and the fiddler was doing a fine job. He stood on the long porch leading to the kitchen door and listened to the melodious notes that drifted through half-opened windows. Then he removed his hat and stepped toward the door.

At first not one of them heard him as he rapped, but then Moses began to bark and Margaret got up and went to the door. John stood with his hat in his hands and fumbled with it nervously, and hoped that he did not look as uneasy as he felt.

Margaret Gee stepped back from the door and John smiled and said, "Good evening Ma'am. I am John Somers. Is Sarah Jackson here?"

Margaret eyed him for a second and she at first, did not recognize this tall young man with bronze skin and gentle blue eyes that seemed not to belong in that dark face.

As she studied him silently Margaret remembered that it was the young man who had walked Sarah here back in April, and she smoothed a strand of hair back from her face and welcomed him inside and sent one of the children to get Sarah, who was in the livingroom with the rest, tapping her toes in time with the music.

Sarah sat beside her brother Peter as he clapped his hands. "Dennis could drag a bow across a violin and make it tell a beautiful story, a happy story," thought Sarah, just as she heard someone call her name.

She rose and went to see what Margaret needed, and turning the corner from the huge livingroom into the kitchen Sarah came face to face with John. She blinked, not really expecting him so soon, and her hands flew to her hair to smooth it and her fingers unconsciously tugged at her dress and apron to make sure they were smooth. Oh, she hoped that she looked alright. Margaret saw Sarah's dark face light up when she recognized the young man and she observed that his did this also. She wondered why Sarah had not mentioned this special friend to her?

Sarah ran to him and he hugged her, lifting her up in the air to look more closely at the smooth lines of her pretty, oval face, from the high and prominent cheekbones to the dark eyes and full lips. He longed to kiss those lips but this was not the place, for real love was a very private thing between a young woman and a man. It was their way. "Sarah, you look lovely!" he exclaimed, and she held him close for a moment and smiled. "John, it is so good to see you," she said and then as he sat her back down she introduced him to Margaret again. Sarah asked if Margaret remembered who he was, and with a nervous laugh the woman said that she did and then she simply said, "Sarah, when you have finished saying hello, bring Mr. Somers in to sit and hear the music with the rest of us," and Margaret made a slight curtsey and left the room.

"Sarah, Sarah...you really are beautiful," whispered John, and her copper face turned crimson, but she was very pleased that he would say this thing.

"When did you arrive in the valley, John?" Sarah wanted to know, and she took the twisted hat from his hands and placed it on the hatrack in the hall. "I arrived two days ago, but I got a job right off. The weather was good up on Guildhall Hill, so I have been haying." Sarah smiled, for in the fleeting minute that she was pressed against John's chest she could smell the scent of hay and clover on his clothing, and she thought this was a clean and beautiful smell. And her heart was very glad that there was no odor of liquor on his breath.

Sarah took his hand and said. "My brothers are here....Peter and Dennis. Dennis plays well, I think. Come, let us go in and listen to the music, John." He followed her in silence, and Dennis glanced up and saw his sister leading John into the room and he nodded to the man an thought to himself, "At least tonight he looks sober." And because John was indeed sober, he did not recognize Dennis and could not recall ever getting into a scuffle with Dennis or John Jackson either.

Dennis stopped playing at the end of a song and Sarah cleared her throat and announced proudly, "My friends, this is another friend of mine. His name is Somers....Mr. John Somers."

Friendly greetings were exchanged all around, and the younger children giggled because now they knew that Sarah had a sweetheart. Margaret looked sharply at her young brood and they stopped their showing off.

Sarah was not paying any attention to the children, but was instead watching the way that John had taken an extra minute when he shook Peter's hand. She saw that he had told Peter that the bear claw on the string around his neck was very fine. Peter, who seldom got attention, smiled from ear to ear, and Dennis also noticed this gesture and decided it was a kind one. He smiled for the first time at John and thought, "Well, he is probably not too bad....when he's sober."

Before John left that evening, Fred Gee invited him to return on Saturday night for the kitchen junket that he and Margaret were planning.

John was pleased and thanked his host, but it wasn't until he and Sarah stood on the porch saying goodnight that he actually decided to attend.

Standing there in the moonlight, John looked like a shy and bashful boy, instead of the rake that he was known to be. "Sarah, would you like me to be at the gathering Saturday?" And he cupped her chin in his hand as he asked this. She met his gaze and answered, "That would please my heart, John Somers."

"You always please mine, woman," he whispered, and then she was in his arms and eager for the kisses that he placed again and again upon her sweet-tasting lips. "Sarah," he said huskily, "In the letter you said about time. You said yes, but not when."

Her tilted eyes crinkled at the corners and bore into his blue ones as she teased him, "I will marry you. I think in "Skamonkas," for September is a fine and beautiful month."

John sighed, "September," the month for corn reaping, is a good time Sarah, if....you mean next month and not...next year." As he said these words his voice was deadly serious, and Sarah tossed her head back and a soft laugh escaped her lips. "Serve you right if I did make you wait until next September, but next month I will share my blanket with you."

"Well, it is about time!" he snapped, and they both laughed together and then were content to hold each other and listen to the night sounds of the cricket and the nightbird, and even the gentle wind that rustled the leaves on the mighty elm trees standing proudly on the river bank.

The winding Connecticut River lay before them, and in its own calm way sang love songs to the night as it continued on, knowing all, seeing all, and leading all her children home.

The northern corner of the wide porch had lines stretched across it, and from these sweetgrass, freshly washed, was hanging and drops of water dripped steadily down upon the wide boards below. Sarah had a line of progression going; washing some of the sweetgrass, drying some, and combing with her ancient comb that part of her supply that was ready for this step in the creation of a basket. It was not work. It was her life. Sarah had accompanied Margaret into town, and while her landlady shopped for food in Lancaster, Sarah sold her baskets to the stores along the street. Lancaster merchants knew Sarah and her workmanship by now and selling was an easy thing. This was a much simpler garnered market than walking mile after mile. The shopkeepers bought in volume, often taking upwards of a dozen at one time. Sarah knew that walking was the slower way, but she also knew that walking was a wonderfully healthy thing for the mind and body. She missed the door-to-door contact of old friends, and she realized that this new wholesale market in town was better for her pocketbook but that the old way was better for her soul.

When Aunt Sarah with her serene smile stood before a door, looking somewhat shy, she was always invited in and was offered sugar cookies, fresh baked bread or in the autumn, apple cider from some farmer's press. As she sold her baskets she was always asked questions about folks that had gone to ailing. Quick consumption was a dreaded fatal cold, with pneumonia-like symptoms that often White doctors could not cure. She could not save people with this sometimes, but she had some patients who were strong and young when stricken, and they had recovered. Sarah treated these with the blossoms of red clover mixed with the root of the comfrey plant for the bronchial congestion. Chickweed for inflammation was mixed with the bark of the white willow, and the salicin in this helped lessen the severity of aches and pains and reduced a fever.

Enroute back from Lancaster, Sarah told Margaret that she planned on marrying John Somers the very next month. Margaret clucked at the horses, raised an eyebrow and responded, "I knew you were friends Sarah, but I'm surprised that this will take place so soon."

Sarah smiled at her friend and said, "It is not soon. It is a very long time that we have felt something special for each other." Sarah was blushing and her dark copper face took on a deeper shade, but her eyes were crinkled with happiness. Margaret simply smiled and said, "Well, we got to get you a suitable dress for your wedding, Sarah." Sarah smiled. "I have that. I brought it with me. Come up when we get home and see what you think of it."

Margaret was not prepared for the beautiful off-white dress that hung in Sarah's meager closet. The lace and the detail of the garment were excellent, and Margaret was elated. "Sarah, it is a beautiful dress. Why, you will be the prettiest bride," and she gave the slender young woman who even she now called Aunt Sarah, a hug and said, "I will make your wedding cake, Sarah, but where will you be married?" Margaret wondered which church the couple would choose, but Sarah answered quickly, "No need for church, Margaret, just a preacher man at his house or.... at your house?"

"Of course at my house, Sarah, for my house is also your house," Margaret said, and suddenly the older woman was weeping, feeling strange inwardly that she should think of this little hired girl as her own daughter.

Margaret got control of her emotions and looked into the hauntingly serene face of Sarah and sniffed, "Don't mind my foolishness, dear," and she dabbed at her overflowing eyes with her apron corners and continued, "It's just that I feel like you're my own child is all." Sarah smiled a warm smile and nodded, "I know. My own family, my circus family and now my White family. It is good, Margaret, that we are family."

The next morning, with baskets piled on her head, Sarah started on foot toward Guildhall Hill. She had not been here this summer, and she knew that almost every farm along the way would want to buy a basket and that she would see new faces and miss old ones, which was the way of this world of constant change she lived in.

She followed the river road until she approached the left-hand turn leading up the mountain. Today we know this road as the Ball Road, its name was not important, but the neighbors all along this river and that road most surely were.

Each farm she passed along the way was in the business of haying. She saw the various hayracks, and hanging from atop the hay barns were hayforks, which through the use of pulley blocks and rope would lift the hay into the haymow. In that loft the fresh-mown hay was dried and stored for food and fodder for the animals. "Storing for winter," thought Sarah.

It was a sweltering day, and before she made the turn toward her destination Sarah had to stop and remove the light jacket that she wore.

All along the river road she had seen men bare to the waist loading hay onto the cumbersome-looking hayracks, and she knew that before many days some of these would be suffering the effects of a very bad case of sunburn, for the White man would and did brown up, but often he became physically sick from the sun, his skin peeling off his body to boot. As she walked along thinking about this, Sarah decided that it was good that only last Sunday she had taken the time to replenish her stock of ointments, especially the swamp tree or tamarack, whose resins and gum as well as the fresh leaves were used as an application for sunburn and other skin irritations.

Sarah was climbing steadily upward now, and she stopped midway of the steep incline, and set her baskets down and rested. She had nibbled on berries along the roadside and was really not that hungry in this mid-day heat and humidity. She chased a deerfly that kept buzzing around her head. Her clothing was stuck to her.

A little brook ran along at the side of the road and she went there, removed her shoes and splashed in the cold clear water. It felt good to her and did seem to make her feel better all over. She replaced her shoes and positioned her load of baskets upon her head and began walking once more, but had only gone a few steps when a scraggly wolf crossed the road in front of her. He had been running, and his tongue was red and hanging out the corner of his mouth. The condition of his pelt was very poor and he looked to Sarah as though he had that disease called mange, because of the scabby patches and hairless spots upon his hide. Some citronella would take care of the mites, Sarah knew, but the dog hated citronella because it burned his eyes, and it would be no different with the wolf.

The wolf paused only a minute and looked at her, but there was no malice in his look. Sarah thought it was a pathetic glance he shot her way, and she whispered, "Roll around in the yarrow leaves, old man," for the yarrow plant was often made into healing ointments for skin problems. The wolf lifted his ears at the soft sound of Sarah's voice, but he whirled then and tore off into the woods, and she thought about all the wolf troubles that people over across the river in Lancaster were having. There, some lost nearly all their sheep herd in one night. Sarah knew she should not praise the wolf and that the White people hated this animal, but she could never hate the wolf because for all of his bad habits, he was a mystical symbol to the Abenaki. He was in fact, the Grandfather.

The terrain was different up here on the ridge of this mountain, and much more of the fields had been cleared of rocks and stumps since the last time Sarah had been there. Like the flat river country below it, all the farms were surrounded by stone walls that wove their way in snakelike fashion to the furthermost corner of a man's land. Many times these stonewalls were used as boundary lines just as the Connecticut River was, because all the land and all the water was now owned by some person and no one else could settle on that land. Sarah shared that very basic Native American belief that no man can own the air he breathes nor the land he stands on, nor could he sell it to another, but the White men did this every day.

Sarah knew that the Abenaki was not usually an owner of land, but was a free wandering spirit that belonged to the land, was an extension of it, in fact. Now with all the changes that had swept across this New England coast, the Dawnland people could roam no more, but that old Grandfather Wolf, he could and he did, still as free as that big old hawk that was circling in the sky, screaming as he dove toward a field mouse far below him.

"Stay free as long as you can, my brothers," whispered Sarah as she made her way along in a sure-footed and steady manner.

She was treated to a tall glass of cold, cold, tea at the second farmhouse she stopped at. These people had not been living here in the valley very long, and they had a young son with a crippled and shriveled right arm. The boy's mother told Sarah that he had the paralysis and he had, at that time, suffered from such a fever that the doctor said he would die, but he had not. "Just his arm is all that died," the youngster's mother proudly said, and Sarah nodded and asked, "He has feeling in the limb?" The boy's mother said that he did, but it caused him pain sometimes. Sarah had already sold two baskets here, and she reached into the pocket of her dress and extracted a small bottle. "Here, make this into tea when he hurts," she said, and started for the door. The mother did not know what the mixture was. If she had asked, Sarah would have told her that the bark of the willow would stop the fever, and the ground root of the sarsaparilla would help the rheumatism that the boy most likely was suffering from.

Sarah went on her way, never quite understanding why these people were so driven to work. Just the work of clearing these fields of rocks and stumps had taken many of these farmers their lifetime. It was their way, thought Sarah, just as leaving things alone, the way they were meant to be, was the way of her people.

The next farm sat at the crest of a steep hill and sloped to flattened fields below, and here the view was stunning; and stepping up and climbing on a rock, Sarah could see all across the valley below her.

She could see the Connecticut River, a thin blue line now, and a scattering of houses that was Lancaster and even Dalton and Jefferson. In the background rose a range of mountains we know as Starr King, and then the Mt. Washington Range seemed to over-shadow all the other mountains near it, and Sarah knew this famous range as the Crystal Hills. She could not think of the actual Abenaki word. She would ask Dennis. He might remember how their father said it.

Reflection upon a forgotten name always caused Sarah sadness, for it was the death of a language, and ironically that forgotten language had been used to name most of the rivers, streams, and mountains in the northeastern United States, until the White men came and changed the names to English words that seldom told anything about what was named. She stopped and ate some "squeskimenak" raspberries that were hanging over the narrow roadside, and she said the name aloud as she brushed off the leaves and dust before she ate the succulent red berries. Directly up ahead of her on the other side of the road she saw some currants and knew that these, Aunt Nel called "pessimenal." Sarah knew that "mskikoiminsak" were strawberries and that the Abenaki name for the gooseberry was "kowakimen," and beechnuts were first called "wajoimenal". She continued on and carried this thought train. "I have not forgotten all the words," and her lips formed the word "taliozigan," meaning boiled meat, and mkuejazigan, which is Abenaki for roast meat. She knew that the "wskidakuam" was the Abenaki word for sap, and that "skootum" was a trout, and that "wataqua" was a pickerel, and "molazigan" was a bass, while "namas" was just a fish.

A robin sat perched on a tree limb near her and began singing, and this brought a smile to Sarah's face. She spoke out loud to the robin, "Hey, brother "kwihkweska," I know your name and recognize your song. I will save some "squeskimenak" for you, if you save some "popokual" cranberries for me...little friend."

Sarah satisfied herself at last that she had remembered more words of her native language than she had forgotten, and this was good, but it was hard to remember and retain the words if you never had anyone to say them to.

As the next farm loomed up ahead of her the robin flew away, and Sarah watched it go and vowed that she would someday teach her own children the dialect and words of the old ones. She would teach them the words even if they also had no one to speak these words to. They would know, for she would tell them.

Someone had to tell the descendants of the Dawnland People all the things that were never written down. The lives and events and legends that were remembered were the unwritten history and heritage of a people proud and silent. That they had lived must be remembered, unless all the world forget they ever did.

On the very crest of the hill she started down the field toward the farm below. As she walked along, she wondered why they had built this house at the bottom of the incline instead of at the top, where they could see the splendor of the New Hampshire hills.

A friendly dog came running to meet Sarah, and she spoke to him and reassured him that she was not an enemy.

She stopped at a water tub that horses drank out of, and she could see the clear liquid streaming and spurting out of the pipe, and then it splashed down on the tub below. Sarah made a cup of her hands and let the cold, crystal water fill her palms, and then she drank. There was one thing she could always remember about Guildhall Hill, and that was that if you tore the topsoil from the Aki, or earth, you would see the blackest dirt anywhere. This was good growing soil for all the green things, especially the maize. The air up here was invigorating to breathe, and Sarah decided that it was a less inhabited place and was therefore a little behind the farms along the river and this was good, because life here and land here was more the way she remembered things as a child, simple and unchanged by either man or crude machines-of-sort.

A woman waved to Sarah from the porch that went across the front of the house. She was lean and tall, and her hair that once had been the color of a fox's-tail was now mouse-colored and turning grey. Her apron was stained and so were her hands, for she was cleaning greens. She rose up from where she sat and greeted Sarah warmly. Sarah smiled, this woman was like Guildhall Hill itself, plain and very strong.

She leveled a gaze at Sarah and said, "Come up here and sit a spell," and Sarah did this, but not before she told the stranger her name and found out that they called this woman by the name of Hannah.

At that moment Sarah heard the most horrible screaming and insane raving that she had ever heard. It startled her. Someone in this house had apparently lost his senses and gone stark raving mad!

Rising to her feet Sarah exclaimed, "What is that?"

The woman called Hannah squinted against the sunlight and then looked squarely at Sarah and replied calmly, "It's jest Gramps! Guess somethin' woke him up! All he can do is rave when he is awake. Been yellin' and crazy for years now." Sarah raised her eyebrows and looked quizzically at the woman. It was hard to imagine living for years with that going on in the background.

"Oh, he has been touched," she said, and Hannah nodded her head. Sarah spoke then. "He is harmful to himself and others?" Hannah reflected before she said, "Yes, he would be, but we restrain him, so no he ain't."

The screams came again and they were more animal than human, thought Sarah, and this was a little upsetting to her for she had never yet actually doctored one whose mind was gone. He was probably very violent, and in older times the shamans made special potions to get rid of these evil mind-stealing spirits that took over someone's body.

"Is he in pain?" Sarah asked, and Hannah said, "Don't really know. Don't think he does either!"

Sarah looked at Hannah and said, "His body must be suffering to make such sounds, I think." Hannah had gone back to scanning her beet greens and as she dusted dirt and an occasional insect from them she said, "We don't give Gramp no medicine. We jest keep him clean and feed him, same as you would a dog."

And Sarah thought, "No, you would shoot a dog and put it out of its misery, but this was a man, so he must linger."

Sarah never forgot her first visit to that back hill home. She was perplexed as to what she should do. She had things and knew of other things, weeds and roots that were sedatives and calmatives, but by the sounds radiating out to the porch this poor creature was beyond all that.

"I am an herbalist. I would be willing to see this Gramp and if I could help him, I would like to."

Hannah spoke then. "You said your name was Jackson...Sarah Jackson?" and when Sarah nodded, Hannah went on. "Well, you must be Aunt Sarah! All of my neighbors talk about you. Alright, Aunt Sarah, I'll take you up to see him, but tain't a pretty sight!"

Sarah did not expect it to be a pretty sight as Hannah led her through the front door and into a hallway, and on up a narrow and darkened stairway that led to a second floor comprised of three bedrooms. From here a ladder appeared at the end of the second floor hallway, and the two women climbed the ladder which led them to an open loft. Just before they started up the climb, Hannah said, "Aunt Sarah, we can't keep a stitch of clothes on him! He tears them to shreds and he bites and scratches if you get near him. Sometimes he eats his food, sometimes he plays in it or throws it against the wall."

The loft was a dark and open little room, with a narrow window from which a beam of light came through. They approached the living form from which the screams had momentarily subsided just a little. He was a very old man, with wild eyes and white hair that was flying around his wrinkled face. He had a few teeth missing in front, and a long and scraggly beard of dingy white hung to his bare chest.

He did not look like a grandfather. In fact, he didn't look like a man, but more like some strange species of unknown animal.

Sarah sucked in her breath, for the poor old man was sitting in his own excrement, and in this little room with almost no air the stench was overpowering.

She fought off a wave of nausea and went and knelt before the wretched figure, saying gently, "Grandfather, it is fine. I have come to help you if I can."

He looked at her with gleaming eyes, and it was at that moment that Sarah could see the angry red marks around his thin wrists and ankles too, for he was shackled to the wall in iron chains and he had pulled and worn the skin off, and one of his ankles actually oozed some green secretion that smelled like gangrene or at least the start of it, but it was hard to discern the odor of the sore, because of the stench of his own bodily wastes.

He was stark naked, and his arms and legs bore the scratches that his own fingernails inflicted. His hair was dirty but his skin was not, so apparently his family did try to keep him washed as best they could.

Sarah turned then and looked at Hannah, and that hard-working woman had tears in her eyes, and Sarah realized that the elderly man was tied or chained here because there was nothing else they could do. He thrashed now, his legs and his arms moving convulsively from time to time.

"I hate to have ya see him, Aunt Sarah, him bein' all mess and naked." And here Aunt Sarah stopped her and gently said, "It is all right. Old Grandfather, he is very sick and old. We are all naked under our clothes, Hannah. I will help you change and bathe him, then I will try to help him."

Glancing at the pathetic little man, Sarah decided that if a man had to exist in this way, with all dignity gone, it was better that he was mad, and did not know it.

Sarah found that cleaning and bathing that violent old man was not an easy task. Hannah had been exactly right! As the two women struggled to turn him and wash his body, he in turn growled and snarled like a mad dog, and they had to duck his flailing legs as he kicked at them. Aunt Nel had told Sarah that caring for and attempting to doctor the raving mad was the hardest chore of all, and now as the elderly one tried to scratch and bite them, Sarah was seeing and understanding some of what her aunt had meant.

In earlier times among her people it was said of the mentally ill, especially the violent ones, that their bodies had been taken over by evil spirits, and often everyone stayed away from these people, all but the medicine men and shamans. Sarah knew that in cases such as this, one of the shamans prepared special calmative concoctions to sedate the inflicted person. They also prayed and chanted to help the effectiveness of the medicines that they administered, and often sweetgrass was packed into a clay pipe and the shaman smoked this and then actually blew the sacred smoke from the medicine pipe into the nostrils, ears, and mouth of his patient. After all, it took the most powerful medicine to get rid of the demons that stole and controlled the minds of their victims.

Sarah gazed down at the bloody shackles that held the old grandfather fast to his chains, and a chill came over her. This picture reminded her of the stories she had heard so often about the southern slaves that were held in chains. "Like a bear," she thought, "caught in a trap that will never be sprung.....a slave to his madness."

Sarah realized that it was the madness that was responsible for the old man's restraints. If they were to let him go, he would run like a wild thing through the fields and forests. He could neither feed nor take care of himself, not even to protect himself from the elements. If they freed him in this condition, it ultimately meant a death sentence sooner rather than later. "They do the best they can," thought Sarah, as she and Hannah struggled and finally succeeded in bathing the man and in getting fresh blankets under his naked body.

Toward the final moments of their chore, exhaustion seemed to overcome this man called Gramps. His ravings became less, and the white froth that trickled down his chin at the height of his rage seemed to abate some. Epilepsy, Sarah had seen it before. This was not as common a disease among her people as it seemed to be with those of White extraction. She knew that the ground roots of the lily of the valley plant were very good in the treatment of epilepsy, and Aunt Nel swore by their effectiveness as a heart stimulant.

Sarah realized that lily of the valley along with small amounts of valerian or the more common moccasin flower or lady's slipper would calm the old grandfather, and therefore lessen his pain and struggling. It would not cure him, nothing that she knew of would, but it would allow him to sleep in a restful way and it would make him more comfortable.

As he slept fitfully in his exhausted state, Sarah applied a mild astringent made of the outer layer of the bark of the birch tree. Some of the oil was also used because it was both antiseptic and fast-healing.

They turned to go, and Sarah touched her hand to the old man's forehead and it was not hot. This was good, she knew, because apparently his sores looked worse than they were and infection had not gotten a hold on his pale flesh, at least not to the gangrene stage.

Tears stung her eyes as she rose to leave. "Sleep, old grandfather...it is best for you," she whispered. "Grandfather....I did the best I could."

The woman called Hannah and Sarah made their way down the narrow ladder to the second floor, and then down a steep stairway that led into the kitchen below.

"He'll never be no better, will he Aunt Sarah?" was the question on Hannah's quivering lips, and Sarah looked at her with compassion and sadness and said, "No. Never better...just more comfortable, is all."

Hannah dabbed at her steel-grey eyes with the corners of her apron and she said, "That's all we ask, Aunt Sarah, that you can make him a little more comfortable." From her medicine pouch that she always wore under her apron, Sarah took the powders that she needed and mixed these with water. "Make him drink this, in this amount," she said, and called Hannah close to observe the dosage of each concoction. "He needs this noon and night. It will lessen the severity of the seizures and calm him so that he can sleep better. I will bring more in a week."

Sarah stayed at Hannah's insistence and enjoyed supper with this family. Here she learned that the illness had befallen the man some five years ago when he had been kicked in the head while shoeing a horse. They said he slept for four days and nights, and that when he woke up he was frothing and had convulsions. He did not know any of his own, and now half a decade later he still did not. The convulsions now only came when he was in a rage. Sarah listened. Some day modern medicine would understand about seizures and even about epilepsy itself, what caused it and what actually cured it. She wondered silently to herself if it was a disease that came on by itself from the inside, or if it was an outward thing, like the aftermath of a terrible injury such as this man had?

Night was coming on fast now, and this grateful family hitched up their old Dolly horse to their very best buggy and carried Sarah home. This was only the first visit of many that Sarah would make to this family. They rode in silence in the warmth of that August evening, and Sarah was just a little melancholy, wishing she had the knowledge and the tools to do more.

Just before she climbed out of the wagon when it stopped in the Gee driveway, Hannah and her family thanked Sarah.

"I wish I could have done more," said Sarah, but this family would hear none of this, and Hannah clucked, "Aunt Sarah...you did the best you could and that's fine." The old dog Moses was waiting for Sarah to scratch his ears at the foot of the steps to the house. Margaret came out to meet her, saying that she was getting worried, and Sarah smiled, knowing that Margaret had been no doubt fretting since supper time.

Sarah stopped on her approach to the porch steps and gazed up at the night stars. They were bright, and as they looked down upon her and all the world below them, Sarah felt that they were giving her a strange inner-peace, even as she reflected upon what the old ones said, which was, "The stars that light the darkened trail see all and know all."

"Don't question or doubt the stars, Sarah," Aunt Nel had told her many times. "It is not for you or me to know the answers to the whys of this life. It is for the stars to know and for us to do the best we can."

Sarah spoke a moment with Margaret, and then descended the landing and started up the stairway to her room. Her carriage was not straight and erect this warm night, because somewhere deep within she carried the feeling that she had somehow lost a patient, and her shoulders were slouched and bent like her head.

Inside the darkened room, she fumbled with a lamp and then got it lit, and with careful fingers she adjusted the flame.

The smell of sweetgrass was strong inside the little room and was intermingled with the pungent aroma of herbs like rosemary and fennel and the like drying, so that they could be used later to quiet an over-palpitating heart when the rosemary was made into a wine or tea. The well known carminative action of fennel seeds was a wonderful aid for infantile colic when mixed with catnip, and it was the very thing that stopped Grammy Gee from "tooting herself to death" with the gastric distress that was known as flatulence.

Tiredly Sarah thought of the comical Grandmother Gee, and knew that in that particular case she had done her best, and it had been good enough to free the spry old woman from a life of embarrassment and what she called "royal fatooting!"

In the flickering glow of the dim light thrown off by the lonely lamp beside her bed, Sarah removed her shoes. She uncoiled her hair and made two long thick braids that fell almost to her slender waist.

She very methodically then removed the medicine pouch from beneath her apron, and simply hoisted the thing and untied the string that let the pouch fall to the braided rug on the floor below. Sarah then unbuttoned her dress, but she was suddenly exhausted and she lay back upon the bed without even removing her garments or turning back the covers.

Her eyes were drawn to the half opened window and the white curtain waving in the night breeze. She sighed a long sigh, and a burst of starlight streamed through the window and momentarily fell upon her face. And suddenly Sarah knew that she had not failed, because one never does when she has done the best she possibly can.

A soft smile played on her full lips and sleep was quick to overtake her. The stars that saw all looked down and observed Aunt Sarah as she lay in a peaceful slumber, uncomplicated by dreams of any kind.

At just about this time, on the crest of a knoll up on Guildhall Hill, an old grandfather (still chained to a wall) lay also in a peaceful sleep. And to the relief of his family, it was his first good rest in many, many nights. Aunt Sarah's herbal medicine was working!

Now Sarah did not know this but those night stars knew that all these things would be.

The twinkling little lights would not tell what they saw or what they knew, because they did not speak, they only listened. They only listened and shined starlight on the darkened pathway of people like Aunt Sarah....Aunt Sarah, who faced head-on the winds of life and did the best she could.

The morning of the kitchen junket arrived and Sarah overslept and Margaret, knowing how late she had arrived home the night before was content to let her rest. During their brief talk at the foot of the stairs Margaret's suspicions had been confirmed: Sarah had been doing more healing of the sick than selling baskets.

Sarah came rushing down the stairs, her hair flying and her clothing a little hastily put on. "I'm late! Oh, Margaret....you should have spoken to me sooner!"

From the sink where she labored over piles of breakfast dishes that were strung with egg yoke and oatmeal, Margaret laughed, "Hush child! I knew you needed your rest."

Washing her hands, Sarah retrieved a clean towel and began drying the dishes that Margaret washed, but Margaret scolded her good-naturedly and insisted that she sit down and have some coffee and a hot muffin, and so Sarah did. As she ate, the smell of a slow fire could be detected through the open window in front of the sink. "I smell beans baking," Sarah said, and Margaret giggled, almost girlishly for once, "Oh, you know that Fred Gee. Can't have a Saturday night without beans. He has them slow baking in a beanhole out back. I forbid him to eat them or let anyone else eat them until after the get-together!" Sarah forced a straight face but she did understand Margaret's concern, considering that her house would be full of company. Finally laughing softly, Sarah said, "You are right. Those beans do have a way of sliding down quietly only to sneak back up on you from behind and blow up." Margaret nodded. "Why do these Connecticut River hardheads demand beans on Saturday night, Sarah?"

Rising from the table to begin her daily chores, Sarah grinned very mischievously and answered, "Perhaps they like living dangerously!"

"He teases for them beans for supper, and he will be!" Margaret warned.

Sarah tied on a clean apron, rolled up her sleeves, and filling a wooden bucket with soap and water, began to mop the floors. As Sarah swished the mop, Margaret checked her rising rolls and then washed windows. About an hour before lunch, the two women sat down at the dining room table and polished silver together.

Margaret was a very meticulous housekeeper, and she especially wanted it to be extra clean on this day with company coming. "I don't mind if the rest of the valley folks see a little dust and dirt at my place if t'warn't for Celia," Margaret said, and Sarah understood. While they rested, Sarah told her friend about the ailing old grandfather who was chained to a wall up on Guildhall Hill. Margaret almost shuddered to think of this. "It must be terrible to live with that old fellow, Sarah!"

As she polished a fork, Sarah answered, "They do their best for him, Margaret. They care for him as he is now....and they love him for the man he once was."

Fred and the younger children were over in Lancaster, purchasing numerous items on the list that Margaret had given them. The husband knew that the chores of cleaning would be easier on his wife and Sarah without children around. He also knew that Margaret always got so nervous and cross whenever her cousin Celia was attending a family affair that he was glad to be out of earshot.

As she tried to remove a water spot on a table Margaret sputtered and Sarah grinned. "Margaret, you're nervous as a long-tailed cat in a room full of rocking chairs!" she exclaimed.

Margaret faced Sarah then and said, "I know. It's just I don't want Celia tellin' everyone I'm a poor housekeeper, is all...and she would if she found any dust! She's dirty clean you know, dirty clean!"

As Margaret wiped a hand across her flushed and perspiring face she went on, "Only reason she's coming here is to try and get her hooks into Dennis, is all!"

Sarah glanced at her friend but said only "Hummmph!" She had surmised why the girl was coming here, but Celia was not her problem—she was Dennis's problem.

Shortly after an early supper and before the guests started arriving, Sarah stole away to her secluded little bathing spot on the banks of the Connecticut River.

The swamp maple was the predominate species that lined the river bank, but at this particular hideaway there were no swamp maples, just a thick stand of pine trees. Within the aromatic shelter of those pines, Sarah removed her white lady's shoes, and the white sand felt hot and good. Under her bare feet she could feel the sand and the pine needles and they felt soft to her touch, and she stripped off her sweat-soaked clothing, unpinned her hair and as it cascaded down her back she walked into the crystal clear water a ways, and then dove under it for a lengthy swim. Before returning to the shelter of the trees, Sarah rested and then scrubbed her body with a little soap and a lot of white sand. The low hanging boughs of the stately pines provided ample cover to cloak her nudity from the eyes of the world, and realizing this she stood up in the water and when the spray and ripples settled, she could see her reflection clearly. Sarah stared at that reflection having no guilt feelings about her nakedness, for this was her natural coat, like fur was to the wolf. She had never been told that being naked was sinful. Her undressed body was a precious thing, a mere shell that held her spirit until she died. At her death this copper colored body of hers would melt into the earth and rocks, and her spirit, free at last, would walk the trail to the stars...or else fly straight to Heaven. Sarah believed that White men as well as Red men belonged to the earth, but that their souls belonged to the Spirit World.

As the sun faded, Sarah could see the slender outline of her body gleaming like bronze upon the rippling water. She saw her long and shapely legs, the curves of her buttocks and the flat of her stomach; these all leading to that small triangle, her woman's part or her secret place. This looked like any other woman's, and her eyes traveled further and she saw her breasts that were small and firm and she was pleased that they did not sag. She knew many her age that looked more like a cow than a woman.

Studying her own image, Sarah wondered why so many White people felt that the naked body was something to be ashamed of, like an unclean thing. The human body was not dirty, it was a natural and beautiful creation. How each man or woman felt about their body was a personal thing.

Since she had been old enough to realize what the word body meant, this is what Sarah had been told: "The body or shell is yours, not to be flaunted or exhibited by one's own self or allowed to be abused or exploited by any other." Aunt Nel had finished, "Respect and love your body, child, for stains and scars upon the body show also upon the spirit."

Reaching for her towel, she began to dry herself with brisk sweeping motions. She dressed quickly, putting on a long green skirt and a white blouse with many, many buttons. As she put on her fresh clothing, Sarah was still remembering her reflection that had pleased but not shocked her. She was glad that she indeed looked so unscarred and womanly. She had respected her body and she was pleased that she had done this thing. In a few weeks she would be married and her husband would be getting no other man's leavings. She had respected herself and thus had honored her man, because love could never be without respect.

This was not a big thing as far as a man was concerned, but to a woman's way of thinking this was a very big thing. At the time her body changed to that of a woman, Aunt Nel had told her these words: "Save yourself for marriage, Sarah. It saves your own self-respect and that of all of those who's blood is also that of yours."

As she combed and brushed her damp hair, a dark blush stole across Sarah's face when she suddenly realized that in four short weeks she would be standing naked before a man for the first time. She would be as bare as that reflection she had studied moments earlier, but it was not the nakedness that was troubling her, it was the uneasy thought of hoping that John Somers would see her...see her and like all that he saw.

Sarah knew that he was marrying her because he in a sense had to, for that was the only way that he would ever know her body. He, on the other hand, was reputed to be a rake and undoubtedly had known the bodies of many, many women. These women knew all the ways to please a man while Sarah did not. This caused a dark look to cross her face as she headed for the house. Then as she walked along the optimist in Sarah took over, and she knew that those experienced women that knew how to please a man did not know how to get one to commit, it would seem. Marriage was a promise of not only love for now, but love for all of your life. As she stepped onto the porch Sarah thought of the handsome face of John and she almost said out loud, "Okay to know many women, John Somers....so long as you only love one, Sarah!"

She would never ask her husband-to-be about any woman or women in his past, for that is what they were and this was the future and she was his future....his forever....his Sarah.

One wagon after another, the neighbors of the Connecticut River valley arrived in South Guildhall that night. Fred and Margaret were both delighted, because save for old Jed and his family, it seemed the entire valley was here. His was the only family not present. The gathering started on the lawn, and after much food and drink that was neither baked beans nor corn liquor, the gathering moved into the house. The spacious living room was cleared of rugs and furniture, and a banjo player and a guitar player joined Dennis in furnishing the waltzes and old-time jigs and reels that made up the music of the day.

Standing back on the sidelines, Sarah noticed the way Celia lifted her feet up high and then crashed them to earth like boulders. Celia was not a bad dancer, just a show-off one.

John had arrived late, and when he entered and suddenly appeared beside Sarah her heart danced within her. He was deeply tanned from his recent days in the hayfields and his light hair made a sharp contrast. His warm blue eyes were the color of a summer sky, and they were laughing as they had been the first night that Sarah ever looked into them and decided that they looked like he'd stolen them from someone else.

"Could I have this dance...Miss Jackson?" was his question, and she nodded and replied, "Of course, Mr. Somers," and then they laughed softly and glided out onto the crowded floor and took their place among the other swirling dancers. He did not tell her that she looked beautiful this night. He did not have to, because his stolen eyes did much talking for John Somers.

Dennis stood like a tall oak tree, a head above the other two musicians. The fiddle was tucked against his barrel chest and he tapped a foot in time with the fiddle that he played so skillfully.

At every break, Celia tended out on Dennis, leaving her dancing partner and running off to fetch Dennis a drink of punch or lemonade.

Her face was flushed and she was putting on her best behavior—she seemed the life of the party. Dennis noticed her. She was telling him what a fine musician he was. He went outside for a smoke and when he returned Celia was waiting for him, and she continued to monopolize his attention all night. John Somers noticed this and said to Sarah, "Is that your brother's girl?" "Seems to be," Sarah replied, and John could tell that Sarah did not care for the young woman with the cold blue eyes and the honey blonde hair. John smiled, "Don't be so serious, Sarah. Men like to be chased by attractive women." Sarah raised and eyebrow and looked up at him. "Oh, and how would you know this thing John?" He smiled down as he spun her slender body in time to the music and whispered, "I'm repeating only what I have heard," and then both he and Sarah laughed. Later as they danced again, John confessed to Sarah, "In all honesty, she has all the earmarks of a snooty little bitch, Sarah." Sarah searched his face and said, "Your blue eyes see very deep, John Somers. I wish my brother's could see that well." He held Sarah close to him and replied, "She is food for his ego is all, Sarah," and Sarah answered with her usual "Humph," but she could have told him that Dennis would marry Celia someday. How she knew this she did not know, but she knew, she just knew.

As the evening wore on the children danced until the sandman came to get them one by one. Two of the Gee children's bedrooms were made into dormitories, and as they conked out the children were carried here and put to bed in neat little rows, three and four to a bed.

Shortly before midnight Dennis played a goodnight waltz, and then

Fred invited everyone still awake to come into the kitchen and have some of his baked beans, fresh from the bean hole and smelling like heaven to this group of Connecticut Valley natives.

The atmosphere was one of fun and frolic and Margaret sliced loaves of fresh made bread, which was buttered liberally and used to sop up the bean juice as this hearty group of farm men and women ate.

"This is the best kitchen junket I ever went to!" exclaimed someone, and when Celia, hanging onto Dennis's arm, made the statement, "Cousin Margaret....you really did outdo yourself!"

Margaret smiled. She had worked so hard, cleaned so hard and worried so much, and now almost forty neighbors were wolfing down those baked beans like there was no tomorrow, but it must be a good party because even Celia approved.

About midway through the meal, Fred rose to his feet and announced that on the second Saturday in September, Sarah and John were going to be married. Sarah's face turned beet red and John gulped hard when Fred, who did have some whiskey hidden in the corn crib out in the barn invited all gathered here to attend the upcoming nuptial.

Margaret gasped. How could she ever make a wedding cake that was big enough for sixty people? Oh, well, she would have to find a way.

Celia had stopped talking and she looked sharply at Sarah. She wasn't prepared for this news and she said to Dennis, "Kind of sudden, isn't it?" Dennis looked at her and replied, "They are old friends. Knew each other before Sarah left the valley."

"Oh," Celia said, and then she went on, "Well, she has got herself a good-looking man, anyhow."

Dennis raised an eyebrow at her. He did not think John Somers was particularly good looking. He thought he was a reformed drunk and that his sister could have made a better choice. Celia saw the dark look and added quickly, "Sarah is pretty, Dennis. Very pretty indeed, why she could have probably had her pick of......" Here Dennis cut in coolly and said, "Well, she chose him...that one. He will be my brother-in-law, and that is that!"

Sarah stared into her plate and said nothing. She read the sadness in her brother's eyes even though she could not distinguish what his lips had snapped at Celia. Sadness too was what Sarah felt for her brother Dennis at that moment. He did not know what sadness in a marriage was, but he would, because into his life had come a rain cloud that would set the course of his destiny, which was one word....Celia.

The days before Sarah's wedding rolled by with such speed that in later years, she actually wondered how so much was accomplished. There was not a minute of that time that wasn't spent at a dead gallop, and this was not a good or sensible way to go through life.

Unlike most brides-to-be, Sarah's days were not full of herself and the planning for a new married life. Instead, they were spent in a bustle of trying to keep up with her daily chores, preparing for her wedding, and gathering the herbs that she needed for her medicinal supplies. The fall of the year was the prime time to harvest the medicine crop. It was the most crucial season of the year, and if the herb-gatherer was not ready, then the time would come and pass quickly and her harvest would be small and less effective. The herbalist must pluck when the plant harvest was ready. Nature waited for no one, not even for Aunt Sarah.

Sarah planned to gather herbs and flowers when there was no dew upon them. During these crowded hours she tried to keep building up her supply of sweetgrass for the baskets. Often, late at night her image could be detected, sitting in her room in the shadow of a lamp as her hands worked either plain plaiting or using twisted overlay strips doing decorative curlicue work. Her baskets often had hardwood splints, and always the Algonquian double-rim hoops. The splints were made from logs that were soaked and pounded until the annual layers peeled off. Once in a while Sarah would weave an Iroquoian-type basket made with splint plaiting and cornhusk twining, but always she returned to her native Abenaki sweetgrass. She noticed one day too that her hands wet or dry smelled of sweetgrass and she smiled, for this was a good scent.

Sarah had come to learn that John Somers himself could weave a basket. He made baskets in the style of the Micmac, with dyed splints and often using more spruce and cedar bark than sweetgrass. He had learned to do this as a child. His grandfather had taught him, and although he did not do it perfectly, still he could create a usable vessel.

Sarah would find that what her future husband actually excelled at was splintering the ash logs to make the splints for the baskets. He was the most accurate man with an ax that Sarah had ever seen. Even Dennis noticed his precision and remarked on it. From the brown ash tree John would use only the back of the ax and this was pounded to loosen the layers so they could be peeled into strips, but still precision strokes were needed and it would take nearly a full day to prepare an average-size log that would yield eight to ten baskets. After the ash was peeled from the log, gauges were used to cut the strips into different widths for baskets. The ash was very hard on the hands, leaving them sore and hurting and also splintered. Sweetgrass was always Sarah's favorite basket material, because she felt sentimental toward it. It was part of her heritage, something as aromatic and sweet as it was mysterious.

Sarah had often been heard to say, as she finished the construction of a new basket, "This grass the earth has given. My hands have made a basket and now this grass lives forever."

Through the years, John Somers had been known to cock his head as if to disagree with Sarah, but then he never did. After all, it was considered Holy Grass, and who knew, perhaps it would live forever. Very often the work of the hands outlives the hands themselves. And so it was with Sarah.

The air was crisp that sunny September morning. The leaves had not yet begun to change. Sarah stood in front of the full-length mirror in the bedroom she occupied here in the Gee household. She wore the off-white silk and lace dress that Lou Ann had picked out for her earlier this spring. It was a beautiful dress, and Sarah's eyes moved from the small seed pearls to the mutton-leg-styled sleeves that tapered to fit her wrists. Her hands smoothed the rows of lace attached to silk that hugged the tight fitting bodice and nipped in at the waist. These fell flat again across her hips and then finished with a bustle in back. Why, this didn't look like her, this looked like someone else! She smiled and her white teeth were visible, and her smile was one of pride and happiness. Sarah had taken extra pains with her hair this morning and it was pinned securely in its French twist, but she had brushed it a little higher today. She was glad that she had long ago decided not to wear the matching hat, and Margaret had removed some of the ivory-silk, and lace ribbon and made a handsome bow with trailing ribbons, and this was what crowned Sarah's head. Her eyes filled with tears as she saw how deep her copper colored skin looked against the ivory dress.

She still looked like what she was, an Indian. She was an Indian in a dress that should be worn by the daughter of a king. Well, her father was not a king but he was a chief, and right now how Sarah wished that he could see her this day.

Her eyes were overflowing now and tears slid down her face. Oh, how she wished that Father was here, and Aunt Nel and Winona too, but they were gone forever. She took a handkerchief from the dresser drawer and wiped her eyes and tried to stop her chin from quivering. She was not alone, after all. She had Dennis and Peter here, and soon she would be marrying the man she loved, and that was really nothing to cry about.

It was true that she would miss the presence of her family, but John and Lou Ann lived too far away. Lou Ann would smile if she could see Sarah now; after all, the dress was a gift from her. As she regained her composure, she reached into a dresser drawer and took just a dab of some perfume that smelled like lilac and put it behind her ear. So many things were rushing through her mind, in these the closing moments of her single life.

Two weeks ago John had found them a place to live. It was a cabin made of logs that sat about a mile up the Ball Road that led to Guildhall Hill. The farmer whom John worked for owned it and hayed the fields out in back but he did not use the place, so he agreed to rent it to John and his new bride at a lower than usual cost, if John would stay and be his permanent hired hand.

John had agreed, and so Dennis and Peter had taken a wagon full of Sarah's baskets and basket materials and boxes containing herbs and drying plants up to the cabin already. Sarah had gone up two days earlier and cleaned the place as best she could, after first driving off a porcupine that had taken up residence under the wood-burning stove in the kitchen. "Thank God, the cabin has a wooden floor," thought Sarah.

This cabin was rough-hewn but appeared to be sturdy, even though it was very dark inside. It possessed only a kitchen and one large bedroom and a small one. For now the small bedroom would hold her working materials like sweetgrass, but later, when she and John had children, at least the first would have a bedroom of its own.

Below she had heard the guests arriving. There was much laughter, and only minutes before she had seen Celia arriving with other neighbors, and Celia wore a very pretty blue satin dress. However, on this particular day it couldn't hold a candle to the one that Sarah was wearing! A smile crossed her lips. This was a good day, because standing here in front of the mirror Sarah had wondered what she would ever do with such a beautiful dress. "I will never wear it again," she said half out loud, but then she knew what it was meant for: she would not wear it again but her children would, for she would make it into dresses for her women children. They too could look like daughters of a king.

Sarah walked to the window and looked down. It seemed half of the valley was gathered on the lawn outside. The minister had come and had agreed to marry John and Sarah under Margaret's rose trellis, and the sun was shining brightly on it now.

Sarah's eyes followed the crowd and she saw Peter seated way off in the background in his best coat and pants. Poor Peter, he would end up staying with her and John, most likely, especially if Dennis went back to Boston. Sarah saw Dennis sitting at the base of a big oak, and who stood beside him brushing dust from his coat but Celia. Dennis was not visibly happy about his sister marrying a "no-account." As she watched the big man who was her favorite brother, Sarah wondered if he realized that one day he would be marrying a "crow woman," the one beside him in fact.

Sarah watched all the heads of dark and red hair below her and then she saw him. He was about the last person to arrive but he was here, and he was walking tall and proud through the crowd. Her heart swelled in her chest, and there was no doubt in her mind that this man was indeed the one.

Sarah saw the sunlight touch upon his flaxen hair, saw his bronze arms reaching out to shake hands with people below, and hoped that she would always feel about this man with the stolen eyes the way she did on this golden "Skamonkas" September day in the month of "Indian Corn Reaping."

Sarah was torn away from the window by the sound of Margaret's work-torn hands, tapping impatiently upon the door.

"Come in Margaret," Sarah said, and Margaret entered in a whirl of skirts and was eager to help Sarah with any last minute details, but she stopped suddenly and surveyed the hauntingly lovely face of the slender young woman before her. Her eyes looked upon the dress and Margaret let out a long sigh. "Sarah, Sarah....you look beautiful!" She stepped forward then and gave Sarah a hug, then straightened back and said, "Well child....you look ready! Are you ready?" Sarah's dark eyes danced and she said that she was.

Seated on the lawn in rows of chairs were the valley people that Fred had invited to Sarah's wedding. She had not planned on so many but it was all right. Margaret had made the wedding cake using one of Aunt Nel's old recipes. Sarah had placed washed rose petals in sugar and water in a closed jar and set the jar to dry on her window sill, and as the sugar and water crystallized the thick syrup turned a pinkish color and this was used in a white cake, using egg whites only, and to Margaret's delight the cake tasted just like a rose smells. Sarah had assured her friend that it would, but Margaret was not sure of it. She had made a boiled sugar frosting and decorated the many layers of the wedding cake with great pains and it was beautiful, and Sarah never told her that the rose cake tasted much better with plain old whipped cream on it.

Margaret walked ahead of Sarah and they made their way carefully down the stairway, and Sarah knew that when she approached the hall below she would walk through the door into a new life. She no longer would be the Gees hired girl, no, she would be John Somers's wife.

All the guests were dressed in their best and seated for the wedding about to take place before them. At a signal from Margaret, Dennis rose and began to play the wedding march, and Sarah appeared and began walking toward the trellis. Smiling, his face lit up like a lamp, was Peter, and he took his sister by the arm and they walked toward where John Somers stood waiting.

This was a big day for Peter because he got to not only escort his sister, but he was also John's choice for best man, and he did both of these jobs just brimming with pride.

It was a simple wedding, a short ceremony where wedding vows were exchanged, and to her complete surprise John had bought a wedding ring which Peter passed to him. When the time was right, John placed the ring on Sarah's finger and tears glistened in her eyes. They had never spoken of rings and many did not wear them at all, but John had desired that she wear his band of gold and so she would from that day on.

John had not expected his bride to be wearing such a beautiful dress and he was proud and pleased, as pleased in fact as she was to be given the wedding ring.

There was dancing and refreshments after the service, and these valley people stepped high to the music and didn't seem to mind at all the fact that they were dancing on hard earth.

The music was provided by Dennis and his violin, and today he was joined by two guitars and a banjo. John and Sarah were the first couple to start dancing, while on the sidelines friends wished them happiness and clapped their hands.

"You're lovely," John whispered in his new bride's ear, and quickly added, "Where did you find that dress around here?" Sarah glanced up at him and said, "I brought it with me from Boston a long time ago." John raised an eyebrow and remarked, "Sarah, You mean you had the dress before you had the man?" "No husband, I had the man long before the dress, only he didn't know it."

As John's blue eyes bored into Sarah's dark and mischievous ones he shook his head and laughed. "Sarah, you always surprise me!" he said, and this was true. It had surprised him when two weeks ago Sarah had informed him that she did not want to go to Portland, Maine for a wedding trip, but instead would rather take a leisurely week and go fishing up in the Paul Stream country in Maidstone, Vt. John was willing, and so it had been decided that they would pack their gear and the morning after they were married and they would head for Maidstone Lake for a week of camping out and fishing.

Congratulations were coming in from every corner of the lawn, and when the cake was served, all agreed it was the most delicious cake they had ever tasted. "It tastes like roses, Margaret....like roses smell, I mean," Celia said to Margaret, and Margaret's eyes met Sarah's and the two women smiled. "This is wonderful, what did you put in this cake?" Another wanted to know and Margaret laughed and said, "I used something Sarah called rose syrup instead of vanilla."

Margaret had no way of knowing it, but from that day on there would be a lot of rose cakes made around the valley.

Dennis put down his fiddle and Sarah noticed that he went directly toward where Celia sat in her blue satin dress, and shortly thereafter they were whirling around in time to the music. It was good, thought Sarah, for it was the first time Dennis had smiled all day.

The afternoon wore on and Sarah changed into a cotton dress. It was white with tiny yellow flowers on it, and had a matching yellow sash that tied into a bow in the back. This was the dress Sarah would wear when she and John climbed into the wagon that would give them a ride to their little log home.

Before they left, Margaret broke down and wept as she and Sarah said goodbye. Celia came, with Dennis by the arm, and wished the departing couple well. She inquired where they were going for a wedding trip and Sarah said simply, "Fishing." Celia stepped back and then began to laugh heartily and Dennis looked at her sharply. It was not a laugh of humor, it was one that was making fun of someone. She was quick to note the glance from Dennis, and she momentarily regained control of herself and said, "Fishing...that just amused me. Sorry, I didn't mean to offend either of you." She said this almost contrite enough so that Margaret and many others believed her, but Sarah didn't. John Somers smiled then and said shortly, "They say Sarah fishes as well as she weaves sweetgrass. I wouldn't want a woman afraid to bait a hook."

Celia visibly cringed. "If I had to bait a hook....I'd faint! she announced and then went on, "besides, fish stink!"

Sarah had turned and was walking toward the waiting wagon. She was ignoring the things that Celia said. She heard a laughing voice in the distance say, "There is more to fishin' than baitin' a hook!" This brought laughter from the group that had followed the couple to the wagon. And as she climbed onto the leather seat, Sarah knew that the words were true. There was more to fishing than baiting the hook, there was the landing of the fish, and somehow Sarah knew from the heart that Celia, the timid fisherman would be very good at landing a fish.

Dennis had told John and Sarah that he and Peter would be over to visit them soon. John had then invited both Peter and Dennis to come to dinner the very next Sunday. "Peter, you were a great best man today. Tell me what you want for dinner."

Peter smiled and said quickly, "Peter, him love Southern fried chicken."

"Fried chicken it is, my man," John announced, and then he climbed into the wagon beside Sarah.

The driver in the front seat clucked to the horses and they were off in a cloud of dust that rose from the sandy driveway beneath them.

Sarah had a somber look on her face even as she waved goodbye to her friends. John said, "There we have only been married two hours, and already we have company coming for fried chicken!"

Sarah looked sharply up at her new husband and announced truthfully, "I don't know how to cook Southern fried chicken. Do you?"

The sun had long set and soon night shadows would be cast all across the valley. John and Sarah waved the wagon away and then turned and began walking toward their little log house. John carried Sarah's one valise, and as they approached the door he stopped and said to her, "I think in White man's fashion I am supposed to carry you over the threshold, Mrs. Somers." He grinned and picked her up as lightly as if she were a child.

Sarah smiled. The bride being carried across the doorway by the groom went down in White custom a long ways. Inside her valise she carried a blanket. She had placed it there only this morning. It was soft and beautifully woven and it was her wedding blanket. This went very deep into Indian custom. This blanket would be her most treasured possession as long as she and John were man and wife. If they ever parted, then they would split the blanket and that would end their married life. As she placed it in the valise Sarah had whispered a little prayer:

"Great Spirit...Father of the wind, let me keep my blanket whole and for a long, long time."

John set her down amid the boxes that were piled up in the kitchen. There were no curtains up yet and even their bedding was not unpacked. Everything was in boxes, from dishes to baskets.

Sarah rolled up her sleeves and found the box that contained the blankets for the unmade bed. She found sheets and blankets and then disappeared into the bedroom to make up the bed. John stepped over and around boxes and then lit one of the lamps on the table, for it was getting dark and it was always dark in this small cabin.

Just then Sarah let out a squawk and then John heard her laughing.

When she lifted the mattress to tuck in the sheet, bells began to ring! Some of her neighbors had been here and tied one cow's bell and two sheep bells to the springs beneath. John came in and they laughed together. "I guess before I go any further we had better tip the mattress up and remove those bells, John," Sarah said, and he chided her with "Or...we could make love and see how they work." Sarah saw the grin that played around his mouth and her eyes crinkled up at the corners and she said softly but firmly, "Remove the bells, John."

John did as she requested and then went out into the kitchen and began unpacking boxes while Sarah made the bed at last. He was looking for the things they would need tomorrow when they started their fishing trek up in Maidstone country. There would be plenty of time to unpack and place things when they returned.

John had fallen into one more vice that Sarah didn't know about, and thus he pulled out a pipe and lit it up. The smell of the sweet tobacco reached her nostrils from the bedroom where she was packing clothes away. She said nothing. A pipe at night was a very relaxing thing and she did not mind this smell. Somehow it seemed natural.

When Sarah went into the kitchen John was on his way to the spring to get them some fresh drinking water. Sarah sighed. There was no pump here, but there was a porcupine trying to crawl in through the door John had left partially open. Sarah chased the quilly pig out into the dusk and threatened, "If you don't go away, I will use your coat to trim my moccasins....I promise you!"

I will live with no running water but I will not live with a sneaky cuss like you!"

"I heard that, Sarah!" John said, and she whirled and told him she did not mean, him.

John went out and split an armful of wood and placed it in the stove. They did not need a fire this warm night but they would need one in order to cook their breakfast in the morning.

Finally, as Sarah packed food away on shelves and in cupboards, John took his pipe and went outside and seated himself on the rough bench that sat beside the door.

Shortly thereafter Sarah joined him, and they sat here enjoying the night sounds all around them. They sat in silence, and once John poked her gently and motioned toward the field to the left, and there a young doe grazed in the new moonlight. She saw them and whirled and bounded away, and when she reached the forest she blended into it as softly as the smoke that rose from John's pipe.

They heard the hum of the cricket and the cry of the night bird, and John put his arm around her. She lay her head on his shoulder and they inhaled the smell of sweetgrass and listened to the Connecticut River slapping along across the field from them. These were the sounds and smells of home, and Sarah felt that there were no better sounds or smells than those here in this valley. They watched the first stars come out and cross the sky, and when John remarked, "The stars seem extra bright tonight," Sarah nodded and answered, "They know all things, the stars." John looked at her tenderly and said, "Then they know that I love you, Sarah. I have dreaded marriage but I know I would have no life without you."

Sarah smiled a knowing smile and said, "There is a time to be single and a time to be married. Your time had come, John Somers!"

He looked at her and then was forced to laugh. Somehow he always felt that she was always one step ahead of him. John removed the pipe from his mouth, tapped it out and then quipped, "So has yours, woman. It is time to go to bed."

She got up and dutifully went in. Inside, in the glimmer of the kerosene lamp, Sarah went to the bedroom and removed her clothing. Then she wrapped herself in the Marriage Blanket and waited for her husband.

He was not long in putting out the lamps and joining her. Stepping into the little bedroom John said, "You wear the blankets of your people," and disrobing he joined her and wrapped the wedding blanket around them both. This was an old Algonquian custom and John felt very married now.

She stood wrapped in his arms with her head resting on his chest and listened to the hammering of his heart. She felt John's lips upon her neck and throat and then upon her mouth, and he was kissing her in a different way tonight, for his kisses had always been wonderful but restrained. Tonight he was very tender but very unrestrained.

As their bodies melted into one, Sarah lost all track of time and of reality almost, for she was aflame with love and desire for her new husband. As the blanket fell away she did not notice. She felt his caresses but she could not see the face above her as he lay her back upon the bed. He whispered things to her but she could not hear, he kissed her and she could not breathe, her heart felt full and her eyes filled with unshed tears but she could not cry. She could only cling to him and love him and show him just how much she was his wife.

Sarah awoke once just before dawn. Her husband lay beside her, and in the darkness she could not see his handsome face but she could hear the beating of his heart. He turned once and reached for her and called her name and whispered that he loved her, and then he fell sound asleep again.

Outside it had clouded up and a soft rain fell on the roof above her. The patter of it was as soft as butterfly wings against a flower, and Sarah felt complete and warm and safe and very anxious and confident to face the days ahead.

She knew that she and John had much to learn about each other and much to learn about living together, but they no longer walked alone along the winding trail. When his back ached Sarah would rub it, and when her heart ached John would kiss away her tears.

The rain suddenly stopped, and Sarah sighed and her eyes closed in a peaceful slumber. This had been a very good day, one that she could remember when the cold winds roared and the snow flakes fell upon a frozen land, and she did, all the years of her long, long life.

Sarah woke up and the sun beamed through the small bedroom window and lit the dark little room up. She reached for her new husband but he was not beside her. She came fully conscious with the wonderful aroma of hot coffee brewing.

She sat up in bed, feeling momentarily embarrassed for being a lazy wife. "John, how long have you been up?"

He stuck his head in the doorway and said, "Not long. How do you like your eggs, my fine lady?" Sarah smiled and the dimples at the corner of her mouth were very prominent. "Oh, John....I would have gotten our breakfast...if you had waited."

"A likely story!" he retorted, with fake anger easily detectable in his voice.

Sarah was up and pouring water into the wash basin. She washed her body by means of a sponge bath that her people called "cat washing."

The breakfast the new groom had prepared for her was delicious. He had peeled and sliced fresh potatoes for pan fries. He was a fine cook and she would never question him nor threaten his superiority in the cooking field. "I'm pretty well packed," John said, and then added, "There are a few clouds but I think they will roll over."

Sarah cleared and washed the breakfast dishes and put the unused food away. Next she turned her attention to the bedroom and tidied everything up in there.

She packed her high leather moccasin-boots for when they arrived in the deep woods later today. She wore a dark brown skirt and a yellow short sleeved blouse with a neck that was low enough to be comfortable in this early September heat.

At eight o'clock in the morning they loaded themselves up with camping gear and began the trek up Route 2, walking toward the North Road in Guildhall. Here they would follow that narrow path and then cross the mountain to the lower end of Maidstone Lake. They would walk most of that day, not even stopping for lunch and only occasionally to rest. This was not a hard chore, for John and Sarah were used to no other mode of transportation than their legs.

"I wish we had a canoe or a boat. We could follow the river all the way to Guildhall with no carrying at all," John said. Sarah had thought of this too and she said, "My father made beautiful canoes." John looked at her.

He had taken her hand now because it was a way to pull her along from checking to see how all her plants and herbs were doing. He grinned. He guessed that when you were into medicine, it was a necessary thing to do, to notice every change in every herb, but if he hadn't taken her hand to pull her along gently they would be all day getting to Maidstone, and it was only a few miles by taking this mountain shortcut.

They walked past farms on the North Road and people smiled and waved at the young couple. Sarah had been to all of these farms either selling baskets or in several cases helping with medical emergencies, like birthings and whooping cough and the like.

Children called to her, "Hello Aunt Sarah!" and she always smiled and waved back to them. John smiled at one point and remarked smugly, "You're too young to be an Aunt." Sarah flashed, "I already am an Aunt. My brother John has an Ivy Rose." John grinned, and they crossed a pasture and headed up a steep incline. John helped Sarah crawl under the hedge fences that were grey and weatherbeaten. "That is a pretty name. I would call my daughter Susan for my mother," John stated as they walked along.

Sarah smiled. She preferred Suzanne herself, but if the name Susan was special to her husband then it was fine with Sarah.

John raised his hand then and signalled that they stop. Sarah was tired and sank to the ground under her load of gear. They sat down with a clatter because there were pots and pans tied to the load and these clanged loudly.

"Look at that stand of birch here Sarah! I could surely have a good canoe out of some of that!"

Sarah scanned the mighty stand of birch trees and she nodded. It seemed that today her new husband's mind was on a canoe.

Sarah opened one of her sacks and withdrew her high-top moccasins and removed the clumsy White lady's shoes from her swollen feet. John saw the red marks and the way Sarah rubbed the soles of her feet. "Do those shoes fit so badly as that, Sarah?" he questioned, and she grinned and answered wryly, "They are all right. Any I've ever had on I think were made by a blacksmith."

John laughed. He sat beside her now and placed his arm around this quiet woman who so often made him laugh. He got up and moved away and came back with both hands full of blackberries. Sarah followed him to the bush and they ate their fill of these. This reminded Sarah that she must dig the root of the blackberry, because in Lunenburg she had a patient with an almost constant diarrhea. She knew that it was a bit too early yet to dig the root, but soon, very soon.

John interrupted her thinking. "Sarah, you have a ring of blackberry juice around your mouth," he grinned broadly down at her.

"Here...take it off, husband John," she said, motioning to her lips. He bent as if to do that and cupped her chin in his hand and then decided to kiss the stains away. This did not work, even though Sarah enjoyed the warmth of his mouth upon hers. When he raised his head she said, "John Somers, you look terrible in a purple mustache!" and then they laughed with and at each other. The sun was in the two o'clock position, and Sarah sat down and put on her moccasins. They felt soft and good to her tortured feet.

As they walked upward toward the pinnacle of this small mountain, the air was fresh with the scent of cedar and pine. The maples were scattered about and the leaves had just started to turn. A small brook that was little more than a spring gurgled along somewhere in the mixture of other forest sounds, hidden by the thick tangles of undergrowth.

They stopped once and saw a family of moose eating, and the animals were content not to do anything but stand and look at the two lovers.

"If I thought that moose could get along on three legs, I'd like to eat the fourth," Sarah said, and John made a short laugh and then as he helped her over a wet and marshy place he said, "Well Sarah, if you don't know how to fry a chicken how do I know you can cook a moose?"

"You don't," she said. "You'll have to bring one home and we will see."

They reached the top of the crest and looked down upon the waves slapping along the shoreline of Maidstone Lake. They stopped and rested again, readjusted their camping gear and then headed down the mountain toward that blue water below them.

The earth here was moss-covered and the oak trees were prominent, and they walked along the shoreline of the lake until they found a spot that they both liked.

This place had the flat ground they needed to pitch their little army surplus tent. There were tall jack pines almost in a semi-circle in back of the site, with branches sturdy enough so that they could hang some of their supplies from the branches, high enough so that a bear could not reach their tools or some drying food. This site also had a white sandy beach.

The campsite had numerous small cedar trees around, and the aroma of the pine and cedar was very refreshing to one used to smelling farm scents like cow manure and the pungent fragrance offered by the backhouse.

John and Sarah put up the tent and lashed it tightly to the stakes that held it. This tent even had a canvas floor and Sarah smiled. This was good, especially if it rained.

To make more room in the small tent, John placed all the canned goods in a sack and hung the sack on the branches of the mighty pine that sat closest to the tent.

Sarah arranged rocks in a circle and dug down in the earth until she had a fire pit, and then she went to pick up the kindling wood and firewood that they would need later this evening, when the moon had replaced the sun that now danced through the forest and splashed brilliant light upon the evergreens scattered between the beech and the maple and the ash trees about.

The mountain ash trees were in bloom. Their orange reddish berries hanging in clusters, stood out brightly in contrast to the dark green leaves of the tree. This tree produced a poisonous berry, but one very much valued by the Abenaki and all Algonquian Indians because it was so effective in the dyes that these Native Americans so often worked with.

Sarah inhaled the clean mountain air and breathed deeply, as if she could not get enough of the very simple sounds and smells offered by land, sky, and water when left unspoiled, the way they were when the Great Spirit put them there.

Inside the tent Sarah placed perishables like flour and sugar and salt, and even ten eggs out of a dozen that made the trip thus far.

The only meat they brought was a little salt pork and a side of slab bacon. Quickly Sarah cut these up and put them into a couple of cans. These tin containers were then fastened with a rope and put to float in the cold mountain water of the lake that stretched before them.

The rope was tied to a tree, and inside the sealed cans the meat was dry and bobbed about on top of the water being pushed along by silver waves that slapped against the shoreline. Occasionally the cans would come together and make a heavy clinking sound. This was fine, for it would keep the curious little animal creatures away, at least for the first night. By the third night they would however be used to the sound, and they would gather in the shadow of the night and peer from stumps and trees at these two uninvited guests who came to share the forest with them.

One side of the tent was lined with staples and the rest of the space was where Sarah would prepare their bedrolls later that evening.

When she was through with her inside tasks she went to see where John was. He had walked on along the shore, and when he returned he told Sarah he had seen a fat buck deer. "Umm. He would taste good over our fire Sarah girl, huh?" and she nodded and replied, "Well, I guess it's deer track soup, husband."

Sarah had removed her high moccasin-boot shoes. She felt the soft grass and moss of the land against her tired feet and the earth felt welcome and cool. Her clothing was soaked with perspiration and the long skirt clung to her long legs. "I trust you scouted around, husband John....and we are alone?" "I did and we are," John answered and Sarah chimed in, "Except for half the animals and noisy loons in Essex County!"

They decided that they would swim, but first John started a fire so that while they were swimming a bed of coals could be building. They stepped out of their clothing and then hand and hand walked into the clear refreshing water. They swam with long strokes then they just began to frolic and play in the water, like the children that lived inside each of their hearts. They would fish tomorrow. Today they would play.

They splashed and laughed and were like two eels, or was it more like two otters, chasing each other around this enchanted pool.

Once John came up under her and took her down, and she spit water and hissed like a cat. He righted her immediately, laughing and saying he was sorry. She was in his arms then and they were kissing, but they would not make love here. Tonight there was a time for loving, but today there was supper to think about.

Sarah had planned on getting this meal, especially since she had played no part in breakfast except to stuff herself.

"I was going to start supper soon, but now you will just have to wait until I dry my hair. Night will come on with speed and I need to dry my hair so I won't get a cold."

"That is okay. I will catch us a couple of fat fish for supper," John said.

Sarah nodded. They stood, their arms around each other, and slowly made their way to shore. Sarah dressed and then towel-dried and brushed her hair with her hands until it was nearly dry. She finished this job with her sturdy old hairbrush.

John kept his word and returned with fish for their supper. He only had one, but it was a huge lake trout and there was no need to catch a second.

He cleaned and washed his prize and then brought it to his wife. He smiled when he saw her face light up. "John Somers! You did catch a fish for our supper....you did!" she exclaimed, reaching for the fat, sleek trout. John smiled, "T'would do me no damned good at all to kill a chicken!"

She joined him in laughter, and he said, "It is all right, Sarah, I should have asked you what to cook. I will cook the chicken...after all, I am a cook."

"Good husband John, you cook the fried chicken next Sunday and I will make a basket to serve it in...me being a basket maker."

For the rest of her days, whenever Sarah heard about chicken in a basket, her mind would go back to this wonderful time in her life.

Sarah rolled the fish in flour and meal and cooked it golden brown over the coals in just a tad of bacon fat. She made a short bread in another pan, and they ate this warm and covered with some of Margaret's blackberry jam. She served John tea and he smiled and told her that she was a wonderful cook...for fish.

"Of course," she said and then went on, "I am an 'Arosaguntacook.' Years ago, the whole tribe went fishing and smoked their catch along the shores of the Saco, the Connecticut, the Amonoosuc, and the Androscoggin Rivers." There was a wistful look in Sarah's eyes when she thought of other days.

Frequently her eyes had wandered to the mountain ash tree, and she had remembered the time when Winona had climbed up one and eaten the berries.

Aunt Nel had whisked her down, and stuck her fingers down the tot's throat until she had vomited the poisonous berries back up. Years later as they traveled with the circus, they had been sitting by their night fire and Sarah said, "I love the mountain ash tree. It makes me think of home." Winona had looked at her sharply and remarked, "Well it makes me think of puke."

Sarah almost had to blink away the tears. Winona had found the man that she knew was the one, but she had never been able to marry him because the eagle in her spirit had claimed all that was earthly in her. "Sarah, look, there is an eagle!" John exclaimed, and pointed up to the huge brown bird with the white head that was circling above them.

"I saw her when I was fishing! I heard the small ones call. She scolded me for taking that fish, I guess she wanted it for her young."

Sarah only smiled, and a warm tear slid slowly down her cheek. She had always wanted her sister to have a home and family of her own. How did she know that she did not?

"Sarah, you're crying! Are you ill?" John's voice was full of love and concern and Sarah hugged him, leaned her head upon his broad shoulder and said, "The peace of this place makes me homesick for....my family, is all, John." He cupped her chin in his hand and with his deep blue eyes fastened intently upon her own dark ones he said, "Sarah, you are still a Jackson but your name is now Sarah Somers. I am your family and later on our children and their children will also be your family, and I see no reason for tears." She knew that John was right.

John held Sarah and then with his handkerchief he wiped her eyes, and hand in hand they took a stroll to stop and watch a family of moose feeding. They headed north, because the beaver were working a section here and John wanted Sarah to see the site of the dam.

The night shadows were falling fast as they approached close to the dam and they still had not seen any beaver, but suddenly the slapping of tails against the water told them that the beaver knew they were there, had either heard them, seen them or possibly smelled them, but now they sounded their alarm.

"These hard-working little furry men, with their sharp teeth build fine houses for their families," Sarah said. "They are very intelligent, our brothers, with their flat tails like paddles." John agreed, and they decided that they would come earlier another night to just sit quietly and observe the beaver at work.

The sun went down in a red glow against the horizon. Suddenly an old porcupine fell from a tree with a grunt. Sarah, who was deep in her own thoughts, was startled by this and cried out. John laughed at her and put his arm around her and they walked on. The cry of the eagle split the air and it soared over them, dipping low and then rising high and calling out the way one would say hello to an old friend.

John noticed this and he laughed and waved back at the big bird, but Sarah did not wave back. Goose-flesh rose in mounds on her bare arms and she whispered, "Hello Sister" as a shiver ran through her.

Later that evening after the nightfire Sarah lay warm and secure in her new husband's arms. She was content, in fact almost happy because she knew that Winona was fine. Silently the one who made the baskets thanked the One who made the eagles, for it was the same God who created eagles and men.

Sarah went to sleep listening to all the night sounds of the forest, soft and mysterious. Once she whispered "Sarah Somers," which was the name she knew she would carry all the remaining years of her life.

Sarah Jackson was no more, and Sarah Somers was the one listening to the cricket and the night bird and the drum of her new husband's heart.

As a light breeze swayed the tall pine boughs above her, Sarah Somers knew that the trail that she must walk led only ahead. A soft smile played across her lips because she was looking forward to walking that trail with John, her husband, her lover, her friend. She also loved this untamed wilderness called Maidstone Lake, where fishing was good and leeches were bad and adhered to your skin as you bathed or swam. This was all right, for they were part of the natural plan.

She drifted off to sleep a while later, thinking how much she loved this mountain air and every bush, berry, fish and animal, yes, every precious bird.....especially the eagle.

On the fourth day of their honeymoon on the shores of Maidstone Lake the air changed. It began with a fierce thunderstorm in the early hours of the morning. The thunder seemed to shake the ground underneath their makeshift shelter. The lightning split the skyline, and they watched it as the great angry streaks went toward the ground.

They were awake in their blankets. They listened to the tapping of the rain upon their storage kettles outside the tent. A nearby pine tree got hit and they heard the crack and hiss, and Sarah rose from her blankets just in time to stick her head outside the tent and see the sparks flying as the top of the mighty tree fell to the ground with a death scream of its own.

She was quick to scamper back to the warmth of the blankets, letting out her breath in a long sigh. "Boy, John Somers—that was a close one!" He nodded and added, "This is the line storm. Now the fall weather will be upon us."

The wind and thunder finally left the area, and Sarah and John were a longer time starting their breakfast fire this morning with everything soggy from the rain.

They drank the coffee in silence and John, being the better cook, made some bannock bread in the heavy skillet. They spread it with maple syrup and ate it with great relish.

Shortly after they had eaten, the rain started up again, but it was a tame rain, a gentle rain, one just right for fishing, and so they took their poles and left the campsite and traveled down Paul's Stream. This was wonderful fishing, and at noon they made a small fire and cleaned fat trout and then cooked them over a bed of coals, fastened to forked sticks that they had whittled. Sarah liked this old way of eating. It brought back her early childhood days when the entire Taxos band camped along the shores of the Connecticut, Ammonoosuc, and Androscoggin Rivers, and smoked the catch on the shore. There were plenty of fish then and plenty of Indians too, it would seem, but now there were not so many of either species.

She always got a far-away look in her eyes when she thought of the past, and John knew that melancholy look now and quickly he said, "I wish

I had a canoe. We could stash it on the lake and come here often in the summer months."

The embers of their noon fire were dying out, and John puffed his pipe slowly to let his lunch digest. Sarah walked around looking for herbs and roots and berries ready for picking. John continued, "In the old days my grandmother said a canoe could be built in fourteen days, and the women did the sewing."

Sarah came and sat down beside him. She listened to the song the brook sang as it bubbled along beside them. Finally she spoke. "I have never sewn on birch bark, Aunt Nel and Father did this. Father and my brothers built many canoes before, in just about that time, I would say." John looked up and a smile brightened his dark face. He thought a minute or two and then said, "Hummm. Two of your brothers are coming to dinner Sunday. Do you think they would help me build a canoe, Sarah?"

She shrugged her shoulders and responded, "I do not know what their plans are, but husband, you can ask them."

The steady rain had continued most of the day and the two fishermen ignored it, took it in good stride, and returned that evening to the campsite looking like two drowned rats. But, they caught enough fish so that Sarah was able to use a small grate which John carried with him, and a second fire was started and Sarah smoked the fish that they had caught. And they would eat them at a later date.

This would be a winter to cope with. Sarah had no garden of her own. Next year she would have corn and beans and squash and potatoes in the root cellar under the little log cabin they called home, but this year she would do her best with what they had.

They had both changed to dry clothing upon returning to the camp. Supper was bacon and beans and a corn meal bread that John called "Johnny cake," and Sarah thought it was delicious. He was a splendid cook, and every day he taught Sarah something new about cooking, simple things but helpful like telling her to breathe through her mouth and not her nose when she peeled onions. She did this and John was right, her eyes did not smart and water. "I've been an onion weeper since I can remember, husband. It is good to not have to cry when I cook with onions." Suddenly Sarah laughed and said, "Bad way to cook in fly-time!"

The cool air was growing more so, and the crisp of autumn could be felt this evening. John and Sarah had put on extra clothing and taken a walk toward the beaver dam. They stopped and sat down on the stout back of an uprooted tree, because from here they could observe the beaver. They watched quietly for any sign of life around this intricately woven mound of interlaced sticks and mud. Sarah had often marveled at the ingenuity of the beaver. No one, no enemy, even the bear, could get into the beaver's lodge. One could only get inside under water, but the lodge itself was on an island with the entrance and escape routes under water.

Her eyes traveled to the top part of the mound where the sticks were not welded together by mud, and this allowed fresh air to pass in and out of the lodge. And yet, once she and Dennis had tried to peer down into an old abandoned beaver's lodge, and even though the top sticks of the venthole were not stuck together, it was impossible for their eyes to see the inside.

John smiled suddenly and said softly, "Even Grandfather Bear can not tear his way into a beaver's lodge." Sarah knew this. Her father had explained early in life that the beaver had more than sharp teeth, His mind was also sharp. He could dam a brook or a stream, he could even withstand the spring floods that often washed out the beaver dams. He did this by carrying in his mouth limbs and trees that often a man could not move, and packing them into the side of a dam being threatened.

Sarah and John both heard the slap of a beaver's tail. They had been seen or heard. They smiled at one another. They had great respect for this particular brother of theirs because he was so very manlike. The beaver lived in colonies, and each colony was ruled over by a chief and they had their own laws. A bad beaver was sent away and given no more respect than a "no-account" man.

"I'd like to see the new kits," Sarah whispered, and John answered, "We will come bright and early in the morning. Perhaps we can catch sight of them." As they walked hand in hand back through the forest, Sarah could smell the fish smoking at her fire. "I once saw an old buck beaver actually swim up under a younger one and rip his stomach out over a female," said John. "They are vicious when they fight."

The night shadows were settling in as they stepped inside the circle of pine trees that sheltered their tent. A southern wind was blowing cold, and together they sensed that they were not alone. They stopped now and could make out the shadow of eight sets of legs. The wolf pack moved stealthily about, quiet and waiting. Now the yellow glitter of their eyes could be seen. They were waiting for a signal from their leader. He walked around, his tongue red, his mouth dripping with saliva. The smoked fish had called them.

John and Sarah had no weapons except a skinning knife. John soundlessly removed it from his belt. Sarah was shaking her head no, because there were too many of the wolves. From the outside perimeter of the dimly glowing fire, other dog-like shapes were taking form. This was a large family or pack, and without a word John put the knife back into the case attached to his belt. He touched Sarah on the arm and they each removed their outermost garment, in John's case a frock and in Sarah's a heavy wool shawl. They stepped away from each other and then from two different directions they ran toward the fire, each screaming the most spine-chilling and blood-curdling sounds they could make, and flailing the air in front of them with their clothing.

The wind had been against them and the wolves were so intent on the smoking fish that they had not heard or smelled the returning fishermen, and so they whirled about in fear and confusion. At the fireside John picked up a sturdy stake that had served as a poker, and he swung this and leaped for the skulking wolves. Sarah dropped the shawl and moved toward the most daring animals. She was now carrying two tin pots and beat on them relentlessly, and sparks flew from them by the force of the blows, and she screamed and charged the wolves and they ran away snarling, their white fangs showing as they did so.

John and Sarah laughed when it was over. For many seconds they could not speak, and when they could John advised, "tonight we had better leave a torch burning. They will be back, Sarah, for they fight just like we do. Hit and run warfare is the way of the wolf and the Indian."

Sarah nodded. She knew that he was right. "I wish we had a gun, husband John," she said.

He replaced his heavy jacket and seated himself before the fire, and then he replied, "I wish we had a canoe."

Sarah looked at him sharply. He was still harping about that canoe he wanted. "Do you think a canoe would scare the wolves away?" Sarah wanted to know and John snapped, "No, but it would take us to hell out of here."

Sarah got that stubborn look on her face. She placed her hands upon her hips and softly stated, "My family name is Wolf! I will not be run off from anywhere by brother wolf! Do you hear that, husband John?"

He sighed and looked at his new bride and said, "Better to run than to be eaten!"

"Hhhummm," answered Sarah as she went inside the tent to prepare the blankets that made up their bed. And later that night she fell into a dreamless sleep. Many times she opened her eyes and listened to see if she could hear the soft sound of a wolf walking around outside the tent. John did not sleep much either, and the cold September air bit through the sides of the tent and Sarah shivered, in spite of the extra blankets.

Just before dawn broke, John whispered in a teasing voice, "nearly daylight and no wolf yet, but if one comes."

Sarah retorted sharply, "If one comes, I'll kill him...you'll cook him!"

John laughed softly. No wolf would ever survive an encounter with his Sarah in the morning, because she was nothing but a grouch!

Thus four days into his honeymoon, John realized it was over.

The wet soggy air had been replaced by clear weather, which brought on a strong cold spell. John and Sarah broke camp a day before they had planned to do so, because indeed it dropped into the thirties the last two nights of their stay. These temperatures could be borne but there was very little pleasure in them. fall had arrived in one fell swoop, and it was time to pack up gear and head back across the mountain into the town of Guildhall, and then to follow the railroad bed to South Guildhall to their log cabin. It pleased Sarah to think about that dark and rough-hewn little place. The hearth was made of simple field stones, but it provided warmth and comfort far more than this canvas tent did.

As they made their way along the old familiar landmarks in Guildhall, John remarked, "I meant to ask you Sarah....have you ever eaten beaver meat?" She nodded, "Yes, but I did not like it. Aunt Nel used to marinate it in whatever spices she had on hand to get rid of the taste of fat, and it did help, but not enough for me to say that I liked the taste of beaver meat." "Hummmnn," John seemed to agree. The tail of the beaver was good, but not the rest"

The leaves had taken on great color since they had been gone, and the brilliant red shades on the maple trees were far more beautiful than any other tree.

At the turn to the road that led to their cabin they stopped and rested a minute. They stood looking over at the mountain ranges to the east across the Connecticut River from them. There on the New Hampshire side the Starr King Range rose. Next came Mt. Washington, the Crystal Hills, with snow on the top already. There was just enough green and yellow left to bring out the red and crimson and russet color of the changing foliage of the mountains. Sarah spoke then and said softly, "Father said this beauty was unsurpassed!" and she inhaled deeply the autumn air. John was not sure exactly what she was saying and he asked, "Do you mean the Crystal Hills?" Sarah shook her head and answered, "No, I mean them all...all of these painted hills of home."

For many years now, the Connecticut River had served as a boundary line between the states of Vermont and New Hampshire, but to the Indian, his fondest memory of that river was that it was his highway to the best hunting and fishing grounds on either side. From the New Hampshire side, the Green Mountains of Vermont rose up before you to the west and these too were painted hills, the painted hills of home.

Arriving at the cabin, Sarah was again confronted by her friend, the porcupine. This time he sat on the flat stone that served as the third step to the threshold and was doing a nice job of eating the wooden door. Sarah picked up a discarded broom that leaned against the side of the small abode and chased the quilly pig out of there, threatening, "You will be decoration for my moccasins yet, you! Go eat some of those outhouses around here. Now that would be making yourself useful!"

In an awkward manner the porcupine headed for the woods in back of the cabin, and John laughed and teased Sarah, "I think he likes you Sarah, poor thing, he just wants a home!"

Placing the broom against the side of the house again, she remarked, "If he moves in husband, he damned well sleeps on your side!"

And together they laughed and went inside the little house and unpacked boxes that were still stacked there. John started a fire in the hearth, and Sarah unpacked and dusted and washed and placed dishes and pots on shelves and into cupboards. There was so much to do. She sighed just thinking about it.

John took two large wooden buckets and went down to the spring and brought back water.

The next day was Saturday and the bride and groom of one week were up early. Inside Sarah hung curtains, while outside John took an ancient scythe and with great long strokes mowed the tall grass that surrounded the little log cabin. Looking out at him, the sun touching on his golden hair, Sarah was proud that she had a man like this, one who would work. Nothing, after all, was so bad as a man who would not work.

The next morning, about an hour before the noon sun was directly overhead, Dennis and Peter appeared walking up the road. Dennis carried his violin and Peter had a package of sticky-buns that Margaret had sent to Sarah and John.

Sarah met her brothers at the door and she could see Dennis looking around, and he seemed pleased with the lawn that before this day had been a hayfield.

Sarah had potatoes roasting on a grate on the hearth, and both her brothers raised their eyes when they saw that it was John who was laboring over a pan of hot grease and frying that chicken that Peter had requested.

At the questions in their eyes Sarah flushed and said, "I never cooked chicken this way. John has many times, so he did this thing for me and for you."

Dennis and Peter smiled and nodded. Dennis had heard from John that Lou Ann was not at all well. She had some kind of a breathing problem. Sarah felt uneasy at this news. She must write to Lou Ann.

Before too long the Jackson and Somers family was seated around the table, which was really not a table, but in fact a rough-hewn pine board that was quite long and had a sturdy bench on each side. And so they faced each other and visited, and enjoyed the golden brown chicken that Sarah's husband had prepared for them.

They spoke of things and Sarah listened, for men liked it when they had a chance to speak with one another. She was only half listening and was clearing the table when the talk came around to canoe making.

She liked the direct way that her husband asked her brother Dennis. "Do you know how to build a birch bark canoe?" Dennis was seated now on one of the benches, and he puffed his pipe contentedly while his dinner digested, and he nodded, "Yes. Not for a long time have I done this, but I know how and Peter does also."

John's face lit up like a candle and he said, "Well, I have wanted a canoe for here on the Connecticut or to stash at Maidstone Lake. Would you be interested in helping me construct one, and we can all be equal owners and share it fairly?"

Dennis thought a minute or two before he answered, and then said, "Well, I will be working over near Concord for Celia's uncle, but I will come and work what I can." He turned and looked at Peter and asked, "What say you brother?" Peter smiled and nodded his consent, and John Somers was so pleased that he slapped his knee and cried, "At last....a boat!"

Sarah did not speak. She only listened. Soon her brother would be working for Celia's uncle, and so it had begun. She washed the dishes, and the men went outside and made their plans for when they would start the canoe project.

One week from that very day, they arrived and stayed for a week with John and Sarah. Dennis would supervise, he would not sew.

Aunt Sarah seated herself on a bench that had been dragged outside, and from here she watched with great interest the construction of a birch bark canoe. Father had done this but she had not paid enough attention, for her interest was in herbal medicine and basket making. But, still it was a wonderful craft to know. If she and John ever had a son, Sarah would like him to be able to build a canoe.

Sarah's hands worked absent-mindedly on a basket as she watched the center sheet of birch bark spread out over a 12-foot canoe frame. From strips of white cedar the end frames were bent. The birch bark edges were turned upward between guide posts secured with cedar stays.

John was very clever with an axe, but on this particular type of woodcraft, Sarah had to admit that Dennis was even better. She watched the sides being raised as birch bark strips were added to the edge of the centermost piece. The men spoke little, but they measured with great care and precision all that they did.

The project was held up one day for rain, but on the fourth day it began again.

The day was hot and the men worked bare to the waist, their muscles glistening in the autumn sun. The canoe was coming into being now, and the end frames were carefully set in place and John was elected to sew the white cedar gunwales on. These gunwales were carefully spread with wood cross-thwarts.

Jack-pine roots were coated with pitch after they were used to sew the seams. Dennis was a master at slicing the thin cedar boards that would be used for the floor boards, once they had soaked enough to make them pliable. Cedar strips made up the ribs of the canoe, and these had been soaked in hot water and shaped like a horseshoe. These were wet and then dried for one day before being driven carefully into place so as to keep the bark from splitting. This took patience, skill, and much attention to detail. This took craftsmen.

On the eleventh day into the project a root strip was sewn the length of the prow seam while a guard strip was placed over the gunwales to protect the careful stitching John had done.

When all the holes and cracks had been filled and sealed with pitch, the canoe was done and her builders called it "The Waterbug."

All along the river while the canoe making was going on, curious valley neighbors came to see the construction of that craft that was made so simply out of birch bark, white cedar, and the roots and pitch given from the jack-pine.

To the White inhabitants of this valley it seemed an almost incredible thing that Peter, John, and Dennis had done, because the canoe was beautiful to the eye, and when they launched it on the Connecticut River, it proved to be a sleek and exquisitely balanced water craft, as tough and strong as the wood and bark from which it was made.

Sarah smiled with pride at the workmanship of her husband and her two brothers....her family. She smiled even more when she overheard the three men say that they enjoyed building the canoe so much that they each wanted their own. And over the years together, they made one for Dennis and one for Peter.

On the final evening of the completion of the Waterbug, Sarah roasted a turkey over her outside spit. After the meal there was the usual conversation about the state of the country, and especially the goings on here in the far reaches of the upper Connecticut River valley.

On the local scene, Grandmother Gee was said to have had a shock and was not doing well. Sarah knew that she must go there.

Identical twins had been born to a family up in Guildhall and Sarah had wished that they had called her, for she had never helped in the delivery of twins. Indians seldom had twins.

Dennis played his violin for awhile and then Sarah served tea and sugar cookies to her family. Dennis told them that John Jackson, down in Boston, said that the talk was more and more about war between the North and the South.

"Do you think it will come to war, Dennis?" Sarah wanted to know, and her brother was a long time answering and finally said, "Yes, I do. Slavery must be stopped."

Suddenly, Sarah had a strange chilling sensation that ran the length of her spine. She knew what her brother said was true. Somehow, she also knew that he would go to war, would be a part of that fight to put a stop to slavery. Peace-loving Dennis was going to war, and he would be getting married soon to Celia. Sarah said not a word, but she knew this was as sure as the sun coming up in the morning.

"Oh," said John Somers, "today on the road when I ran into the Gee family, Sarah, they told me to tell you that some old Jed somebody was dead." Sarah's expression did not change but she lifted her head and said, "Oh?" and her husband went on, "It happened in the middle of the night. He was thought to be drunk and beating his horse, and the horse broke free and stomped him to death right there in the barn."

"Whew! Stomped to death by his own horse," said Dennis, and John added, "Margaret Gee said they are not going to do anything to the horse."

And Aunt Sarah being an Indian naturally thought like an Indian. If she did not respect you when you were alive, then she liked you no better when you were dead.

Dennis spoke, "Not going to do a thing to the horse, huh?"

"Well I should hope not!" snapped Sarah, and then she blurted out, "That horse has got a lot more friends than old Jed had!"

John began to laugh. Dennis looked at his sister and asked with a wry smile, "You think this man went to heaven, Sarah?"

"Yes, hog heaven...he is there," Sarah answered.

"You wouldn't be a relative of Nelemano Jackson, would you?" Dennis asked.

"Yes," confessed Sarah, "I've got all the earmarks!" And this was true, because she was indeed like her Aunt Nel, especially noted for calling a spade a spade.

The first year of Sarah's married life was spent in that dark little cabin, chinked with moss between each log. It did have wooden floors made of wide rough boards that were held together by wooden pegs.

Sarah was glad to have a wooden floor, especially in a makeshift cabin such as this, for so many of them had no floor, only hard packed dirt. She was also appreciative of the fact that the cabin had a good sized root cellar. The later days of September, the first month of her dwelling there in the cabin, had seen her make three trips to farms where she simply swapped white ash baskets and sweetgrass baskets for sacks of potatoes, bushels of carrots and onions and a variety of winter squash. Next year she planned to have these things growing in her own little garden out in back of the cabin, but this year she must barter baskets for them.

Sarah had managed to find the time to replenish her medicinal herb supplies. winter was always the hardest time of year, with inclement weather and always colds and fevers abounding.

In October of that first year she had stood at the graveside of her friend Mrs. Elizabeth Gee, known as Grammy Gee to most of the valley. Many friends came to honor the good life she had lived.

The funeral was held in a church, and this was the first time Sarah had attended a church funeral. She found the organ music comforting to the ears, and the minister spoke words of hope and everlasting life to the family and friends of the elderly lady, who had in one way or another touched many of them. This was good, thought Sarah; now the bent but spry grand dame was at peace, never to hurt or want for anything again.

Tears silently slid down the sides of Sarah's face. It was very hard to say goodbye to a friend who had somehow always managed to make Sarah laugh. She smiled softly and wiped her eyes and thought suddenly, "The world according to Grammy was an interesting place."

On the way home Sarah spoke to her husband. "I wish Aunt Nel had had a gathering like that to say goodbye to her. She was like Grammy, forceful and strong and deserving of praise for the good trail that she walked."

John took her hand and replied, "Good works are never forgotten, Sarah."

"Yes," she said, and then went on, "They are branded forever in the hearts of others."

November came and the trees were bare. The ground was dry and not yet frozen, but well on its way. As soon as the permanent snow came John banked the little cabin with balsam boughs, all around the foundation and up to just under the small windows.

Peter was a frequent visitor, and he and John had built up a substantial woodpile to draw from when the cold winds blew.

One night when snowflakes fluttered by the windows and woodsmoke curled softly, John and Sarah were startled by a heavy pounding on the door.

John pulled on clothing and answered the door and Sarah stood holding an oil lamp. She was wrapped in a discarded housecoat of Margaret Gee's and it was big, but it was wooly and warm. The fire in the fireplace had burned low and the cold rough boards felt very uncomfortable to Sarah's bare feet.

A local farmer came in. He was very distressed. He asked if Sarah would help. He thought his daughter was bleeding to death.

She nodded and very quickly she was bundled up and climbing into the waiting wagon. Her medicine bag was clutched tightly in her hand, and she just hoped that inside it were enough good medicines to help the young woman in trouble.

The middle aged man with a hard face and gnarled hands slapped the horses briskly and the wagon flew up the road. At the door of the farmhouse Sarah was greeted by a woman with fly-away graying hair and a face tight with strain.

She took Sarah's coat, and as always Sarah asked, "Did you try to get a doctor?" The woman said, "Yes, he is away on a baby case."

Sarah briskly rubbed her cold hands together and then rolled up her sleeves. She followed the farmer's wife up the stairway to the dimly lit bedroom of a young woman no more than twenty years old.

The girl's loss of blood was clearly evident even in the dim lighting afforded by kerosene lamps. Her red hair was wet with perspiration, and when Sarah leaned closer she could see the glassy blue eyes and cheeks that were warm with a high fever.

"What is her name?" Sarah had asked on the way up the stairs, and was told it was Lisa.

Going quickly to the bedside, she reached and took one of the thin and trembling hands and she smiled and said, "Lisa.....I am Aunt Sarah. Don't be afraid......Aunt Sarah will help you."

The bed covers were lifted off and Sarah could see that there had been profuse bleeding. This could be a hemorrhage during the monthly menstrual cycle, but the girl was so young that Sarah doubted this. She saw that Lisa's mother had recently applied clean towels, and upon examination they were holding. Lisa's mother left to get another lamp.

Sarah pulled the covers up and asked the question that she must. "Lisa, could this bleeding be that perhaps you might be possibly with child?" "No!" cried the girl, and Sarah touched her shoulder and said, "Listen child...listen to Aunt Sarah. You be quiet and don't get yourself upset. To give birth is a very natural fact of life, just as to miscarry is in some cases when something is not just right."

The girl relaxed a slight bit, and Sarah opened her little medicine bag and began looking at her little vials of herbs and tonics. She asked for tea so that she could add one particular concoction to it, and the girl's mother went silently to get it.

Sarah sat back down on the bed. She smiled and with a gentle hand stroked the girl's damp forehead.

Sarah was thinking of a word that was becoming more and more frequent in the treatment of young women—abortion.

"Lisa, you think about what I tell you. My business is healing the sick, not telling their business to anyone else, ever. If this was a natural termination of a pregnancy, then we have little to fear from infection."

The girl rolled her eyes and looked at Sarah, who continued rubbing her patient's forehead and speaking calmly. "Now....if this bleeding was caused by an outside thing, we must concern ourselves and be very careful of infection. Do you understand, Lisa?"

The girl looked at Sarah and read kindness and honesty in her eyes, and she nodded that she did understand.

For a long moment Sarah did not speak to Lisa, and then she smiled and asked softly, "How far along do you think you were, Lisa?"

"Almost two months," the girl sobbed, and Sarah comforted her. She patted the girl's trembling hand and continued, "Um. Now did it happen child, or did you make it happen?"

Lisa looked at Sarah and simply stated, "I made it happen. He can't marry me. He is married already, came in hayin' and left right after. I didn't want Pa to know, so.....I threw myself down the stairs earlier this evening...so as to get rid of it."

Sarah swallowed hard. To end a human life was a hard thing to think about, especially the most helpless and vulnerable of all human life—a baby. When she spoke her eyes were solemn and she replied, "What is done is done." She was inwardly thankful that the girl had not tried to abort the child by some makeshift metal tool, like a button hook or a coat hanger such as Sarah had heard about. At least this method of destroying life would probably not take the mother's life. In many cases, infection from the "killing-instruments" that fearful and tormented women used, often did. Lisa had no broken bones, just bruises.

"Lisa, your child is no more. If you will have others I do not know. The blood flow is much better and you will not die yourself, and often that is the price paid for this type of thing. I have powders for the infection, and I have other things to take the fever away and to lesson the pain." The young girl sniffed and nodded. Sarah put two different things into the tea. The first was a hearty amount of the inner bark of the slippery elm, for inflamed membranes, and the second was some ground-up black cohosh root which was a sedative, a relaxant and an antispasmodic that helped the normal pain of menstruation.

The girl sipped the tea and calmed down some. Sarah would also give her a mixture of devil's claw and echinacea root to detoxify and fight off infection.

After drinking the tea the girl settled back against the pillows and whimpered, "You think I'm a terrible person, don't you?" But Aunt Sarah nursed the sick. She was a healer, not a judge.

Sarah shook her head and smiled. "Lisa, I think you are what I see, a frightened little girl that has lost a lot of blood...and a child. That is the pain I can give you nothing for.......but in time even that scar will hurt less." Sarah once more pushed the covers back to make sure everything was fine, and she said, "You have learned a hard lesson, Lisa, learn from it. And from here on, live with nature, Lisa, in harmony with it....not changing it to your liking. If you do this thing you will have lived well and walked a good trail. Respect all life, child, especially the unborn."

Sarah sat in a wicker chair, wrapped in a blanket. She never left the side of the bed. In the morning the fever was down and Sarah was sure that Lisa would be physically well. Whether she would ever be emotionally well again was something she could not say. Some got over this, some did not. If she could handle guilt, she could survive.

The girl hung onto Sarah's hand like a lifeline. She was able to eat a light breakfast, and when Sarah was leaving she whispered, "Aunt Sarah ...I think Ma knows! Please don't tell my Pa ... Pa, he's funny ... he would never understand." Sarah promised that she never would tell, and she never did.

Her work was done here, and as she started for home she couldn't comprehend one thing. What was it about men in general that they could make babies, could create life, but could not understand that sex and babies went hand-in-hand, with or without a wedding. Weddings were optional, after all, but the act of mating was the natural way in which the earth was populated.

Sarah mulled the words "Pa would not understand" over in her head, for these were words she had heard before in similar situations. It seemed to Aunt Sarah that the Pas of the world could understand and live with the murder of the unborn, easier that they could with a little condemnation.

Aunt Sarah returned home, but her heart was heavy within her chest when she thought of Lisa and all the misguided young women like her, who could spend the rest of their lives missing a part of themselves they could never get back, while chubby, ghostly baby fingers pointed at them.

As the shadow of the little log cabin rose up in front of her dark eyes Aunt Sarah was very glad that she was home. She was also glad that she came from a race of people who took the time to tell their children about the facts of life with a straight tongue, facts that were complete even to the part about baby fingers pointing.

The first autumn of Sarah's married life was one of the happiest times in her memory. In the course of that year, she had seen the buds and little green things grow into flowers and herbs, and the maple leaves had changed from green to rose and gold and ended up in russet red.

She loved the maples in this beautiful northern valley. They gave their sap in the spring to be made into syrup and maple sugar. This delicious health food would sustain the children throughout the severe Vermont winters. Like people, these maple trees had their beautiful time of life when bedecked in autumn finery. They also did get sick and old and die like every living thing, but even then the maple tree gave, for it was cut and split for firewood and there was no wood that could warm cold feet like rock maple. Sarah often thought "Even in its death flame...still it gives."

The last hard frost had gotten the maples and the corn and the bright orange pumpkins too, all up and down the Connecticut River. Snow had arrived early and now it was on the ground for good. The earth was still and white, and the once brilliant maple leaves were lying under that heavy snow. The ducks had quacked their final parting cries as they headed south to a place where the sun would shine and the days were warm. Sarah always felt a tug on her heart when the ducks flew south, for a part of her heart longed to go with them as her ancestors had done since time immortal.

John and Dennis seemed to respect each other, while Peter just accepted John as another brother. John was kind to Peter and Sarah was pleased, and he and Dennis had joined her and John for one last fishing trip before the snow arrived. The fish were fat and life was good.

At a chicken pie supper up at Guildhall, Sarah had been told about her brother Dennis and his plans to marry Celia at some future date. Sarah digested this with her meal and said nothing. The chicken pie and biscuits were delicious and the news was not news to her. She had known this thing would happen.

Through that first winter John worked in the woods cutting pulp for the farmer he worked for. Wherever they needed a man he was there, and still sometimes on clear winter evenings he would tell Sarah about his experiences in the logging camps in Maine and he often would offer to make something for a lunch after supper. He loved to cook, and he was such a good one that frequently Sarah would feel bad that a man who could make an apple-pan-dowdy like him had to waste eight hours of the day cutting or hauling out wood.

She had told him that if he had rather go to Parmacheenee to work she would either stay or go with him, but he said no, this year there had been enough changes and adjustments in their lives. December landed, with all the snow and sleet that could be expected from that month. The snow was quite deep for so early in the season and a hard flu was about. Sarah used more of her herbal medicines up during the first fifteen days of that month than she had dispensed in all of October and November together. "A Blackberry winter," thought Sarah.

Sarah was up early each morning getting John off to work before daylight. He would not return before dark. Inside the little cabin Sarah busied herself making baskets. She spent a lot of time making one out of ash for John. It would be a fishing basket and she would give it to him for a Christmas present.

Two nights before Christmas John came riding home in a wagon. He was singing and carrying a large dead goose with a three-foot stretched neck.

In the spirit of Christmas, the good farmer that employed him had given John a freshly killed bird. Thus John left the farm, walking through the softly falling snow, whistling as he went. He had not walked far when a wagon stopped and another neighbor offered him and the dead goose a ride. In keeping with the spirit of Christmas, the driver of the wagon gave John a drink out of his whiskey flask. John had not taken a drink in a very long time, and it tasted wonderful to him, that hot and burning liquid gold. At the other man's insistence he took another and still another, and by the time Sarah heard him singing, she knew that he was intoxicated.

Looking out the window Sarah could see the snowflakes swirling around her husband's head. The bloody bird was dragging behind him in the fresh snow. The bird would be plucked in the morning, but tonight she would sever the stretched neck of the goose. She would chop his neck off and leave him in the shed tonight. John approached the door, goose and all.

With a cry she headed for the door. She didn't want that bird in here just yet. Out the door she went at a gallop, stopping in the little shed long enough to seize an axe, and so she met her husband and the goose. Her face was stern and her color high, and to a guilt-ridden John she was an ominous sight, her voice sharp and her weapon held high and menacing.

"Stop right there, you!" she snapped, and John looked at her and stopped his singing. His eyebrows shot up and he stared blankly at her and dropped the bloody bird to the ground with a soft thud. He said, "Hell, Sarah.....I ain't drunk enough yet to be scalped!"

His feet were unsteady, but he was trying to be brave and indignant and Sarah, despite her apparent disgust, had to smother a laugh.

John pointed at the goose on the floor. "Frank gave me this, Sarah. It's Christmas! I lied...I said you could cook a goose."

Now John was trying to be funny. Sarah raised the axe high in the air, and with a shrill cry she lunged for the long-legged man in front of her who wiped the drunken grin off his face and bolted for the safe haven of the house.

"I can't cook a goose, eh Somers?....Well, I'll damned well be cooking yours if you don't go inside and sober up!"

The next morning from his sickbed John said, "I'm sorry, Sarah! I'll not drink again. I didn't mean to break my word...I was just happy, but I did break it just the same." He was grim for a moment and then he repeated, "I'm sorry and I won't drink no more, Sarah!"

From the plucked goose that she was laboring over Sarah answered, "I can overlook a mistake John, but I cannot live with a drunk! Either you stay sober or I live alone. Now....it is finished." And it was finished for good, the drinking part of her husband's life, but even then the damage had been done. He did not realize the early warning signs of liver disease but Sarah already had. This saddened her, but what was done was out of her control. She knew that he had injured his health by drinking, but her concern was that he drink no more and that she do the best she could to keep him healthy and strong as long as she could. You see, Aunt Sarah did not know that John suffered from another disease called alcoholism, which was the forerunner of his liver problems. "He has the thirsty-weakness," she often thought, not realizing that it took tremendous strength on his part and not weakness to maintain sobriety for her.....not himself.

On Christmas eve Sarah was delighted when John placed a package under their small tree. She had decorated the tree with popcorn and cranberry ropes, but she was not sure if John would buy her anything.

When he went to bed that night Sarah slipped the fishing basket she had made him under the tree, and in the morning they were both delighted to see that the other had cared enough to give.

She pulled the bright red-fringed shawl out of the package and wrapped it around her shoulders. "Husband! It is my finest gift!" she exclaimed, and John kissed her playfully on the nose and argued, "No, I have that already....you....and next this fishing basket."

John took over the actual cooking of the bird, and Dennis and Peter came and enjoyed Christmas dinner with the newlyweds, and after the feast they sat around and visited and talked of many things, but somehow the subject always got around to the war that most certainly seemed to be coming between the North and the South.

As they had for years, the rumors of slavery abounded, only now people were listening and caring. On both sides of the issue men were taking a stand on what they believed was right and what was wrong. It was very clear to Sarah as she sipped her tea that Dennis would be going to war. She had known he would marry Celia, and she also knew, he would be a soldier. She thought it ironic that this brother, so gentle, would be the one to take up arms against slavery, and still she did not think it so strange, for her father always said, "Beware when a good natured dog gets mad!"

"I'm buying a farm outside Lunenburg. Got it nearly paid for, Sarah. Celia will stay there if I have to go," Dennis said, and his sister calmly listened and nodded.

She knew that he would have to go, but she also knew that he felt it was a thing that had to be done. Slavery by itself would not die, it was an evil thing that must be killed, so that all men could live free upon this earth which they inherited.

John shook his head. "I hope it's over and done with. I hope it ain't a long skirmish."

Sarah refilled the cups with steaming tea and again said nothing, but inside her heart she knew that it would be a long war, this civil strife that would pit White man against White man over freeing the Black man. At times Sarah wondered whether an Indian or a Red Man should have a part in this at all, but then she knew that there was no race that so loved to roam the earth in freedom as did the Indian. He could not live in captivity, and to his way of thinking, death and war were a part of living....of living free.

Snow flakes fluttered through the air and the snow was piling up higher all the time. Dennis and Peter decided that they had better head back home before dark, and as they hugged their sister goodnight, she was sorry that they had gotten onto the subject of war, but it was there.....it was all people talked about.

As her two brothers headed out into the night Sarah called to Dennis, "Bring Celia with you sometime, brother," and he nodded, but she knew he would not. Sarah just knew these things, knew them just as she knew that Dennis would go to war and that he would come back safe when it was over, to the Connecticut River valley, to hunt the deer and fish the streams like his oldest grandfather's grandfather had.

She watched the long silhouettes of her brothers as they walked away. They seemed to blend into a oneness with the night shadows and the softly falling snow. When she could see them no more, she closed the door against the cold and then crossed the room and stoked the fire into a good-natured burst of glowing flames.

As the coals and embers spit and crackled in the hearth, the leaping flames brought to mind the campfires of long ago. It was a quote that she had heard for as long as she could remember. She knew her father and his family were most likely not the first to say this, but it was such a good example of the free-roaming, free-living lifestyle of the Indian people. "We take life as it comes and live for freedom, accepting war and death, to be always free to hunt and fish and wander."

The men said this for a joke and often laughed even as they said it, but it was true. "War and women are always near to a man, but the cougar and the white-tailed deer a man must go and find. He must heed the cry of the old wild goose, he must trail the herds and always follow the river," said Sarah.

John was changing a lamp wick and noticed the strange and faraway look on his wife's face, but he had not heard quite all that she said. He cocked his head at her and said, "I heard not what you spoke, Sarah." "I spoke the truth, John, I spoke the truth," replied Sarah softly, and then she smiled and took her place in the old rocking chair by the fire. And as her nimble fingers plaited on a sweetgrass basket the small cabin was filled with the fragrance of sweetgrass, the fragrance of summer itself.

John spoke to her then. "Are you all right, Sarah?"

"I am fine, husband. I am warm and happy. I just want to sit awhile and smell the sweetgrass, for it tells me there's another spring coming, war or peace."

John scratched his head. He did not always understand the workings of a woman's mind, especially this one, this gentle Sarah that he loved so.

There had been instances when Sarah had predicted the future to a degree of accuracy that almost frightened him. However, for the most part she was quiet and thoughtful and a woman not given much to talking at all.

Rising and banking the fire, John said, "Sarah, my love, if you had lived in Salem they'd a called you a witch and burned you at the stake."

She met his eyes and he saw that compelling twinkle in those mystical eyes, and she replied, "Maybe they did! But I don't think so." He laughed and jested "Wrong color?" And Sarah met his challenge with "If I was there....I was." They both laughed, and now it was she who rose from the chair and John took her by the hand and they walked toward the bedroom, putting out lamps as they went.

"I'm glad your family came for dinner," John said, and Sarah answered "Me too, and thank you husband. This was a fine Christmas."

The young lovers reached for each other, while outside the wind had picked up and snowflakes were whirling in a frenzy of white. Later when the wind died down the temperature would really drop. Sarah was glad that John had placed extra rock maple on the fire. The maple tree (that giving tree) would burn and keep them warm inside the cabin. Outside, blue ice would be forming on the snake-like back of the Connecticut River, the one in fact that Dennis would follow and fish when the war was over, and Dennis came marching home.

In January, the snow lay heavy upon the earth. The ground was frozen deep beneath that frigid cloak. People stayed in their houses for warmth and journeyed away from home only when they had to. Sarah heard news from her valley neighbors when she ventured out on a baby case, or to treat the influenza that struck without discrimination throughout this once-green valley.

In February, Dennis was married, and John and Sarah and Peter did not attend the wedding. It took place at the home of one of Celia's relatives, and though it was not a fancy affair, Sarah was sure that it would be too fancy for her.

In March, the biting winds were less severe to the nose and the days were a little longer. winter was finally letting up a little, the terrible grip it held upon this land.

April came with rains hard and constant. The land was soaked and the small brooks and fields were brimming over. Sarah was eating dandelion greens in late April, and in mid-May the fields that she had dug these greens in, were under water. The Connecticut River was over her banks and sweeping away anything that got in her path on those verdant upper Coos Meadows that separated Lancaster, New Hampshire and Guildhall, Vermont.

From her herb gathering on Tarritine Ledge, Sarah looked out across, what a stranger would see as a huge lake, that buried the meadows in a watery grave. This river was beautiful when it sung to you, but when the song became a roaring threat it was awesome and very deadly.

Filling her collection of herbs and early roots to the brim, Sarah began her trek down near the highway. The fields would not lie in their watery tomb very long. The water would drop and the meadows would surface, sometimes silt-covered, but most of the time they would be richer and more fertile than ever before. It was nature's way.

Sarah was hungry now. She had not eaten enough breakfast. As a matter of fact she had not eaten any. These mornings lately found her in a state where the smell of John's breakfast cooking made her quite nauseated. This was a new experience to her. She had always enjoyed her first meal of the day, but then of course she had not always been two months pregnant.

She was pretty sure last month, but now when she skipped her second month, it seemed certain, especially coupled with the fact that she felt dizzy in the mornings, something she had never experienced before.

This condition was only temporary, Sarah knew, just as the situation with the over-flowing river. The river would go back to normal water level, and within a couple of months Sarah would be able to eat again in the mornings. She, like the river, would go on and survive.

When she told John, he smiled and simply said "Do you want a man-child or a woman?" "I desire a man-child," Sarah said. He smiled at her and said "If it doesn't work out that way....remember, I'd rather have a girl child first, because little girls are special."

And so on through the warm and later hot days of summer, as her abdomen began to swell, Sarah would think of these words. Well, it would seem that either a boy or a girl would be appreciated by at least one of the wishing parents.

In June, Dennis had left The Green Mountain State with one of the first Vermont volunteer regiments. He was on his way to the Civil War.

The Sunday before he left, Dennis and Celia came and had dinner with Sarah and John. Peter also came, and a meal of pot roast and gravy tasted good. John had treated them all to a spice cake with a boiled maple frosting. Even Celia agreed that it was as fine a cake as she ever tasted.

John Somers and Peter planned their first fishing trip of the season. Sarah would go. She would go fishing and do all the outdoor things she could until she grew so huge with child that she could not, and then she would stop, but not before. Sarah was not sick, only pregnant.

Dennis could see that his sister was obviously with child, but he said nothing. Celia only asked, "Which do you want—a boy or a girl?" Sarah looked at her and said calmly, "I want a boy.....John wants a girl." As she sipped her tea Celia said, "Funny, how men all want girls. If we ever have children, Dennis wants a girl."

"Perhaps that is the way it is meant to be," said Sarah, and then she laughed, "At least one of the parents is bound to get their wish."

Celia's eyes fell on some dried yellow string beans that had been strung on a rope across one wall. Swallowing a laugh, she asked, "What are those?" Sarah's face got red. She was still used to smoking fish and drying vegetables in the old way, and besides, that was how she preserved all her herbs and most of her medicinal roots that wound up in her medicine powders.

"That is Little Britches," Sarah said, and looking at the rope of brown beans hanging there it did look like a row of "little trousers or britches." "Do you eat those?" was Celia's next question, and Sarah nodded her head yes, for these were excellent when washed and soaked. They could be boiled with salt pork and made an acceptable vegetable to accompany any meal.

Celia bent over laughing, and the longer she laughed the more angry Sarah became. She would never go to Celia's house or to any other woman's house and do a thing so rude as to point and laugh and ridicule the way another preserved their staples.

Sarah was picking up the dishes from the table and she set them down with a force that broke a plate into three pieces. Celia saw the deep crimson flush on Sarah's cheeks and she said, "Oh Sarah, don't take offense. I could just imagine Dennis eating the likes of that." With her hands on her hips Sarah faced the mocking woman and snapped, "Hummmm. Well, he has eaten the likes of that, many times in his life." Celia rose then and said haughtily, "Well he won't be feeding me any of that! Those old Indian ways are a thing of the past. Dennis lives in the future."

Whether it was her condition that made her so ill-humored no one was ever quite sure, but Sarah shot back, "Dennis lives like something he will never be......a White man!"

Rising to her feet Celia said, "Of course he is a White man. He surely would not go back living like an Indian."

"No," said Sarah, "but you cut Dennis and he bleeds Indian. He was born an Indian. He will die an Indian.....you will never change what is!"

John and Dennis came immediately into the kitchen from where the sharp voices of the two women came.

"Dennis, I'm ready to go!" snapped Celia, and Sarah turned and set more dishes into the sink with a crash, this time breaking a cup. John and Dennis looked at each other and Dennis quickly got his wife by the arm and they retreated from the little cabin.

After the sound of the horses' hooves could be heard no longer, John asked, "Sarah, what are you mad at?"

Washing the dishes now Sarah said, "She made fun of my beans....of my "Little Britches," and I'm tired of it!"

"Oh," her husband said, smiling. He had never seen Sarah get upset this easily. She was slow to anger as a rule.

"Dennis and I were looking over the birch bark canoe to see how it fared the winter when we heard you two growling at one another."

"Growling! That's all I did was growl! I should have bit her!" Sarah exploded in an outburst of tears. John laughed and came and put his arms around her. "There Sarah...don't cry. Now it is all over and done with."

"It will never be over and done with, John. How can she ever love a man when she hates what he is? We will always be Indians to her and she is ashamed of us! Ashamed of Dennis too, if you could read her heart." John listened and knew that the words his wife said were true. Celia would never make Dennis Jackson completely into a White man, even though she would spend many years of her life trying. In a hard to understand way John felt sorry for Celia, sorry that she had chosen to make Sarah Jackson Somers her enemy because she had thrown away such a good friend.

"I didn't say goodbye to Dennis," Sarah whispered, and John smoothed her hair and said that the next day they would walk over to where Dennis lived and she could say farewell. This is exactly what they did. Dennis came to the porch and spoke with them and then shook hands with John, and kissed his sister good-bye. A short time later up the road came Dennis in his wagon, complete with milk-jugs thumping around in the back. He stopped beside John and Sarah and gave them a ride home.

Sarah was very grateful for that kindness. Her feet had begun to swell if she did much walking, and today she had done a lot.

Climbing out of the cumbersome farm wagon, Sarah smiled at Dennis. "When you come home, brother, we will fish the river." "We will, sister, and my niece or my nephew, whichever will fish with us," said Dennis.

Sarah made a broad smile. "Yes, we will follow the river when you return, brother...we will follow the river."

Suddenly Dennis stopped the wagon. He turned and called to Sarah then. "Sister, have you got any Little Britches already cooked?" With a smile darkening her copper-colored face Sarah turned and said, "No brother, but I have just finished some of Aunt Nel's fry bread and I have a fresh jar full of honey butter.

Honey butter was nothing but unsalted home made butter mixed half and half with honey, or strawberries, or whatever you had.

Dennis ate this with great relish. Then he smiled and said "I could eat the whole damned jar, Sarah. Haven't had any of that for years. Tried to get Celia to ask you how to make it, but she said she wouldn't like it. She is a headstrong woman."

Sarah looked at Dennis and thought "She is a crow woman, that one, and a carrier of bones." All she actually said was, "Here Dennis, take the rest of the jug of honey butter with you, and when you come home, I promise to make you some strawberry butter out of preserves, if I have to, but I will make some, I promise."

Getting up to go, Dennis took the jug with him. He smiled at her and teased "Honest Injun, Sarah?" She made a broad and rare full-smile, and then she made a solemn face and met his level gaze and answered, "Honest Injun, Brother." Dennis drove away then, and he was laughing as he did this. Sarah smiled and waved goodbye to him. Her heart was glad that Dennis had not forgotten all the old ways completely. After all, he still knew who you could trust to take an oath.

Sarah headed for the cabin, not realizing that three long years would go by before she would see her brother again and be able to keep her promise. What she did realize was that even if his wife accepted him for the good White lifestyle that he lived, deep in his own heart, Dennis Jackson, like his sister, knew who he was and that he was not ashamed of it.

Sarah stared over at the Crystal Hills across the river, and suddenly she remembered the Indian name on her lips and then said it out loud. "Agiochook.....Agiochook....the Crystal Hills." In ancient times the Dawnland People had believed that the Great Spirit himself lived at the top of that mighty range, and they were afraid to journey there. Sarah, however did not believe this.

Her belief was that the Great Spirit lived where he always had...in the land beyond the stars. He had created "Agiochook" and every other creature. She had no doubt of this, and she also knew that he would watch over Dennis as he did all of his children. He was the God of the Indian, and He was the God of the White Man also. He was One.....and He was bigger than "Agiochook," bigger than life and bigger than death. Why, He was even bigger than this necessary war that would for a time stop brother Dennis from following the river. Dennis had remembered part of his heritage today, and Sarah had remembered a name long lost in her subconscious. She smiled, for these were good omens....two very good omens, and life was good.

The summer passed like that fleeting, longed-for season always does, and by the time the corn was ready to eat Sarah had taken from her own garden all the green vegetables that she could stuff into her root cellar. She always referred to it as "our cache," the name given long ago to platforms built high enough in tree branches to keep bears, wolves, and other predators out of the food supply. These were usually covered with birch bark or something similar to protect the store of foods from the elements. A cache was a hiding place.

The root cellar was an inside cache, was all. Her garden had been a good one, and her back had ached as she hoed it and picked the weeds out one by one.

Sarah hadn't minded garden work before, but then her ankles had never swollen before, nor had she had a belly that protruded out in front of her. She was clumsy now as she moved around, and the heat of August made her back ache terribly as she tried to gather up her harvest.

John helped where he could, but he was not a good gardener. He often stepped on the plants, because when they were little and needed the most nurturing, he couldn't distinguish a small carrot from a weed. Sarah usually sent him from the garden on some errand that she thought up, just to get him out of there.

In July, John had taken work in a logging camp in Parmacheenee, Maine. He had worked for that company before, and they offered him fine wages for his cooking skills. He came home every two weeks for a three-day week-end, taking a train out of Berlin into the South Lancaster railroad station.

Sarah was glad that John had a chance to make good wages, especially with their baby coming.

She filled her days with hard work, knowing that this was the way to sleep at night, especially if you were not used to sleeping alone.

John had shared her desire to have more money, but he hated to leave her in this condition and be so far away.

Sarah had assured him that she was fine, arguing that she was strong and knew what to do and that she would be perfectly all right by herself for these few months before the actual birth.

One cold bitter night in late November when the moon looked pale and yellow and all the earth looked dead, the wolves came.

Sarah had gone to bed early that night after giving up working on a basket because her back ached so. She stoked the fire and banked it, and then stood and watched the frosted window panes before she retired.

She had not slept well, and sometime after midnight she heard them howling. It was an eerie sound in the night, and by the tone of their hungry cries and trumpets she thought she heard five distinct howls. It was a mournful sound, and she knew the wolves were in the cedar swamp in back of the cabin, and that they were coming very close to the little cabin that had become her prison, more-or-less, since the early November snows came.

She lay in her bed and knew she was safe, and yet felt something that was new to her, a thing called anxiety. She wished that John was here beside her. She would undoubtedly go to sleep and not worry much about the howling wolves.

Rallying from a half-sleep, Sarah realized that the wolf pack was very near to the little wooden frame building that John and Peter had made for the sheep. They were bedded in straw, and yet they were not very comfortable this night, she knew. They had ears too, and the sheep in her sheepfold could undoubtedly hear the snarling and baying of the wolf pack.

The howling became louder still, and sounded very dismal on this lonely winter night.

Finally, Sarah clumsily made her way up out of bed. She put on her shoes and hastily pulled a large robe that had been discarded by Margaret around her swollen body.

In the kitchen she stoked the fire and lit a couple of lamps. The frost was half way up the window panes, but even in that little space Sarah could see the wolves circling the sheepfold. She did not know what to do really, but she knew that she had better be doing something or she would have dead sheep out there!

She pulled an ancient shawl around her shoulders, and picking up a lantern lit it and started for the shed. In the shed she found her garden hoe. She had not used it since summer, but it had a sturdy handle on it and it was sharp to the touch.

Stepping out into the chill of that frosty air, she momentarily caught her breath. It was cold! She could see the wolves, now leaping and dancing around. In their hunger they had become very bold and very brave. The leader was a big male with baleful eyes, and he even had the audacity to stand on his hind legs and scratch and dig with his sharp claws on the door of the small building that sheltered the sheep from the elements. Inside the sheep cried and bleated, and it seemed to Sarah that they were begging for their lives, but the wolves had no mercy on the gentle sheep inside.

This angered Sarah. These bold ones who would show her little spring lambs no mercy would be getting no mercy from her.

She began walking toward the pack then, in a slow deliberate gate, because that is how she walked now in this eight month of her pregnancy.

They saw her, were aware of her presence, but they did not seem to care. A couple of them stopped and trotted a few steps toward the woods and then sat down to see what the leader would do. What he did was turn and look directly at Sarah, and against the white snow she could see the red of his tongue hanging out. He watched her with baleful eyes and snarled, and she saw yellow-white teeth flashing. He moved toward her, but she did not step back. She faced his snarl and walked toward the leader.

She clutched the lantern in one hand, and in its dim light she saw not five but six lurking figures in the darkness. She set the lantern down and took the hoe, getting a good grip on the handle with both hands, and then she spoke to the pack and her voice was not a request but instead, a command.

"Go back where you come from, brothers! Find your own food....these sheep are mine."

The leader took a step toward her, and the thick fur on the scruff of his neck was standing. He drew his lips back and she could see the deadly fangs, and he made a strange sound and seemed about to spring. Sarah raised the hoe above her head and met his cold stare with one just as cold. "Come ahead brother, I'll rip your throat out with this hoe....come on, Sarah is no sheep. You kill Sarah maybe, brother......but you die too!"

She started toward him, knowing that she and her baby might both die here in the frigid snow and darkness. She also knew that she faced one who felt safety in numbers, one who often, one-on-one, was known to be quite cowardly. She knew this, just as she knew she was not.

Sarah clenched her teeth and waited for the spring, but the wolf at the last minute jumped back and sideways, and snarling and growling he began to slink away. The pack followed him into the night shadows.

Sarah swung the hoe and called after them "And don't come back, I tell you brothers, you do....you die!"

Snapping and yelping, they retreated to the woods and back to the cedar swamp that was their home. Sarah picked up the lantern and carefully made her way back to the shelter of the little cabin. Once inside she sat down and put the teapot on. Suddenly she was aware of some sharp and stabbing pains in her abdomen. She rubbed her huge stomach and said, "Now look, you.....I have had enough excitement for one night. You don't belong here until next month, so you just settle down and behave yourself, and all your life, you let no coward scare you!"

She drank her tea, and the little life within her did settle down, and Sarah went back to bed and slept quite well until morning.

Two days later her brother Peter stopped by to see if she was all right, and she told him about the wolf incident. Now Peter was not a hunter, for he would get turned around in the woods, but he had always shot at targets and he had a gun of his own.

"Sarah, me come and stay in the little room with the baskets in it. I have my gun. It would scare them away for good."

Sarah thought about this and she decided that perhaps this might be a good idea, especially with the baby due next month and John away for another week.

And so Peter came and stayed evenings with Sarah. One night they heard the wolves, and the minute they began to get close Peter went out and fired his antique rifle twice into the air, and the wolves stayed away from the cabin.

Sarah enjoyed Peter's company. He sometimes helped Sarah construct the sweetgrass baskets, and he always chopped the ice off the spring and carried her water. This was good, because although a simple task, it was one that she had come to dread since she could not bend down now. "And White women have ten and fourteen children," she thought.

Peter missed Dennis and Sarah did too, but she was quick to reassure Peter that Dennis was a crack shot and a skilled outdoors-man and that he could take care of himself.

John returned at the end of the week, and by that time the first week in December was upon them. He decided that he would not return to the logging camp until after the baby was born. He had cleared it with his superiors before he left, and once Peter had told him about the wolf pack and Sarah with her hoe, John decided that he would not have returned to work until after their child was born, even if he had not already gotten an okay from the company.

The day after John returned, Margaret Gee's sleigh drove up in front of the little cabin. She climbed out and Sarah welcomed her with a strong hung.

Margaret smiled when she recognized one of her old dresses that Sarah was wearing now, for it was the only thing she could get around her. She did not mention this, but as the two women had tea and cookies Margaret said that Celia had stopped in. She had had a letter from Dennis and he was fine. They had seen no combat yet, but they had been forced to sleep out of doors in torrential rains, and many were getting sick. Sarah listened. She was glad that Margaret would pass on this information to her because Celia never would.

Margaret laughed and explained that Celia had told every bit of gossip in the Connecticut River valley. Sarah smiled and looked at her friend Margaret and simply warned, "Hummmm. The dog that brings the bone...also carries the bone."

Margaret laughed and agreed. "Ain't that the truth! I was very careful what I said, believe me!" Then Margaret approached the reason for her visit. She knew it was time for Sarah to deliver, and she was hoping to talk her into coming home with her and having the baby at her house. Sarah thanked her but declined, saying "Your house is lovely, Margaret, but mine is fit enough for this birthing." Her friend did not press the issue but made John promise that he would come and get her when the time came. She did not want Sarah to be alone.

In the midst of a snowstorm one week before Christmas, in the middle of the night, Sarah woke up and got up awkwardly from the bed.

A low backache had been what originally brought her out of a light sleep, but now she realized that her time was here.

Beside her John asked, "What is it, Sarah? Is it time for the baby now?" She sat on the side of the bed and calmly said, "Yes it is time, husband."

He jumped out of bed with a speed that made Sarah laugh softly to herself, in spite of the discomfort she was feeling now from the pains in her abdomen and back.

"I'll go get some help, Sarah. I'll get Margaret!"

Standing up, Sarah got her bearings, and began to walk the floor. "You will get nobody unless I tell you!" she snapped.

Sarah felt confident that she knew what to do. For three days now she had been sipping the special tea made of wild raspberry leaves, which were a relaxant for the uterine muscles. She did not expect a hard labor. She was young and strong, and childbirth was a natural thing. Already out of sweetgrass she had fashioned a birthing basket, and when the cycle was completed, from a squatting position her man or woman child would drop into this, onto the soft folds of clean white cotton sheet-blankets.

John was flying around the cabin like a leaf in the wind, and Sarah had set him to boiling water. Then she placed a heavy broom handle across the backs of two chairs.

As her pains became harder and John said, "I don't care what you say Sarah, you can't have this baby by yourself!"

When she could speak, she wet dry lips and answered, "I am not alone...you are here."

"Please Sarah...let me get a woman."

Now Sarah was working hard and she was impatient, and she told her husband, "We made this baby without any help, John...we can bring it into the world without any help!"

Sarah was absolutely right, too. When her pains were very close she squatted over the basket on the floor between her legs. She had the chairs in place so that she could, if she needed to, drop to her knees and push on the sturdy broom handle while having a pain, but this was not necessary and suddenly she called to John, "Come quickly,....help me....it is here," and he ran to her, and together they eased the new and slippery life into the basket below. At that moment Sarah felt weak and unsteady on her feet, but her vision cleared and John mustered up a strength he didn't know he possessed. He even helped in the process of tying the tiny knots in the umbilical cord and then by cutting between those knots, separating this newborn child from its mother.

Sweetgrass was burning in a dish on the stove, and in the tiny basket lay a baby girl with masses of unruly straight black hair that would one day be the color of her mother's.

Sarah eased her way back and lay down upon the bed. This was the time to go to bed, after the labor was done, she thought. This is why Margaret or no other White lady could come to help. They would hinder.

"It is a girl baby, husband John...is she all right?" Sarah asked, and even though she was momentarily drained, she was more concerned with how her child was.

Her labor had been short, but she was suddenly very sleepy. She smiled as John handed the newly cleaned and prepared bundle over to nuzzle at her breast. As he did so, he said, "She is not just all right, Sarah, she is perfect!" His face was beaming with fatherly pride.

Sarah whispered, "My little Christmas Carol....brought by a new snow storm." Then her face clouded, and as she touched one of the new little pink hands she asked, "You wanted to call her Susan.....didn't you John?" He smiled. "Susan was my mother. You are this snow child's mother, Sarah. Carol is a fine name."

Through half-closed eyelids Sarah mumbled, "Not Carol, husband John. Caroline will be her name.....Caroline Snow Somers."

"That name is good and right for her, Sarah," John said.

Sarah answered, "Yes, good and right, like the snow that guided her to us this night."

The seasons arrived on time and then melted strangely together, as springs and summers, golden autumns and frigid winters all came and passed away into history, like the smiles and tears that were shed during that time by the sturdy inhabitants of the upper Connecticut River valley. The soil here was rich and black and fertile, but indeed it was the river that was the very heart of this valley.

In the shadow of that river Sarah continued to spend her days, weaving her baskets and studying the herbal and plant life around her, because she knew that plant life, animal life, and human life.....all things were connected.

She was often heard to quote, "the mightiest tree.......to the most bitter of all the berries......each of these is important to us and all of these are life to us."

Aunt Sarah's reputation as an herbalist grew, and when the child Caroline was around two years of age John took a job in the logging camps and Sarah and the child stayed alone. Caroline was simply bundled up and taken along when Sarah responded to a sick call. And it would have pleased Aunt Sarah so much, as Caroline grew into a youngster of eight, if she had shown any interest in herbal medicine, but she did not. She was a bright and strong-willed woman child, this hazel-eyed girl with a disposition as changeable and stormy as the wind that howled the night she was born.

Most times Caroline had a calm disposition, but then like hissing sparks her temper would flare and she was the spitting image of Winona, thought Sarah so often. One day after disciplining her daughter for a stomping tantrum, Sarah said to John quietly, "Our Storm Child has eyes that change with her clothing and moods." He laughed. "You should have named her "Storm Woman", perhaps? the husband queried, and Sarah with a strange and faraway look on her face answered, "I should have called her Eagle." He did not understand, she saw, but she didn't explain the logic of her words. She must not disturb her sister's spirit by speaking her name. That old superstition ran deep inside her heart, and yet so very many of Winona Jackson's traits and mannerisms were so clearly visible in the child Caroline that it was little wonder the old ones said, "Blood is thicker than water." If seeing is believing, this was so, thought Sarah.

When Caroline was six years old, Sarah bore a son. He had come into this world with little trouble. He had been born in the heat of late August after a day of blackberry picking, and even though Sarah was tired when the labor started, still she was ready. She had been drinking the concoction mixed with raspberry leaves for many days now, and this labor was even shorter than with her first child. She was alone when this baby arrived, and while her daughter Caroline slept through her afternoon nap undisturbed in the next room, Sarah delivered the boy herself and then cut the cord between them. Looking down into his perfect dark little face, she felt a rush of pride, even before she removed him from his birthing basket which she straddled. She clucked and fussed over him, and gently washed the child and wrapped him in soft blankets, and then lay down beside him on her bed. He was plump and healthy, and her heart beat with delight, for she knew that when her husband returned that evening he would have such a fine man-child to greet him.

That was the way John found them, Sarah and the child dozing peacefully. He was elated! The fact that no supper was ready didn't enter into his mind. He woke Caroline from her nap and prepared the evening meal, and much to his dismay Sarah walked to the table and shared it with him and her daughter. John clucked and scolded and carried on like an old mother hen, and finally to escape his fussing Sarah returned to bed without partaking of her beloved second cup of tea. As she left the table she said coolly, "John, you are a worse pain than any I had all day!" She was inwardly glad that when she delivered the new baby, John had been too far away to interfere with her work! Aunt Nel had been so right, thought Sarah, when she had insisted, "There are babies.......and then there are the real babies......men!" Aunt Nel meant sick men, of course.

Caroline had been napping so soundly that she really didn't notice her brother until after supper. If she had awakened while the actual birth was going on, Sarah would have explained that she was giving birth, just as she had when Caroline walked in on the cat having kittens. Birthing was another part of living, just like dying was, and children should be told the truth about the beginning and the end of life on earth, so that they would understand and never be afraid of either one.

Little Caroline looked down at the infant nuzzling at its mother's breast, and said "Why, he is as noisy as a kitten, mother." Sarah nodded her head and then was forced to laugh a little later, when she saw the way the young one was scrutinizing her brother's upturned little face.

Before anyone could speak the girl said, "Why his eyes are open and I bet he can see!" "I think so," said Sarah, and Caroline burst out with, "Why, Mother! Where are his teeth? He hasn't a single tooth in his head!" "They will grow in later, Caroline, when he is bigger," Sarah whispered softly, and Caroline ran a hand through her new brother's dark hair and said "That's good! Who wants a toothless brother hanging around for the rest of her life?"

Sarah concealed a smile. She knew that someday Caroline would learn the value of that boy child. She would learn that life holds many gifts for us, but fewer are more valuable than a brother—with or without teeth.

Caroline's face broke finally into a broad smile, and she said simply and to the point, "Well Mother and Father, I like him. Of course he will be pretty useless for awhile, but I'm glad we're going to keep him, and if his teeth don't grow in we'll have Uncle Peter whittle him up some!"

The new parents laughed again and Sarah thought to herself, " Winona Jackson, Eagle Woman.......you will never be dead as long as this child Caroline is alive."

Caroline, with the aid of her father, was allowed to sit in the rocker and hold this little boy, and it was there that she really began to think of him as her little brother. And throughout all the years ahead, if Caroline had a fault it was being overly protective of her younger brother.

Smiling down at him she said, "I like this boy! I like him even better than Harvy the goat......and he smells so much better too!"

Sarah and John looked at one another. They knew that Caroline had picked out the goat's name because it was her favorite name, she had said.

"Well then it is settled, Caroline," said Aunt Sarah. You named the goat, now you can name this boy." Caroline smiled, and then she said after a minute of thinking, "I'd like to call him Harvy....Harvy the boy, of course!" And so it was done, but when the child was out of earshot John questioned, "Sarah, do you think you should have named the boy for a goat?" Sarah snapped back, "I didn't name him for a goat!" I let Caroline name him and she called him Harvy." Sarah had that stubborn look on her face and John said, "I would like his middle name to be John, like my own Sarah. Do you like Harvy John?" "Yes," smiled Aunt Sarah, "It is like a melody, that name. I like it very much, husband."

Harvy was a quiet little boy, and when he was only five he astounded friends and family with the mellow sounds he could create on a crude willow whistle that his father had carved for him. He had the gift of music, and at ten he was slow in reading and math skills but he was a fine guitarist. Harvy at twelve had mastered the flute, and what he lacked in brains he certainly made up for in talent. At thirteen he played three instruments beautifully but could not read a note. He played by ear. With that old willow whistle he could imitate the call of every bird in the valley. He could play their songs and mimmick their soft calls and warbles, and he loved the forest and had rather spend the day fishing and playing his flute than to be in school or around many people.

He like his mother was not much of a talker, but he was a good listener and a good son and his mother was proud of him. She did not know then that he had inherited his father's thirst for rum, and that because of this he would never be the musician that his uncle Dennis was. Sarah could understand sickness but she could not understand weakness. If she had known that Harvy's adult life was ruled by an illness out of control, she would have accepted him and his drinking problem as she would one inflicted with a disease. Sarah however did not understand, and what she actually knew was that the apple had not fallen far from the tree.

As John's hair turned very silver, Sarah's own dark hair was showing strands of grey, but only here and there. Caroline had turned into a beautiful young woman of seventeen, and with her mother's firm guidance and gentle discipline she had mellowed from the wild thing that she was and Sarah was indeed proud of her. She was proud of Harvy to a degree, but saddened that he was not ambitious like his sister. From door-to-door, from a child to manhood, Harvy carried his mother's baskets. He carried them on his head, of course. He was not a mean person and he was honest. He was just a man who liked his rum too much. Sarah was proud that he was such a fine musician, but heartbroken that he was not all that he had the potential to be. She saw no fire in his dark eyes, only a placid acceptance of life ... of a life without dignity.

Sarah would say to John, "That boy ... he is not a bad man. Why does he have to be so weak, John?" Sometimes Sarah the herbalist used to wish that if he had to be something he would not be weak, that he would be sick instead of weak, never realizing that indeed her son was sick, as all alcoholics are.

Through the years she had told both her children all the legends and the stories of her people, of their forefathers, but the fact that Harvy was the grandson of an Indian Chief meant nothing to him. He was not a man of pride, this Harvy ... Harvy, Sarah's only son, and though she loved him he was still the biggest disappointment in Aunt Sarah's life.

One day as she despaired over the discovery of her son lying in a drunken stupor in the woodshed, her husband said, "Sarah, don't cry. He might find a young girl someday. One that is special, and he will change for her ... I did for you."

And as mental images of her father's last years crossed her mind, Sarah knew that Harvy was very much like that man who fought the train, so long ago.

She wiped her eyes and said, "He will not change, husband. He gets the thirst from Father and you ... he gets the stubbornness from me. That one ... he will never change. He spends his time between bottles and he lives only for Harvy."

And Aunt Sarah wept for her son, that shiftless one who did not realize himself that he had so much more than he had not.

Aunt Sarah went on quietly living in this peaceful valley. She had returned to it many years ago, heartbroken over the death of her only sister, and she had started rebuilding her life one basket at a time.

She still gathered her herbal medicines and made her concoctions and poultices, and her patients would testify that they worked.

Sarah tried unsuccessfully to interest Caroline in the world of herbal medicines, but she could not. Caroline had no interest in caring for the sick. She was an average basket maker, though, and did work hard to help her mother with this trade. Caroline was a seamstress, and her stitches were fine and her embroidery work was lovely to behold, but she saw no benefit in knowing the signature of medicinal herbs and plants, even though her mother stressed time and again that even not wanting to know for the sake of her own health surely was a shame. At this point Caroline would laugh and say, "Oh mother, you are so old fashioned! And besides that ... I'm never sick!"

With great sadness in her voice, one day Sarah answered her carefree daughter, "Caroline, you are a dumb puppy. The mother wolf teaches her young to feed upon witch grass to provoke vomiting. The cub bear..that one, he too listens to his mama, and eats the roots of the fern to heal his troubles. But Sarah's cubs ... no, they will not learn to take and use the medicines from the earth. One day a life could depend on this ... even your own, my daughter."

Caroline listened with proper respect, but she did not take it to heart. There were doctors around the little valley towns now, and they possessed fine medicines which they gave to their patients.

Many times the young daughter had heard her mother state that when it came to medicine and illness, "Anything we needed ... we truly had been given."

Caroline knew that her mother spoke the truth, but she also had to question whether her mother and her ancient concoctions could possibly be as good at healing the sick as could a doctor who was a trained and skilled professional. Book learning had to count.

She decided that her mother's medicines worked for her generation but modern people needed modern medicine, and so she never took the time to learn that the root of the fern was good for swollen joints, or that uncurled ferns with their snakelike appearance were used to expel worms. She completely missed the importance of trying to understand that the herbalist associated the characteristic of each plant with a part of the human anatomy. The only single clue that Caroline could remember was her mother's claim that "What is sweet to the taste is bitter to the stomach, and what is bitter to the taste is sweet to the stomach."

Sarah stubbornly tried to persuade Caroline to learn that the color of a plant or herb, its shape and where it grew, were all part of the clues to what it would heal. She wished the girl would learn only the basics: red flowers were blood purifiers, and yellow and spotted flowers were medicines for the liver; but Caroline was a modern-day woman with interests in sewing and dancing, and no desire to learn the wonderful medicinal secrets from her mother. And because of this, all this good medicine would go to the grave with Aunt Sarah when she began her long sleep.

As her children grew to maturity, they sprouted into tall and independent young people. Caroline was pretty and carefree, with many, many friends. She enjoyed being the life of the party, and if she had a bad fault, it was that of excusing her brother Harvy for everything he did and being ready to protect him at all cost, against all odds. He could do no wrong, this shiftless young man that was her only brother.

The seasons changed and the years rushed by, and some of Sarah's best memories were of the time when Dennis returned from the Civil War. He still had his fiddle. Dennis came home a tall and thin giant, and there was a strange sadness in his dark eyes that was not there before that conflict. It seemed that food rations had been scarce, and often the men had had to sleep out in the elements, and the southern rains and swamp encampments had taken their toll on her brother. Sarah was sure that his lungs had been damaged, because he was so slow to gain any weight back and he had a cough that came on with the onslaught of any cold. Dennis seemed to have no resistance against either a cold or a fever, and Sarah was worried. Sarah made coughwart-syrup for Dennis.

Still, when Caroline and Harvy were young there were many good camping and fishing trips along the Connecticut River, and in the glow of their nightly campfires a new generation of Jacksons heard the history of the ones passing. These were good story telling hours too, and Sarah could shut her eyes and hear again the voices of her children as they begged her, "Please Mother, do tell us the legend of the No See Ums." And with the night stars flickering overhead, Sarah would tell her children this story that she had been told also in the shadow of the night stars and in the glowing embers of a campfire.

Sarah would settle herself back comfortably, and then she began this often repeated legend of her people. "Long, long ago.....when no White men were here and the Dawnland People roamed and fished and hunted at will, there was still a menacing thing about that caused the people much fear and displeasure. He was a great black bird, bigger than an eagle and more deadly than a wounded black bear." Here Sarah would spread her arms wide in order to show her audience what she had been shown, which would accentuate the size of the bird's wing-span, which was longer than the height of three warriors, and its great curled talons were the size of hunting arrows.

Only the spitting coals of the fire could be heard now as Sarah continued her story.

"The people wanted to put an end to this bad bird called "Mosquito," because he swooped down on our lodges and carried our babies away. One day Mosquito carried off a young maiden, and her sweetheart was very angry and determined to avenge his love. He armed himself with nets and thongs of rawhide, and he sat out in the middle of a field and waited for the great bird to come and it was very bold now, so it did, like a bolt of thunder out of the bright sky. But the warrior waited, chanting his death song as he did so, and when the Mosquito dived low to make his kill, the warrior rose quickly and finally engulfed the Mosquito in his trap of rawhide thongs. Then from everywhere, every corner of the field, the people rose up and fired arrows into the struggling bird of prey. The sky was black with arrows and the warrior died, but happily because he had avenged the maiden."

Sarah poked the fire with a stick and continued, "Well, now a great feast was held as word passed through the mountains that the Mosquito had been destroyed. They left his body there to rot away and they danced, the people did, and they did not know that even as they danced in celebration of ridding the forests of this creature, that from his vile and rotting body, thousands of tiny, almost invisible mosquitos were already infesting the woodlands, and these we call No See Ums. They still pester us and bite us just as they do the White men, who call them midgies. The people made a great mistake by not burning the carcass of the bad Mosquito, and now he is gone, but his children live on to spoil the season of summer to this very day."

Aunt Sarah finished her story and always remembered one time in particular when Caroline had said quickly, "Mother, do the White people know where their midgies come from?" And before Sarah could answer, Harvy replied, "Sure, they probably think they brought them with them from Europe, like everything else!"

Here the Jackson family burst out laughing, but there were times too that this family bent in sorrow and shed tears, and bravely tried to console each other, as one-by-one a generation ceased to be.

"Live well, my children," Sarah was often heard to say, because she knew that when they one day reached the Land beyond the Stars, if they hadn't shined here, they would not shine there, in that place where no one ever sheds a tear—or says goodbye, again.

Aunt Sarah knew that her husband was dying. For some time now, she had administered to him the strongest pain killers that were available and known to her that Mother Earth or Aka grew. It wrenched her heart to see his healthy, copper-colored skin pale and turn into that yellow-gray color that she knew all too often as the death pallor. Both their children had been told, and John had also gone to the doctors in St. Johnsbury and Lancaster, but unfortunately they could do nothing for him except to confirm Aunt Sarah's diagnosis of incurable liver disease. The medical doctors had a name for this, cirrhosis.

John had not been able to work in the woods since late November, and Sarah had kept food on their table by selling her baskets. After one sick call she took a young fat rooster home under her arm. He was an ugly bird but he did not scare Sarah. She knew that this fine fighting rooster would make her hens very happy, and in the spring she would have some baby chicks, thus insuring her food supply of poultry as well as eggs. Caroline named the rooster "Napoleon Bones Apart" because, she said, he had the longest and most crooked legs she had ever seen on a bird. Napoleon Bones Apart was also a foul tempered fowl.

It was the night before Christmas eve, and Aunt Sarah knew that her husband John had not many more to see. The bloat in his abdomen had already started.

In the middle of the afternoon the sky became overcast and it began to snow. John and Sarah were working on baskets and had listened to Caroline sing and Harvy accompany her on his guitar. They were practicing Christmas carols for a school program that they were both appearing in that night.

As the afternoon passed, Sarah arose from her basket plaiting and brushed the curtains back and looked outside. "It isn't building up, John. It is very big flakes."

She had been taught from childhood how to read the weather. This was not a big storm. There had been no warning ring around the moon, and big flakes meant little snow, whereas little flakes meant big snow. "Big snow....little snow," she repeated more to herself than to anyone else in the room.

John smiled at her. "I know you always liked the snow, Sarah, and especially at this time." She nodded her head in agreement, for it was so. This was the North, and in the North frigid below-zero temperatures could be devastating to the leaf life and the green things sleeping under the ground. These green gifts needed sun and also rain in the summer months, but they badly needed the insulation of a blanket of snow to cover and protect them for their journey to life in the spring.

John rose to his feet and began putting away the basket tools. His clothing was just beginning to show the significant amount of weight that he had lost since early fall. He looks so thin and so tired, his wife was thinking, but he interrupted her thoughts. "Sarah, it is a warm snow. Are you going to the school play tonight?" She told him that she was, and he decided that he would go with her and she was very pleased.

After supper Caroline and Sarah cleared the dishes away and then began putting on their best clothes and brushing and rearranging their hair. When Caroline finished primping, Sarah brushed her own hair back into its French twist. She studied her reflection in the mirror as she did so, and found that here and there she detected a tiny line on her smooth dark face which she had not noticed the last time she had taken time to do this.

She turned from the looking glass, knowing that there were more and more grey hairs visible each year. She smiled to herself when she remembered that foul-smelling brew that her father used to mix up by steeping butternut shells. It was to add oil to his hair, he always claimed, and it did and made it shine. It also made his hair stay very black, until he began drinking more and didn't pay so much attention to his personal grooming habits.

She had smelled that concoction brewing so many times, and had seen her father combing it through his greying hair. Aunt Nel never used this on her hair, and Aunt Sarah decided that she never would either.

The Somers family had no sleigh to ride in, and so with John and Sarah each carrying a lantern they ventured out into the softly falling snow. Aunt Sarah never forgot this night. It was not cold, and the sound of their boots made squeaking noises on the snow-covered road. Harvy and Caroline walked ahead of them and then wanted to carry the lanterns, and so their parents let them light their way and they followed along behind, walking hand-in-hand up that narrow ribbon of a road that led to the one-room school on the flat in South Guildhall.

Other valley families passed them as they walked, and the bells on the sleighs jingled, and all could see the white puffy clouds made by the horses' breath as they passed. People waved to them as they forged on. Most of these wagons were already filled to capacity, as many of these valley families were big ones.

They arrived at the school and took their places, and Sarah was pleased to see Dennis and Celia and their younger daughter Nelemano, called Nellie by her mother, who would not use the Indian name.

Dennis was playing some violin songs, and he did not know that Caroline would be singing a solo this night. Neither did Caroline's parents, who thought she was singing with a group.

John and Sarah seated themselves and removed their heavy coats, and no sooner had they sat down when little Nellie Jackson wriggled free from her mother's grasp and sprinted away toward her Uncle John and Aunt Sarah. She climbed up onto Sarah's lap and hugged her. "Aunt Sarah, I didn't know you'd be here tonight ... and Santa Claus too," she said.

Aunt Sarah held the cute little girl in the bright red pinafore up in front of her and said, "Nelemano ... you are the prettiest girl here tonight. Santa will bring you something special, I know."

Little Nellie looked up at Sarah's dark face and said, "I want a doll. I want some red ribbons for my hair and ... most of all, Aunt Sarah, I want a fuzzy little kitten."

Celia scowled and shook her head no. She and Sarah had made their peace, and so were polite and civil to each other when they met. The child went on to say, "Mother says no red ribbons, but Santa will bring me white ones. Mother says I can have a jewelry box but I can't have a kitten." Smiling at the child, Aunt Sarah questioned her. "Well, what does your father say?" Nelemano's face broke into a broad smile and she giggled. "He said...'wait and see, Nell, wait and see'".

The teacher, a slim frail woman with kind grey eyes, announced that it was time to begin the play. A hush settled over the audience and the entertainment began. The younger grades all had parts in this play and it began with Santa Claus arriving, right on time to end the skit, and handing out hard candies and oranges to all the children.

Next came a trio of violin, guitar and flute, in which Dennis played his ancient fiddle. After a few moments Caroline stood poised at center stage, and Harvy couldn't be seen at all, but softly in the background, guitar chords could be heard as he strummed his guitar. Pretty Caroline stood very still for a long minute, and then she began to sing "Silent Night." She had a beautiful voice, clear and pure and true to every note. The crowd became very silent, for few if any of those assembled here had ever heard such a talent. When the shock wore off, Sarah found that her eyes were smarting with unshed tears of pride. Why, Caroline should be a singer, that obviously was what she did best, and she was very calm, handling herself like a professional entertainer.

Aunt Sarah never forgot how proud her husband looked, sitting there quietly and hearing people whisper about what fine musicians his son and daughter were. It was good that they had come here tonight to listen and to sing along in celebration of Christmas.

At the end of the evening the Somers family rode home with Dennis and his family, and many of the church-going neighbors decided that if this Indian family believed in Christmas, they were fair game to be converted, and this started months and even years of trying to get Aunt Sarah and her family to join a church.

The women came often after that, and Sarah was always gracious to them but never joined a church. It was hard for her to explain to these well-meaning church people that she did not have to go to a church to know where God was. He was everywhere. He did not build the churches, He created the stones and the trees that the churches were made from. He was in each drop of rain and each evening sunset, and He was in her heart always. Finally Aunt Sarah was quoted as saying, "I don't want to join a church. I believe God is there, but He also is with me ... and we walk well together, Him and Sarah. You honor Him on Sundays, I honor Him each day that I live well."

The unsuccessful conversion of Aunt Sarah to join a church was a thing that came and went like a fad every few years from then on. This Dawnland woman, who believed in God but not really in churches, lived a good life and at the same time resisted conversion.

As this particular Christmas Eve came and went, Aunt Sarah walked through the snow and crisp air toward her brother's house. In her arms she carried some honey and some cough tonic for Dennis. For Celia she had brought jam and preserves, and for little Nellie she carried a basket made in the shape of a jewelry box. Sarah talked soothingly to the little basket as she trudged along that Christmas morning.

The memoirs tell us that Aunt Sarah had been gone from the Jackson household almost five minutes before little Nellie took the cover from her new basket. Inside that basket sat a fuzzy grey and white kitten, and around its neck a bright, red ribbon was tied and a note read, "Merry Christmas, Nelemano ... my little friend ... love from Santa."

Aunt Sarah appears to not only have believed in God, but in Santa Claus too! She often said, "A smile on the faces of little children ... that is the true wealth of the earth."

The legend says that the "Owaissa," or a Bluebird, sang to Aunt Sarah that bright morning. She smiled and said, "Owaissa, life is good." And for the most part she felt that her life was good, this independent basket maker who survived 108 years of change, resisted conversion and would die as she had lived, an Indian ... not a convert.

In the years that lay ahead of her, when sorrow bent her proud head low, Aunt Sarah would draw upon her memories of days when life was good, like walking through the softly-falling snow on Christmas Eve, she and John walking hand-in-hand and still in love, oblivious to the cold or to the fact that their trail together was almost walked, or even that thick ice was forming on the top of the Connecticut River, flowing up ahead.

Aunt Sarah's face was lined but not wrinkled, as seventy-five years of living showed itself in the crow's feet around her deep-set dark eyes, in the grey that now was the dominant color of her once black hair, and even in the sag of the shoulders that a few years back had defied her age as well as the law of gravity, which in the end pulls every living thing back to the earth from whence it began.

The dog days of summer had passed now, and the early September sun fell warm upon her proud and almost haunting face. She was heavy-laden with baskets today, but somehow in the splendid early autumn sunshine she did not feel burdened. She felt anticipation, not tiredness.

These baskets would not be going to the stores in nearby Lancaster or door-to-door around the valley. Aunt Sarah was taking them to a market that came only once a year, the area's only agricultural display, which was and is still called the Lancaster Fair.

Following Route 2 along, Sarah found her eyes drawn again to the ledge called Tarritine. This old and much-frequented Abenaki camping place had been named originally "Tarritine Ledge" by members of the Mic-Mac tribe who came to trade and fish with the Connecticut River Indians, so long ago. This name spoke nothing of the ledge itself, only that it was inhabited by "Tarritines," which is what the Mic-Mac people called the Dawnland people.

Aunt Sarah stopped and rested just a bit, and continued to cast her gaze upon that wonderful vantage point. She would have to go there before cold weather set in, just to feel that rock-strewn earth beneath her feet and reassure herself that she had not nor never would forget this place, her first memorable home.

Aunt Sarah began to walk ahead. It was hard to make her eyes move away from that ledge that was so much a part of the life and very existence of a people long silent. The Abenakis had roamed all the region north of the great Fifteen Mile falls on the Connecticut River on their annual hunting and fishing treks.

Tarritine Ledge was more than a camping place to Aunt Sarah and the Dawnland People, it was home.

Jack Frost had recently touched the scattering of maple trees along the crest of the ledge, and if Aunt Sarah looked hard enough up toward the top, she felt she should be able to see the makeshift tents and tepees of her Bear Clan family. Where did they go, those tepees? They should be there, perched on the highest point and best vantage place along the river. "They should be there," thought Aunt Sarah, for she knew that they were there long before there ever was a South Guildhall or a Lancaster either. But times had changed, and in this all-White-world history had been written not about the Indian, but indeed out around him.

Aunt Sarah dropped her proud head and continued to walk on down the road. Her heart was always sad when she realized that the little Indian village that actually crowned the rocky-top of that ledge had passed silently away into history, as unnoticed and as noiseless as the wood smoke that curled softly from the wigwams that once stood there.

Sarah Jackson Somers squared her shoulders and quickened her pace, because she knew it was little use to dwell on the past. Nothing had happened to her but life. Life happened to all living things and all living things changed. Only the dead stayed the same.

The first year of the Lancaster Fair, 1870, she and John had walked down this road together, and once they were over on the actual fairgrounds the sights and sounds had reminded her of the circus, and of Winona. Winona had been gone so long then, and now John was also gone.

Aunt Sarah stayed beside John's bed for three days and three nights before he left her. He did not know that she was there, but she did.

From an old trunk Aunt Sarah removed a wool blanket, beautifully designed in bright Native American schemes and colors. The fringe on the edges of the Wedding Blanket were long and flowing. Sarah folded the blanket, and then into the plain board casket she placed this wedding blanket, beside John.

With eyes red and swollen from weeping, she said this: *"Great Spirit, ... Father of the wind, a long, long time ago I asked that I may keep my blanket whole ... Now, my man John, he takes the blanket with him to wait for me, to wrap me in it when my day is done ... to wrap me in it like his love for me, and mine for him."*

It made the neighbor ladies feel satisfied that Aunt Sarah allowed a minister to speak at John's funeral. "How come you did that, Mother?" Harvy asked, and softly Sarah answered, "To ease the minds of all our friends, my son. I am not converted yet, and I doubt that your father heard a word."

Harvy Somers laughed then and so did his mother, because she believed that wherever John Somers was, he was also laughing, laughing and healthy and happy, that very handsome man who carried a blanket and waited for ... Aunt Sarah.

Sarah stopped and adjusted the load of baskets that she carried. She was sure that somewhere between here and the other side of the river, someone would stop and offer her a ride in some kind of a wagon. Aunt Sarah was beyond the ledge of her childhood days now, and her aging though still bright eyes fell on the Crystal Hills or Agiochook, the famous White Mountains of New Hampshire.

On the last day that he lived, her late husband had asked her to tell him the legend of Passaconaway's last ride. With Harvy and Caroline also seated by his bed and listening, Aunt Sarah took John's feeble hand in hers and repeated this tale.

"One hundred and twenty winters had Chief Passaconaway seen. He was tired now, and withered like an old oak tree. His warpath days were over, and he dwelt alone in a wigwam on the outskirts of what had been the once vast Penacook domain. On a cold, cold, winter evening, while Passaconaway's fire burned low and the north wind howled, other howling could be heard. This new howling grew louder, and soon a pack of great silver wolves dashed through the night sky. They ran swiftly, and they were harnessed to a hickory sled that was holding a throne. The throne was covered with beautiful furs of ermine and mink and beaver pelts, and the spirit team raced across the frozen lake called Winnepesaukee, and north toward the Great Stone Face, and faster and faster they ran and then they stopped directly in front of the wigwam of Chief Passaconaway. The fire was out in the wigwam now, and the proud old chief took his place upon the throne of furs, and this phantom team of silver wolves, amid yelps and snarls, carried the old warrior on his last ride.

The famous chief felt the snow and ice biting into his copper skin, and a smile crossed his face. He began to sing and chant his death song. And lone trappers, camped on the icy shores of frozen streams below him, heard the howling of the wolf team and heard the unmistakable death chant of Chief Passaconaway. Shivers ran up the spines of the men who listened as the death chant echoed through the mountains all around them.

Then on up the side of the steep slopes of Agiochook itself, that phantom team pulled Passaconaway. The Algonquian tribes all feared to walk in the shadow of the White Mountains, Agiochook, for it was the home and dominion of the Great Spirit, but Passaconaway did not walk here. He was riding as a special guest of the Great Spirit.

He chanted his death song even louder now, and on toward the summit of those Crystal Hills the sleigh was carried. Just before it reached the very pinnacle of Agiochook, the wolves broke their harness and ran howling off into the wilderness. Then the hickory sled burst into flames, and Passaconaway too was wrapped in leaping tongues of fire. Like a fiery comet he shot across the northern sky, and there he vanished amid the stars......for all eternity."

As Aunt Sarah repeated this legend, John went to his long sleep. She smiled softly as she remembered that this being his favorite legend, it had been good that the last earthly sound he ever heard would be the sound of Aunt Sarah's voice telling him that story, as he himself embarked on his last journey.

In the ten years following her husband's demise, Aunt Sarah lost first Caroline and then Dennis. Caroline was happily married and living in Gorham, New Hampshire. Aunt Sarah's warning came in the form of a dream. She was climbing down from Tarritine Ledge, and from the cold and freezing snow around her she saw him as he emerged from a whirl of blowing snow, that teary-eyed Grandfather Wolf. He howled only once and then he loped away, and Aunt Sarah awoke in a cold sweat. She had not long to wait, for early the next morning she received word that Caroline was gravely ill with influenza. Aunt Sarah packed her medicine bag and boarded the next train, but when she arrived at Caroline's side, Caroline was gone. Was that a scream escaping from Aunt Sarah's lips? No, it must be someone else, she was too strong for that, you see.

Not long after Caroline was buried in her husband's family lot in Lunenburg's Riverside Cemetery, Sarah would get her second loss. Few things in her life was she any less prepared for than losing either her daughter or her brother Dennis. This time there had been no wolf or messenger owl, or even the flaming star. No, there had been nothing to warn her, almost as though this death was not supposed to be. She thought of her powerful brother Dennis. No, a cold could never kill that mighty man, but pneumonia could, and it did. When the doctor gave Dennis up, then it was that Celia sent for Sarah. Aunt Sarah entered the room and walked to the bed and brushed her hand across her brother's cold forehead, and she knew that Dennis was not unconscious, he was dead.

Celia was tearing at Aunt Sarah's coat sleeve like a mad woman and screaming over and over, "Sarah, can't you give him some medicine?" Tears welled in Aunt Sarah's eyes, and she turned and gave the frantic woman an icy stare and then she shook her hands off and said, "I have no medicine for the dead, Celia ... no medicine for the dead." And then Aunt Sarah walked back to the bed, and bending close to his ear she whispered, "Brother, I am so sorry. I wish that she had called me," and with that she walked out of the house without another word, or even a backward glance.

At the end of the long driveway she heard little Nellie's feet come running after her. "Aunt Sarah, the doctor said ... Mother said Father is..." Here the child burst into tears, and Sarah bent and hugged her thin little body to her heart.

"Oh, Aunt Sarah ... is Father all right? Is he really happy?" This was what her niece wanted to know, and Aunt Sarah smoothed her fine dark brow, and told the truth with strong conviction,

"He is happier than he has ever been, Nelemano ... And when we see him next, child, it will be forever."

As Aunt Sarah wiped the tears from her own eyes with the back of her hand, a shattered little Nelemano asked, "But why do people die, Aunt Sarah?"

With a clean handkerchief Sarah dabbed at her niece's swollen eyes and answered, "Because, my beloved niece, it is how we finish life. It is finishing what was started on the day we were born. Your father's walk is done here, but he waits for you ... there on the other side."

Nearing the wooden bridge that led to Lancaster, Aunt Sarah began to think of other things, like when at age sixty-five she diagnosed pains in her chest and her shortness of breath as heart disease. This was about the time many women had this trouble. The body must run out of something or just get tired from all the energy it took to go on living.

At that time she told her son Harvy and her friends, "My illness needs time to heal. This heart has known much sorrow and I am tired. I need only the peace of these mountains and the clean fast-moving streams of the forest," and she went deep into the woods and stayed in a small wigwam by a brook for a whole year. She knew how to get away from civilization and she knew where to find the foxglove, or digitalis, that fine diuretic which had so many good benefits to help a tired heart. That year of Aunt Sarah's sabbatical, Harvy watched out for his Uncle Peter, who worked at the Lunenburg-Dalton Ferry. Harvy also came every two weeks on Sunday and left his mother canned goods. He was always sober, knowing how she despised his drinking. He had not believed his determined mother when she said, "All I need is the peace of the mountains and the clean fast-moving streams," but Harvy had to believe her when she came out of the woods one year later, and lived another forty-three years.

One night, stirring her nightfire, Aunt Sarah remembered the day she came home and found Napoleon Bones Apart and all her chickens, staggering and flopping around the yard. The flock had found some of Harvy's sour mash for home brew and eaten it, and Napoleon Bones Apart was the drunkest bird of the bunch. Aunt Sarah was furious, seeing Napoleon with his wings flapping, flat on his back trying to say, "Cock-a-doodle-doo."

She raged, "Harvy Somers, you drunken lout! See my birds! Come out here! Look at my helpless Napoleon Bones Apart! What have you to say for yourself and your still? Look at my chickens.....look at my precious Napoleon Bones Apart! What do you have to say about him, Harvy John

Somers?"

"He can't hold his liquor worth a damn, Ma!" exclaimed her son with a broad grin. Sarah took a broom to him and drove him out of her sight, but finally she had to join the girlish laughter in the background. And she turned only to see Caroline bent over and trying to decide who was the funniest, Old Bones Apart, flat on his back, or her brother Harvy, trying to hop over downed chickens and stay clear of the broom his mother was so angrily flailing at the back side of his lap. "Reformation of a rooster is hard work, Harvy," laughed Caroline.

Caroline's wonderful wit and laughter, it was good to remember the good times too, thought Sarah, and there had been so many...so many.

The clip clop of horse's hooves and the rumble of a wagon were the sounds that brought Sarah to the present.

The wagon pulled to a stop beside her, and a fair-skinned woman with light hair piled high on her head, smiled down from the wagon at Aunt Sarah. Aunt Sarah smiled. This was "Birdie" Call, her nephew John's wife.

"Get in the wagon, Aunt Sarah," said Birdie, and Aunt Sarah who was just realizing she was tired, was pleased to see Birdie's hand reach out to help her board the wagon. "Thank you, Birdie," said Aunt Sarah as she settled herself back against the wooden seat and arranged her load of baskets on the floor by her feet.

"I'm going to the fair, Birdie," she said, and Birdie good naturedly answered, "John and I always go and take the children. They just love the fair, you know." Aunt Sarah smiled. Yes, she knew. This fair was the biggest family reunion in the upper Connecticut River valley.

Someday, when she was older and when her legs refused to carry her long distances, she would go to Tarritine Ledge, and there she would bury all of her medicinal tools. She would no longer need them, or more correctly she would not be able to effectively heal herself or others.

All these things passed through Aunt Sarah's head when she thought of Tarritine Ledge, and she must have been saddened, having no one to pass on the wealth of her herbal medicines to, but today as she climbed down from the wagon she was thinking about the fair, and she picked up her load of baskets and headed straight for that small exposition. Aunt Sarah could smell the popcorn and hear the carnival music playing. The scent of good cooking odors and even the smell of animal manure were familiar. Somewhere in the distance dogs were barking, and many bright colored flags and feathers waved high over the barkers heads.

Memories and thoughts about her circus years flooded her brain, and now she could see the tents and smell the sawdust. For just a moment Aunt Sarah felt that if she turned her head, she should see Winona Jackson walking along beside her, smiling and inhaling all the sounds and smells of long ago.

Many of Aunt Sarah's friends were gone now, but she knew that what ones were left, she would see today at the fair, and she would bet the fox a chicken that she would return home tonight and have sold every basket.

A band began to play lively music then, and tapping drums made little children want to march in time with the beat. Aunt Sarah was no longer young and she could not march or run or even dance anymore, but she could walk, she could still walk, and she did, straight ahead toward the roar of the crowd and the smell of sawdust, and she thought only of the future.

Autumn was here in the beautiful upper Connecticut River valley, and soon the painted hills would abound with magnificent color, and then snow would lay white and heavy on the earth. But, come spring, there would be so many healing herbs to gather, new babies born, and sick babies to make well, and new baskets to be made.

A hint of a smile tugged at her lips and that golden sun fell warm upon Aunt Sarah's face. And yes, life was uncertain, but life was very good.

The End

OVER A CENTURY

LAST OF THE ST. FRANCIS TRIBE DEAD IN LUNENBURG HOME

MRS. SOMERS JOINS HER OWN

Last Wednesday one of Lunenburg's oldest, and, in a sense, most interesting resident passed quietly away while sitting in her wheel chair to which she has been confined for several months.

Mrs. Sarah Somers was born in Pennsylvania in a wigwam, a pure blooded Indian of a tribe nearly extinct. With the few remaining members of the St. Francis division she migrated to Maine and from there to Lunenburg.

Some of the older residents can still recall the Jackson family in their wigwams on what is now known as the Maillet farm. "Sarah" is remembered as a young woman of unusual grace and beauty. She married John Somers and to them three children, John, Carrie (Mrs. Leighton) and Harvey, were born. Harvey is the only survivor. He and a niece from Guildhall were the only relatives present at the funeral.

In the death of Mrs. Somers the tribe of St. Francis is gone. We are glad to remember her as one who lived for approximately 100 years without once being untrue to the traditions of her fathers. Her kindness to her friends, her thrift, her honesty, both of word and deed, are well known to all her neighbors. She was deeply and intensely religious with the simple yet unswerving faith of her people.

Up to a few months ago Mrs. Somers lived in a little house on the Gilman road with her son Harvey. On account of a serious illness she was then taken to the home of Adelord Forest where she has been cared for ever since. Her funeral was held from the Forest home, Rev. R. H. Mercer officiating. Tributes of flowers were sent in by friends and neighbors. Her body was placed in the tomb awaiting burial beside her husband in the spring.

EPILOGUE

For ninety-two years this woman of the Dawnland supported herself by gathering the green gifts from the earth and making baskets. During the very final months of her life she was an invalid, confined to a homemade wheelchair in a rest home in the town of Lunenburg, Vermont.

A man I know was just a boy at the time that Aunt Sarah was a patient, being cared for at his father's rest home. He explained that every evening the other patients at the home gathered around the kitchen table for a friendly game of cards, all except Aunt Sarah. She did not play cards, but every night as the game began she would be wheeled to the table, where she could sit unnoticed outside the circle of players and observe the game.

Many times Aunt Sarah's head would droop toward her chest, and her old and bird-like eyes would close in gentle sleep, but one cold night in February of 1931 Aunt Sarah's head dropped for the last time.

She had died so quietly that no one realized that she had slipped away and gone to her last sleep, except that small boy who noticed Aunt Sarah's eyes were open.

Aunt Sarah was a woman of peace, and she died peacefully in much the way that she had lived 108 winters of her life, silently and with dignity, outside another White Man's circle ... looking in.